Pr⸻ ⸻or Rosie Goodwin:

'A⸻ ⸻ed writer . . . Not only is Goodwin's characterisation
and⸻ ⸻logue compelling, but her descriptive writing is a joy'
Not⸻ ⸻ham Evening Post

'G⸻ ⸻win is a fabulous writer . . . she reels the reader in
sur⸻ ⸻ingly quickly and her style involves lots of twists and
tur⸻ ⸻hat are in no way predictable' *Worcester Evening News*

'G⸻ ⸻lwin is a born author' *Lancashire Evening Telegraph*

'R⸻ ⸻e is the real thing – a writer who has something to say
and⸻ ⸻nows how to say it' Gilda O'Neill

'R⸻ ⸻ is a born storyteller – she'll make you cry, she'll make
you⸻ ⸻ugh, but most of all you'll care for her characters and
lose⸻ ⸻ourself in her story' Jeannie Johnson, author of *The Rest
of C⸻ Days*

'He⸻ ⸻tories are now eagerly awaited by readers the length
and⸻ ⸻eadth of the country' *Heartland Evening News*

ROSIE GOODWIN

Tilly Trotter's Legacy

headline

First published in Great Britain in 2006
by HEADLINE PUBLISHING GROUP

First published in paperback in Great Britain in 2007
by HEADLINE PUBLISHING GROUP

2

ISBN 978 0 7553 3488 9

Typeset in Bembo by Avon DataSet Ltd,
Bidford-on-Avon, Warwickshire

Printed and bound in Great Britain by
CPI Antony Rowe, Chippenham, Wiltshire

Headline's policy is to use papers that are natural, renewable and
recyclable products and made from wood grown in sustainable forests.
The logging and manufacturing processes are expected to conform to
the environmental regulations of the country of origin.

HEADLINE PUBLISHING GROUP
A division of Hachette Livre UK Ltd
338 Euston Road
London NW1 3BH

www.headline.co.uk
www.hodderheadline.com

Contents

Part One
Fated for Sorrow

Chapter One

'COME ALONG, WILLY. We shall be late for the train at this rate.' Tilly's son was standing at the window with his hands clasped behind his back, staring out across the grounds of Highfield Manor. Or that was how it appeared. In truth, his mother knew all too well that he could see no more than a few yards in front of him now. Blind in one eye, the sight was steadily deteriorating in the other. The knowledge brought her small white teeth nipping down on her lower lip, but then forcing a brightness into her voice she again urged him, 'Come along then, slowcoach.'

With his hands held out in front of him, Willy reluctantly turned and lumbered towards the shape that was his mother. Once at her side, she looked into his eyes on a level, for at five feet ten inches, Tilly was tall for a woman. Taking his elbow she led him from the elaborate drawing room past Peabody, who was waiting in the hall with Master Willy's coat and Tilly's warm cape folded across his arm.

'Your cape, madam.' As the butler advanced on her, Tilly inclined her head.

'Thank you, Peabody.' She turned slightly as he draped the cloak around her slight shoulders before asking, 'Is everything in hand for Miss Josefina's homecoming tomorrow?'

'Oh, yes, ma'am,' he assured her solemnly. 'Peg has been up since the early hours preparing the menu and baking, and Fanny is already in the process of giving the house a thorough cleaning.'

'And the fire has been lit in Miss Josefina's room to air it?'

Again he nodded vigorously. 'Yes, ma'am. For the last two days now.'

Tilly smiled her satisfaction at him before tying the ribbons of her bonnet firmly beneath her chin. Trimmed with a single feather, it was elegant in its simplicity. Today she was dressed in a dark blue taffeta day dress that rustled and billowed about her legs as she walked, and set off her blue eyes to perfection. Steve McGrath, her fiancé, liked her to dress in blue. In fact, he had requested that she wear blue for their wedding, but she didn't want to think about that yet. First she would get Josefina home and settled back in. Then she would break the news of her forthcoming marriage. No doubt it would come as a shock to the girl, for she had always known Steve McGrath as no more than a family friend and the under manager of the mine that Tilly owned.

Peabody hurried to the front door and opened it for them, and as they emerged onto the steps of Highfield Manor, Tilly saw Ned Spoke waiting for them below with the carriage, the horses pawing impatiently at the ground.

'Safe journey, madam,' Peabody called as she led Willy down the steps, and Tilly turned to raise her hand in farewell.

Once she and Willy were settled in their seats, Ned leaned in and tucked two heavy travelling rugs across their laps.

'To keep the chill out,' he explained good-naturedly. 'You have a long journey in front of you, lass.'

'You're quite right, Ned,' Tilly agreed, 'but it will be made slightly easier by the fact that we are staying in a hotel tonight before we begin the journey home tomorrow. I dare say we'll all be glad of a rest once we get to Liverpool, and I'm sure Miss Josefina will, after her long sea voyage back from America.'

He closed the door and seconds later, the carriage drew away.

Tilly looked across at her son. A young man of almost twenty-one now, he was looking very handsome in a new tweed suit with his fair hair neatly brushed and flat against his head. Not that it would stay that way for long. Willy's hair had a life of its own, which no amount of brushing or Macassar oil could tame.

As the carriage bowled down the drive past the line of rowan trees, Tilly's thoughts moved to Josefina, and a feeling of apprehension settled around her more closely than the fur-lined cloak she was wearing. In the letter her adopted daughter had written to her, telling of her intentions to return home, she had sounded very different from the girl who had gone back to America, to the border country between Texas and Mexico, some time ago in search of her natural family. In that aim, she had eventually been successful. Yet her family had been nothing like she had expected. Josefina had found them living in abject poverty and it seemed to have broken her spirit, for they had shown her no affection, were only interested in the money she might be able to give them.

And what would the young woman's feelings be now, towards Willy? This was the real reason why Tilly had agreed to accompany him on this journey to the docks, for until recently she had been adamant that Willy should go to meet Josefina alone. Tilly was well aware that before Josefina had gone, her feelings towards Willy had not been those of a sister towards a brother. But since her departure, Willy had suffered a great loss – and whereas only days before, he had been looking forward to the girl's homecoming, he was now so confused that he didn't seem to know how he felt.

Tilly glanced at her son. White-faced and gaunt, he stared vacantly from the carriage window, and she guessed that he was feeling as apprehensive as she herself.

When Josefina had left, Willy had been in love with Noreen Bentwood, the daughter of a local farmer. Now both Noreen and Simon, her father, were dead following on from a terrible accident in which their carriage overturned, and Willy was the father of a newborn baby girl, who was being brought up by Lucy, Noreen's mother. Tilly had the distinct feeling that Josefina would not be happy to discover this, for she had always demanded all of Willy's attention ever since she was a little girl, and had never been good at sharing him, even then.

Tilly sighed. Not that Willy was showing a great deal of interest in the child. It was almost as if, since Noreen had died, he wanted to forget everything connected with the horror of her death – the child included. And had Tilly not insisted that he visit the little one every Sunday at Brook Farm, she doubted he would have gone there at all. It was strange now she came to think of it, for immediately following Noreen's death he had been all for keeping the child at Highfield Manor. It was she who had talked him out of it and persuaded him that the child would be best cared for by Lucy. Tilly was ashamed to admit that it had not been purely for the child's sake. She had prayed that at long last she was about to know some peace when she and Steve became man and wife, and she had no wish to take on the responsibilities of another child. And so, Lucy had taken the child back with her to Brook Farm and Willy's interest in her had waned, as had his excitement at Josefina's homecoming.

As if he could somehow read his mother's disturbed thoughts, Willy suddenly asked, 'Are you all right, Mama?'

'What? Oh yes, pet. Yes . . . I was just wondering how we would find Josefina. I mean, it must have come as a great shock to her when she found her natural parents. Especially when they shunned her, poor lass.'

Willy's head bobbed in agreement. 'It is as you say. But you know – Josefina always had a great deal of spirit. I'm sure that she'll cope with it. Especially when she gets home to us.'

Tilly pursed her lips and turned her attention to the view beyond the carriage window. They were approaching South Shields now and would soon be at the train station, where the first leg of their journey to Liverpool would begin. She could only hope that he would be proved to be right.

They reached Liverpool at tea-time, after an exhausting journey involving three changes of trains, at Newcastle, York and Leeds. The sky was darkening and the rain was coming down in cold blistering sheets. Tilly instructed a carriage that was waiting outside the station to take them straight to the docks, and after lifting their overnight valises into the luggage compartment, the driver urged the horses forward through the busy streets. Muddy roads slowed their progress and so by the time he finally drew the horses to a halt, the *Mauritania*, the passenger ship on which Josefina had travelled, was already docked.

As the driver helped Tilly down from the carriage she saw that passengers were already beginning to disembark; the whole area was alive with activity. Muscled seamen with ruddy faces were dragging huge trunks down the gangplank, followed by finely dressed men and women, whose eyes scanned the crowds assembled on the dock for signs of those who had come to meet them.

Tilly waited impatiently until Willy was at her side, then after instructing the driver to wait for them, she lifted her skirts with one hand and taking her son's elbow with the other, began to pick her way through the crowds. The stench of rotten fish and unwashed bodies hung heavy on the air, and the cobbles underfoot were treacherously slippy. At one point she had to steer Willy around a dead rat that was almost as big as a cat. A flock of seagulls were noisily squawking as they picked at its remains and Tilly wrinkled her nose in distaste. But at last they were almost at the bottom of the gangplank and she stared upwards, waiting for a sight of Josefina. As a tremor ran up her son's arm, she snatched her eyes away from the steady stream of people disembarking to glance at him. His nervousness was transmitting itself to her. Would it be her daughter who was returning to her, or some stranger who now felt she belonged to no one?

Tilly didn't have to wait too long to find out, for suddenly a small, dark, elfin-like face appeared and her heart skipped a beat. *Josefina.* She was dressed in a dark green velvet suit, and about her shoulders was draped a short cape trimmed with fur. A matching hat and muff completed her ensemble and she looked every inch the lady and absolutely enchanting.

Unlike the other passengers, she looked to neither left nor right as she made her way down the steep incline, but kept her head held high.

Tilly's heart flooded with love for the girl she looked upon as her own. When she reached the bottom of the gangplank, Tilly leaped forward and placing her hands on her shoulders, stared into Josefina's eyes as tears glistened on her lashes.

'Aw, hinny.' She slipped easily into the term of endearment her granny had once used to her as Josefina stared stiffly back at her. The only sign of emotion she showed was a slight tremor of her lips as she replied, 'Mama.'

As her eyes travelled past Tilly they came to rest on Willy and now she said, 'Hello, Willy. I was wondering if Noreen would allow you to come and meet me.'

Willy's mouth opened and shut but the tense moment passed when Tilly took command of the situation. Explanations could wait until later on, when they were out of the atrocious weather.

'Come on, you two. There will be plenty of time for chatting later at the hotel.' Clicking her fingers she caught the attention of a burly sailor who was wrestling an enormous trunk from the bottom of the gangplank. Extracting a shining half-sovereign from her purse she instructed him, 'Will you bring Miss Josefina Sopwith's luggage to the Ship Hotel in South Street. There will be another of these waiting for you.'

Tipping his cap respectfully, he greedily pocketed the coin. 'Yes, ma'am. Consider it done.' Just for a second he glanced regretfully at the row of whores in low-cut dresses who were standing against the huge warehouse walls that lined the quay. Still, he consoled himself, there would still be some there by the time he got back from the hotel, and the extra money would allow him to be a little choosier. Whistling merrily, he went about his work as Tilly steered Willy and Josefina back towards the coach.

The driver eyed Josefina curiously, but made no comment as he held the door open and ushered the two women inside.

As the carriage rattled away across the cobblestones, Tilly took Josefina's hand in hers and squeezed it affectionately. An uncomfortable silence had settled over them and she was keen to break it.

'You must be tired after your journey?' she said sympathetically as she shook the girl's hand gently up and down. Willy seemed to have lost his tongue, no doubt following his sister's spiky remark about Noreen. Oh dear. The sooner Josefina was put fully in the picture, the better it would be. But first, let them get settled into the hotel.

As Tilly swept into the foyer of the Ship Hotel, more than a few eyebrows were raised. She ignored them. Tilly Trotter had become used to stares and they no longer troubled her. At fifty-one years of age, she was still a fine-looking woman, if somewhat different from what fashion dictated a woman should be. Taller than most of the men whom she passed on her way to the desk, Tilly held herself erect, a striking figure with her white hair and unlined face. When the people looked from her to the dark-skinned, foreign-looking girl beside her, who also bore herself as every inch the lady, the eyes grew yet wider. And then there was Willy. A fine young man, smartly dressed – he looked every inch the gentleman – but the way he held his arm out in front of him told of his near-blindness.

Coming to a halt in front of the desk, Tilly informed the man there: 'Mrs Matilda Sopwith and family. I have booked us a suite of rooms. We have luggage in a trap outside, and await a trunk from the *Mauritania*.'

The man's rheumy eyes ranged down the page of the book in front of him and he nodded. 'Yes, madam. Your suite is all ready.' Reaching behind him, he snatched a key and, passing it to a porter who was hovering close by, he told him, 'Escort Mrs Sopwith and her family to their suite on the second floor, Benjamin. Then fetch their luggage in for them.'

'Yes, sir.' Benjamin, who looked to be no older than twelve or thirteen at most, immediately doffed his cap and hurried towards a broad staircase with Tilly and her entourage following closely behind.

At the door to their suite he timidly asked, 'Will that be all, madam?'

'Actually, there is something else you could do for me.' Crossing to an ornate gilt mirror that was hanging above the fireplace, Tilly undid the ribbons of her bonnet and drew it from her head. Patting her hair into place, she then lifted her purse and tossed him a shiny shilling. 'Could you have a tray of tea and sandwiches sent up to us, please? It will warm us and keep us going until dinner-time.'

'Certainly, madam.' He backed from the room with the money clenched tight in his fist and Tilly turned to find Josefina undoing the buttons of Willy's overcoat. A wave of affection swept over her. Although she was only half his size, Josefina had always mothered Willy, and now that she had returned, it looked set to continue. Laying her bonnet on a small table at the side of the roaring fire, Tilly undid her cape and shook it before draping it across the back of a chair. Then holding her hands out to the welcoming flames she urged, 'Come and sit over here, you two. You'll soon be warmed through.'

Josefina led Willy to a wing chair and pressed him into it before removing her own cape and bonnet. As Tilly watched her she felt a moment of concern. Josefina had always been small, but now she seemed positively tiny. Her jet-black hair was combed into a tight chignon on the back of her head and her smouldering black eyes looked too big for her face.

'Have you been eating properly?' Tilly asked, then flushed when Josefina tossed her head and answered rudely, 'Did *you* eat properly when you were being tossed about on waves ten foot high, Mama?'

As Tilly recalled her own sea voyages to America and

back, in what seemed a lifetime ago now, she suddenly felt foolish. 'Of course I didn't. Forgive me, my dear. That was a silly question to ask.'

Still Willy had uttered barely a word and the urge came on Tilly to shake him. Why was he behaving like this? She, better than anyone, knew how much he had looked forward to Josefina's homecoming, and yet now that his sister was here, it seemed that the cat had got his tongue. But she wouldn't worry about Willy for now. It was Josefina who needed her attention. Drawing the girl to a small settee and sitting beside her, she asked, 'So how are you really, pet?'

The kindness in her voice brought a stinging to the girl's eyes. She looked at this woman, this strong, loving woman who had been the closest thing to a mother she had ever known, and suddenly the tears welled up inside her and they had to find release or she would surely drown in them.

They spurted from her eyes like water from a dam as Tilly gathered her into her arms and rocked her to and fro. 'That's it, hinny. Let it all out now. There's nothing like a good cry to set things right, so me granny always told me.'

Deeply distressed to see her so upset, Willy sat on the edge of his seat, looking helplessly on. He could only ever remember Josefina crying once in the whole of their lives together, and the fact that she was crying now told him how very deeply distressed she must be.

When Benjamin arrived back with their luggage, it was Willy who rose and fumbled his way to the door. He did the same when a maid in a starched white apron and a frilled cap wheeled a trolley set with an assortment of sandwiches and fancies and a most welcome pot of tea to the side of the fire.

'Shall I pour for you, sir?' she asked, her eyes tight on Josefina, and Willy almost snapped her head off.

'No, that will not be necessary. Kindly leave us. Can you

not see that my sister is distressed?' The words were uncharacteristically sharp for him and the little maid almost tripped over her skirts in her haste to be gone.

Rising quickly, Tilly crossed to the trolley and poured them all a cup of tea, then pressing a bone china cup and saucer into Willy's hands she told him, 'Sit down there by Josefina. We all have a lot to talk about.'

She was about to pass Josefina her tea when the girl buried her head in her hands and sobbed afresh. 'Oh, Mama, did you see the way she looked at me! As I once had pointed out to me, I am neither fish nor fowl. Too learned for my own kind but the wrong colour to be accepted by yours. Oh, why did I come back! I belong nowhere, and never will!'

'No . . . no, that isn't true, my dear. You belong here with us,' Tilly comforted her. 'But I *had* to let you go. You would never have rested until you had discovered your roots. Now you are home where you belong and you can put it all behind you.'

But even as she looked at the tearful girl she wondered, *Could she?*

Chapter Two

THE NEXT DAY, they were all seated on the train that would take them home. The last time she had made this journey, Tilly had been returning to Highfield Manor as a widow following the untimely death of her young husband, Matthew Sopwith, after an attack by Indians on their homestead near Fort Worth in Texas. Willy and Josefina had only been tiny children then, and she remembered wondering what her faithful staff would think of Josefina, whom she had adopted after being led to believe that she was her late husband's illegitimate child. Part-Mexican, part-Indian, the girl was beautiful – but in a way that would always appear outlandish and not a little savage to the narrow-minded inhabitants of the little mining village near Jarrow.

Of course, the villagers always jumped at any chance to besmirch her reputation. From the age of sixteen, Tilly had been spurned as a witch by the locals, thanks to a string of tragedies and a feud with the hated McGrath family. And true, Tilly had admitted it to herself: she *did* seem to have a power that bewitched some men, leading to violence and scandal of all kinds. Once, her housekeeper Biddy had said, 'You seem fated for sorrow, lass,' and Tilly could only agree.

What was more, as her own son Willy was the result of a twelve-year liaison she had had with Mark Sopwith, her late husband's father, could she really blame the gossips? They had viewed Josefina as just another of her sins.

'Hmm, 'tain't the most joyous of homecomin's I've ever seen,' Peg remarked as she held her feet out to the flickering fire in the kitchen. Tilly had arrived home not an hour since with Master Willy and Miss Josefina, and Peg was enjoying a few minutes' rest before she started to dish up the special celebratory meal she had spent the best part of two days cooking and preparing for them.

Ned Spoke, who was enjoying a welcome mug of tea after leaving the horses in the care of the stable-boy, nodded in agreement. 'Ee, they've got faces on 'em as long as pike-staffs. Hardly said a word to each other all the way back from the station, from what I could gather. Still, happen they're all just tired. When they've got a hot meal in their bellies an' they've had a good night's sleep in their own beds they'll probably feel different again.'

Fanny, who was basting the leg of lamb that she had just lifted from the oven, remarked, 'Don't know why they couldn't have invited Mister Steve over. Miss Josefina's got to get used to the fact that Tilly an' he are goin' to be wed at some stage.'

'I doubt she even knows about it yet,' Ned confided. 'From what Tilly whispered to me out there on the steps, they ain't even told Miss Josefina that Willy has a bairn yet. Huh! I don't mind bettin' there'll be a song and dance when she does find out. You know what she's always been like with Master Willy. Never liked anyone goin' closer than an arm's length to him, she ain't, so she's not goin' to take very kindly to the fact that he's a father.'

The two women nodded in agreement as they pondered on his words, but when the bell sounded from the drawing room, Fanny quickly straightened her cap and smoothed her starched white apron before heading for the door.

She found Tilly pacing up and down, but she stayed her steps when Fanny entered the room. 'Has Steve called in today?' she asked.

Fanny nodded. 'Yes, Tilly.' After all the years they had known each other she rarely addressed Tilly as 'ma'am' unless in the presence of company, and today was no different. 'I believe he called in on the way back from the mine late this afternoon to see if you'd arrived back yet.'

'And did he leave any message?'

'Not so far as I know, though you'd have to ask Peg to be sure 'cos it was her that he spoke to.'

'Thank you, Fanny.'

As the woman turned to leave the room she paused to ask, 'What time will you be wantin' dinner served?'

Tilly glanced at the ormulu clock on the mantelshelf and shrugged. 'Oh, about six, I should think. Willy and Josefina are just changing after the journey. Thank you, Fanny.'

Fanny flashed her a smile and hurried back out into the hallway, where she almost collided with Steve McGrath.

'Hello, Fanny. Tilly in there, is she?' he greeted her.

Fanny nodded. 'Aye, she is. An' talk of the devil, she was just askin' if you'd called round yet.'

'And here I am!' Steve handed his hat and coat to Peabody before striding to the drawing-room door and disappearing through it.

Fanny gave the butler a cheeky wink before hurrying on to the kitchen. Only the trusted staff as yet knew of Tilly and Steve's impending marriage and the news could not have pleased them more. Most of them had known Tilly all of her life, and to their minds she was overdue a little happiness.

When Tilly turned from where she was gazing down into the fire, to see Steve striding towards her, her smile lit up the room.

'Why, I was just asking Fanny if she had seen you,' she told him.

'So I understand.' Taking her into the circle of his arms he kissed her soundly before stepping away and asking, 'So how did you find Josefina?'

Tilly's shoulders slumped and the smile left her face. 'Not good, I'm afraid. And she and Willy are so strained with each other. He told her about Noreen's death but he hasn't told her yet about the child.'

Steve raised his eyebrows. 'Whyever not? It isn't something that he can keep quiet for long. Josefina is bound to find out about her one way or another.'

'I know, but I thought she ought to hear of it from him. I didn't feel it was my place to tell her.'

'And have you told her about us?'

Tilly's downcast eyes were his answer and he sighed heavily. 'Aw, well. Things will fall into place. They usually do. Meantime . . . I've missed you, madam.'

She giggled like a girl. 'Why, I was only away for one night.'

'Aye, and that was one night too long. I can't wait for the time when we can be together for always.'

She was in his arms again, and as his lips found hers she forgot everything but the joy he could light in her. When the drawing-room door suddenly opened, they sprang apart as if they had been burned, and turned to see Josefina staring at them with a look of incredulity on her face.

'Oh, pet.' Tilly felt like a child who had been caught out

in some dreadful misdemeanour, and hot colour suffused her cheeks.

'Steve and I . . .' she began '. . . that is, I was going to tell you when you had settled back in. But we're . . . Well, the thing is . . . we're going to be married.' There, it was said, and had she slapped the girl, Josefina could not have looked more shocked.

'I see,' she said eventually. 'And when is this marriage going to take place?'

Steve straightened his shoulders as he looked calmly back at her, and his cheeks too were now stained with annoyance. 'As soon as she'll have me,' he informed her. 'I've waited long enough. But she wanted to get you home and settled before we planned the date. Now that you *are* home, I can see no reason for delaying. You and Willy are adults now so I think it's time your mother thought of herself for a change, don't you?' He wasn't going to take any nonsense from this young lady!

Josefina was saved from having to answer when the door opened yet again and this time it was Willy who fumbled his way into the room. Although his eyesight was restricted, his other senses were not, and he instantly picked up on the chilly atmosphere. 'Is something wrong?' he asked.

'It all depends what you class as wrong,' Josefina told him sulkily. 'Mama has just informed me that she's going to marry Steve. Is there anything else that has happened whilst I've been away that you haven't told me about?'

Willy cleared his throat. There would never be a better opening for him to tell her about his child so he nodded. 'There is, as a matter of fact. You see, I told you about Noreen's death. What I have omitted to tell you is that before she died, she gave birth to a child . . . my child.'

Josefina's hand sprang to her mouth and Tilly took a step

towards her, for she had the awful feeling that her daughter was about to faint. However, the girl waved her away as with her eyes still tight on Willy, she asked, 'And where is this child?'

At this point, Tilly began to walk towards the door. 'I think it might be best if Steve and I left you two alone for a time. You have a lot to talk about. Dinner will be served at six, and seeing as Steve is here now and you know of our intentions, I'm going to ask Fanny to lay another place at the table. He may as well dine with us now that he's here.'

Once out in the hallway, Tilly released a deep sigh and Steve drew her close to his chest. 'Well, it seems that there is nothing left to hide.' His voice was soft as he witnessed Tilly's deep distress. 'Admittedly, she could have learned of these things a better way, but what's done is done. I for one am glad that everything is out in the open. After all, we have nothing to be ashamed of, do we?'

As Tilly looked up into his dear face a wave of love washed over her. A love tempered with guilt as her thoughts turned again to the promise she had made to Matthew, her late husband, on his deathbed. The promise was one he had begged her to make, before he died. *I shall never marry again*, she had told him, as he breathed his last, yet here she was about to become Mrs Steve McGrath.

When some time later they made their way into the dining room, they found Willy sitting alone at the table.

'Where is Josefina?' Tilly asked as Steve held her chair out for her.

Willy's face was clouded as he replied shortly, 'She decided she wasn't hungry.'

Tilly and Steve exchanged a glance that said more than a thousand words as Fanny pottered into the room with a steaming tureen full of soup.

The so-called festive meal was eaten in silence until Steve eventually asked Willy, 'So, has a name for the child been decided on yet?'

'Mrs Bentwood did say that she might call her Sarah. It was her grandmother's name, I believe.'

'I approve of her choice,' Steve told him as he helped himself to another freshly baked roll. 'How do you feel about it?'

Willy shrugged his shoulders. 'It's as good a name as any, I dare say.'

The uncomfortable silence settled yet again, broken only by Fanny when she came to clear the dirty dishes away before serving the main course. Tilly noticed that she looked tired, but then that was hardly surprising. Soon, Peg would be going to live with her sister in America and so for the past weeks, Fanny had not only been doing her own household chores but she had been working alongside Peg in the kitchen in readiness for when she took over the cooking duties. Tilly made a mental note to put the word out that a new housemaid would be required, not that she expected to find anyone from the village. Despite all her best efforts to help the people there, there were still some who thought of her as a witch. In recent years, she'd had two rows of new cottages built for the miners who worked in her mine, and the majority of the workers had moved into them gladly. They would have been fools not to, for the new cottages had stout wooden floors and outside water closets; they were light and roomy, with good-sized fireplaces in which to burn the coal she allowed them for free. Tilly gave a tiny sigh. She had made donations to the church, too, but all in vain. She was still shunned and knew now that she always would be.

Her lips moved into a wry smile as she thought of the effect the news of her forthcoming marriage would have on the villagers. Up until now, she and Steve had managed to keep it quiet, but of course it couldn't remain so for long. Word of what was happening up at the Manor usually spread like wildfire, and no doubt it would only be a matter of time before it reached the village. Then the cat would really be amongst the pigeons. Steve looked at her enquiringly as he wiped his mouth with a napkin. 'So, what's so funny then?'

'I was just wondering how the villagers will react when they hear of our marriage.'

'They can react how they like,' he replied, grinning, then on a more serious note he asked, 'Have you heard how Lucy and the bairn are faring?' He saw Willy's ears prick up but made no comment.

'We're going to ride over to see them tomorrow, aren't we, pet?'

Willy nodded somewhat reluctantly as Tilly continued, 'I'm going to give Lucy the deeds to the farm and the cottage, plus I'm going to make her an allowance each month so that she and the child won't have any financial worries. It's the least I can do in the circumstances. I want to ensure that they live in comfort.'

'And will that salve your conscience, Mama?' Willy's question made Tilly almost choke on the wine she was in the process of swallowing.

'And just what is *that* supposed to mean?' she asked when she had caught her breath.

Her son answered quietly, 'Well, you were keen enough to get the child away from the Manor, weren't you?'

'It was Noreen's dying wish that her mother should have care of her,' Tilly pointed out indignantly. 'You *know* it was, Willy.'

'Oh, I know all right. But I didn't see you putting up much of a fight to keep her here. Were you worried that it would be left to you to bring her up?' But before Tilly could answer him he scraped his chair across the fine woollen rug and stood up. 'If you'll excuse me, I'm rather tired. I think I'll retire now.'

'But you haven't even had your main course!' Tilly exclaimed.

He waved aside her concerns impatiently. 'No matter. I seem to have lost my appetite, so I'll bid you both good night.'

Fanny passed him as she carried in a large covered silver dish to the table. It smelled delicious.

'Where's Master Willy off to?' Placing the dish in the centre of the table, she took in Tilly's flushed face at a glance. 'There's a leg of lamb in there as would feed an army an' Peg's gone to no end of bother to welcome Miss Josefina home.'

'I know she has, Fanny, and I'm so sorry. It seems that neither Master Willy nor Miss Josefina are in very good spirits. But never mind. Tell Peg whatever Steve and I don't eat tonight can be made into a stew tomorrow.'

'Hmph!' Fanny declared, and turning about she flounced away to fetch the vegetables, wondering why everyone had gone to so much trouble in the first place.

Later that evening, when Steve had returned to his cottage, Tilly mounted the stairs and tapped at Josefina's bedroom door. At first she thought the girl must have retired to bed, for there was no reply. She was just about to move on to her own room when the door suddenly opened a crack and Josefina stared out at her. Then, leaving the door ajar, she moved back into the room. Tilly followed her. Crossing to the window, Josefina stood with her back to her mother as she gazed out past the heavy damask curtains into the foggy night. Her hair was released from the elegant chignon she had

23

worn earlier and was now woven into two long black plaits that reached to her waist. She was dressed in a voluminous white lawn nightgown that made her skin look even darker and billowed about her legs when she moved.

The overall impression was of a very young girl, and Tilly had the urge to rush across the room and snatch her into her arms. Josefina was hurting deep inside, and it showed in her every movement.

'Could I have a tray sent up for you, pet?' she said quietly. 'You really should eat something.'

There was silence for a while until Josefina muttered brokenly, 'They were living like animals, Mama. No . . . that is an insult to an animal, for even they try to protect their young and keep their dens clean. I had never realised that such poverty existed.'

Tilly joined her hands and pressed them tightly into her waist. It was a habit she had formed over the years when she was distressed. And she was distressed now. Oh yes, she could have told Josefina what her natural mother was really like. But would it have done any good? And the answer came back: No, it wouldn't. Josefina would never have believed her. She had to go and see for herself, and God willing, now that she had done so, she would come to terms with her beginnings and learn to go on. She had to, for what alternative was there?

Before she could make any comment, Josefina's voice came to her again, and this time she said, 'Does Willy still love Noreen?'

At a loss for words, Tilly's mouth opened and shut for a time before she replied. 'I think he certainly *did* love her, but Noreen is gone now. You must give him time, Josefina. I know that he was looking forward to you coming home.'

'Was he?' Josefina's voice was laced with pain as, turning to the woman who had been a mother to her, she caught hold of Tilly's face and held it, so that the older woman was forced to look into her eyes. 'What is the child like? Willy's daughter?'

Tilly's tongue slid across her dry lips. 'She's a bonny little bairn,' she said gently. 'I would be a liar to say otherwise. Why don't you come with Willy and me tomorrow to meet her?'

Josefina pulled away. 'I don't *want* to meet her.' The words, laden with jealousy, flew from her lips like bullets from a gun as Tilly looked on in astonishment. She had not expected Josefina to be happy when she discovered that Willy had fathered a child by another woman, but never in her wildest dreams had she dreamed to see the response she was getting now.

With a toss of her head, Josefina flung herself onto the bed. Crossing to her, Tilly laid her hand tenderly on her shoulder. 'The child – Sarah, as we think Lucy is going to name her – is here now, my dear. There is nothing we can do about it. But it should not affect your relationship with Willy. Once things settle down there is no reason why you cannot be as close as you once were.'

Arms folded tightly across her chest, Josefina scowled unbecomingly. There will be no talking sense to her tonight, Tilly thought to herself, and she made to leave the room. At the door, she paused to look back once across her shoulder, before closing it softly behind her, and as she walked the short distance to her own room she found herself thinking, Why does nothing in my life ever run smoothly? For it seemed that every time she found herself with happiness within her grasp, something always happened to spoil it.

Chapter Three

'ARE YOU QUITE sure that it's wise to venture out in this, ma'am?' Ned Spoke asked with concern. Then, at her look, he joined his hands together and stooped low. Tilly placed her foot in them and allowed him to hoist her into Lady's saddle before taking the horse's reins from his hands.

'I know this countryside like the back of my hand, Ned,' she assured him as she slipped her feet into the stirrups. 'It would take more than a bit of fog to make me lose my way hereabouts.'

'It's more than a bit of fog,' he said stolidly, nodding towards the stable door. 'You can barely see a hand in front of you out there. 'Tis as thick as porridge. Why don't you let me get the carriage ready? I could have you there in no time.'

Knowing that Ned meant well, Tilly smiled at him. 'Stop worrying, lad. We'll be back before you know it. Master John and his wife are coming for dinner today to welcome Miss Josefina home, so we won't be gone for too long, will we, Willy?'

Willy, who was seated astride his own horse, nodded in agreement although his face was sullen as his mother urged her horse past his. With her legs astride her mount in her riding breeches and her knee-high leather boots, and her straight figure, Tilly could have been taken as a young man. She had stopped riding side-saddle, as ladies of the gentry were expected to ride, some years ago when she returned from America. It had caused yet another stir amongst the local people and given them something new to gossip about for months. Now it was accepted. After all, Tilly Trotter, as she was still known, had always been a law unto herself, they had muttered.

Once outside, the pair turned their horses and began to trot along the drive. As Ned had told them, the fog was so thick that they could barely see a hand in front of them so the journey was made in silence. When they eventually rode into the yard of Brook Farm they saw Lucy's son Eddie Bentwood, staggering towards the farmhouse door laden down with a huge basket of logs for the fire.

Tilly climbed down from her mount and after tying him to a post she asked, 'Is your mother in the kitchen, Eddie?'

'Aye, she is. She's just fed Sarah an' when I came out she were trying to rock her off to sleep.'

Tilly smiled. So, the child's name was definitely decided upon then. Sarah. She rolled it around in her head and decided that she liked it as she strode towards the door closely followed by Willy, who was still scowling.

They found Lucy with the baby in her arms walking up and down the length of the flagstoned kitchen.

'Hello,' she greeted them as Tilly made straight for the baby. Willy stood by the door, his hands clasped behind his back as he looked on, making no attempt to approach the child.

'May I?'

'Of course.'

Tilly held her hands out to the blazing fire to warm them before taking the child from Lucy's arms. Staring down into her face she could see nothing of Willy there. The child might have been a miniature copy of her mother. Her hair was surprisingly thick and already had a tendency to wave. It was dark, as were the eyelashes that were now curled on alabaster cheeks as she slept peacefully.

'She's very beautiful.'

'Aye, she is. She reminds me of Noreen at her age.' Pain flitted briefly across Lucy's features as she hurried away to fill the kettle at the sink before thrusting it into the heart of the fire. 'No doubt you'll be glad of a cup of tea to warm you both up. It's bitter out there.'

'That would be very nice. Thank you.' Tilly watched her pottering about and guilt, sharp as a knife, stabbed at her. This poor woman had been forced to live in Tilly's shadow all of her married life because of Simon Bentwood's obsession with her. Added to that was the fact that Willy, her son, had inadvertently been the cause of Lucy losing her daughter, and yet still she could take the trouble to make them both welcome. Tilly wondered if she would have been as generous as Lucy, had she been put in her position. But no answer was forthcoming.

Eddie had finished stacking the logs to the side of the fireplace, and as his mother moved about, laying the heavy earthenware mugs on a tray, he told her, 'I'm away to feed the beasts, Ma.'

Her eyes as she looked back at him were gentle. 'Thank you, son,' she said.

Seeing this as an opportunity to escape what was fast becoming for him a very uncomfortable situation, Willy offered, 'I'll come and give you a hand.'

If Tilly found it strange that her son did not wish to

spend time with his daughter she made no comment until both young men had left the room and then she asked, 'Are you managing, Lucy?'

'Oh aye. I've become good at managing.' Colour stained Lucy's cheeks as she realised her answer might have caused offence, but Tilly made no reply. Instead she gently laid the child into a crib at the side of the fireplace and joined Lucy where she was now pouring boiling water into a large brown teapot.

'You have decided on a name for her then?'

'Yes, we thought Sarah Jayne. Do you like it?'

'I think it's a beautiful name.' Reaching into a pocket inside her jacket, Tilly now drew out a formal-looking document and laid it on the table.

'What's this then?' Lucy raised her eyebrows as she stirred the tea in the pot before covering it in a thick woollen tea cosy and leaving it to mash.

'It is the deeds to Brook Farm,' Tilly told her. 'As of this day, it is yours, Lucy.'

When the other woman's mouth fell into a gape, Tilly went quickly on, 'I have also instructed my solicitor to pay you an allowance that should be more than adequate to cover your needs, every first of the month from this day forward.'

Lucy had had very little since marrying Simon Bentwood, including his love, but what she did have aplenty was pride. 'That won't be necessary,' she said quietly. 'We are not quite charity cases yet. Eddie has long since done the outside work. He had very little choice, with Simon's back being the way it was, and I can earn enough to feed us with the dairy products I sell at market. So thank you. But no, we won't be needing your help—'

When Tilly suddenly held her hand up and stopped her mid-flow, Lucy was surprised to see the tears glistening on her lashes. '*Please*, Lucy. I of all people know that you must hate me. I find it very sad, for under other circumstances I feel that you and I might have been friends. But now we have a mutual interest in our granddaughter, so if for nothing else, will you please let me do this for her?'

She watched the emotions flit across Lucy's face. Another refusal was hovering on her lips but then her head bowed and she said in a low voice, 'I don't hate you, Tilly. None of what happened was your fault. The blame lay all with Simon and his obsession with you. And yes, I agree, under other circumstances we could have been friends, for I have to say that I admire you. You have had to live with the stigma of witch attached to your name given by ignorant people who knew no better, and yet you rose above it. So, if it makes you feel better then yes, I will take what you offer and thank you kindly. In truth, all I have is the farm and Eddie, and now, of course, Sarah to care for.' As her eyes moved to the sleeping infant in the cot her face softened. 'She's a bonny bairn, isn't she?'

'Oh yes. She is that, all right.' Both women stared at the baby in silence for some moments until Tilly remarked, 'Are you feeling well, Lucy? You look a little pale.'

Lucy grinned ruefully. 'It's no doubt having to get used to doing night feeds again. I had forgotten how tiring a newborn could be.'

'I could always get someone in to help if it is too much for you. A girl from the village perhaps?' Tilly offered.

Lucy shook her head. 'Thank you, but no. It gives me pleasure to care for the child. Once she is sleeping through the night it will become easier.'

The silence settled again until Lucy asked, 'Is Josefina safely home?'

'Oh yes, but I have to say she is changed.' Sadness creased

Tilly's brow as she sipped at the steaming tea Lucy had pushed towards her. 'She went to America in search of her natural family, which I suppose is understandable. That she would wish to know who they were, I mean. Sadly, they were nothing at all as she had hoped they would be, and it was a bitter blow to her. I could have told her before she left that they wouldn't welcome her with open arms but it was something she had to see for herself. I will never forget how easily they parted with her when I offered to take her to live with me when I was in America. And then that was something else I had to bear when I first returned to England with the child in tow. Everyone thought that she was mine, but then the villagers have never missed an opportunity to berate me. My back should be broad by now.'

Both women were smiling now as they looked back at each other, and some of the strain between them lifted like mist in the morning. However, a sudden commotion out in the yard brought them both springing from their seats and running towards the door. When Lucy threw it open they saw Willy and Eddie squaring up to each other like two opponents in a boxing ring.

'What's all this then?' Lucy cried as, lifting her grey serge skirt, she skipped across the yard to stand between them.

Eddie scowled. 'I was just telling His Lordship here that anyone can make a child, but it takes a man to keep one!'

'Enough!' Lucy's face was as livid as his as she pushed him none too gently towards the cottage door. 'Have we not seen enough heartbreak lately without you starting?'

The anger seeped away as Eddie hung his head in shame. Taking his elbow in a firm grip, Lucy propelled him back through the door and Willy followed sheepishly.

Once back in the kitchen the easy atmosphere of minutes before was gone and although the two young men now kept their distance, the atmosphere between them was such that Tilly felt she could have cut it with a knife. Nor could she fail to notice that Willy studiously avoided looking towards the child, and this, on top of the heated words he had just exchanged with Eddie, brought her lips together in a straight line. Perhaps in time things will right themselves, she thought to herself. It is still early days yet. After all, when Noreen died, Eddie had lost a beloved sister so it was only natural that he should want to lay the blame for her loss at someone's door.

As her eyes roved the room she could see why Lucy loved it here at Brook Farm so much. In many ways it was very basic and yet Lucy had managed to transform it into a very comfortable home with her knick-knacks and the colourful rugs on the floor. Pretty curtains hung at the small leaded windows and the smell of a joint of pork that was roasting in the oven filled the room with its delicious aroma. The huge oak dresser, which took up almost all of one wall, was laden with Lucy's treasured collection of fine china that she had accumulated across the years.

As Lucy saw Tilly looking around she seemed to read her thoughts and smiled sadly. 'I realised in a very short time of marrying Simon that ours was not destined to be a marriage made in heaven. And so I suppose I poured all my efforts into this house and the two children that resulted from our coming together. You must forgive Eddie's outbreak. He and Noreen were very close and he misses her cruelly. For some long time I still loved Simon as well. Oh aye, for many years my love for him was strong but gradually he wore me down until I could stand no more. Sometimes I thought of returning home to my folks. But then there were the children to consider and so I stayed and our lives fell into a pattern. Now there is Sarah to think about.'

At this last remark, Willy bowed his head with shame but

Lucy's hand reached across the table to cover his as she told him, 'You must not blame yourself for Noreen's death, Willy, despite what Eddie here might have said. Had Simon allowed you to marry her when you wished to, things would have turned out differently. I sometimes felt that Simon's possessiveness of her was unnatural.' Her lips quivered but then her chin was held high again as she told him, 'What is done is done. We all have to go on now for Sarah's sake, if nothing else . . .'

Swallowing the lump that had formed in her throat, Tilly said softly, 'Simon wasn't *always* a bad man, Lucy. When I was young he was my salvation, but life took our paths in different ways.' She had no idea what had prompted her to say this, except perhaps the fact that she was sitting in his house, in his kitchen, with his wife. And strangely she was remembering the young Simon Bentwood who had come to her aid on more than one occasion when she was little more than a lass.

Lucy shrugged. 'Be that as it may. Life changed him and there is no turning back the clock.'

It was at that moment that Sarah whimpered and Lucy immediately rose from the table to gather her into her arms. The child's eyes fluttered open and as they settled on her doting grandmother's face the whimpering gave way to a contented gurgle. In that moment Tilly knew that she had made the right decision in persuading Willy to let Lucy care for her. As long as the child had her she would want for nothing, least of all love.

The journey back was even worse than the one going, for if anything the fog had thickened. It swallowed up every sound, and as they made their slow way home Tilly had the uncanny feeling that she and Willy might have been the only two people left in the world. Had she not known the countryside so well, she had no doubt that they would surely have become lost.

When they finally trotted into the yard, Ned sighed with relief. 'Eeh, I were just gettin' worried!' he exclaimed as he helped Tilly down from the saddle. 'Another half an hour an' I'd have had a search-party out lookin' fer you. Still, you're home safe now. An' how did you find the little 'un?'

Handing him the reins, Tilly smiled. 'She's beautiful, Ned. But have Master John and Miss Anna arrived yet?'

'Yes, ma'am. About half an hour or so since.'

She nodded, then taking Willy's elbow she steered him towards the steps of the Manor. Peabody met them at the door, looking as relieved as Ned had to see them. Taking their hats and riding crops, he announced, 'Master John and Miss Anna are waiting for you in the drawing room. Shall I have a tray of tea sent in to warm you up, ma'am?'

Tilly rubbed her hands together. 'That would be lovely, Peabody. Thank you.'

As they entered the room, Anna instantly rose from her seat and crossing to Tilly, kissed her soundly on the cheek. 'Oh my goodness!' she recoiled. 'You are frozen through. Come over to the fire and get warm.'

John watched his wife lead Tilly to the fireside chair, and once again the thought that plagued him flashed through his mind. Anna would have made such a wonderful mother. Why wasn't it happening? Why were they still childless?

'Y . . . you're . . . very b . . . brave to venture out in this, Tilly.' As John's hand gestured towards the fog outside the window, Tilly grinned.

'Misguided might be a better choice of word,' she replied jocularly then, 'So how are you both?'

'Oh, we're very well,' Anna replied for him. It was a habit that Tilly noted she had adopted of late – speaking for her husband, who had a cruel stutter. Tilly found it endearing, and thought how pretty Anna looked today. The young woman was wearing a soft grey dress with a high collar that all but covered the terrible purple birthmark that ran down across her chest from beneath one ear. The neckline was trimmed with white lace, as was the bodice of the dress, and the flowing full skirt accentuated her tiny waist, making her appear like a little doll. John was watching her with open adoration shining from his eyes, but that was nothing unusual, for Tilly was aware that her brother-in-law worshipped his wife and that his love was returned. Her thoughts ran down the same road that John's had taken only moments before. If only they could have their own child . . . The irony of the situation suddenly struck her full force. Here was Willy with a child that he now appeared to have no interest in, and here were a couple who would have given their right arms for one.

She had no time to ponder on it, for just then there came a tap on the door and Fanny appeared. 'Dinner will be served in one hour, ma'am.'

'Thank you, Fanny. I'll pop up and get changed then.'

Fanny bobbed her knee and disappeared back the way she had come as Tilly rose to follow her. 'If you'll excuse me I shall be back down shortly.' Once in the hallway with the door safely closed behind her, her shoulders sagged as she made her way to the sweeping staircase. The visit to her granddaughter had emotionally drained her, and the words Eddie had spat at Willy were still ringing in her ears. Anyone can make a child, but it takes a man to keep one. She hoped that in future she would not have to count Eddie Bentwood amongst her enemies.

Up on the galleried landing, Josefina was coming towards her. Today she was dressed in a sea-green dress made of taffeta that set off her dark colouring to perfection. The girl was very aware of where Tilly and Willy had been, but chose to make no comment on it. Instead she asked, 'Have John and Anna arrived yet, Mama?'

'Yes, pet. They're in the drawing room with Willy. Go down to them and I'll join you as soon as I've changed. They are so looking forward to seeing you again. And . . . I feel I should tell you. I have asked Steve to join us for dinner too. We haven't told John and Anna about our plans to be married yet. We wanted to wait until you were home so that you could share in the celebrations with us.'

From where Josefina was standing the news did not warrant a celebration, but she refrained from saying so and simply moved past her mother without a word.

When Tilly rejoined them in the drawing room some short time later, Steve had arrived and he looked her up and down appreciatively. She was looking especially charming in a low-cut gown made of silk. It was one she kept for special occasions, and she saw John and Anna exchange a puzzled glance as Steve took a seat by her side on the chaise longue. Tilly felt herself blush as she tried to envisage what their reaction would be to the announcement. Would they be unhappy about it, as Josefina obviously was?

It was halfway through the meal when she found out. Steve suddenly stood up and with a proud smile on his face announced, 'John, Anna, Tilly and I have something to share with you. I'm delighted to tell you that I have asked Tilly to be my wife and in agreeing to do so, she has made me the happiest man in the world.'

Tilly held her breath as she stared into their dear faces. For a moment they looked positively stunned, but then John suddenly leaned across the table and started to pump Steve's hand up and down with a delighted smile on his face.

'W . . . why, this is m . . . marvellous news. Congrat-ulations. And about time t . . . t . . . oo. What d . . . do you say, Anna?'

Anna caught Tilly into an embrace and kissed her soundly on the cheek before answering, 'Why, it is as you say, John – marvellous news. We wish you both every happiness.'

Happiness. The word spun round and round in Tilly's head and what she said to herself was, 'Oh, *please* let it be so.' She had craved happiness all of her life but each time she had attained it, some cruel twist of fate had snatched it away from her. As she looked into Steve's shining eyes she offered up a prayer. *Please, Dear Lord, do not take him away from me, too, for I do not think I could bear it.*

Even as the words were being silently uttered Steve was striding round the table. Once in front of her, he produced a small leather box from his waistcoat pocket and, taking from it a beautiful emerald and diamond ring, he slipped it on to the third finger of her left hand.

'There we are then, Tilly Trotter. It is official. Now all we have to do is set a date for the wedding.' And so it was done.

Chapter Four

DARKNESS WAS CASTING its cape across the countryside as with a deep scowl on his face, Randy Simmons strode through the village. For many years, the ageing farmworker had had a cushy job as cowman at Brook Farm, but since the missus had finished him because she said she couldn't afford to keep him on any more, he had been forced to take work in Rosiers' mine. Oh, Mrs Bentwood had made all the right noises, telling him how sorry she was and making sure that he had enough to tide him over, but that had done nothing to soften the blow. The only comfort to be had was that Rosier was Tilly Trotter's rival.

As he thought of the witch and her blind bastard of a son, Simmons gritted his teeth and hatred coursed through him. Never once did he stop to think that it was he himself who had brought about this turn of events, for Randy Simmons it was who had made sure that Simon Bentwood knew about Noreen's affair with Willy. This had led to the girl's imprisonment by her father, her subsequent flight to Newcastle, and her job in Proggle's Pie Shop near the waterfront. Worked half to death until close to her confinement, Noreen was eventually found by her father and brought home – when their trap capsized and Simon was killed. Hours later, Noreen herself died, after giving birth to a bairn.

Randy Simmons cared nowt for the tragedy. All he knew was that now he was forced to work deep in the dark bowels of the earth, with barely a sight of daylight. After being used to working in good clean air, it was this that got to him more than anything else. This, and the fact that he had also lost his cosy billet and was now having to stay in grimy lodgings in South Shields, with cockroaches for bedmates.

However, today he had heard something that had made his ears prick up. Something that, if used wisely, might just get him his revenge. He had been following some men up the steep pit bank after a hard day's work when he overheard one of them talking about a forthcoming marriage. Normally, talk of a marriage would have made him curl his lip. It was *who* was getting married that had interested him. Tilly Trotter and Steve McGrath, no less. The news had taken the wind out of his sails for a start. But then he had got to thinking about it and it came to him like a flash from the blue. There was someone who needed to be informed of this news. Someone who would *not* be happy to hear it. And it was to this same person that he was going right now.

He hurried past the two rows of new cottages that Tilly Trotter had ordered to be built for her workers following the last disaster at the mine. For some long time they had stood empty, for the villagers had a deep fear of the woman and her reputation as a witch. But then they had begun to move into them, one family at a time. They would have been fools not to, for the new cottages were twice as big as the hovels they had lived in before, and were light and airy, with two rooms up and two rooms down to each.

Now there was only one left habitated of the original ones and it was to this that he was heading now. A lighted oil lamp in the window told him that the person he wished to see was in, so he strode to the door through a tangle of weeds and rapped on it sharply.

Minutes later, it creaked open and he found himself staring into the face of an old woman who looked more like a witch than ever Tilly Trotter did. 'Mrs McGrath?'

'Who wants ter know?' She peered at him in the light of the lamp that she held high in her wrinkled old hand.

'Me name is Randy Simmons, missus. I have some news that you might like to hear.'

She frowned, and for a moment he had the feeling that she was going to close the door in his face, but then curiosity got the better of her and holding the door wide she told him, 'You'd best step within.'

Once inside the cramped room he took his sooty hat off and twisted it in his hands as he glanced about him. He found himself standing on a hardpacked mud floor, and it was all he could do not to wrinkle his nose, for the smell of damp and unwashed bodies was overpowering.

Crossing to a rough wooden table, the elderly woman slammed the lamp down, then hitching her shawl more tightly about her scrawny shoulders, she demanded, 'Well then? What is it that's so important it couldn't wait till morning?'

'Hmm.' He cleared his throat and then began. 'I used to work for Simon Bentwood at Brook Farm. That were before Miss Noreen died, that is. Soonever she an' the master passed away, the missus told me she couldn't afford to keep me on an' I found meself out of a job. An' all because of that blind son o' the witch!'

'An' what does that have to do wi' me?' Her eyes were screwed into slits as she peered at him through the gloom. The corners of the room were in deep shadow and he was just about to answer her when he saw something scuttle along the skirtingboard. He shuddered. Rats. He had always had a fear of the damn things, even when he was working on the farm. But they had been nothing to the ones he now encountered down the pit. Fat as butter they were, an' twice as nasty. He could remember his very first day, when he had been working knee-deep in water. He had chanced to look down, to see one idly swimming past not six inches from him, and his screams had echoed off the coal seams as he went full length only to come up coughing and spluttering from the filthy, icy water. The rest of the men, once over their panic, had never let him live it down.

Dragging his eyes away from the corner with an effort he looked back at the woman and told her, 'Word has it that your Steve is to be wed.'

Her eyes stretched wide with surprise for a moment before she asked, 'Oh aye? An' who is it he's goin' to be marryin'?'

'The witch – Tilly Trotter.' There – it was said, and now he had the satisfaction of seeing her drop heavily onto a hardbacked chair as shock registered on her face. After a few minutes rage took its place and he smiled to himself. He had been right to come here, for rumour had it that no one hated Tilly Trotter as much as the woman he was facing now. If anyone could prevent her happiness it would be her, and now that he had planted the seed, all he had to do was sit back and watch it grow.

'Over my dead body,' she suddenly declared, emphasising her words as her fist slammed on the table. 'Where did you hear this?'

'Rosiers' pit is full of it, missus. There ain't no mistake, I promise you.'

'An when is this *farce* supposed to be takin' place?'

'That I can't tell you,' he answered truthfully. 'But you bein' Steve's mam, I thought you had the right to know.'

As she slowly rose back up from the chair, Randy Simmons had the strangest feeling that she had grown, for where her back had been hunched, now she stood tall. 'That witch has hounded me an' mine all her life,' she grated. 'But soon it will be time to end it. I tell you now, so listen well. I will kill that woman if it's the last thing I do – you mark my words. An' I don't care if I die meself in the doin'. From now on, Tilly Trotter's days are numbered.'

A chill ran up his spine as he saw the venom in her eyes, and suddenly the need was on him to be gone. Turning abruptly, he stumbled towards the door. Once he reached it, he flung it open and staggered out into the cool night air. Then he took off through the village as if he had just encountered the devil himself, leaving the cottage door swinging open behind him.

Left alone, old Mrs McGrath looked around at her humble abode. Here was she, living in poverty, whilst that she-devil up at the Manor wallowed in luxury. And now, as if to add insult to injury, she planned to marry her youngest son, when not so many years since, she had been the cause of the death of another of her brood, Hal. Her eyes filled with tears as she thought back to the broken body they had carried home on a door from the foot of the gorge. And it was Tilly Trotter who had been responsible for it, though she had walked free whilst they buried him. Mrs McGrath did not allow herself to dwell on the fact that Hal had lain in wait for Tilly with the intention of raping her. After all, had Tilly not cast a spell on him, he would never have contemplated it. Nor did she think that although her husband, who had worked down Tilly's mine, was now dead and buried beside Hal, still Tilly allowed her to stay on in her cottage, rent free. No, all she could think of now was her need for revenge.

Crossing to the door she gazed up at the sky and there she made her curse. 'Tilly Trotter, from now on your days are numbered, for I will never rest easy till I wreak my revenge.'

Turning about, she made her way back inside with only the rats that lurked in the shadows for company. Tapping her gnarled fingers on the tabletop she stared off into space for some time and slowly an idea began to form. It might not be possible to get to Tilly straight away, for she was surrounded by the Drews who had always looked out for her. But what she *could* do was get to them – or one of them at least. Sadly, Biddy Drew, who had been the closest thing to a mother Tilly had ever known, had long since passed away. But there were still Peg and Fanny, whom Tilly regarded as sisters, not to mention the lads. It was no secret that Tilly looked upon the Drews as her family, and if anything should happen to them . . . She smiled into the darkness revealing blackened stumps that were rotting in her gums, and slowly her wicked plan began to form.

Randy Simmons meanwhile was going on his way as fast as his legs would carry him. He had the strangest feeling that this very night he had set wheels in motion that would not be stopped.

Chapter Five

PEG SWIPED A tear from her cheek with the back of her hand as she pressed another article of clothing into the trunk Tilly had thoughtfully provided. She had also ensured that Peg was completely rigged out with new clothes from top to bottom, and Peg had no doubt that when she set off for America, she would feel like a queen. There were just three more days to go, and then the journey would begin. Her feelings were mixed, for whilst she could hardly wait to see Katie, her sister, again, the thought of leaving those she held dear here at home was painful. Katie had made the journey to America with Tilly some years ago following Tilly's marriage to Matthew Sopwith, and when Matthew died, Katie had chosen to stay there and marry Doug, one of the ranch hands who worked on Matthew's spread.

One big regret was that she would not be here to see Tilly wed Steve McGrath. She had actually offered to postpone her journey until after the wedding, but Tilly would not hear of it. 'Absolutely not!' she had cried. 'You are long overdue a little time to yourself, Peg. Besides, I don't want a big fancy do. The quieter the better, as far as I'm concerned. We don't want to give the villagers anything more to gossip about, do we?'

'But who will help you choose your wedding outfit?' Peg had asked, and Tilly's eyes had twinkled with amusement.

'Haven't I just told you it's going to be a quiet affair? I shall probably wear a respectable two-piece costume or a day dress that can be worn again afterwards. After all, I am hardly what you would class as a blushing bride, am I?'

This had brought their two heads rushing together as their laughter joined. Tilly had spoken the truth, for she had loved four men in her life, beginning with Simon Bentwood. Fate had sent them on different paths but then she had known love with Mark Sopwith, the master of Highfield Manor, when she was little more than a girl. Their love for each other had begun when they had been trapped together below ground in the mine he owned, which now belonged to her. The accident had resulted in the master losing both of his feet, and Tilly coming to the Manor at his request to care for him. Their relationship had developed into that of a husband and wife, and it had stretched on for twelve long years, although Tilly had always refused to marry him. A smile tweaked the corners of Peg's mouth as she recalled the uproar it had caused in the village. Sadly, when Mark died, Tilly was carrying Master Willy and because she had never wed him, that young upstart, Miss Jessie Ann, Matthew's sister, had banished her from the house with little more than the clothes she stood up in, and two small shares that Mark had bequeathed her.

Tilly had then caused yet more of a stir when she married Master Matthew, Mark's son. They had left for America shortly afterwards, but again happiness was snatched away from Tilly when Matthew was badly injured in an Indian raid. Shortly afterwards, he too had died, leaving Tilly a widow. She had returned to England with Master Willy, who was only a small child then, and Miss Josefina, who Tilly had been led to believe was the result of an affair Matthew had had with a young Mexican-Indian girl. And now here she was, about to marry Steve McGrath, and Peg could not have been more pleased about it, 'cos at the end of the day it had always been as plain as the nose on your face that he worshipped the very ground Tilly walked on.

Peg's mind skipped back in time and she was moment-arily saddened as she recalled the young Simon Bentwood and thought how different his and Tilly's lives might have been, had they come together . . . Over the years Simon had turned into an embittered, twisted man. Funny thing life was, when you came to think of it. But then she supposed that coming together with three out of four loves wasn't bad. She herself had only known one and he had died leaving her a widow, though if what Tilly had said was true about there being a shortage of women in America, then who knew what life might yet have in store for her?

Her thoughts were interrupted when Fanny bustled into the room with some freshly ironed petticoats folded across her arm. 'Here you are then. Might as well put these in your trunk whilst you're at it. How's the packing going?'

Peg shrugged her plump shoulders. 'It's all but done now, but I still can't believe that I'm really going. I shall miss you all so much.' Suddenly snatching a clean white handkerchief from the pocket of her apron she rubbed it around her face as tears sprang from her eyes and rolled down her cheeks.

Fanny crossed to place her arm about her. 'Here, give over now,' she chided gently. 'You'll have me at it in a minute an' all. An' then the pair of us will be no good to neither man nor beast.' The two sisters held each other tightly for a moment before Fanny gently disentangled herself from Peg's arms.

'I wasn't going to say anything, but Tilly has organised a

bit of a do for you tomorrow night,' she told her. 'Sort of a leavin' do, I suppose you could call it. Anyway, I'm only warnin' you 'cos I don't want you burstin' into tears. An' anyway, now that the plans are under way there'll be no hiding it from you.'

'Aw.' Peg was deeply touched and for the moment rendered temporarily speechless. Eventually she regained the use of her tongue and asked, 'Will it be just us lot?'

'Ah, now that *would* be tellin'. What I will say is be sure to put your best bib an' tucker on, eh?' Fanny tapped the side of her nose and left the room with a throaty chuckle.

Peg turned back to the trunk and began to rummage through it until she came to a dress that was made from fine soft wool. It was one that Tilly had bought for her a couple of Christmases ago and was one of her particular favourites. Laying it neatly across the back of a chair she then straightened her hair and went about her business with a spring in her step.

In the village at that very moment, a carriage pulled up at the door of the vicarage and a smartly dressed lady stepped down from it and looked about her. It was many years since she had seen the village but it had changed little, apart from the two rows of new cottages that now ran on past the church.

Turning to the driver she pressed a coin into his hand and asked him, 'Would you mind waiting for me, please?'

'O'course, ma'am. 'Tis my pleasure.'

She smiled, then lifting her skirts she marched up the path that led to the vicarage door. The door was opened by an elderly lady who peered out at her suspiciously.

'Good afternoon,' the visitor said courteously. 'Could you tell me if the parson is in, please?'

'Aye, I could. But who wants ter know?'

'Tell him that Mrs Ross would like to see him, if you would be so kind.'

When the door was closed in her face and she heard the woman's footsteps receding down the hallway, Ellen smothered a grin as she thought, Well, *she* certainly didn't go to charm school!

Minutes later she heard the footsteps approaching again and once more the door swung open. 'Parson Portman will see you now,' the woman told her shortly.

Ellen stepped into the hallway of the house that had once been her home. As the woman led her towards the drawing room at the rear, Ellen was saddened to see how drab it all looked. When she had been mistress there, she had made sure that there was always a large vase of flowers on the hall table, and pretty pictures had hung on the bare walls.

When the woman left her at the parlour door, Ellen tapped on it lightly.

'Enter!'

Straightening her back, Ellen walked in and was once again disappointed. This room, like the hallway, was bare of ornaments of any kind and looked very much like the sober-faced man who was staring at her with open curiosity alight in his eyes.

'Please, do sit down.' When he motioned towards a chair, Ellen perched primly on its edge.

'What can I do for you then, Mrs er . . .?'

'Ross, sir. My name is Ellen Ross and my husband George was the parson here before you.'

His eyes stretched wide with surprise, taking the wrinkles from his face. So this was the notorious Ellen Ross who had danced with the so-called witch Tilly Trotter in the vestry, then got embroiled in a murder case, causing her poor husband to flee abroad to become a missionary. He composed himself before asking, 'Is your husband not with you, madam?'

'No. Unfortunately, Parson Ross passed away many years ago in Africa. But that is not why I am here, so I will get straight to the point. During the time I lived here in the village I became acquainted with a certain young woman by the name of Tilly Trotter. Would you happen to know if she still lives hereabouts?'

He coughed uncomfortably before replying, 'Oh yes. She is certainly still hereabouts. Mrs Sopwith, as she is now known, is the mistress up at Highfield Manor.'

Now it was Ellen's eyes that almost started from her head. 'Are you quite, *quite* sure of that fact?' she questioned him.

Nodding solemnly, he rose and paced about, his hands folded in a tight grip behind his back. 'Oh yes, everyone is aware of Tilly Trotter hereabouts. But then, I dare say I have no need to tell you of her reputation. I am expecting a visit from her any day now, as there are rumours that she is about to marry again. No doubt she will be asking me to officiate at her wedding, but the trouble is—'

'The trouble is, it sounds as if *you* are as small-minded as the people who live hereabouts!' Ellen too rose now and there was a touch of colour in her cheeks as she said in a low voice, 'I have to say, I would have expected more charity from a man of the cloth.'

He stared back at her indignantly as she turned on her heel and made for the door, her full skirts billowing about her. She had discovered what she wanted to know and saw no point in staying any longer.

However, with her hand on the door knob she paused to look back at him, and what she said now was, 'I am saddened that a man of your intelligence should listen to idle gossip. Tilly Trotter was unfairly pilloried as a child and it seems that nothing has changed. And now, sir, I will bid you good day.' So loudly did she bang the parlour door that it danced on its hinges, causing her a measure of satisfaction. She then swept past the old woman who was watching her with her mouth hanging slackly open and did exactly the same with the front door.

Once out in the sunlight again, Ellen Ross looked up and down the village street. So . . . Tilly Trotter was now the Lady of the Manor, was she? Well, good for her. It certainly beat the title of witch. Ellen could hardly wait to see her.

When the swaying carriage drove in through the gates of the Manor, Ellen's excitement grew, and by the time it drew up outside the steps she was almost beside herself. She had the driver lift her trunks down onto the drive, and after paying him a modest tip she stood and gazed about her. It was as she was standing there that a man turned the corner of the house and strode up to her with a pleasant smile on his face. When she smiled back, he tried to think where he had seen her before – and then suddenly he exclaimed in some surprise, 'Why, it's Mrs Ross, ain't it!'

'Yes, it is – and aren't you Arthur Drew?'

'That I am, ma'am, and it's right pleased I am to see you. Does Tilly know you're comin'?'

Ellen giggled, making her appear quite girlish, and that was the moment that Arthur, who had always been a confirmed bachelor, lost his heart to her. The years had been kind to her. She still had the slim figure that he remembered, and the same sweet smile that had made him make the trek to Sunday school each week to drop off the young 'uns. As he was making these observations, she was eyeing him and thinking what a handsome man he had turned into. Stretching her mind back into the past, she tried to gauge how old he might be now. He would be a few years younger than herself, if her memory served her rightly . . . Then she remembered why she was here and asked, 'Is Tilly home?'

'Oh aye, as far as I know she is. An' I don't mind betting she'll be right pleased to see you.'

'I do hope so. Particularly as I've come unannounced.' As she glanced down at her luggage, Arthur quickly told her, 'You go in out of the cold. I'll bring this in for you.'

He watched as she tripped lightly up the steps, her skirts swirling around her, before bending to hoist one of the trunks into his strong arms.

Peabody answered the door within seconds and looked at her enquiringly.

'My dear man,' she trilled. 'I am an old friend of Mrs Sopwith's. We haven't seen each other for many years and I'm afraid I've come completely out of the blue. I would like to keep my name a secret for the time being. Do you think she would see me?'

Warming to her smile just as Arthur had, Peabody beamed back at her. 'I shall certainly find out for you, madam. Meanwhile perhaps you would care to wait in the drawing room. There is a good fire in there. Now, may I take your cloak?'

As she gave Peabody her cloak, bonnet and gloves, Ellen's eyes swept around the impressive hallway. Tilly had certainly done well for herself, it seemed. After following him into an equally impressive drawing room, Ellen felt the first stirrings of doubt. Had she been too impulsive in coming here? After all, she and Tilly had not seen or heard from each other for many, many years – and Tilly might not be pleased to see her, particularly now that she was the Lady of the Manor. Her presence might dredge up memories that were, to say the least, unwelcome.

Even as the thoughts were swirling around in her head, the sound of the door softly opening again brought her turning from the window, where she stood, gazing out. A woman was walking towards her, a woman no longer young, with hair the colour of driven snow, but this only seemed to add to her ethereal beauty. And then it hit Ellen Ross like a blow between the eyes: this woman was Tilly! Much taller now but still with the same straight figure, the same bright eyes that seemed to be able to look right into your very soul.

As emotion rushed through her, she took a step forward with her hands outstretched, and said, 'Oh, my dear!'

As recognition dawned in Tilly's eyes, her hand flew to her breast and she stared incredulously across the room. And then the years slipped away, and suddenly she could see them both in her mind's eye, and she and the parson's wife were young again, dancing up and down the vestry with their skirts held high and their laughter ringing in the dusty air.

'Oh, *Ellen*. I never thought to see you again.'

'Nor I you, my dear. But here I am.' As one they covered the distance between them and Tilly, who was rarely seen to cry, was sobbing as if her heart would break as she stared into the dear face that had once meant so much to her. In all the long years apart, she had never forgotten Ellen Ross or the kindness she had shown her, and now here she was like an answer to a prayer.

Clutching her hand as if she feared she might disappear again, Tilly drew her across the room and pressed her down onto the sofa. Then skipping across the room she pulled on the tasselled bell-rope that hung at the side of the fireplace. Fanny appeared within minutes and courteously bobbed her knee, sneaking a curious glance at their visitor. 'Yes, ma'am. What can I get for you?'

Fanny could have counted on one hand the times she had

seen Tilly truly happy, but this was certainly one of them, as she was to tell them all in the kitchen, for there was a smile on the mistress's face that stretched from ear to ear.

'Fanny, could you bring us some tea, please? A large pot, I think. Oh . . . and perhaps we could have a nice piece of fruitcake to go with it. I know it's not long until dinner. You *will* be staying for dinner, won't you, Ellen?'

'Well, I really ought to be getting back . . .' Seeing the disappointment settle across Tilly's face, Ellen came to a sudden decision. 'Of course I will. I'd be delighted to. Thank you.'

As Fanny hurried away, Tilly rushed back to Ellen's side and taking her hands in her own again, she asked, 'So, have you come from your parents' house? I received your letter saying that the parson had died when I was living in America. I shall tell you all about that soon, but first, let me say how sorry I am about Mr Ross. He was a kind and good man.'

Ellen gave a long, sad sigh. 'I'm afraid I didn't stay with my parents for long when I returned to England. I was ill with the fever at first, but when I recovered, I knew I had to leave them. Poor Mama and Papa. I had become the black sheep of the family after the trial, and eventually I chose to return to Africa. It is a wonderful place, Tilly, full of the most astonishing sights.' She squeezed Tilly's hands. 'I am now on my way back to live temporarily with my mother but thought I would make a special trip to the village and call in at the vicarage to enquire if you still lived hereabouts. When Parson Portman told me you were now the Lady of the Manor you could have knocked me down with a feather. You've certainly done well for yourself, my love.'

With a shrug of her shoulders Tilly looked towards the window. 'You could say that in some ways, but in others, my life has been far from easy,' she confided.

Looking tenderly at the beloved woman who had taught

her to read and write when she was nowt but a young raga-muffin, living in a small cottage with her gran and granda, and roaming the hillsides like a young goat, Tilly commented, 'Time has been kind to you,' and now it was Ellen's turn to shrug.

Tilly could hardly believe that she had changed so little. Her hair was still a rich dark brown, with barely a trace of grey, and her figure was slim and girlish. Only her complexion, which was more sallow than before, bore witness to her years in the Dark Continent. At that moment, the door burst open and Josefina swept into the room, only to stop in her tracks when she saw Ellen.

'I'm so sorry, Mama. I did not realise we had a visitor.'

Ellen looked mildly surprised as she stared back at the exquisite dark-skinned girl, then standing, she politely extended her hand. Josefina took it as Tilly introduced them.

'My darling, this is Ellen Ross. She lived in the village when I was a girl and was married to the parson. Ellen, this is my daughter, Josefina – and ah, here is Willy, my son.'

By now, Willy was fumbling his way across to them with his hand extended too.

'I'm very pleased to meet you,' he told her sincerely. 'Mama doesn't tend to have too many visitors, apart from family, of course.'

Ellen warmed to him as he pumped her hand up and down. He might have gone on doing so, but a squeaking noise heralded Fanny wheeling in a tea-trolley that looked to hold not only fruitcake, but enough food to feed an army.

'Ah, is that ham I can smell?' Willy sniffed at the air appreciatively, and, after supplying the visitor with a plate and napkin, and offering her a platter of dainty sandwiches, while her mother poured out the tea, Josefina began to load a plate for him.

Turning her attention back to Ellen, Tilly asked, 'Do you really have to go on to your parents' house tonight, Ellen? Couldn't I tempt you to stay? We have so very much to catch up on.'

Ellen hesitated, and then seeing the anticipation in her friend's eyes she said quietly, 'Well, if you're quite sure it would not inconvenience you and your family, I would love to stay. To be honest, my mother has no idea at all that I'm coming so she certainly won't miss me.'

Without even being asked, Fanny turned about and almost skipped towards the door. 'I'll go an' prepare a room in the grey wing then, shall I, pet?' In her excitement at their having a visitor she had reverted to her native endearment for Tilly, but Ellen noticed that Tilly did not seem to mind a jot being addressed so by a maid. The whole set-up looked strange to the parson's widow, for here was Tilly with two children, one who appeared to be half-blind and the other of a different race. And where was the father of the children, Tilly's husband? Or perhaps she should say fathers, for these two could not have come from the same man. Tilly certainly hadn't been lying when she said they had a lot to catch up on, and so began what was to be the first of many nights Ellen would spend at Highfield Manor.

Dinner was a merry affair. Although it was many years since they had last met, Steve and Ellen chatted their way through each delicious course with the ease of old friends. At one stage during the meal, Ellen found herself thinking back to the distant time when Steve had tipped her off about Hal McGrath's plan to put Tilly in the stocks, and the events that had then led to her killing Burk Laudimer in the girl's defence. She shuddered at the memory but then pushed it away; it was best left in the past now. She was determined that nothing should spoil this night.

However, although Ellen was doing all she could to be cheerful, the atmosphere between Josefina and Willy remained strained. Tonight, Tilly was so thrilled to have Ellen with them that she chose to ignore it and left the pair of them to get on with it. At least Josefina had made the effort to join them instead of having a tray sent up to her room as she usually did, so that was something at least.

Eventually the talk at the table turned to the renovations and extensions Steve was doing to the cottage he and Tilly were to live in. 'I've already got men working on a fine stable-block,' he told them animatedly, 'and I've also now added another two good-sized rooms to the living quarters downstairs, above which I intend to build a bedroom. Of course, it will still be nothing like what Tilly is used to here, but it should be comfortable all the same.'

Tilly smiled across at him proudly. She would have lived in a barn with him, had he asked her to. 'I'm sure it will be lovely,' she assured him, then, 'Shall we all retire to the sitting room? Biddle will serve coffee, and a glass of port or brandy for those that want it.'

'Who is Biddle?' Ellen asked, and Tilly winked at her with amusement twinkling in her eyes.

'Biddle is the footman and as old as the hills. He's been here for years but I haven't the heart to retire him. He's like one of the family.'

As they all rose and began to make their way from the room, Ellen giggled. 'You've certainly come a long way, Tilly Trotter,' she teased, 'what with Biddle the footman, and Peabody the butler – not to mention the little maid I've seen and the cook. Oh, and of course, I saw Arthur Drew outside too.'

'Jimmy is here as well,' Willy told her. 'Arthur and Jimmy tend the gardens and do all the odd jobs about the place. Rather well too, I might add. At one time we had all the Drews here, didn't we, Mama?'

'Yes, we did, dear.' Tilly's face clouded as she thought back to Biddy, who had passed away some time ago, but then she brightened up. She wouldn't be sad tonight with Ellen here. She intended to make the most of every single minute of their time together. After all, for all she knew, more years might pass before they saw each other again. Smiling widely, she ushered them all into the sitting room where Biddle was waiting to serve the after-dinner drinks.

Chapter Six

MUCH LATER, WHEN Josefina and Willy had retired to their rooms, and Steve had returned to the cottage, Tilly drew Ellen to the velvet sofa at the side of the fireplace in the drawing room.

'I've been longing to get you all to myself,' she told her excitedly. 'There is so much to tell you I scarcely know where to begin.'

'I know exactly what you mean,' Ellen replied with a trace of sadness in her voice.

Tilly cocked an eyebrow as she held tight to her friend's hand. 'Have you not been happy then, Ellen?'

The older woman's slight shoulders shrugged imperceptibly. 'What *is* happiness, Tilly? I have been loved and cared for . . . but not perhaps as a wife should be.'

Tilly remained silent until Ellen composed herself and went on. 'After George and I left the village following the unfortunate episode when you were put in the stocks, and I was charged with the manslaughter of Burk Laudimer, we travelled to the heart of Africa. Oh, the tales I could tell you of the sights I have seen and the places we visited! Tribes of people with skin as black as midnight, who had never looked on white men or women before. All those different languages and beliefs took some getting used to you know. George certainly had his work cut out converting them, I don't mind telling you. Shortly after moving out there, he became firm friends with a gentleman named Doctor David Livingstone, a Scottish missionary who dedicated himself to exploring and evangelising Africa. Oh Tilly, he was such a truly remarkable man and George was completely in awe of him. His wife Mary was a wonderful woman too, and whilst the men were off on their travels she and I often stayed behind and I helped her to care for their children. They had six – Robert, Agnes, Thomas, Elizabeth, Zouga, who we called William, and little Anna.'

Ellen paused for a moment, as if she could see them there before her, then she told Tilly solemnly, 'It was just as well I was there, for Mary was often plagued by ill-health. More than once she was struck with partial paralysis, which was not helped by the difficult life she was forced to lead. There are all sorts of insects and diseases out there – you can't imagine what it's like. Anyway, we moved about quite a bit in the course of our work, though I never once heard her complain, for her love of her husband was such that she would have followed him to the ends of the earth. Our main settlement was in the Valley of Mabotsa, which is about two hundred miles north of Kuruman. It was whilst David was building the settlement that he was mauled by a lion. His arm was so badly damaged that he never had full use of it again.' She shuddered. 'That poor family! At one point, Mary's ill-health caused David to send her and the children back to England for four years to recover. It was during those years that I embarked on expeditions with the men, and the sights we saw will remain etched on my mind for always.'

Ellen's face became animated as her mind slipped back in time. 'I can remember David's words when we set off as clearly as if it were yesterday,' she murmured. ' "I shall open up a path into the interior or perish". Livingstone was convinced, you see, that Christianity and civilisation would deliver Africa from slavery and barbarism. On our journey we followed the Zambezi River to the Indian Ocean, and on the way we encountered the most spectacular waterfalls you could ever imagine in your wildest dreams. The Africans had named it "Mosi-oa-Tunya" which means "The Smoke that Thunders", but David renamed it "The Victoria Falls" in honour of our Queen. Oh Tilly, it was such an emotional moment.'

Tilly's head bobbed in agreement as she tried to contemplate it. 'It must have been. But what of you and George? You have spoken of him very little up to now. Did you have any children?'

Ellen played nervously with the buttons on her bodice. Eventually she confided in a small voice, 'No, Tilly. We never had children – although it was always my greatest wish – but then that was hardly surprising. You see, George and I . . . Well, our relationship changed after we left England.'

'In what way?'

Ellen sought for the right words to describe what had happened. 'The thing is, George was some ten years older than me, as you may remember. After the incident in the village he became very protective of me. Oh, he was always kindness itself and would have moved heaven and earth for me, but . . . I think in his eyes I became more of an errant child than a wife and we stopped . . . well, doing the things that a husband and wife do.'

As the implication of her words sank in, Tilly's brow furrowed into a deep frown though she made no comment and eventually Ellen began her narrative again.

'I sometimes got the impression that he saw me as some

sort of puppy that he could pamper and spoil. I know, of course, that that side of a marriage is not everything, but there were times when I became so frustrated that I had the urge to return to England and leave him to it. I think perhaps I might have, but Mary and I had started a small school for the African children and I became so immersed in running it that I was able to put other things aside for long stretches at a time – and then, of course, George died.'

There was a moment's silence, then Ellen picked up her story again. 'Mary and I ran the school together until she died in 1862. It was a great loss, as we had become so close. David was absolutely devastated. He had her buried beneath a tree in Shupanga and then sadly went on with his journeys. He had hoped to keep his children with him, but it soon became clear that the climate was affecting their health too, but what was there for me to come back to? And so I gave it much thought and decided to stay as a teacher in the school that Mary and I had started.'

Seeing Tilly's amazed expression, Ellen smiled wryly. 'Never mind about me. It seems that life has not been straightforward for you either. Tell me all that has been happening.' But as she spoke, the clock on the mantelshelf chimed midnight and Tilly saw the older woman stifle a yawn. They had been so busy talking that the time had just slipped away.

'There will be time enough for that tomorrow,' she promised. 'I'm afraid I've been very selfish. Look at you – you can hardly keep your eyes open. Please tell me that you will stay for just another day at least. If your parents are not expecting you, surely just one more day won't hurt?'

Ellen smiled sadly. 'Actually, my father died some years ago. There is only Mother left now and from the letters I have received from her recently, it seems that she is confined to bed with arthritis. No doubt I shall have to take on the role of nursemaid when I do return. Poor Mother. So yes, as long as you're quite sure that my being here isn't inconveniencing you, I would love to stay another day, or even two if you will have me.'

'Oh Ellen.' The brightness in Tilly's eyes told of the pleasure her friend's visit had evoked in her. 'You can stay for as long as you like. My fiancé and I will be planning our marriage soon and it would be wonderful to have a friend to share in the arrangements. I may now be mistress of the Manor, but I can assure you I have few friends, apart from the ones in this house, of course. That is something that certainly hasn't changed with the years. But come now. I shall show you to your room and then tomorrow you must come to meet Sarah, my baby granddaughter, with me.'

When Ellen gave a start of surprise, it was Tilly's turn to smile. 'As I said, I have a lot to tell you – but not now. You look as if you're about to fall asleep at any minute.'

'I think I just might.' Ellen stifled another yawn. 'And as much as I'd love to come with you in the morning, I'm not sure that I'll manage it. Perhaps I could meet your granddaughter another time?'

'Of course you can.' Hoisting Ellen to her feet, Tilly linked her arm through hers and together the two women made their way from the room and up the wide staircase.

As they climbed, Ellen stared in awe at the magnificent portraits that hung at intervals on the fine flocked wallpaper, including one of Tilly, which Mark had commissioned many years ago. Her eyes stretched even wider when Tilly opened the door to what she called the grey room.

For many years past, Ellen had lived in very primitive accommodation, sometimes little more than a glorified mud hut, so this room appeared very luxurious indeed. A large four-poster bed draped with curtains in a soft grey patterned brocade stood against one wall, and matching curtains with elegant swags hung at the full-length window. The walls were papered in a delicate shade of blue, and a welcome fire was blazing in a pretty fireplace. A huge, finely carved mahogany wardrobe and a mirrored dressing-table and stool stood against another wall, whilst on the third wall was a washstand, with a willow-pattern jug and bowl. The lamp on the bedside table washed the room with warmth as Ellen gasped with delight.

'Why, Tilly, it's absolutely beautiful! I shall be afraid to move in here,' she stuttered.

Tilly crossed to the bed to make sure that Fanny had placed a stone hot-water bottle in it. 'I hope you'll be comfortable, but if there is anything at all you need, don't hesitate to pull the bell-rope there.' She pointed to a tasselled rope that was hanging at the side of the bed, then gestured at Ellen's trunk, which Arthur had placed to one side of the door.

'I didn't get Fanny to unpack it for you as I wasn't sure how long you'd be here,' she said. 'But if I can persuade you to stay for a while, she will do that for you in the morning.'

Ellen's delighted laughter rang around the room. 'Oh Tilly,' she spluttered, highly amused, 'although we did have an entourage of servants in Africa we sometimes had to live in accommodation that left a lot to be desired, so I'm quite sure I shall manage to do my own unpacking.' She spread her hands to encompass the room. 'And it has been many years since I slept in a room such as this. I think I shall be *more* than comfortable. In fact, you may have to come and drag me out of bed in the morning.'

Tilly's laughter matched her guest's now, although she

promised her: 'There will be no fear of that. You lie in for as long as you like and recover from your journey.'

With a final smile she slipped from the room and began to walk along the labyrinth of corridors that would take her to her own room. The whole house was fast asleep and Tilly could have heard a pin drop as she quietly entered her bedroom. Once there she stepped out of her dress and hung it neatly across the back of a chair before crossing to her washstand where she washed herself from head to toe in the now cold water that Fanny had placed there for her some hours before. She then slid her nightdress over her head and took the pins from her hair, allowing it to spill down her back in all its shining glory. Despite the fact that it was snow-white, it was still thick and she smiled at herself in her dressing-table mirror as she brushed it and twisted it into two thick plaits that hung to her waist. It had been an eventful day with Ellen turning up out of the blue like that. Many a time she had thought of her over the years, but she had long since given up hope of ever seeing her again, which only went to make her surprise arrival today all the more enjoyable. The only thing to mar the day was Josefina's reaction to Ellen. But then that hardly surprised Tilly at all. Josefina had always been jealous and possessive of her, and since her return from America she had been even more demanding, if that was possible. But at least she got on well with most of the servants, whom she loved with the same kind of loyalty that characterized her bonds with Tilly and with her brother. Josefina was self-contained, and passionate, and quite unlike anyone else, Tilly had come to accept.

Still, at least Willy and Steve had gone out of their way to make Ellen feel welcome, and no doubt Josefina would warm to her if Tilly could persuade her to stay long enough. Laying down the silver-backed hairbrush that had been a present from Matthew in the early days of their marriage, she rose from the stool and crossed to the bed. Clambering in, she snuggled down beneath the covers with a tired smile on her face. At last, good things were beginning to happen in her life, and with this happy thought in mind she finally drifted off to sleep.

The family were at breakfast in the dining room the next morning when Ellen entered and smiled sheepishly. 'I'm so sorry for being late,' she apologised to them all, trying hard to hide her shock when she saw that Tilly was dressed in a pair of fine suede riding breeches. 'I'm afraid the bed was so comfortable that I had a problem dragging myself out of it.'

Tilly's eyes were bright as she beckoned her to the table. 'I told you not to worry about getting up,' she scolded her gently. 'I could see how tired you were. Anyway, I've had a place laid for you so do help yourself from the sideboard.'

Ellen helped herself to a liberal portion of bacon and kidneys. When she was seated, Tilly asked her, 'I take it that you slept well then?'

'Like a log might be an apt description,' Ellen smiled.

'Good. I shall be going to see my granddaughter, Sarah, shortly, but I shall be back for lunchtime. Whilst I'm gone, please feel free to have the run of the house. There's a rather well-stocked library at the end of the hallway, or perhaps you might like to take a stroll around the grounds?'

'Oh, I'm sure I shall find something to entertain myself,' Ellen assured her, after swallowing a mouthful of bacon. 'Will you all be going to see Sarah?'

'No, just Willy and me.'

Ellen could have sworn she saw a flicker of resentment pass across Josefina's features at Tilly's words, but she said nothing, and Ellen thought that she must have imagined it.

Although Willy kept up a constant stream of chatter throughout the meal, she noticed that Josefina said very little, and Ellen's curiosity was awakened. Who was this dark-skinned girl that Tilly had introduced as her daughter? There seemed to be nothing of Tilly in her at all. Had Tilly been married to a black man at some point, she wondered. She had said nothing about any African connection last night.

When the meal was finally over they took their coffee into the morning room and Tilly pointed to a pile of news-papers that Biddle had placed on the small table at the side of the fireplace. 'Do feel free to look at those while we're gone. And as I said before, should you need any help with your unpacking, Fanny will be more than happy to assist. We're having a small party here tonight for Peg who is going to live on my late husband's ranch in America, with Katie, her sister.'

'Oh, was your husband the father of Willy and Josefina?' Ellen asked innocently.

'No, he wasn't,' Josefina answered before Tilly had had time to open her mouth.

'My brother and I are what is termed as bastards . . . aren't we, Mama?'

A stunned silence settled on the room until it was broken by Tilly, when she said, 'That was quite uncalled-for, Josefina.' Then, turning to address Ellen, who was wishing she could have bitten her tongue off, she told her, 'I'll have time to explain everything to you later. But for now, Willy and I will have to be off. Lucy will be expecting us.'

As he marched towards the door, close behind his mother, Ellen saw the young man glare in his sister's direction before closing the door smartly behind them. Josefina was visibly pale as she rose from her seat with tears glistening on her long dark eyelashes. Ellen would have liked to comfort her, for there was an air of such abject misery about the girl that the woman's kind heart went out to her, despite her outburst of minutes before. She hesitated, and during that time, Josefina got up, her head in the air, and waltzed from the room, slamming the door resoundingly behind her. Ellen winced and then shrugged. As Tilly had promised, she would tell her all about it when the opportunity arose and until then she would have to contain her curiosity.

The sun was riding high in a cloudless blue sky when mother and son reined their horses to a halt in the yard of Brook Farm. Even so there was a nip in the air, and Tilly's cheeks were glowing as she made her way into the kitchen where Sarah was propped on the horse-hair settee gurgling contentedly as she watched Lucy potter about the room. Of Eddie there was no sign and Tilly was glad, for following his outburst of some weeks ago, the atmosphere was still strained whenever he and Willy were present.

As usual, Willy hovered by the door, nervously fiddling with the rim of his riding cap as Tilly crossed to the child and gathered her into her arms.

'So how are you all, Lucy?' she asked as her eyes moved to the woman who was bending to press the large black kettle into the heart of the fire. She was concerned to see that this week, Lucy looked even paler than she had the week before, and dark circles were beginning to form beneath her eyes.

'Oh, bearing up,' Lucy replied with none of her old sparkle.

'Willy, go out and bring in the cakes Peg has made, would you? They're in the bag on the back of Lady's saddle.'

The instant that Willy had left the room, feeling his way, Tilly crossed to Lucy and looking deep into her eyes she asked, 'What's wrong? And don't say nothing. You're as pale as a ghost. Is Sarah still disturbing you at night?'

'No, no, not at all. The child is an angel and sleeps through most nights now,' Lucy told her.

As she straightened, Tilly noticed for the first time the slight swell of Lucy's stomach and for a time she was so shocked that she was rendered speechless. Her mind began to do rapid calculations. Yes, it could be possible that Lucy had become pregnant just before Simon's death. The timing would tie in with the swelling she had just noticed. But why hadn't Lucy said anything? She was getting on for having another child, yet stranger things had happened. Why, old Mrs Pearson down in the village had given birth to her youngest at forty-seven, and as Tom her husband had said at the time, you could have knocked him down with a feather, for he had thought her childbearing days were long over. The next thought that entered Tilly's head brought her teeth clamping down on her lip. If Lucy was pregnant, how would she cope with two babies to care for?

At that moment, Willy came back into the room with a blast of cold air that sent the flames licking up the coalhole. He placed the bag Peg had prepared down on the table and Tilly felt the moment for asking Lucy straight out if she was carrying a child was gone; for now at least. But what she would do was try to get to the farm on her own in the week and ask Lucy straight out. If the answer was yes, then Tilly would insist that she allow her to get some help in. She was more than aware that since they had stopped children going down the pit, a move with which she was wholly in favour, there were any number of young girls in the village who would jump at the chance of being given a position on Brook Farm. If Lucy would allow it, that was, for Tilly had discovered that Lucy was fiercely independent and welcomed help from no one.

Deciding not to dwell on her fears for now she lightened

the mood when she told Lucy, 'I had an unexpected visitor yesterday. Ellen Ross used to be the parson's wife in the village when I was a girl but she and her husband moved abroad many years ago and he became a missionary.'

'Really, and have you not heard from her since?' Lucy asked affably.

'Only once, which made it all the more pleasant when she arrived yesterday.' Tilly shifted Sarah into a more comfortable position in her arms before going on. 'I'm hoping to persuade her to stay for a while at least. We're having a little party for Peg tonight, sort of a farewell do, I suppose you could call it. I can't begin to tell you how much I shall miss her though. She's like a part of our family, isn't she Willy?'

He nodded.

'Well, I gather the Drews have been your family ever since your gran an' granda died, is that right?' Lucy replied as she poured the steaming water into the teapot.

Some minutes later, Tilly brought up the matter that had been playing on her mind for weeks past. 'Lucy, I was thinking . . .' She broached the subject tentatively, unsure how the other woman would take what she was about to suggest. When Lucy raised a quizzical eyebrow, she took a deep breath and went on, 'Should we not be thinking about having Sarah christened now?'

To her relief, Lucy's head wagged in agreement. 'I've been thinking much along the same lines myself.' Her eyes softened as they settled on Sarah who was now sitting on Tilly's lap happily playing with the collar of her blouse. 'I think Noreen would have wished it. The trouble is, I'm not sure if Parson Portman will agree to do the ceremony. After all, Sarah *was* born out of wedlock and therefore she could be classed as a . . .'

When her voice trailed away, Tilly's face flushed with

annoyance. 'He would have to be absolutely heartless to refuse,' she said curtly. 'Particularly allowing for the circumstances that led to Sarah's birth. After all, it's common knowledge that she *would* have been born in wedlock had Simon allowed it, so why should the child be punished?'

A slight shrug of her shoulders was Lucy's answer and now Tilly told her with determination, 'Leave it with me. I shall go to see him myself. There is one thing I would ask of you though. If the parson does agree to do it, would you allow me to throw a small party to celebrate after the service up at the Manor?'

'Why would we want to have it there?' Willy snapped, breaking the silence he had maintained since entering the room.

Tilly's eyes were like chips of ice as she glared back at him. 'Because, Willy, whether you want to face your responsibilities or not, Sarah is your child and, may I add, my grandchild.'

Willy's head drooped in shame and after a time he slowly covered the short distance between them and hesitantly stroked the child's hand. Instantly she clung on to his finger and colour suffused his face as Tilly smiled at him encouragingly.

'Why don't you hold her? She doesn't bite, you know.'

When she pressed the baby into his arms he stared into her face. His vision in one eye was gone altogether, and the vision in the other was blurred, but it was enough for him to see close up that the child was a miniature copy of her late mother. Tears clogged his throat and as he forced them to stay there, he had the sensation of drowning. He had held on to his memories of Noreen and tried to convince himself that she was the only woman he would ever love. But it had been hard since Josefina had returned home, for the sound of her voice was enough to set his pulses racing as Noreen's once had. And here was the fruit of their love in his arms. How could he ever love wholly again whilst Sarah was there as a constant reminder of the wrong he had done? Already the picture of Noreen's face was fading in his mind – until he looked at Sarah, that was.

Tilly's hand on his arm was gentle as she told him, 'There is no shame in caring for the child, Willy. Nor any shame in moving on with your life.'

His eyes moved to his mother's and she saw a look of incredulity settle across his face. How can she say that? he was thinking. Had it not been for him, Noreen would still be alive. And in that moment the guilt that never left him was unbearable, and he knew that he would have to live with the weight of it for the rest of his life: it stretched before him like a life sentence.

Suddenly thrusting Sarah back into Tilly's arms he turned on his heel and strode clumsily from the room, knocking into a chair, as Tilly and Lucy exchanged a glance.

Lucy now took the baby from Tilly before telling her softly, 'Go after him, pet, he's hurting.'

Tilly lifted her hat from the table and after kissing Lucy and the bairn on their soft cheeks, she strode from the room straight-faced, thinking, Dear God, why was there always something to worry about?

Chapter Seven

TILLY ARRIVED HOME to find the Manor buzzing with activity as the plans for the party got underway. A heavy cloth had been placed over the table in the dining room and now that it had been lifted to the side of the room, Biddle and Fanny were busily loading it with food for the night. Great meat pies took up one end, together with all manner of freshly baked rolls and savoury pastries fresh from the oven. On the other end stood a large dish of strawberry trifle, which was a particular favourite of Master Willy's, made with bottled fruit from the estate, along with cakes, and apple-and-blackberry pies whose fragrance made Willy's mouth water with anticipation.

'Oh, Peg, whatever shall I do when you're gone?' he teased as he placed his arm around her plump waist. 'There is no one who can make a strawberry trifle like you.'

Flushing with pleasure at the compliment she wagged a wooden spoon at him. 'You'll get by. Now stand aside, please, else we'll be having this party after I'm gone.'

He chuckled as he watched her make her way to the door, but the smile slid from his face when Josefina suddenly appeared, looking none too pleased.

'Are you quite sure it is such a good idea, allowing the

staff to have their party in here, Mama?' she asked haughtily. 'Surely they could have held it in the kitchen? It isn't as if there isn't room in there.'

At this, Willy walked out of the room without so much as a word and now Tilly told her sharply, 'Really, Josefina, what has got into you! I sometimes think if there were prizes for airs and graces you would win a first. Why shouldn't Peg have her party in here? She's almost like family to us. In fact, there was a time when the Drews were all I had in the world. You would do well to remember that, my girl. I'm only sorry that they all can't be here.'

Josefina sniffed before turning about, and in a rustle of skirts she flounced out the way she had come. Tilly tapped her riding crop against the side of her breeches in annoyance. She had hoped to keep the party a secret from Peg until Fanny had admitted that she had told her about it. Now, here was Peg helping to prepare her own do. And as if that wasn't bad enough, now Josefina was on her high horse. Now that Tilly came to think about it, she had rarely been *off* her high horse since returning home, and her mother's patience was being stretched to the limit. Sometimes she had to resist the urge to scream at both her and Willy, for the two of them seemed to be wallowing in self-pity. Still, she decided that nothing should spoil this night for Peg so she would go and get changed and then come down to help with the preparations. She was just leaving the room when she almost collided with Ellen, who was carrying a great tray of homemade biscuits in her hands.

'What's this then?' Tilly greeted her and Ellen laughed.

'I got roped in to help. Not that I mind, you understand. I used to absolutely love parties, though I cannot remember the last time I went to one.'

'We can soon remedy that,' Tilly smiled back. 'Though I

have to say that it doesn't seem quite right, a guest having to help with the preparations.'

'It doesn't seem quite right that a member of staff should be allowed to hold a party in the mistress's dining room,' Ellen retorted with a chuckle. 'But as I am fast discovering, this is no ordinary household. However . . .' Her face became serious now. 'As much as I appreciate your invitation I shall have to decline.'

'But why?'

'Because I'm afraid my trunk doesn't contain anything suitable to wear to a party,' Ellen told her regretfully. 'As you can imagine, there wasn't much call for party dresses where I have been living.'

Tilly eyed her up and down. Ellen barely reached up to her shoulders but apart from the height difference the two were of a very similar slim build.

'Come with me,' she ordered in a voice that brooked no argument, and the instant Ellen had laid the biscuits on the table she took her elbow and began to steer her towards the staircase. 'I might just have the solution to your problem.'

Once inside her bedroom, Tilly flung her wardrobe door open and began to sift through the dresses within. Finally she withdrew a gown in a soft sea-green and held it up for Ellen's approval.

'I think this one might be just right for you. Why don't you try it on?'

'Oh, Tilly. I really couldn't. It's far too fine,' Ellen objected.

'Nonsense.' Tilly began to undo the buttons as Ellen reluctantly took off her dress. Then Tilly slipped the other over her head and smiled with satisfaction as it settled about her. The colour was perfect for her and apart from the length, it fitted her like a glove.

'You look beautiful in it,' Tilly told her. 'And seeing as I never wear it you'd be doing me a favour if you took it off my hands.' She picked up a pretty pin-cushion that Josefina had made and embroidered for her when she was a child, with the letters T T intertwined in slip-stitch, and took some pins from it to mark the place. 'Now let's take it off and I'll get Gwen, our little maid, to alter the hem for you. She's absolutely wonderful with a needle and thread. By the time she's finished with it, you'll think it had been made for you.'

"Thank you, darling Tilly.' Ellen watched Tilly sail purposefully from the room with the dress tucked over her arm and then she crossed to the window to stare out across the grounds. Down below, Arthur was tending to the flowerbeds. His shirt-sleeves were rolled up to the elbows and she saw that his muscled arms were already beginning to tan despite the earliness of the season. Much to her deep embarrassment, Ellen's heart skipped a beat and she turned hastily away from the window. Whatever is the matter with me? she thought to herself, although she already knew the answer, and then began to pull on her old dress again. Perhaps it would not be such a good idea to stay here for too long, after all.

Downstairs, Willy had retired to the library to escape all the hustle and bustle of the party preparations. Steve would be coming tonight, along with John and Anna who wished to say their own goodbyes to Peg. They would then stay the night in the room that had been theirs whilst they had lived here, before returning to Felton Hall in the morning.

He had just lit his pipe, a habit his mother thoroughly disapproved of, when he heard the library door open. Without even turning from the deep wing chair he knew that it was Josefina. There was a certain scent that she always wore that he would have recognised anywhere. For a while she was unaware of his presence and she crossed to the floor-to-ceiling bookshelves and began to peer at the titles there. Suddenly, some inner instinct told her that she was not alone and she swung about to find Willy watching her through a haze of smoke.

'Oh, Willy . . . it's you. You startled me,' she said quietly. She had the distinct impression that he had been avoiding her since she had returned home, no doubt because he was still grieving for Noreen. Even as the thought occurred to her, jealousy, sharp as a knife, pierced at her heart. But why was he avoiding her so? Surely he could see that she loved him? Noreen was gone and could never come back. So why could he not turn to her?

'I was looking for something to read,' she said unnecessarily, and with the old twinkle in his eyes, Willy retorted, 'Why don't you try Voltaire?'

It had always been a joke between them, for Voltaire's *Candide* was the book that the late Mr Burgess, who had once been a tutor to the children at the Manor, had once instructed Tilly to read.

Seeing Willy smile made Josefina relax, and crossing to him now she said all in a rush, 'Oh, Willy, I missed you so much whilst I was in America.'

Conflicting emotions flitted across his face as he saw the open adoration in her eyes and for a time he seemed to be wrestling with some inner demon. But then the closed look she had come to dread brought his lips together into a tight line before he replied, 'No doubt it was just all things familiar that you were missing, Josefina.'

Had he slapped her across the face she could not have looked more hurt, and turning about she made silently for the door, closing it equally silently behind her.

Once he was alone, Willy flung his pipe into the back of the fire and buried his face in his hands. 'Why is everything such a mess?' he asked of the empty room, but the only answer he got was the spitting of the logs as they settled into the iron fire-basket.

Upstairs, Josefina was lying curled up on her bed and sobbing as if her heart would break. She had come home with such plans for the future. She had hoped that she and Willy would be married and live happily ever after. But as the days moved on and he distanced himself ever further from her, her dreams were dying. Turning onto her back she stared up at the elaborate ceiling rose high above her and the thought in her mind now was, It would be best if I were to leave here once and for all.

Steve was the first to arrive that evening looking very smart in a new melton coat and a satin waistcoat over a silk shirt. Tilly met him in the hallway and his eyes were full of admiration as he took her into his arms and kissed her soundly. As usual, Tilly's dress was plain but elegant and she looked stunning. It was a lovely peacock-blue colour that emphasised the colour of her eyes and her snow-white hair.

She smiled when she saw that his hair was still damp and guessed that he must have rushed home from the mine, where he was now manager, to wash and change. Sometimes she worried that he was doing too much, for as well as working at the pit, he spent every spare minute he had overseeing the work on the cottage where they would live once they were married.

'You look tired,' she commented as she tenderly stroked his cheek, but he just laughed. 'I'm as fit as a butcher's dog,' he told her. 'The only tiredness I suffer from is waiting for you to set the date for the wedding.'

'Oh, Steve.' Concern brought a frown to her brow. 'I *do* want us to be married. You know I do, more than anything. I just need to get Josefina settled properly back in. You must have noticed how strangely she has been acting since she arrived home from America? And Willy's attitude towards her doesn't help. They were as close as could be before she left, and I thought that it would be the same when she got home, but Willy is also in a strange mood. Sometimes I feel like banging their heads together, for it's as plain as the noses on their faces that they love each other. Why can't they see it? And anyway, as for us getting married – the cottage is nowhere near ready yet, so there is really no rush, is there?'

Steve placed his arm around her waist. 'True, the cottage is not quite ready but it shouldn't be too long now. And as for Willy and Josefina – I shouldn't worry about them too much. You know what they say – true love never runs smooth. Look at us for an example. There were times when I thought I'd die before you ever looked the side I was on, but it came right in the end, didn't it?' His eyes flicked towards the dining room and now he asked, 'Am I the first to arrive?'

'Yes. John and Anna are due at any minute. I'm so looking forward to seeing them, though I wish it could have been in happier circumstances. I really don't know how I'm going to cope without Peg. I feel as if I shall be losing a sister.'

Steve's head bobbed in understanding. He would miss Peg too, for he had grown close to the Drew family over the years through his association with Tilly.

The clanging of the doorbell interrupted their thoughts, and when Peabody answered it, John and Anna spilled into the hall. They were hand-in-hand, and the sight brought a warm feeling to Tilly's heart. It had been she who had introduced them some years ago, and from that day on she had believed in the saying, love at first sight, for if any two were made for each other, it was this young couple walking towards her now.

'Tilly.' They both kissed her soundly then turning his attention to Steve, John said, 'H . . . hello, Steve. You're looking v . . . very smart t . . . tonight.'

Steve shook John's hand with a happy grin on his face and told him, 'Aye, well, you have to make an effort when you're engaged to be married to the Lady o' the Manor.'

They were all laughing now and after Peabody had taken their coats, Tilly ushered them towards the dining room. John whistled through his teeth when he saw the spread laid out on the table. 'C . . . crikey, T . . . Tilly. You've cer . . . certainly done her proud.'

'It was the least I could do for her after all she and her family have done for me,' Tilly smiled. Moments later, Willy joined them, followed by Arthur and Jimmy who were dressed in their Sunday best and looking rather uncomfortable. Crossing to a table that was laden down with drinks next to the main table, Tilly asked, 'Right then, what would you like? It will be me serving you tonight for a change.'

'I'll er . . . I'll have some ale, if that's all right with you, Tilly,' Arthur told her. Soon everyone in the room had a drink in their hand and as the rest of the staff trickled in, including Peg, the atmosphere became relaxed. Tilly had got Arthur and Jimmy to carry the piano through from the day room and once Ellen appeared, looking very pretty in the dress that Tilly had given her, she sat at the stool and began to play for them.

Soon the wine and beer were flowing like water and everyone was helping themselves to the food as Tilly looked on with satisfaction. A thought suddenly occurred to her, and she covered her mouth with her hand and stifled a giggle.

Cocking an eyebrow, Steve asked, 'Oh aye, an' what's tickling you then?'

'I was just wondering what the villagers would say if they could see us all now,' she grinned up at him. 'Can't you just hear them? "There she goes again," they'd say, "not knowing her place." But what *is* my place, Steve? I've lived a long time but I'm yet to discover where I belong.'

'Well, that's easily remedied. I can tell you exactly where you belong and it's with me!'

Their laughter joined as Fanny suddenly flew past them in Biddle's arms, the couple dancing up and down the length of the room. Then Peabody was partnering Peg, and even he seemed merry tonight. Jimmy was dancing with Gwen, whose cheeks were glowing, for it was no secret that she worshipped the very ground he walked on. When Steve asked, 'Don't you think we ought to join them, madam?' Tilly giggled, then he bowed dramatically and, offering his arm, said, 'May I?'

'You may, sir.' And then she was in his arms and they were twirling up and down and Tilly couldn't remember when she had last enjoyed herself so much. At some stage, Biddle took over the piano-playing, which was somewhat of a surprise, for Tilly had never known that he could play. And then she was further surprised when Ellen waltzed past, clutched tight in Arthur's arms. She was looking up at him with a rapt smile on her face and it struck Tilly what a nice-looking couple they made.

As if reading her thoughts, Steve leaned down to her and whispered, 'They look bonny together, don't they?' When Tilly nodded in reply he went on, 'Did you say that Ellen had been widowed?' Again she nodded, and though not a further word on the subject was spoken they each knew what the other was thinking.

Anna's laughter rang around the room as John sped by with her gripped tightly to him, and Ned Spoke, who had positioned himself at the side of the drinks table, was swaying with a smile that stretched from ear to ear.

At one point Tilly noticed that Willy and Josefina were sitting in the deep bay window watching the proceedings but making no effort to join in. She shrugged. Tonight she would ignore it, for she wanted nothing to spoil Peg's last night.

It was almost on eleven o'clock when Jimmy stood and shouted, 'Speech, Tilly! Surely there should be a speech?'

Tilly blushed becomingly as Steve nudged her towards the centre of the room and a hush fell amongst the assembled crowd. Looking around at all the dear familiar faces, she swallowed the lump in her throat and began, 'It was many years ago following the deaths of my granny and granda that I happened across Katie Drew by sheer chance. I had no one in the world and nowhere to call home, so she took me to hers out of the goodness of her heart, and there I met Peg and all her brothers and sisters. From that day on, my life changed for the better, for I was accepted into that family's hearts as I had never been in the village. Over the years, Biddy Drew became the nearest thing to a mother I had ever known and you . . .' she spread her hands to take in the rest of the Drew family dotted about the room '. . . you all became the siblings I had always longed for and been denied. Sadly, Biddy left us some time ago, but I think I can speak for us all when I say that we feel her loss every single day. We can take comfort from the fact that if there is a heaven, she will be happy there, for that woman had a heart made of solid gold.' The lump was swelling, and gulping now she looked towards Peg. 'Peg, on behalf of us all I want to wish you a safe journey. You will be missed more than you could ever know, but it's time for you to have a life of your own instead of being constantly at our beck and call. My life has been enriched for having known you. I love you as a sister, Peg Drew, and you will go knowing that, and every one of us here, will never, ever forget you.'

'Aw, Tilly, hinny.'

Ned Spoke pressed a none too clean handkerchief into Peg's hand as tears exploded from her eyes to run in rivers down her plump cheeks. And then they were all around her in a tight circle and as her eyes passed from one to the other of them she tried to lock their faces away into her memory, for she knew that after tomorrow she might never look on any of them again.

It was long after midnight before the dining room was empty of everyone but Tilly and Steve, and then taking her into his arms he looked around ruefully. 'Oh dear me. It looks like someone's going to be busy tomorrow.'

She looked around the untidy room. 'Aw, well. I've told them all to have a lie-in. Peg and I will be off early, so no doubt it will be cleaned up by the time I get back, and what if it isn't? I'm hardly deluged with visitors, am I?'

His lips found hers again and for a time she gave herself up to the pleasure of his closeness before pressing him away from her and sighing, 'Go on, you. Get yourself away whilst you have the chance or I just might keep you here.'

He groaned but obediently turned about, and she followed him to the door where he kissed her good night. 'Are you quite sure you don't want me to come with you tomorrow?' he asked. 'It's a long journey back all on your own.'

'I shall be fine,' she assured him. 'Now get yourself off. I want you to keep that pit of mine running smoothly.'

He frowned. 'I need to talk to you about that, Tilly. Number three is filling up with water again, faster than the pumps can drain it. But still, not tonight, eh? We don't want to spoil it.'

She stood shivering on the steps until he returned from the stable-block with his horse, then watched until the night mist had swallowed him up before turning and making her way to bed, yawning. Tomorrow was going to be a very long day.

Chapter Eight

THEY WERE STANDING on the steps of the Manor with every single person that Peg held dear huddled about them. It had surprised her, for she had said her goodbyes the night before and after the party she had not expected any of them to be up so early. Even Miss Ellen was there, standing next to Master Willy and Miss Josefina. Ned had brought the carriage around to the front steps and her luggage was stowed in the hold and all ready to go.

'You be sure and write now,' Fanny told her, and Peg could only nod in answer, for she was too full to speak. And then Tilly had hold of her elbow and she was steering her down the steps, which was just as well, for Peg could hardly see through the tears in her eyes.

They were all waving and she was hanging out of the carriage window waving back until they had all disappeared behind the rowan trees that lined the drive. Peg dropped heavily back into her seat as Tilly squeezed her hand.

'This is it then, Peg. There's no going back now.'

'Aye, pet. As you say, this is it.' Peg watched the gates flash past and it came to her that this would be the very last time that she would see them. And then she fell silent as she tried to mentally prepare herself for the train journeys and the long sea voyage ahead of her.

The train station was heaving with people when Ned drew the carriage to a halt outside, and as Peg saw the train standing there her eyes almost started from her head. There were clouds of black smoke billowing up to the roof and the platform smelled of engines and burning oil. As Ned trundled along behind them with Peg's trunk a loud announcement that the train would be departing in fifteen minutes caused Peg to almost jump out of her skin.

'Ah, we shall go to the buffet room and have a cup of tea then,' Tilly told her as Peg's nervousness attached itself to her. 'Ned, would you get a porter to put Peg's trunk into the luggage van, please? And then you might like to join us for a cup of tea before you start back to the Manor.'

'Aye, I'll do that, Tilly,' Ned told her affably. 'Make sure as they put plenty o' milk an' sugar in mine, would yer?'

He hailed a porter as Tilly led Peg into the buffet room, which seemed to be bursting at the seams with people. Peg looked about uncertainly as Tilly left to fight her way to the counter. The room was grubby to say the least and Peg had the urge to set to and clean it, though not in this outfit, of course. She was wearing one of the new day dresses that Tilly had treated her to, with a matching hat sporting a single feather that curled around its brim in a warm burgundy colour. It was by far the smartest outfit that Peg had ever owned and she was chary of sitting down on the grubby chairs for fear of marking it. She looked around at the walls, which might once have been white but were now a dirty grey. The dull brown doors were scuffed and scratched from the many feet that went in and out of them, and to her mind every one of the tables looked as if it could do with a good scrub. But then, she must get out of this way of thinking now. From this day on she would no longer be a servant but a woman in her own right. The thought chased the nervousness away and brought a smile to her face. By the time Tilly returned with three chipped mugs full of tea, Ned had taken his place at Peg's side. They all looked down into the lukewarm liquid, which seemed to have a film of grease floating on it.

'Aw, well. At least it's wet and warm,' Ned shrugged, ever the optimist. 'Nothin' like you make it though, Peg. Now *you* make what I term a good cup o' tea. Strong enough to stand your spoon in an' sweet enough to rot yer teeth. That's probably what I'll miss most about you when you've gone.'

'You cheeky devil, you!' Peg playfully swiped her bag at him and they sipped at the tea until the announcement came to inform them: 'The train to Newcastle is now boarding.'

A surge of people swept past them and were soon clamouring to get aboard. Tilly and Peg felt themselves being carried along. Peg planted a final kiss on Ned's cheek then she was being led into a ladies-only carriage, where Tilly pressed her into a window seat. She could see Ned standing there on the platform, furiously waving his hat, and then there was an ear-splitting screech and the great black train throbbed into life before slowly chugging out of the station. Peg was almost beside herself with excitement, for she had never been on a train in her whole life. Suddenly she felt that she was embarking on a great adventure with the rest of her life spreading out in front of her . . .

It was late the following evening as the carriage approached the village, but Tilly hung out of the window and shouted to Ned, 'Could you stop at the vicarage on the way home?'

She was bone tired after the long journey to see Peg

safely on her way, but now seemed as good a time as any to approach Parson Portman about Sarah's christening.

'I will that, Tilly.' Instead of taking the lane that led to the Manor he turned the horses in the direction of the village, and minutes later he drew them to a halt outside the vicarage before climbing down to help Tilly from the carriage.

She straightened her hat and smoothed down her skirt, then with her back stiff she walked up the drive as if she was about to do battle. And do battle she would, if the parson put up any objections.

His housekeeper answered the door on the first knock and as recognition dawned in her eyes she glared at Tilly suspiciously.

'Is the parson in?' Tilly enquired imperiously.

The old woman visibly bristled. Just who the bloody hell did this little upstart think she was, coming here bold as brass to this God-fearing house when everyone knew that she was a witch?

'What if he is?' she asked ungraciously, and now it was Tilly's turn to bristle as she snapped, 'Kindly inform him that I am here and I wish to see him.'

'Hmph!' The old woman slammed the door and shuffled away only to return minutes later.

'You'd best come in,' she told Tilly shortly, and Tilly sailed past her into the hallway.

'He's in the last room on the right down the corridor,' the woman told her before stomping off to the kitchen. Tilly set off in the direction she was told before her nerve could fail her, and within minutes she found herself face to face with the parson, who was looking decidedly uncomfortable.

'How can I help you Mrs, Miss, er . . .'

'Sopwith. Mrs Matilda Sopwith,' Tilly's voice was cool as she looked back at him and he had the good grace to lower his eyes. 'I have come to arrange the christening of my granddaughter, Sarah. I was rather hoping you might be able to perform the ceremony in the church within the next few weeks?'

His already ruddy cheeks seemed to redden even further as he stuttered, 'I er . . . I am not so sure that I can do that . . . Mrs Sopwith.'

'Oh, and why is that?' Tilly asked, although she already knew the answer to her question.

'Well, the thing is . . . I understand the child was born out of wedlock and the Church has a policy that—'

'Ah,' Tilly interrupted him. 'So we are down to Church policies, are we? May I ask you then, when is the stained-glass window that I donated the money for going to be installed? It seems to be an awful long time in arriving.'

Whereas before his cheeks had been red, they now drained to the colour of bleached linen and his chest heaved to such an extent that his rounded stomach strained against the material of his vestment. It was a well-known fact that the parson liked to live the good life, and even though Tilly rarely ventured into the village she got to hear all that went on there through the staff. One of the rumours claimed that the majority of donations made to the church ended up in the parson's belly – either by way of good food or whisky, to which he was known to be partial.

'Now,' she said, 'let's see. About Sarah's christening . . . how about a week on Sunday after the morning service? I *do* hope that you can manage that day. If not, I shall have to have a little word in the Bishop's ear, don't you think? About my donation, I mean. Of course, I'm *sure* that you would already have told him about so sizeable a gift to the church. I find it rather rude that he has never acknowledged it though, don't you?'

In his haste to get to his diary the parson almost tripped over his vestments. 'Mmm, now let me see.' He ran his hand, which was visibly trembling, down the list of dates before exclaiming, 'Why . . . as luck would have it I think I *could* do the service on that day.'

'Oh, how *very* fortunate I am,' Tilly replied, and her voice was sugar-sweet as she flashed him a dazzling smile. 'I shall look forward to seeing you at the church on that date then. You will of course let me know the time, will you not?'

'Oh yes, Mrs . . . er . . . Sopwith. Of course.'

Tilly inclined her head before sweeping from the room, leaving him open-mouthed. What the villagers said about her was true then. She really was a witch. But, oh dear, whatever would they say when they learned that he had agreed to christen the Trotter bastard in the house of God?

The atmosphere in the Manor was subdued when Tilly arrived home, for each of the people there were feeling Peg's loss already. Ellen hurried to meet her as Tilly passed her bonnet and cape to Peabody. 'Oh, my dear,' she said, 'you must be absolutely exhausted with all that travelling. Did Peg get off all right?'

Tilly smiled ruefully. 'I must admit to feeling a little jaded around the edges, but it's nothing a good strong cup of tea won't cure. And in answer to your question, yes, Peg did get off all right. The last I saw of her, she was leaning so far over the rail of the *Mermaid* that I was afraid she was going to fall into the sea before the ship had even set sail.' Turning to Biddle who had just appeared, she asked him, 'Could you have a tray sent to the drawing room, please?'

'Of course, ma'am.' He hurried away as Tilly took Ellen's arm and told her, 'I promised Steve I would ride over to the cottage this evening to see how the extensions are coming along. Would you like to come with me?'

'Won't I be in the way?' Ellen asked dubiously. 'You know what they say, two is company and three is a crowd.'

Tilly laughed. 'Oh Ellen, don't be so silly. Of course you won't be in the way.' Just then, as they made their way to the drawing room, a wicked smell of burning came to them from the direction of the kitchen, and Tilly wrinkled her nose. 'Oh, goodness me. It smells as if Fanny isn't settling too well into her new role as cook,' she commented.

Had she but known it, she had just given Ellen the opening she had been waiting for, and she seized on it now when she said, 'You know, Tilly, I was hoping to talk to you about that. But let's get you sat down and then I'll put my proposition to you.'

Curious now, Tilly sank onto a fireside chair but she said nothing more until Biddle had placed a tray down between them and Ellen was pouring the tea.

'Well, what is this proposition that you want to put to me then?' she finally asked as Ellen handed her a fine bone china cup and saucer. In her mind she was comparing it to the chipped, greasy mug she had been served with in the buffet bar with Peg. However, Ellen's next words brought her thoughts sharply back to the present.

'I was wondering if you would consider employing me as your new cook,' Ellen said. 'Now don't look so shocked, Tilly. I have already spoken to Fanny about it and she is not at all happy about her new role, believe me. By her own admission she could burn water whereas I, believe it or not, am a very passable cook.'

'But . . . Ellen,' Tilly stuttered when she had got over the first shock. 'How could I ever possibly employ you? You are a lady!'

To Tilly's utter astonishment, Ellen threw her head back and laughed. 'Oh, my dear Tilly,' she gurgled. 'I am about as much of a lady as you are. I was married to a parson who left me widowed with little more than my fare back to England, and if you do not employ me I shall be forced to seek work elsewhere anyway. I cannot live on fresh air and I certainly have no intentions of living off the charity of my mother. So what do you say? I know Fanny would love to resume her job as ladies' maid, and I would be in heaven if I could be in charge of the kitchen. Won't you please say that you will at least think about it?'

'Well, of course I will,' Tilly said reluctantly. 'But it just doesn't seem right somehow.'

'Nonsense.' Ellen spread her hands to encompass the elaborately furnished room. 'Look at yourself, Tilly. There are those who would say you are not a lady either, if truth be told.'

That at least Tilly could agree with, and she sipped at her tea as she pondered on what Ellen had suggested. 'If I agreed to this, and I say *if* . . . I certainly wouldn't want you working long hours,' she said finally. 'Perhaps you could just do the cooking and leave the kitchen work to the others? Then, when Steve and I are married, might you consider taking on the role of housekeeper here? I would like to leave Fanny here with Willy and Josefina, as I shall have no need of staff once I am in the cottage. I will then get a new cook in here so that Fanny can continue to do what she prefers to do.'

Ellen nodded enthusiastically. 'Oh, Tilly! I cannot think of anything I would rather do.'

'Then if you are quite sure that this is what you really want then yes, of course I will employ you.'

Ellen flung her arms about her and the two women embraced before Tilly told her, 'There is something I would like to ask you now. It is something that I have always longed to do but never dared to attempt on my own.'

'Yes?' Ellen's eyes were bright as she stared back at her expectantly.

'Well, the thing is,' Tilly went on, 'ever since you told me about the little school you ran in Africa an idea has been growing in my mind. As you are probably aware, a new law has stopped young children from going down the pit – a fact I am most happy about – and now there is a growing need for children to learn their letters and numbers. I have always longed to teach others, as first you and then Mr Burgess once taught me – but can you imagine the reaction I would get if *I* were to open a school in the village? Why, no one would ever let their children attend if I were the teacher, whereas if it was *you* . . .'

Ellen looked amazed and delighted. 'Oh, I think it's a marvellous idea, Tilly! I gained so much pleasure from it when Mary and I ran our little school. Well, it was scarcely more than a mud-hut really, but I so enjoyed it. When George went off on his expeditions with David Livingstone it gave me something to occupy my mind. Have you thought yet where you might position the school?'

'I have, actually. Not too long ago I had new cottages built for the miners who are employed down my mine. I'm sure that Steve could arrange for some work to be done on one of the old ones in order to make it suitable for use as a schoolhouse. He has builders working on our cottage now and I've no doubt that they could soon renovate and adapt one of them. All they would really need to do is lay a proper floor and do some repair work, put a couple of extra privies in – that sort of thing. I haven't spoken to him about it yet, of course. But if you think it might work I could put it to him tonight.'

'I think you should,' Ellen agreed. 'I would just love to see Parson Portman's face when he learns of your new venture though!'

'Speaking of Parson Portman, I called into the vicarage to see him about Sarah's christening this afternoon on my way home,' Tilly confided with a twinkle in her eye.

'Oh, you didn't!' Ellen exclaimed, for after her brief meeting with him, she was in no doubt at all that the man was as small-minded as the rest of the villagers where Tilly was concerned. 'Did he send you away with a flea in your ear?'

'Not at all,' Tilly chuckled. 'In fact, the date is set for a week on Sunday.'

When Ellen looked amazed, Tilly leaned towards her and tapped the side of her nose. 'I may not get down into the village very often but I hear what goes on there. It seems that our Mr Portman is rather partial to good living, and we all know that this wouldn't be possible on the wage that the Church pay him. So, it appears that he is not averse to dipping into church funds and donations – including a quite sizeable one that I gave myself not so long ago. As you may imagine, when I first suggested that Sarah should be christened there he threw his hands up in horror. But when I mentioned that the Bishop had not acknowledged my donation, he became, how shall we say . . . much more pliable . . . and decided there and then that he could christen her, after all.'

'Oh, Tilly.' Ellen was swiping tears of amusement from her cheek whilst she clutched at her side with the other. 'You are truly incorrigible.'

'Needs must,' Tilly replied soberly, then unable to keep a straight face for a second longer she fell against Ellen and their laughter echoed around the room.

Chapter Nine

A S TILLY AND Ellen reined their horses to a halt later
that evening, Steve hurried from the cottage to greet
them. Tilly had not visited for a couple of weeks and
could scarcely believe the changes that had been made in that
time.

'It's almost doubled in size,' she gasped as he helped her
down from the saddle.

He nodded proudly. 'It certainly is, but it's nowhere near
finished as yet. As you can see, the new parlour is all but done
and the main bedroom, which will sit above it, is coming
along at a fair old trot. That should be finished mid-week and
I think I can guarantee that the view from the windows at
the back, which will look down over the rise and the land
that I bought from Mr Pringle, will be quite spectacular. I'm
also adding another room on next to the parlour that will
lead into a library where you can read all Mr Burgess's books
to your heart's content. And of course, the old sitting room is
at present being turned into a kitchen.'

He moved to help Ellen down from her horse and led the
two women on a guided tour. Workmen were still busily
banging and hammering nails in, and they raised their hats
reverently as the women strolled past, though they did look

askance at Tilly's riding breeches, for as one was later heard to say, 'Whoever heard of a true lady wearing pants?'

To Tilly's relief, Steve was all in favour of her employing Ellen, and if he was mildly surprised he managed to hide the fact well. Once the cottage was finished he had no doubt that it would be more than big enough to accommodate staff there too, though Tilly was against the idea of having anyone at the moment. Still, he was going ahead with having servants' quarters built above the new stable-block just in case she changed her mind.

'But how are you managing to live amongst all this chaos?' she asked eventually.

'To tell the truth, I've been sleeping in the little room beneath the eaves where all Mr Burgess's books are stored at present,' Steve said. 'It's about the only part of the cottage that hasn't been touched as yet, and for all it's tiny it's also quite comfortable.'

He had no need to tell Tilly this, for it had been her room many years ago when she had lived with and nursed the kindly old teacher who had eventually left the cottage to her in his will. And soon it would be her home yet again. As the thought occurred to her, Tilly had the sense of coming full circle and it felt right. Perhaps it was time to set a date for the wedding, after all? At the rate the extensions to the cottage were going up it could be habitable within weeks, so what was to stop her moving in? When a picture of Willy and Josefina sprang to mind, followed by that of young Sarah, she impatiently tossed her head. Whenever she thought of her granddaughter, those thoughts automatically included Lucy, and the sense of unease that had always warned her of impending disaster in the past sprang to life in the pit of her stomach. Lucy was looking worse with every week that passed. Tilly was convinced that she was carrying a child now, although Lucy had never said as much. And what about Willy and Josefina? Should she throw caution to the winds for once in her life and leave them to it?

Her thoughts were disturbed when Ellen sidled up to her and whispered, 'Have you mentioned the school yet?'

'No, I haven't. But we can soon remedy that.' Turning to Steve, who was in deep conversation with a workman, Tilly muttered her apologies and drew him away. Then, with her face animated, she told him, 'Ellen and I want to start up a school for the children down in the village. Do you think your workmen could make one of the old pit cottages into something suitable for that purpose?' Then, seeing his expression, she asked, 'Don't you think it's a good idea? It really wouldn't take that much work.'

A mixture of emotions flitted across his face. Taking her arm, he led her to the top of the rise and out of earshot of those that were present. Then, leaning towards her, he told her, 'I think the idea of starting a school is fine, Tilly. You know that I am all in favour of children being educated. But the thing is . . . well, I wasn't going to tell you this but . . .' He took a deep breath before going on. 'I had a visitor a couple of days back. A very unwelcome one. It was me mam and she called me everything from a dog to a devil.'

When Tilly's face registered her distress he took her hands in his and pressed them to his heart. 'Now don't take on,' he pleaded. 'We both knew she wouldn't be pleased when she heard that we were finally coming together, and my back is broad – I can take anything she cares to throw at me. But the thing is, I would feel differently if she was to direct her anger at you again, and if you start up a school you'll be laying yourself wide open to her.'

'Didn't she do enough the day she almost blinded my son?' Tilly asked brokenly.

Steve bowed his head in shame. 'I don't think she'll ever feel she's done enough to you,' he told her truthfully. 'And I'm scared, Tilly. So scared that she might do something to stop us coming together. I've waited all my life for you and I couldn't bear it if anything were to happen to you now.'

He pulled her into the circle of his arms and for a moment she was content to be there, but then her chin jutted with determination and she looked deep into his eyes.

'I will open this school, Steve. With or without your blessing. I'm truly sorry to go against your wishes, but you know, I learned to handle myself many years ago. I had to, and ask yourself, what can your mother do to me now? She's an old, old woman. If you can't bring yourself to instruct your men to make the necessary changes to one of the cottages then I shall ask someone else to do it.'

As Steve looked helplessly back at her he knew that Tilly would have her way and so he reluctantly told her, 'All right then. I'll get one of the men to pop down into the village tomorrow and take a look at what needs doing. Happy now?'

'Yes.' She nestled against him again for a while before telling him, 'How would you feel if I also told you that I was ready to set the date for our wedding?'

'Aw, Tilly, I would feel wonderful. When did you have in mind?'

'Hmm. Let me see now.' She patted her chin thoughtfully before grinning at him and suggesting, 'How would September suit you?'

'Well, of course, I shall have to consult my diary,' he teased and then their laughter joined and floated on the wind down the rise.

Tilly was in a happy frame of mind as she and Ellen made their leisurely way home. At the top of the hill that looked down on the Manor they reined their horses to a halt to gaze down on the vast estate.

'The cottage will feel very small to you after you have become used to such space,' Ellen commented.

Tilly nodded in agreement as she admired the daffodils that were peeping from the hedgerows. 'It probably will. But you know, Ellen, I feel I shall be happier back there in the cottage than I have ever been in the Manor. I have lived and loved two men within the walls of that place, and I want Steve and me to have a fresh start.' When she climbed from the horse, Ellen followed her and as the horses began to graze on the fresh spring grass, Tilly sat down and let her mind drift back into the past. As yet, she had told Ellen none of the circumstances that had led to her being the Lady of the Manor so Ellen silently took a place at her side and listened with rapt attention as Tilly began.

'After you and the parson left, the villagers burned my granny's cottage down. The shock gave her a stroke and she died soon after. I stayed for a time with Simon and his first wife, but she made it plain that she hated the very sight of me, so after a while I moved back to the outbuildings of the cottage. Not long after that, the master – Mark Sopwith that is – invited me to move to the Manor and become nursemaid to his children, which I did. To cut a very long story short he then had an affair, and when the mistress learned of it she took the children and moved back to live with her folks, which meant that I was out of work with nowhere to go once more. It was then that I met the Drew family, and from that moment on, my life took a change for the better, for a while at least.' Tilly smiled fondly. 'They welcomed me into their home and treated me as one of their own, and eventually I took a job down the mine.' A shudder ran through her as she remembered the all-enveloping darkness and the rats that would swim past her as she worked knee-deep in water.

'It so happened that the master was visiting the mine one day when there was a flood and a cave-in, and he and I found ourselves trapped together in the pitch darkness. We were there for three whole days, during which time I was convinced that we were going to die, but we didn't and eventually they dug us out. The master had been badly injured and they had to amputate both his feet. Anyway, the outcome of that was that he asked me to return to the Manor to be his nurse, so I did. Of course, at the time I was still deeply in love with Simon, and some time later word reached us that his first wife had died. So one morning, I set off intent on declaring my feelings for him.'

Tilly laughed bitterly as she recalled the terrible hurt and disillusion she had experienced that day. 'When I got to Brook Farm I found him naked in the barn cavorting with the very same woman with whom the master had had an affair – so that was the end of *that*. From then on, my relationship with the master changed and we ended up living together as man and wife for almost twelve years. He asked me to marry him many times and I always refused, but then I found out that I was having Willy. I would have married him then, but he died before I had the chance to. And so, once more I was sent from the Manor – this time by Miss Jessie Ann, his daughter, and I moved in with Mr Burgess, who lived in the cottage that Steve is working on now. By then Willy had been born. My poor boy Willy.' Her voice broke for a moment. 'I was carrying him through the marketplace one day when Mrs McGrath aimed a stick at me and it hit him instead. That was what caused him to be near-blind. Master Matthew took Willy and me back to the Manor after that, and he and I grew close, and eventually I ended up

marrying him. Funny when you come to think of it, isn't it?
– that I loved both father and son? Anyway, Matthew and I
returned to his ranch in America and it was there that we had
an Indian raid, which resulted in Matthew's death and the loss
of my hair colour.' She tugged at her hair as if to add emphasis
to her words. 'I was very ill for a while following the raid. I
suppose it was the shock. And I had yet another one when I
first looked in the mirror and saw that my hair was snow-
white. And so I came home and the rest you know.'

'And Josefina?' Ellen asked tentatively. 'Where did she
come from?'

'Whilst we were in America I was led to believe that
Josefina was Matthew's illegitimate daughter, so it seemed
natural that I should adopt her and bring her back to England
with Willy and me. I have since found out that she wasn't
Matthew's daughter, but by then I loved her as my own so she
remained here with us.'

'Oh, Tilly.' Ellen's eyes were bright with unshed tears.
'What a terrible life you have led.'

'Not really,' Tilly denied. 'I have known the love of two
good men and now I have Steve. Perhaps at last with him I
shall be allowed to live the happy-ever-after life I have always
sought?'

Ellen made no comment but deep inside she prayed that
this time, Tilly would be right.

The following week was spent in preparations for Sarah's
christening, and now Ellen came into her own, for just as she
had said, she turned out to be a surprisingly good cook. By
the middle of the week the thrall in the huge walk-in pantry
was laden with all sorts of cakes and fancies for the great
event.

It was on the Thursday before the big day when Josefina

finally met Sarah for the very first time. Tilly had been into Jarrow and purchased some fine white silk, which Gwen had then transformed into the most beautiful christening robe that Tilly had ever seen. Ned took the carriage to bring Lucy and the baby back to the Manor so that Sarah could have a fitting, and as Lucy carried her into the drawing room, Josefina's eyes fastened on her. She was nothing at all as the girl had expected her to be, for she had no look of Willy being her father, and Josefina was secretly glad about that. The child had blossomed under her grandmother's loving care and was now a round bright-eyed little girl, with a ready smile for everyone. Everyone but Josefina, that was, for when she leaned over the child, the baby instantly let out a loud wail and held her arms out to Tilly, who happened to be the closest.

'It's probably because she hasn't met you before,' Tilly told Josefina, whose lips had set in a firm straight line. The girl didn't reply but simply stormed out of the room. Deeply embarrassed, Tilly told Lucy, 'You will be so pleased when you see the christening gown. Gwen has really excelled herself.'

Gwen, who was standing close by, flushed with pleasure, which increased when the gown proved to be a perfect fit. The instant Tilly took it off the child she whisked it away to be ironed, and after settling Sarah on the rich Indian hearthrug, Tilly poured Lucy a cup of tea. She could see at a glance that Lucy's stomach had swollen even more, and so when Willy made his excuses and left the room, she finally asked the question that had been on her mind. 'Are you having another child, Lucy?'

Lucy took the proffered cup from Tilly, but instead of answering her question she simply said, 'It looks set to be fine for Sunday. Let's hope the rain holds off, eh?'

Realising that she wanted to change the subject, Tilly was just plucking up the courage to ask her again when Peabody knocked on the door and announced, 'Master John and Miss Anna, madam.'

Tilly had not been expecting visitors, although it was always a pleasure to see John and Anna. Glancing apologetically at Lucy, she looked towards the door and seconds later the unexpected guests burst into the room like a breath of fresh air.

'Hello, Till . . . Oh, *look*, John. This must be Sarah, with her other grandmother.' Everyone else in the room was instantly forgotten as Anna dropped to her knees beside the baby in a cloud of silk skirts. Lucy looked on fondly as Anna billed and cooed at her and John grinned.

'That's i . . . it th . . . then. You'll h . . . have to prise her a . . . away from Anna now,' he told them, then remembering his manners he said, 'H . . . hello, Mrs B . . . Bentwood.'

'Oh, call me Lucy, please.'

'So,' John addressed Tilly now though his eyes stayed fast on Anna who was rocking Sarah on her knee. 'A . . . are we all set f . . . for the big day?'

'Yes, we are,' Tilly told him with a smile. 'All we have to do now is hope that the showers hold off. After all, we don't want the star of the show getting a drenching.'

'Where are W . . . Willy and J . . . Josefina?' John was mildly surprised to find neither of them there, particularly Willy, for Sarah was his daughter after all.

Lowering her head to hide the faint stain of embarrassment that had coloured her cheeks, Tilly replied, 'Oh, you've only just missed them. No doubt they'll be back again in a minute.'

Thankfully, Biddle wheeled a tea-trolley in just then and the uncomfortable moment passed. The rest of Lucy's visit proceeded uneventfully, although when Biddle reappeared to tell Tilly that the carriage was waiting to take Lucy and Sarah home, Anna's face fell a foot.

'Oh, do you really *have* to go so soon?' she asked Lucy. 'Sarah and I were just getting to know each other.'

Lucy smiled as she lifted the baby from her arms. 'Never mind, pet. You'll get to see her on Sunday again, and she'll be in all her finery then, thanks to Tilly. I thought we were going to have just a small affair but it's turning into quite an event.'

'It isn't every day our granddaughter gets christened,' Tilly pointed out with a smile. 'So if we're going to do it we may as well do it in style. It will certainly give the villagers something to gossip about anyway.'

Lucy nodded with a wry smile on her face. 'You're not wrong there. But anyway, I must be off. This little madam will want her feed soon and I can assure you she is nowhere near as angelic when she's hungry. She certainly has a good pair of lungs on her.'

Tilly followed her out to the carriage, silently cursing Willy for not showing more of an interest in his daughter. Josefina's attitude she could understand, for she had never liked anyone to take Willy's attention away from her. Still, as Tilly had discovered on the path of life, things had a habit of working out in the end, and no doubt this time would be no different. She kissed the baby's chubby cheek and then waved the carriage away until it disappeared round the bend in the drive.

Chapter Ten

ON SUNDAY MORNING Tilly stood next to her son and stared out across the lawns surrounding the house. As was customary at this time of the year, there had just been a heavy shower that had left everything looking fresh and green. Newly washed, she thought, as the sun peeped from behind a cloud. The shower had stopped as abruptly as it had started and now the lawns began to steam in the warmth of the sun.

'Ah well. Better to have the rain now rather than later,' she commented.

Willy, who was feeling very uncomfortable about the christening, nodded in agreement. Behind them was a bustle of activity as the servants began to prepare the room for the celebrations that would follow the church service.

'Willy.' His mother's voice had a tentative edge to it now as she asked, 'You will *try* to enjoy today, won't you?'

'I do know how to conduct myself in company, Mama.' His voice was as cold as ice and brought Tilly's hands tightly together at her waist as he turned about. 'And now if you will excuse me, I shall go and get changed.'

She watched him walk from the room, his hand held out blindly in front of him. There was that awful feeling again,

Rosie Goodwin

that she always got before something went wrong, a sense of unease hanging over her like a cloud. Pushing her concerns away as best she could, she hurried away in a swish of skirts and went to see if she could assist in the kitchen.

It was a grand procession that set off from the Manor that day. Tilly, Steve, Willy and Josefina accompanied by Lucy and Sarah went in the first carriage, and John and Anna with Eddie and Ellen followed close behind. In the third carriage were Phillipa, Steve's daughter, with her husband, Lance, and their two sons.

The congregation was just leaving the church following the morning service when Ned Spoke reined the horses to a halt outside. Although Tilly held her head high, she could feel the animosity of the people coming towards her in waves as Ned handed her down from the carriage.

'Stuck-up little trollop! She thinks she's bloody royalty,' a voice floated down the winding path to them, but ignoring it, she reached into the carriage and took Sarah from Lucy's arms. Then, *'Huh! I never thought I'd see the day dawn when the parson u'd agree to baptise a bastard. What the bloody hell is he thinkin' on?'*

She smiled reassuringly at Lucy, who she saw had begun to tremble. 'Ignore them,' she advised in a hushed voice. 'And just remember, their insults are not aimed at you. It's me they are trying to hurt.'

Lucy climbed down from the carriage, and as her skirt strained across her stomach, Tilly felt her eyes resting on it yet again. Once more it seemed to have grown and yet she could have sworn, if asked, that Lucy had lost weight everywhere else, for her arms were stick-thin and her eyes seemed to have sunk deep into her pale face.

Sarah was playing with the ribbons on Tilly's bonnet and she smiled down at her, but all the time the feeling of

106

foreboding was growing inside her and she had the urge to clamber back into the carriage and to tell Ned, 'Take me home!'

By now the rest of the family were gathering around her.

'Please may I carry her?' Anna asked, and inclining her head graciously, Tilly passed the child across into her eager arms. When Lucy had asked Anna to be Sarah's godmother, Anna had almost swooned with delight and was determined to take the role seriously. Now she stood with the godfathers, Eddie and John, waiting for the last of the congregation to file through the lych-gate. When the path was clear, they began to make their own way through the drunken tomb-stones that lined the twisting route to the door of the church, where Parson Portman was waiting for them with a face as dark as a winter's day. And so the service began and Sarah Jayne Sopwith was welcomed into the arms of the Church.

The atmosphere was light when they emerged back out into the sunshine some time later, made more so by the laughter of Steve's grandsons, Gerald, who was twelve and his ten-year-old brother, Richard, who looked surprisingly like Steve and was full of mischief.

Phillipa and Lance were doing their best to stop the boys from playing a game of Tig amongst the tombstones, whilst Tilly smiled indulgently, her arm tucked through Steve's. The sun was riding high in a cloudless blue sky now and Tilly felt herself slowly begin to relax. The service had been beautiful, despite the fact that the parson had obviously not wanted to perform it, and Sarah had behaved like an angel. And now they had the party at the Manor to look forward to.

Tilly and Steve were leading the procession, with John and Anna, who was still holding tight to Sarah, following close behind. It was as they rounded the corner of the church that they came to an abrupt standstill, for standing in the middle of the path in front of them was old Mrs McGrath, and her face was twisted with hatred.

Wagging a gnarled finger towards Tilly she cried, 'Why, you devil's spawn, it's a wonder as the church roof ain't fallen in wi' the likes o' you darin' to step inside it. As for *you* . . .' Her wrath was directed at Steve now as she screamed, 'How could you even *think* o' marryin' the witch when she has yer brother's blood on her hands?'

Releasing Tilly's arm, Steve took a step towards her, hoping to defuse the situation. But if anything, the nearer he got to her, the more incensed his mother seemed to become. 'Keep away from me. Yer no son o' mine. Yer nothin' but a traitor,' she screeched.

'Ma, please. This is neither the time nor the place,' he implored her, but she merely swiped his extended hand away with a strength that astounded him. Tilly noticed a small group of villagers huddled beside the lych-gate watching and listening, and in that moment she was sure she would die of shame. For this to go and happen on this day of all days . . .

Now it was her turn to try and calm the woman, so stepping forward she said, 'Can't we let the past go, Mrs McGrath? You lost your son and my son lost his sight. Surely enough is enough? It is Sarah's Christening Day and she is an innocent in all this.'

'Innocent? Huh! Yer wouldn't know the meanin' o' the word if it were to slap yer in the face. What she is, is the bastard o' *your* bastard, an' from where I'm standin' she should never have been allowed into the church.'

Colour stained Tilly's cheeks now as she drew herself up to her full height and said, 'Please step aside. I have no wish to stand here arguing with you. My guests have a party to attend.'

Old Mrs McGrath's hands clenched into fists of rage.

'Why you . . .' She was beyond anger now and suddenly she launched herself at Tilly with her dirty nails extended. The attack was so unexpected that if Steve had not grabbed Tilly she would have gone her full length on the path. As it was, she toppled sideways and collided with Anna, who still had Sarah in her arms. As Anna lost her footing, she clung on tight to the baby in her arms before landing heavily on the ground. A mutter of horror went up. Sarah had been contentedly gurgling but now her loud wails pierced the air, and as Anna turned on her side she, too, began to scream. The whole of Sarah's face was awash with blood, which had run down on to the virgin white silk of her christening robe. And then to Tilly everything seemed to happen in slow motion, for suddenly she was back in the marketplace again and it wasn't Sarah that was screaming, but Willy, on the day that Mrs McGrath had robbed him of his sight. A deadly silence, broken only by the baby's pitiful wails settled on the churchyard, and then John was springing forward and helping a very shaken Anna to her feet, whilst Lucy grabbed the child and hugged her to her breast.

'Oh my God. My dear God. What have you done to her?' Lucy sobbed as she tried to stem the bleeding that seemed to be coming from a deep gash that ran all down one side of the infant's face.

Steve stepped forward and, turning to John who was trembling like a leaf in the wind, he ordered, 'Get round to the doctor's house as quick as you know how and tell him we are on our way. I think this may need to be stitched.'

'No, no.' The groan came from deep inside Tilly as she leaned heavily against the church wall. This should have been a good day. A happy day. Oh, why did these things always have to happen to those she loved?

Old Mrs McGrath was backing towards the lych-gate and

from a long way away Tilly heard Lance say, 'She must have cut her face on the stones on the corner of the church as Anna fell.' And then there was nothing but a comforting darkness as her eyes fastened on her tiny granddaughter and she saw her life's blood seeping out of her.

The next she knew, Tilly found herself lying on the sofa in the kitchen at Brook Farm with Steve hanging over her, his face a mask of concern. For a moment she was disorientated, but then as the events came back to her she shoved him aside and sat up abruptly. As the room swam around her, she said thickly, 'Where is Sarah? Is she going to be all right?'

'She's still down at the doctor's, lass,' he soothed her as he heard the panic in her voice. 'I knew you wouldn't want to go home until you had seen her so I brought you here. They shouldn't be much longer now.' Crossing to the fire, he pushed the kettle into the flames and set about preparing the teapot, for he couldn't bear to see the raw pain in her eyes. And to think that it was his mother who had once again done such a terrible thing!

As Tilly looked around, she saw that Willy was slumped in a chair at the side of the fireplace with his head bent, Eddie was standing to the side of the window gazing out across the farmyard and Ned Spoke was sitting at the table not quite knowing where to look. And all the time she was crying, although there was not a tear to be seen, for the tears were trapped inside and she felt as if she might drown in them.

When they heard the sound of the carriage rattling into the farmyard some time later they all stood as one and gazed towards the door. There was the creak of the carriage door opening and then approaching footsteps, and then Lucy appeared in the doorway. The front of her dress was stained with the blood of the child who had cried herself into an exhausted doze in her grandmother's arms. And now the tears that had been locked inside seemed to be rising up through her like a tide as Tilly erupted in a sob and cried, 'Oh, Lucy! I am so very sorry. To think that our little Sarah has had to suffer as Willy did because of the villagers' hatred of me.'

Lucy carried the child to the crib and laid her gently down before turning to Tilly. Her face was the colour of putty and yet she seemed to place no blame on Tilly, for her eyes were kindly as she looked back at her.

'The blame for what has happened lies with old Mrs McGrath, not with you, so don't whip yourself. It was you she was aiming to hurt, not Sarah.'

'Will she be all right?' Tilly asked tentatively, scarcely daring to look into the crib at the child, whose head was heavily bandaged.

'Aye, she'll survive. The doctor . . .' Lucy gulped deep in her throat as the sounds of the child's terrified screams rang in her head. 'The doctor gave her some laudanum to calm her so that he could stitch the wound. It runs all the way from here to here.' She traced her finger down along her cheekbone before finishing, 'She will bear the scar of this day for the rest of her life. But at least her sight is intact so I suppose you could say she fared better than Willy.'

Tilly felt as if her heart was about to break. Sarah was, or had been, such a bonny bairn. Everyone had said so, and now for this to happen . . .

The sound of yet another carriage rattling into the yard heralded the arrival of Anna and John. Anna was so distressed by the turn of events that she forgot her manners, rushing into the room without knocking and crossing to the crib.

'That stupid old woman should be horse-whipped,' she declared vehemently, and then realising that it was Steve's mother she was talking of, she said more calmly, 'I'm sorry,

Steve. I know she is your blood, but when is she going to call an end to this stupid witch-hunt she has against Tilly?'

Steve spread his hands in a helpless gesture as Anna tenderly stroked Sarah's damp curls from her brow, then turning his attention back to the table he poured strong tea into the mugs he had placed there and passed them around.

After a time he suggested, 'Would you like me to take you back to the Manor, Tilly?'

She rose unsteadily. 'Yes, please . . . unless there is anything I can do for you, Lucy?'

'No, thank you, there is nothing anyone can do,' Lucy told her with a note of deep sadness in her voice.

'Then why don't you come back with me to the Manor for a few days? This has come as a great shock to you and there are many willing hands there that would help to care for Sarah whilst she recovers.'

'Oh yes, Lucy. Tilly is right,' Anna urged her. 'I would be more than happy to stay over for a few days. There is nothing urgent that needs attending to at Felton Hall, is there, John? I could even have her in my room with me at night so that you could rest and I could watch over her?'

A refusal was hovering on Lucy's lips, but then as her hand settled on her swollen stomach, and she saw the longing in the younger woman's eyes she hastily made a decision.

'Could you manage here on your own for a while, Eddie?'

He nodded solemnly and so Lucy looked back at Tilly and told her, 'Very well then, but only for a short time. Thank you for the offer. I shall just need to get some of her things together.'

'You go on, Tilly,' Anna suggested. 'John and I will bring Lucy and Sarah over shortly.'

As Tilly moved forward, the floor came up to meet her,

and so Steve took her arm and propelled her to the door. Willy followed close behind with a deep frown on his face. Josefina had been taken directly back to the Manor from the church and he could only imagine what her reaction would be when Lucy turned up on the doorstep with his daughter in tow. Still, it couldn't be helped. The poor little mite was going to be in a lot of discomfort for the next few weeks and with Lucy looking as ill as she did, it was up to them to give her all the help they could.

The journey was made in silence, and when they eventually drove up to the steps of the Manor they found Ellen, who had accompanied Josefina home, waiting for them.

'Oh, my dears.' Her voice was laden with sadness. 'I am so sorry for what has happened. Tilly, I have put the guests in the dining room but I think only Gerald and Richard have managed to eat anything. How is Sarah?'

'Scarred for life, from what I can gather.' Tilly's voice was flat and lifeless. 'Lucy will be bringing her to stay in a while. Anna and John are back at the farm with her now, collecting her things together. It was the least I could do for them after what has happened, especially with Lucy looking so ill. Do you think you could ask Fanny to prepare some rooms for them, Ellen? Oh, and Anna and John will be staying too.'

'Of course.' Ellen bunched her skirts together and hurried away in search of Fanny whilst Steve and Tilly handed their hats and coats to a sober-faced Peabody before moving on to the dining room. They found Phillipa and Lance waiting for them, and as Tilly looked at the beautifully laid table and the iced cake that Ellen had so lovingly prepared, the tears rose in her throat again for it seemed to be mocking her. How could what had started out as such a wonderful day have gone so terribly wrong? And all too soon the answer came back as something Biddy used to say echoed in her head. *You are fated for sorrow, lass.*

But why did the sorrow always target those she loved?

Upstairs, Josefina almost collided with Fanny, who was rushing along the landing with her arms full of clean sheets.

'Where are you going with those in such a hurry?' she asked curiously.

'Madam has asked me to get some rooms ready for Miss Sarah an' Mrs Lucy, Miss Josefina,' Fanny told her breathlessly. 'Oh, an' Miss Anna and Master John are stayin' over too.'

Josefina stared at her as if she had taken leave of her senses. 'Miss Sarah and Mrs Lucy staying *here*? Are you *quite* sure?'

'Oh yes.' Fanny's head bobbed. 'I'm quite sure, miss.' She hurried on her way, leaving Josefina to stare after her open-mouthed. Whatever was Mama thinking about? Having Willy's bastard to stay, indeed. And how was she supposed to bear it? As if the fact that Willy had loved another woman wasn't bad enough, she would now be forced to look upon the results of their love under her very own roof.

At that moment she became aware of someone moving towards her, and when she raised her head she saw Willy feeling his way along the wall to his room.

'Is this true, what I'm hearing?' she snapped.

He stopped and said tiredly, 'It all depends what you're hearing.'

'Well, that Mama has invited Lucy and . . . that child to stay here.'

'Yes, it's true. Why? Don't you think it's the least we can do under the circumstances? The poor child is injured, possibly scarred for life, and Lucy is in shock. At least here there will be plenty of people to help her with Sarah.'

'Just as long as I'm not expected to!'

The words had slipped out before she could stop them and she saw his face harden as he said angrily, 'Oh, don't worry, I'm sure you won't have to even look at her if you don't wish to. Funny though . . . I always thought you had a heart, Josefina. Now I'm not so sure.'

He moved on without another word and now her hand clamped across her mouth to stifle the sob that was rising in her. Willy was right; she knew he was right. Sarah was just a baby and she hadn't asked to be born. So why was it that each time Josefina saw her it was like a knife twisting in her heart? And now the baby would be living here under the same roof, and she would be forced to see her every single day.

Josefina was always brutally honest with herself, and she knew that she wouldn't be able to bear it. She should never have come home, she thought for the twentieth time, for she now realised that she no more belonged here than she did in America. Willy would never look at her whilst Sarah was there between them as a constant reminder of Noreen. Turning slowly, she returned to her room, and as she went an idea began to form in her head.

It was very late. Beyond Josefina's bedroom window there was nothing but darkness and the hoot of a lonely old owl in a nearby tree. As the evening had progressed the house had gradually become quieter as everyone retired to bed, worn out with worry and sadness. Half an hour ago she had heard Peabody bolting the doors in the hall and then Fanny's footsteps as she passed from room to room extinguishing the lights. And since then . . . only silence.

Shrugging her arms into her cape, the young woman lifted the small carpetbag she had packed with a few bare essentials, then easing her door open she peered up and down the landing. Everywhere was as quiet as a grave so she softly stole to the top of the stairs and tiptoed down them.

Once at the huge front doors she turned the enormous key and slipped through them onto the steps beyond where she paused to look up at the imposing house that had been her home for almost as long as she could remember. Then, like a thief in the night, she stole away with blinding tears sliding down her cheeks.

Part Two
A Time to Love
and A Time to Hate

Chapter Eleven

'HOW IS SHE today?' Tilly asked as she entered the day room. It had been decided that the family would dine in there this morning, for after the events of the day before, the dining room had not yet been cleared from the party that had never taken place.

Lucy was sitting in the deep bay window with Sarah, whose thumb was jammed in her mouth, snuggled against her breast.

'Not quite so fretful,' Lucy told her. 'She slept for most of the night.'

Anna was in the process of pouring out some tea and now she added another cup and saucer for Tilly. The latter was quick to notice that Anna looked almost as tired as Lucy did, but then she supposed that was to be expected, since the two women had taken turns throughout the night at sitting next to the child's crib.

'Why don't you both go upstairs and snatch a couple of hours' sleep after you've eaten?' she suggested. 'I can look after the baby for a while, and you both look as if it would do you a power of good.'

'Thanks, Tilly, but no. If I'm not here when she wakes up she'll scream the place down,' Lucy told her.

Anna passed them both their tea just as John strode into the room. 'Ah, j . . . just in t . . . time by the lo . . . looks of it. They always s . . . say that ev . . . everything looks bet . . . better after a good strong b . . . brew.'

Anna exchanged an affectionate glance with him as she poured him out a drink and once he was seated, she asked, 'Did you sleep all right?'

'N . . . not really. I c . . . couldn't get off wi . . . without you there.'

Tilly's face softened as she saw the way they looked at each other. At least she had no reason to worry about those two, for it was clear that they adored each other with a passion. If only they could have a child their happiness would be complete. But still, there was plenty of time yet. After all, had she not lived with Mark as his wife for twelve years before falling pregnant with Willy?

As if thinking of him had conjured him from thin air, the door opened and Willy waltzed into the room, his hand groping out in front of him. Tilly hurried across to him and led him to a chair, thinking how strange it was that Josefina wasn't down before him. Despite the fact that their relationship had been strained since Josefina's return, she still nonetheless hovered about him. Oh well, Tilly thought, it had been a long day yesterday, and the girl had no doubt decided to have a lie-in – not that Tilly could ever remember her doing so before. She had always teased Josefina that she was an early bird, for she was usually the first down in the morning as she waited for Willy to put in an appearance.

From his seat, Willy now turned his head in the direction of Lucy and asked, 'How is she today?'

It was the first time Tilly could remember him showing any interest in the child, and she was pleased to hear the concern in his voice. There was little to be seen of the baby's face, for it was still swathed in bandages, and Tilly suddenly wished that they could stay on forever – for what would they see when the bandages were removed? Would she be permanently scarred, as the doctor had warned? They would know soon enough. The doctor had promised to ride out to the Manor later in the morning to change the dressings and check that no infection was setting in. Her stomach churned at the thought of it and the further distress it would cause to the child, although of course, she knew that it had to be done. During the long night that had just passed when she had lain in her bed tossing and turning as she relived the day's events, Tilly had already decided that if the scar was as bad as the doctor had intimated, then she herself would take Sarah to the finest doctors in Shields and ask what could be done to lessen it.

At that moment, Sarah began to whimper. Willy's head snapped round in her direction with a look of deep concern on his face, and, in that instant, Tilly realised that he did love his daughter. But why then didn't he show it? Could it be that he was afraid of what Josefina's reaction might be if he did, or was it that every time he saw her, he was reminded that because of him, Noreen was dead?

'Why don't you hold her for a while, pet, so that Lucy can get something to eat?' Before he could reply, Tilly lifted the fretful infant from Lucy's arms and deposited her on his lap. One eye was lost in a swathe of bloodstained bandages, but with the other she surveyed him solemnly before lifting her chubby hand to explore his face. He broke into a tentative smile, which brought forth an answering one from Sarah. Tilly experienced a small thrill of satisfaction. If she could bring father and daughter together, then at least something good would have come from the terrible events of the day before.

A tap at the door brought all heads turning towards it, and when Peabody appeared and announced, 'Mr McGrath is here, madam,' Tilly felt faint with relief. She could cope with anything if Steve was there. When he walked in past Peabody, Tilly forgot herself as she launched herself at him.

'Oh Steve. I'm so glad to see you,' she told him in a rush.

Placing a protective arm about her waist, he greeted everyone in the room before telling her, 'I called in at the mine to make sure that everything was running smoothly then thought I'd better get over here to see how young Sarah is.'

'She's not too bad,' Tilly told him, 'but we will feel better when the doctor has been out to see her again. I was thinking, we could perhaps take her to a doctor in Shields if we're not happy with the way the wound is looking?'

'Well, we could,' Steve agreed doubtfully, 'but you know, Tilly, I doubt there would be much more another doctor could do now that the wound has been stitched. We just have to hope that it heals and that with time it will fade.'

Looking towards Lucy now he asked, 'What do you intend to do about my mother's attack, Lucy? I had a visit from the South Shields police this morning and they want to know if you wish to press charges. The same applies to you, Tilly. After all, it was you that she attacked.'

'Oh no.' Tilly's hands clasped together at her waist. 'Ask yourself – what good would it do if I were to bring charges against her? It would simply give the villagers something else to talk about and make them hate me all the more. I just wish that it had been me that had been scarred rather than an innocent child.' Her eyes were bright with tears, and once again Steve found himself hating the woman who had given birth to him as he felt his fiancée's pain. Why couldn't his mother just leave them alone to get on with their lives? Or better still, why didn't she just die! Even as the thought popped into his head he knew that it was wicked, but he couldn't take it back. Oh no, he meant it, wicked or not, for from where he was standing it seemed that his mother would hound Tilly for as long as there was a breath left in her body, just as his brother, Hal, once had.

'Lucy, have you thought where you wish to take this?'

Lucy shrugged, her eyes dull and tired. 'As Tilly has said, there is nothing to be gained from dragging this unpleasantness on. What is done is done and the rest, as far as I am concerned, is best left alone. All I want is to be left in peace, whatever that is.'

As they were talking, Fanny was loading their breakfast onto the sideboard. 'Breakfast is served,' she told them, and thankfully the tense atmosphere was relieved for now as they all helped themselves to the food.

Once back in the sanctuary of the kitchen, Fanny's shoulders sagged as she dropped onto a chair at the side of the table. 'Eeh, the atmosphere back there is so thick you could cut it with a knife,' she told Ellen sadly. 'They've all got faces as long as fiddles, but then I dare say you would hardly expect 'em to be leapin' with joy, would you? Not after what happened yesterday. And that poor little bairn, eh? An' she was so bonny. The double of her mother, they reckon. Life ain't fair at times, is it?'

'Huh, as far as Tilly is concerned that's rather an understatement,' Ellen muttered.

Meanwhile, Gwen was dunking the christening gown she had so lovingly stitched up and down in hot soapy water in a deep tin bowl on the enormous wooden draining board. 'Can't see that I'll ever get the stains out of this,' she grumbled. 'People usually like to keep robes as a reminder of their child's Christening Day.'

'I shouldn't worry too much about it,' Ellen told her with a trace of anger in her voice. 'I really can't see that anyone will want to remember this one after what has happened. And all this food . . .' She waved her hand toward the mountain of plates piled on the dresser. 'It will probably all go to waste now, for we will never be able to eat it.'

'Why don't you send some of it down to the people in the village?' Gwen suggested innocently, and when Ellen almost snapped her head off she clamped her lips shut and flushed.

'The way I feel about them at the moment, especially Mrs McGrath, I would see them all *starve* before I would offer them a crust,' Ellen ground out through gritted teeth. 'They have pilloried Tilly almost all of her life and yet she has done nothing to deserve it. Witch, they call her. Huh! Anyone would think they were still living in the Dark Ages.'

'You ain't wrong there.' Ned Spoke was sitting with the rest of the staff at the large scrubbed oak table with a mug of strong tea in his hand and now he told them, 'I had to nip down to the blacksmith's in the village at first light and the whole village is agog wi' what happened yesterday. They were all out cacklin', an' when I put in an appearance they turned their noses up at me like I were a dirty smell. Not that it bothered me, mind.'

'Perhaps I ought to come with you the next time you have cause to go in?' Jimmy suggested, which caused Ned to throw his head back and laugh aloud.

'I appreciate the offer, me laddo. But the day I'm afeared o' that lot will be the day you put me in me box. If there's any witches hereabouts, it's that lot back there. Between you an' me, I reckon as Tilly *should* press charges against the old harridan, but I wouldn't mind bettin' a month's hard-earned wages as she won't. Too soft by half she is, if you were to ask me.'

A ripple of agreement passed through them, apart from Ellen, who said, 'Well, I don't agree with you there, Ned. Like Tilly, I feel that there is nothing to be gained from it. After all, were they to lock old Mrs McGrath up, it would merely fuel their fire against Tilly. By ignoring their attacks she is rising above them and showing everyone what a true lady she really is.'

'Aye, well, be that as it may, I just wonder where this is all goin' to end,' Ned finished, and as his words echoed around the kitchen a cold finger traced its way up Ellen's spine.

'Madam is waiting for you with Miss Anna in the morning room, sir,' Peabody informed the doctor as he took his hat and coat with a polite bow. 'If you would kindly follow me I have been instructed to show you straight in.'

The doctor gripped his large black bag and followed the straight-backed butler along the hallway.

They found Tilly pacing up and down the room, and Lucy sat with Sarah cradled against her on the ornate chaise longue in the deep bay window.

'Ah, Doctor Murray. Thank you for coming.' Tilly nodded towards Sarah. 'She had a fairly reasonable night, apparently, but she seems to be running a temperature today.'

Hearing the deep concern in her voice, he smiled at her kindly. 'I shouldn't worry too much about that. It is probably due to the shock that she suffered yesterday, or to the laudanum I was forced to administer whilst I sutured the wound. Anyway, let's have a look and see how it is today.'

As soon as he approached her, Sarah began to whimper and tried to hide her face in Lucy's chest. Tilly warmed to the young doctor, who had not long taken over in the village, when he produced a sugar bag from his pocket.

'Look what I have for you, Sarah,' he said gently, and

when her chubby hand reached out for it he gave it to her and tousled her hair.

'Now then. You sit there like a good girl, eh? And I'm going to take this nasty bandage off and see how you are today.'

As he began to gently unwind the bandages, Tilly's heart thumped loudly against her ribcage and she had to force herself not to look away. And what she was thinking was, Oh Steve, I wish you were still here. I don't know if I'm strong enough to face this without you. He had left some time ago to return to the mine so, gritting her teeth, Tilly waited.

When the bandage was removed and she looked on the ugly red wound that ran all the way down one side of Sarah's tiny face the urge came on her to cry aloud and she had to resist it. Anna was standing at the side of her and now her arm came around Tilly's waist as she too fought back tears.

Sarah's face had smacked against the stones on the corner of the church as Anna had fallen so the gash was ragged. All around it, the skin was scraped away and her poor little face was swollen and bruised.

Seeing their mutual distress the doctor assured them, 'The grazed skin will grow back. Young skin is amazingly resilient. And of course, the swelling will go down too, given time. I do promise you I did the very best I could with the stitching, although you must appreciate that it isn't easy when it is a young terrified child you are dealing with.'

Tilly could see that what he said was true; the stitches were neat and close together, but still it did nothing to take away the horror of seeing the child's face so disfigured. And to think that it was she who should have been maimed. Oh, why couldn't it have been her? Steve would have loved her even if she was scarred, she was sure of it. Most of her life was behind her now, but Sarah's was only just beginning and she had been so bonny!

'I'll take the stitches out sometime next week.'

As Tilly suddenly became aware that the doctor was talking again she pulled her thoughts sharply back to the present.

'By then most of the swelling should have gone down and the bruising should be fading too,' he went on.

'Will . . . will the scar ever fade?'

Tilly's voice was little more than a whisper as she stared him straight in the eye, and somehow sensing that she was a woman who would appreciate the truth, he told her, 'I doubt it will ever fade completely, though even if I do say so myself, because the stitching is so neat it should heal in a nice straight line. What I mean is, there will be no puckering of the skin to highlight it. I envisage that for some time it will be an angry red weal, which should fade in time to a smooth white line.'

'Is there anything that could be done to make it less noticeable? We could take her to a specialist?'

He shook his head. 'I doubt it, though of course, you are quite at liberty to seek a second opinion. Thank God, the wound is a good way away from her eyes, which means that her sight will be unaffected. Had it been any closer we might not have been so lucky.'

Lucky! The word bounced around in Tilly's head and now she had the urge to laugh. A loud hysterical laugh that she knew if started she would never be able to stop.

As she stood there he was scrutinising her closely, for since moving to the village he had heard many tales of Tilly Trotter, the witch. This lady standing in front of him, and he had to admit that she looked and acted every inch the lady, was nothing at all as he had expected her to be.

From the rumours he had heard he knew that she must be at least fifty years of age now, and yet her skin was clear and unlined, which belied the snow-white hair piled neatly on top of her head. Her eyes were deep and unfathomable, giving her an air of mystery, and her clothes were simple but elegant. Her figure was slim and she was tall for a woman. So tall in fact, that she was looking into his eyes now on a level, and he found himself thinking, I like this woman. She has great strength and a great warmth about her.

Turning back to his patient he asked, 'Would it be possible to have a bowl of boiled water with perhaps a little salt in it?'

'Of course. I shall fetch it straight away,' Anna answered, and taking her arm from Tilly's waist she hurried away, returning only minutes later with the water and a large white towel.

Nodding his gratitude the doctor now turned towards Sarah who was happily sucking on her sugar bag and more contented than she had been at any time since the attack had occurred.

'Now then, my pretty little lady. Let's see if we can clean you up a bit, eh?' he asked her gently and she sat compliantly while he tenderly cleaned the wound as best he could. He then proceeded to wrap a clean bandage about her head. 'Just to keep it clean and to stop her touching it and getting an infection in it,' he explained. 'I shall call back again tomorrow, and let us hope that in another couple of days it will be healed enough for us to leave the bandage off and let the air get to it.'

'Thank you.' Lucy inclined her head and he thought, Here is another woman I could like, a woman of dignity. As his eyes settled on her swollen stomach, he smiled.

'Ah, I see we have a happier event to come. Don't hesitate to pop by and see me, should you have any problems.'

When Lucy blushed and lowered her eyes, he stood up, and after rinsing his hands in fresh water, he dried them on the towel Ellen was holding out to him and snapped his bag shut.

'Right then, ladies. I shall be back tomorrow morning bright and early, but please send for me if you are at all concerned, and I shall come straight away.'

Tilly walked with him to the front door where she shook his hand warmly. 'Thank you for your kindness and all you have done for my granddaughter,' she told him.

'It is my job, Mrs . . .?'

'Sopwith.' Tilly held her head high. 'Although it will soon be changed to Mrs McGrath.'

McGrath? His eyes narrowed. Surely that was the name of the woman who had attacked her outside the church yesterday? As Tilly let him out he wondered if he would ever get used to the ways of the people hereabouts.

It was almost lunchtime by now and Sarah had fallen into an easy doze. Tilly and Lucy were taking advantage of the fact and were enjoying a cup of coffee in the morning room when the door suddenly burst open and Fanny spilled into the room,

'Tilly . . . it's Miss Josefina,' she gasped breathlessly.

Tilly's eyebrows drew into a frown. Placing her cup down on a small side-table she demanded, 'What do you mean, it's Miss Josefina?'

'Well, I . . . I went into her room to tend the fire and make her bed an' I saw that it hadn't been slept in.'

Tilly's heart was racing again and the bad feeling was back. 'Of course it must have been slept in!' She was trying desperately hard not to shout. 'She probably made it herself.'

'Miss Josefina *never* makes her own bed, Tilly. I felt right off that somethin' weren't right so I took the liberty of checking her wardrobe an' some of her clothes have gone. An' her carpetbag is missin' an' all. You know the one I mean? She always uses it when she goes to stay overnight with Master John an' Miss Anna.'

Striding past her, Tilly hoisted her skirts and took the stairs two at a time. She stood in the doorway of Josefina's room for a moment looking around. Then, marching over to the elaborately carved wardrobe she flung the door open. At first sight everything seemed to be there but then she realised that the dark green travelling suit Josefina favoured was missing. Slamming the door she then crossed to the large tallboy where she saw instantly that a number of petticoats and drawers were missing too. Finally she moved to the dressing-table on which Josefina kept her jewellery box. Willy had bought it as a Christmas gift for the girl many years ago, and Tilly knew that she valued it amongst her most precious possessions. It was as she stared at the blank space where it usually stood that she knew without doubt that Fanny was right. Josefina was gone.

Crossing to the bed, she slowly sank down onto it and stared blankly off into space. And now once more she was consumed with guilt. Josefina had never really been herself since returning home, but Tilly had been so taken up with seeing that Sarah was well provided for, and making her own wedding plans that she had left the girl to it. And now she was gone, and knowing her daughter as she did, Tilly had no doubt at all that unless Josefina wanted to be found, she might never set eyes on her again.

She was still sitting there when Fanny swept back into the room some minutes later. Seeing the look of utter desolation on Tilly's face, the servant wrapped her arms around her, and as Tilly's head bowed onto her chest and the tears finally came, Fanny muttered, ''Tain't bloody fair that so much trouble should be placed on one pair o' shoulders, for if it ain't one thing 'tis another!'

Chapter Twelve

'DID PHILLIPA SAY if she would be calling in today?' Tilly enquired as she looked across the breakfast-table at Willy, who was pushing the food around his plate.

'Not so far as I know,' he replied listlessly. 'Though you never know when they're going to turn up. Sarah will begin to wonder who she belongs to soon, she has so many mothers.'

Ignoring the sarcasm in his voice she wiped her mouth on a fine linen napkin and slowly rose from the table. Since the day of the christening the Manor seemed to be bursting at the seams with people. It was just as well, for Tilly felt that if she had been left to her own devices, she might have gone stark staring mad. As she walked towards the door she turned just in time to see Willy push his plate away. 'You should eat, Willy,' she said. 'Starving yourself isn't going to bring Josefina back.'

'Huh! Do you think I don't know that?'

Josefina had been gone for almost four weeks now and even though the house was full, yet still it seemed empty without her.

The pain in his voice stabbed at her like a knife as he

stumbled away from the table. 'Why don't you go out into the garden and get some fresh air?' she suggested. 'Anna is out there with Sarah.'

He shrugged but made no answer so with a slight lift of her shoulders she left him and climbed the stairs to her room. On the way she met Fanny staggering along with an armful of fresh laundry.

'Ah, Fanny. Is Lucy up yet?' she asked.

'Not so far as I know.' Fanny shifted the mountain in her arms to peer at Tilly over the top of it. 'Master John an' Miss Anna are up and about though. I reckon they've taken Miss Sarah out into the garden.' Leaning closer she lowered her voice and told Tilly, 'When I went into the nursery not so long back to strip Miss Sarah's cot I heard Miss Lucy bein' sick in the closet. She don't look too well at all, does she?'

'No, she doesn't. I've asked her to let me get the doctor to take a look at her but she won't hear of it. In fact, she almost snapped my head off when I suggested it. But that's enough about that. How are you coping with all the extra bodies in the house, Fanny?'

'Oh, I'm fine, Tilly. It's nice to have a houseful again. An' I have to say I ain't never seen Miss Anna look so happy. The little 'un's comin' along fine too, ain't she, since the doctor took the stitches out an' the bandages come off?'

Tilly repressed a shudder as she recalled the day Fanny was referring to, for Sarah had screamed all the way through the process like a wounded animal. And each scream had been like a nail in Tilly's coffin until she had placed her hands over her ears and fled from the sound. Still, as Fanny said, she seemed over the worst now, although it broke Tilly's heart each time she looked at her poor little face. At that moment they heard someone sprinting up the stairs. Fanny moved on and Tilly waited until John suddenly erupted onto the landing.

'G . . . good morning, T . . . Tilly.'

'Good morning. And where are you off to in such a rush?'

'Oh, Anna thinks that Sarah n . . . needs a shawl. It's still a . . . a bit ni . . . nippy out there, being s . . . so early.'

Looking into his bright face she asked him, 'Are you quite sure that you and Anna don't mind staying on here to help with Sarah? What I mean is, you've only been home once since the day of the christening and that was only to get some clothes.'

'Oh, w . . . we don't mind,' he assured her. 'I've n . . . never seen Anna . . . looking so happy, have y . . . you?'

'No, I haven't,' she admitted, and now there was a trace of sadness in her voice. 'But you know, John, I have the feeling that Lucy may wish to return to the farm soon. I hope Anna won't be too upset when Sarah goes?'

The smile slid from his face as he shrugged. 'Well, i . . . it won't m . . . mean that we'll n . . . never see her again, will it?'

'No, no, of course not,' she assured him. 'I'm sure that Lucy won't mind you visiting the farm whenever you wish.'

He nodded before going on his way and Tilly went to her room to change into her riding gear. As she came out onto the steps of the Manor some time later in her riding breeches she saw Anna spreading a blanket on the grass beneath the branches of the enormous oak tree. In all the time she had known her, Tilly had never seen Anna looking so bright, to the point that even her birthmark no longer seemed to trouble her. John too seemed happy, for loving Anna as he did, if she was contented then so was he.

Tilly stood and watched them for some minutes, thinking what a happy family they made, before turning in the direction of the stables. Recently, she had taken to riding for the sheer pleasure of it. It didn't matter that she had no place to go. Each morning as regularly as clockwork she would get Arthur to saddle her horse and she would ride it into a lather, as if she were trying to escape from the demons that were chasing her.

Ned would leave with the carriage early each morning just as he had when Noreen had gone missing, but now he was searching for Josefina. So far the search had proved fruitless but still Tilly sent him out each day and continued to live in hope of him finding her.

Arthur was waiting for her and he tipped his cap respectfully. 'Morning, lass. I've got Lady all ready for you. I think she's enjoying all this exercise.'

As Tilly approached the horse he bent to give her a leg up and once she was astride his face became serious as he asked, 'How is Master Willy bearin' up?'

'Not good, Arthur. And neither am I, if truth be told. I miss her so much. I just wish I'd realised how unhappy she was and then it needn't have come to this. Goodness knows how she will survive. She has been brought up as a lady. What will she do for a living?'

'Miss Josefina is a canny lass,' he told her solemnly. 'An' besides, you never kept her short. No doubt she'll have enough to live on for a while without having to find work.'

'I doubt it,' Tilly sighed. 'She didn't ask for any of her allowance from the safe so it may be that she has very little.' Then digging her heels into Lady's sides she set off at a trot down the drive. As she was coming out of the gates she decided to pay Steve a visit at the mine. He had been so wonderful since Josefina had left that her love for him had grown tenfold. Not once had he mentioned their wedding, although sometimes when she was in his arms she could sense his impatience. Soon, she promised herself. I will set the date for the wedding soon. Avoiding the village she broke into a gallop across the fields and by the time the mine came into sight she had broken out in a sweat.

When she reined Lady to a halt in front of Steve's office he came out to greet her and helped her down, then after tying the horse to a post he led her into the office and took her in his arms. 'Any news?' he enquired after he had kissed her soundly.

'Nothing at all.' Her eyes fastened on the grimy office window and she shuddered as she saw through it the roadway that led down into the bowels of the earth. It was strange, but since being trapped down there with Mark Sopwith she could never look on that entrance now without trembling.

'And how is Sarah?'

His voice interrupted her gloomy thoughts and she tried to answer him truthfully when she said, 'Much better, I would have to say, and thriving on all the attention. Anna has heard that goose fat is good for softening scars so she has taken to rubbing it onto Sarah's face three or four times a day. It's Lucy I am most concerned about at the moment. I'm sure that she is pregnant now, Steve. But the pregnancy doesn't seem to be going well. She looks really ill but won't hear of me fetching the doctor to her.'

'Well, she has gone through a lot in the last year, hasn't she?' he pointed out. 'And at least whilst she's with you she can rest. Has she said anything about going back to Brook Farm yet?'

'No, not yet. But I have the feeling that she is missing her home so I don't think it will be long now. Then I'll have another problem on my hands.'

'Oh, and what's that then?'

'Anna,' Tilly told him simply. 'She absolutely dotes on Sarah. She has even taken to sleeping in the next room to the nursery with John now. She says she does it so that Lucy can get her rest but I have other thoughts on the matter.'

'Mmm. She has got close to her,' Steve admitted, as he doodled with a pen on the blotting-paper on his desk. 'But then I think we all have. She has made Phillipa quite broody, and Richard absolutely adores her. I bet there has never been a time when you have had so many visitors?'

'No, there hasn't, and yet . . .' Tilly's head drooped. 'The house still seems empty without Josefina.'

'Look, if anyone can find her, it's Ned.' Taking her hands in his, Steve smiled down into her face. 'She can't have gone that far, can she? Now, how is Willy?'

'Taking it very badly. Not so long ago he was out of his mind with worry when Noreen went missing. So when you think of how that ended, it's no surprise he's worried, is it?'

'Aw Tilly, you mustn't let your mind go down that path. You know what they say, lightning never strikes twice.'

'That might be true of other people, Steve. But what you are forgetting is that I am a witch – according to your mother and the villagers, at least. Sometimes I think they must be right too, for if there is trouble it has a way of finding me.'

'Don't talk so daft,' he scolded her, then hoping to turn her mind to other things he nodded towards the pit entrance. 'Number three is flooding again. We've got the pumps going full on down there.'

'Then get everyone out of there and don't take any chances,' she told him shortly.

'Don't worry, I already have – apart from the blokes who are mannin' the pumps, o' course. Anyway, I dare say I'd best get back to work. Just 'cos I'm engaged to the boss don't give me licence to shirk, does it?'

He led her out into the warm sunshine again, and once

she was back in the saddle asked her, 'Why don't you come over to the cottage tonight? It's very close to bein' completed now an' at the stage where you need to decide what you want to put in it, furniture wise. Are you planning on bringing stuff over from the Manor?'

She shook her head. 'No, I'm not. To be honest, Steve, I want nothing in there other than what you and I have chosen – apart from Mr Burgess's bits and pieces, that is. I rather like his bookcases and thought they would look well in the new library.'

'Your wish is my command,' he told her with a comical little bow, and then slapped the horse's flank. 'Now be off with you. You're too much of a distraction, woman. Oh, an' when you come over to the cottage tonight, a bit of that rabbit pie that Ellen makes so well wouldn't go amiss. I dare say I'll not feel like cookin' when I've done here.'

She coaxed the horse into a trot and soon the mine was far behind her. It was as she was nearing the rise that over-looked the Manor that she saw Randy Simmons swinging towards her with a snap tin tucked under his arm. Slowing the horse to a walk she inclined her head at him but he merely scowled at her as she passed by. She shrugged. No doubt the old fellow was blaming her for losing his job at Brook Farm. But then her back was broad and she was used to being held responsible for everything that went wrong within a twenty-mile radius of here. Whatever it was, the villagers would always find a way of laying the blame at Tilly Trotter's door.

Urging the horse on, her thoughts turned once more to Josefina, and again she asked herself just as she had every single day since the girl had vanished: *'Where in God's name can she be?'*

★

At almost that exact same moment, Josefina was entering a pawnbroker's shop in Durham. It was gloomy inside, and once she had left the bright sunshine behind, she had to stand for some seconds to allow her eyes to adjust to the light. Once they had, she saw a man with a mop of wild grey hair and a rounded stomach staring at her curiously over the top of a pair of gold pince-nez that were perched precariously on the end of his nose.

He frowned, for here was a contradiction if ever he'd seen one. The girl looked a bit like the pictures he had seen of Red Indians, with skin the colour of olives and hair as black as a raven's wing. And yet she was dressed as a lady.

'Yes?' His voice was abrupt as she set her carpetbag on the dirty floor and looked back at him from tired eyes.

'I have an item of jewellery that I think you may be interested in.'

His eyes widened with surprise. She spoke like a lady as well. Her voice was well-modulated and her tone refined.

'Oh, aye. An' where did you get it from? It ain't hot, is it? I only deals in honest gear here.'

'I assure you it is mine to sell,' she told him coldly, drawing herself up to her full height.

'In that case then, let's have a look at it.'

Josefina bent to her bag and after rummaging about for a while she withdrew a brooch in the shape of a butterfly. It was made of solid gold, with diamonds set into its wings that were fashioned to look like dewdrops. Tilly had bought it for her three Christmases ago and the girl had always treasured it, but now she saw it as the possible means of getting the train fare to Liverpool.

Placing it on the counter, she stood back as the man took an eyeglass from his waistcoat pocket and examined her brooch.

'Mmm, it's a quality piece, I'll give you that. But that poses me somethin' of a problem. You see, round here, folks don't go in for things like this. How much were you wantin' fer it?'

Josefina was nonplussed for the first time since entering the shop and stammered, 'I er . . . I'm not sure. What will you offer me?'

'How does a guinea suit you?'

'One guinea?' The girl's voice was incredulous. 'But it cost many, many times that amount.'

'I ain't disputin' that, but as I said, pieces like this ain't easy to sell hereabouts. That's me best offer, so take it or leave it.'

Her shoulders suddenly sagged and her eyes filled with tears as she cursed herself for a fool. Why had she rushed away from home like that before asking Tilly for her allowance? She could have told her that she needed money to buy a present or something and her mother would not have doubted her. As it was, the amount she had brought with her, which had seemed quite sizeable at the time, was going nowhere at all. Hence the need to start pawning her jewellery, especially as she had now decided to make her way to Liverpool. During the last weeks she had stayed in places that were little more than hovels – places that she had never dreamed existed. Perhaps in Liverpool she would be able to start afresh. Get a job in a respectable place where no one would know her. And she would always have the option of travelling abroad, to a distant land where her colour was not the exception, but the norm.

As she stood there trying to decide what to do, she became aware that the man was looking her over very closely. Suddenly leaning across the counter he told her, 'That looks a fine bit o' material in that there coat you're wearin'. I'll tell you what I'll do. I'll add another two bob to the brooch fer your coat. An' then yet another shillin' fer your hat.' He sighed cunningly. 'Too generous for me own good at times, I am.'

Josefina's mouth fell into a gape. Why, he was trying to buy the very clothes from her back!

'But this is the only hat and coat I have with me,' she told him. 'What am I supposed to wear if I sell them to you?'

'No problem there, lass. I can sort you out a nice shawl an' a straw bonnet. The stuff you're wearin' is too fancy fer around here anyway. It'll make you stick out like a sore thumb, an' being the good judge o' character I am, I have an idea you don't *want* to stick out. So what do you say?'

Josefina slowly began to undo her coat, then after untying the ribbons of her bonnet she laid them both on the counter.

The pawnbroker rubbed his hands together, then crossing to a large brass till he opened it and began to count her money out. After placing it on the counter he turned and started to rummage through a pile of what looked like rags before tossing a rather bedraggled straw hat and a shawl that was so dirty the original colour was indistinguishable onto the counter.

'There y'are then. Never let it be said that Jake Hammond ain't a fair man.'

As he popped the brooch into the top pocket of his coat, Josefina slowly lifted her money and the hat and shawl from the counter. She was almost at the door when his voice stayed her. 'You ain't from round here, are you, lass?' he asked. 'Have you run away from home?'

Her chin was high again now as she looked coolly back at him. 'I came in here to sell you a brooch, *not* my life story. Good day, sir.'

His eyes gleamed with amusement as the shop bell tinkled behind her. She had some spirit, he'd say that for her, for all she weren't knee-high to a grasshopper. An' even though her skin was dark, she was quite exquisite when you studied her.

'Alfred!' His voice sliced through the silence and almost instantly, a tall dark-haired man with one eye sewn up appeared from the door at the back of the shop as if by magic.

'Yes, Mr Hammond?'

'The young lass that left the shop just now – I want you to follow her an' tell me where she goes. You can't miss her. She were a bonny, dark-skinned little piece.'

'Right y'are, Mr Hammond.' The man stumbled out as Mr Hammond lifted Josefina's hat and coat and hung them on a hanger.

Alfred spotted her straight away. The colour of her skin and the dress she was wearing made her hard to miss in an area like this. The streets were busy as it was market day, which made it all the easier for him to follow her without drawing attention to himself. She was carrying a carpetbag that looked to be of a good quality, and across her other arm was slung a shawl that seemed to be strangely at variance with the rest of her attire.

Her first stop was at a pie stall and he watched her buy a pie, which she then ate as she went along through the stalls that lined the streets. Eventually she turned off into the back streets and he saw her approach the door of a house that had a *Lodgings* sign hanging in the window. She stood for some time on the chipped doorstep talking to a woman before turning disconsolately away and proceeding down the street. The same thing happened at another house in the next street but her third attempt was successful, and he watched a blowsy woman with enormous breasts nod her head and then admit her.

Making a mental note of the address, Alfred hurried back to tell Mr Hammond where the lass was staying.

Chapter Thirteen

'AW, TILLY. THANK God you're back. There's all hell kickin' off here,' Fanny cried, the second Tilly set foot through the door of the Manor.

'Why? Whatever's the matter?'

'It's Miss Lucy. She got up this mornin' an' decided that it were time she were takin' Miss Sarah back to Brook Farm an' we can't stop Miss Anna cryin'.'

Tilly had half-expected this reaction after seeing how taken Anna was with Sarah.

'Where is Miss Lucy?' she asked calmly.

Wringing her hands together, Fanny nodded in the direction of the staircase. 'She's up in the nursery, getting all Miss Sarah's things together.'

'Thank you, Fanny.' Tilly strode purposefully in the direction of the nursery and once there she tapped at the door.

'Come in.'

Tilly stepped into the room to find Lucy busily folding Sarah's clothes into a large valise. 'So you feel ready to return home now, do you, Lucy?' she asked.

'Aye, Tilly, I do. Though I don't know what I would have done without you over the last weeks and that's a fact.'

She paused in the act of what she was doing to cross to

Tilly and gather her hands into her own, and what she told her was, 'You've been grand to us. But the thing is, Eddie is back there at the farm all on his own, and for all you've made us welcome, Sarah an' I don't really belong here. You do understand, don't you, Tilly?'

'Of course I do,' Tilly told her gently, returning the pressure of her hands. 'But please know that we'll always be here for you, Lucy. You and Sarah are family now.'

'I know.' As the two women looked deep into each other's eyes an unspoken understanding passed between them and Tilly had to choke back the tears that had risen in her throat.

'I er . . . I think Anna is taking it badly,' Lucy said. 'The fact that I'm taking Sarah, that is.'

'Yes. Yes, she would do – but don't worry about it. I'll see to Anna once you've gone. Now I'll go and get Arthur to bring the trap round. I'm afraid Ned has taken the carriage into Shields today.'

'Looking for Josefina, is he?'

'Yes, just as he has almost every day since she left. There is still no sign of her, though. I'm beginning to wonder if we'll ever find her now.' This was Tilly's deepest fear, one that she had never voiced before.

'Oh, you mustn't say that, lass!' Thanks to her own, terrible experience with Noreen, Lucy knew what Tilly was going through, knew the toll it must be taking on her. She must give her some hope to sustain her. 'While there's life there is hope, and I'll guarantee that Josefina is alive somewhere. You'll find her, all right.'

Tilly nodded, then turning about, she stumbled blindly from the room.

Once back downstairs in the hall, the sound of Anna's sobs directed her towards the drawing room. Her sister-in-law was seated on the settee with John, who had his arms wrapped tightly about her. As Tilly entered the room, he turned tortured eyes to her.

'Sh . . . she's taken it b . . . badly – the f . . . fact that Sarah is going h . . . home,' he told her falteringly.

Tilly nodded, then moving towards them she laid her hand on Anna's heaving shoulder. 'Don't cry, my dear. We all knew that Sarah staying here was only a temporary arrangement.'

'I know it was – but I'll miss her so much,' Anna sobbed.

'What you have to remember is that you are Sarah's godmother,' Tilly pointed out gently. 'And as such, Lucy would never stop you from seeing her. She might even allow you to have Sarah to stay with you from time to time at Felton Hall. In fact, I'm sure she would, particularly after her own baby is born.'

'D . . . do you really think she would?' Anna asked, brightening a little.

'I have no doubt about it. Now dry your tears and come and say goodbye for now. You don't want Sarah to see you crying, do you? It would frighten the little lass.'

Anna took the handkerchief that John was holding out to her and after noisily blowing her nose she took a shuddering breath and dabbed at the tears on her flushed cheeks.

They all stood on the steps and waved as Arthur drove the trap down the drive with Sarah sitting on Lucy's lap next to him. Then, as one, they turned and walked slowly back into the Manor.

'I th . . . think we ought to b . . . be thinking of going h . . . home too now, d . . . darling,' John told his wife.

She nodded in agreement. 'You are right, John. We have imposed on Tilly for far too long.'

'Nonsense. It's been a pleasure to have you here,' Tilly

assured her. 'In fact, I don't know how I would have coped without you, with all that's been going on. First the incident with Sarah – and then Josefina going missing. It hasn't been easy.'

John patted her arm sympathetically. 'Things will t . . . turn out all r . . . right in the end, T . . . Tilly.'

'Will they, John?' Tilly wasn't quite so sure, for when had things ever gone right where she was concerned?

Despite the warmth of the day, the night had turned nippy. Josefina drew the shabby shawl about her shoulders and hurrying along the landing, made her way down the uncarpeted wooden staircase, avoiding the lime wash that was flaking from the walls. As she reached the tiny lobby that led directly onto the street, the front door opened and she almost collided with a great bear of a man who was carrying a large jug of ale in his hands.

'Why, hello there, pet. Would you care to come an' join in the party?'

The sounds of drunken laughter were issuing from a room further along the hallway. As his fetid breath hit her full in the face Josefina turned her head and told him politely, 'No, thank you. I am just going for a stroll to get a little fresh air.'

'Ooh! Hark at Little Miss Lah-di-dah! *Ai am just gewing for a strooooll . . .*'

Ignoring his mimicking, Josefina slipped past him, and once she was out on the cobbles she breathed a sigh of relief. The room she was staying in was so dirty that she could barely bring herself to sit on the bed, let alone lie on it, but at least it was better than being out on the streets. First thing tomorrow she intended to get a train to Liverpool. At least it was familiar, from her journeyings at sea. However, once there, she had no idea what she would do, for she was trained for nothing. As a vision of her comfortable bedroom at the Manor floated in front of her eyes she had to stifle the urge to cry. They would all be sitting down to dinner now and she wondered what they would be having, causing her stomach to rumble with hunger. And Willy – would he be missing her? She doubted it. He was too taken with Sarah and memories of Noreen to worry about her.

She had reached the end of the street now and was attracting more than a few curious glances from the women she passed, who were standing in huddled groups on their doorsteps gossiping.

Pausing, she looked up and down, then deciding that one way was much the same as another she lifted her skirts and began to cross the dusty street. She had only walked a few yards when she became aware of footsteps close behind her. Turning quickly, she was confronted by a man who seemed to tower above her. One eye had been crudely stitched shut but despite his deformity he had a friendly smile on his face.

'Evenin', miss. It's bonny fer the time o' year, ain't it?'

'Yes. Yes, I suppose it is,' Josefina replied, hesitantly.

He fell into step beside her and considering him to be harmless, Josefina made no objection. They had walked some way when he asked, 'From around these parts, are you?'

It was growing dark now and Josefina was glad of the fact, for it hid her blushes. 'No. I'm hoping to move on to Liverpool tomorrow.'

'Ah, yer folks live there, do they?'

'No. I . . . I don't have any folks.'

If he heard the tremble in her voice he tactfully chose to ignore it and went on in a friendly tone, 'Managed to find somewhere to stay, have you?'

Josefina shuddered as she recalled the man she had just encountered in the hall of the lodging house.

'Well, I have,' she told him dubiously, 'but I have to say I'm not really looking forward to sleeping there.'

'Why's that then, lass?'

He was the first person who had spoken to her kindly in weeks and she felt herself warming to him as she told him, 'It's rather er . . .'

'Mucky?' he finished for her.

She nodded miserably. 'That is rather an understatement. The room I have been given smells of damp and all sorts of unpleasant things.'

'Problem is, to get something better, you need to move to a better area and that would cost a lot more money. Could you afford it?'

'Not if I'm to keep enough back for my train ticket tomorrow,' she sighed.

'Hmm, then that poses us a slight problem, don't it?'

When he came to an abrupt stop to stare thoughtfully off into space, Josefina stopped too. She had been surrounded by love and kindness for most of her life, and had never had cause to distrust anyone, least of all the kindly man standing next to her.

'I know what you could do,' he suddenly told her with a note of excitement in his voice. 'I could take you back to my lodgin's fer the night. Salt o' the earth, my landlady is, an' I'm sure she'd let you have a room at a reduced rate just fer one night, if I was to ask her.'

Josefina hardly dared to believe her luck. 'But why would you do that for me, having only just met me?' she asked innocently.

He shrugged his broad shoulders. 'Why wouldn't I? It don't hurt to help one another, does it? Seems to me yer a bit down on yer luck an' in need of a friend.'

A warm feeling started in the pit of her stomach and slowly spread through her as she really smiled for the first time in weeks, and Alfred found himself thinking, Lordy, she *is* lovely, just as Mr Hammond said. They'd no doubt get a really pretty penny fer this one, 'specially wi' her high-falutin' ways.

'So, are you up fer it or what then? If you want to come wi' me we'd best not leave it too late.'

Just for an instant she hesitated, but then her head bobbed eagerly up and down as she told him, 'I'd love to. Thank you. But I shall have to go back and get my things.'

'O' course you will. I'll tell yer what, I'll come wi' you, an' then if whoever it is you're stayin' wi' cuts up rough I'll be there to back you up.'

Side-by-side they retraced their steps until she came to the door of the house where she had thought she would be staying.

'Do you want me to come in an' try an' get yer rent back for you?'

'No.' She smiled her gratitude. 'It isn't worth arguing about, really. I'll just get my things and leave. That way we should avoid any trouble.'

'As you will.'

She hurried inside and almost flew up the rancid stairs, only to reappear moments later clutching her bag.

'Blimey, that were quick,' he laughed.

'Well, to be honest the room was so filthy that I didn't want to unpack my bag, so all I had to do was collect it. I haven't even told the lady of the house that I'm leaving, but then she has no cause for complaint. She has secured a night's rent for nothing.'

He took her bag from her and swung it up as if it weighed no more than a feather.

'The name is Alfred, by the way,' he told her as he extended his hand, and as she shook it she told him, 'I'm Josefina.'

And then he was off at a fair old trot, with her almost running behind to keep up with him as she lifted her skirts from the dirty cobblestones.

After a time they passed the pawnbroker's that she had visited earlier in the day, and a pang of regret pierced the girl's heart as she saw the brooch her mama had given her with love, twinkling in the gaslight, as it lay on a velvet pad in the window. She said nothing but continued to follow the man called Alfred until eventually they came to a street where the houses were much bigger – three stories high, detached and standing slightly apart. Even so they still had an air of decay about them, and as Alfred saw her looking at them he told her, 'This used to be the nobs' part o' town but they're mostly all owned by a landlord who crams folks in like sardines an' charges 'em an arm an' a leg fer the privilege now. Me landlady's house is just slightly further up.'

Josefina was beginning to tire from the effort of keeping up with him now, so when shortly afterwards he paused in front of a house, she sighed with relief.

'This is it then, me beauty. The end o' the road.' Taking a key from his pocket he placed it in the door and swung it open, standing aside for her to pass him. She found herself in a large airy hallway that was surprisingly clean. One of the doors leading off it now opened and a thin, elegantly dressed lady tapped her way along the highly polished tiles to meet them.

'Ah, Nell. This is Josefina, a friend o' mine. She's lookin' fer lodgin's fer the night. Do you think you could find room fer her?'

Nell eyed Josefina up and down before saying pleasantly,

'I don't see why not, if it's only for the one night. Would you like to come through to the parlour?'

Josefina inclined her head but her face remained straight, and for the first time since meeting Alfred a finger of unease wormed its way up her spine. There was something about this woman that she didn't like. Admittedly, she seemed friendly enough, but her expression reminded Josefina of a snake that she had seen in America that was just about to strike. Her eyes were cold and remained so even when she smiled. The girl followed her along the hallway and into a comfortable parlour. Heavy drapes hung at the windows and a large aspidistra plant on a stand with barley twist legs stood next to an oil lamp that was casting a warm glow about the room. There was no doubt that this house was much cleaner than the one Josefina had just left, so why then, she wondered, did she feel like turning about and running from it?

'Would you like some tea, dearie?'

The woman's voice brought her thoughts sharply back to the present and now remembering her manners, Josefina nodded. 'Yes. Thank you. That would be very nice.'

The woman turned and left the room, and so smoothly did she glide that Josefina got the impression that her legs were not moving beneath her bell-like, grey alpaca skirt.

'Nice place, ain't it?' Alfred asked as he perched uncomfortably on the edge of a straight-backed chair.

'Er . . . yes, yes it is.' The urge was growing by the minute to stand up and run as fast as her legs would take her, and suddenly Josefina knew that she could not stay there. Perhaps if she were to return to her original lodgings and sneak back in, they might not notice? Even that rat-hole seemed preferable to this.

A sound from above made her start. She looked up

towards the ceiling. 'Did you hear someone cry out then?' she asked Alfred fearfully, once all was quiet again.

'No. Can't say as I did.'

Silence stretched between them until the woman returned carrying a large tray, which she placed on a small table.

'Now, Josefina. Do you take milk and sugar?'

'I er . . . yes, please.' She would drink the tea and then make some excuse to leave.

While the woman was pouring it out with her back to her, Josefina glanced around the room. It was utterly respectable in every way, she had to admit, so why then did she feel so uncomfortable?

'Here you are. And, of course, here's a cup for you, Alfred.'

'Look, this is really most kind of you,' Josefina told her, 'but I feel that I am unfairly imposing on you. I think perhaps it might be best if I were to return to my original lodging house.'

'Nonsense, dear. You're more than welcome. Though, of course, if you don't wish to stay you don't have to. But drink your tea and see how you feel then. If you're still of the same mind, then Alfred will walk you back, won't you, Alfred?' As she spoke she was pressing a cup and saucer into Josefina's hand.

Feeling that she had no alternative without appearing very rude, Josefina sipped at it. She briefly wondered what sort of tea it was. It was certainly not the brand that was used back at the Manor, for it was curiously flavoured with a strange aroma to it. Nonetheless, she drained the cup. It was then that the most peculiar thing happened, for as she reached out to place the cup and saucer back on the tray, they slipped from her hand to shatter on the varnished floorboards. Her head suddenly felt too heavy for her neck to hold up and her legs would not respond when she told them to stand up. And yet she could still see and hear perfectly well, which only made things worse, for what she heard now struck terror into her heart.

'Ah, that's better. She'll give us no trouble now. You've done well this night, Alfred. Jake will be well pleased with you. This little beauty will fetch a fair old price, make no mistake.'

Alfred grinned from ear to ear as he bent to lift the broken crockery onto the tray. And then there were more footsteps in the hallway and when the door swung open, Josefina swivelled her eyes to the side to see the pawnbroker standing in the doorway. He added his praise to the woman's, who Josefina was later to discover, was his wife.

'Ah, so you got 'er then?' Crossing to Josefina he traced his finger along the outline of her small heaving breast. 'Didn't I tell you she were beautiful, Nell? I reckon the Captain will pay a good price fer this little 'un. An' the way she talks . . . Huh! Like one o' the gentry. A rarity indeed; an' just look at the skin on her. It's like black silk. You've done well, Alfred. There'll be a bonus in this fer you, me lad. Now, should we get her upstairs while she's still quiet?'

The woman was bending over Josefina's carpetbag, and when her hand emerged holding the jewellery box that Willy had given her as a present, a scream rose in the girl's throat, but it was trapped there and all she could do was look helplessly on.

'Well, would you just look at this now.' The woman turned it this way and that, allowing the light to play on the lid, which was intricately inlaid with mother-of-pearl. 'Now this is what I call quality. It's rosewood, if I'm not very much mistaken, and a right fine piece. You're not going to put this in the shop, Jake Hammond. I've never seen one like it and it will look fine in my front window.' When she opened the lid her smile broadened yet further. 'And just look what's inside! Seems the brooch she brought into the shop earlier on wasn't the only quality piece she had. These pearls are as smooth as a baby's bottom.'

Alfred was advancing and Josefina felt herself being lifted. Her eyes flashed fire but he merely smiled as he made towards the door with her clutched tight in his arms. She wanted to scratch at his face and scream and shout but it was as if she had been paralysed for she couldn't move so much as a single muscle.

And then he was carrying her up the staircase and she could hear Nell and Jake following behind. Once at the top he started along a landing that seemed to go on forever. At the end of it was yet another staircase and she realised that this must be the one that led to the attics. He began to climb again. It was narrow here, and dark, and Nell had to hold her oil lamp high so that they could see where they were going. He eventually stopped outside a door and after fumbling with a key, Jake unlocked it. And then all hell seemed to break loose when he opened it as a small dark shape lunged towards it.

'Let me out, yer lousy bastards, do yer hear me?'

In the light from the lamp that was spilling into the sparsely furnished room, Josefina saw a young girl struggling with Nell. The tussle was over in no time at all as Jake caught one arm and Nell the other and the pair dragged her back into the room. And then Alfred slung Josefina onto a hard mattress, and whilst Nell and Jake still had firm hold of the other girl he went towards the door. Bringing her arm back, Nell smacked the girl so hard around the face that her head rocked on her shoulders and she slid to a heap on the bare floor.

'Now behave yourself, else you'll not be fed again tomorrow,' she warned as she followed Alfred. Jake was the last to leave, and as he slammed the door shut the room was plunged into darkness. The girl's sobs echoing around the room and the sound of receding footsteps was all that could be heard for a while, but then the sobs slowly subsided to dull hiccuping whimpers and Josefina heard her crawling across the floor towards her.

A trembling hand squeezed her arm and a voice from the darkness told her, 'Try not to be too scared. You've bin drugged the same as I was. It'll wear off in a bit an' you'll be able to move again.'

Although Josefina could not even move her head, tears were spilling down her cheeks now and the girl's hand came up to gently wipe them away. She then clambered up onto the bare mattress at the side of her and wrapped her arms around Josefina's quivering body. 'There, there,' she soothed as a mother might to a child. 'Don't be frightened, I've got yer. I'm Beth, by the way. That lousy bastard, Alfred, got me 'ere last week under false pretences. He told me there were a job as maid goin' an' then they pulled the same trick on me as they 'ave on you. But don't think about it fer now. Try to sleep an' come mornin', whatever it was they gave yer will 'ave worn off.'

Josefina was sure that she would never be able to sleep, and in her head she was crying, '*Mama . . . Willy, where are you?*' All too late she realised what a fool she had been, for they had loved her, but pride and jealousy had stopped her from seeing it. And now it was too late and she had the awful feeling that she would never set eyes on their beloved faces again.

Chapter Fourteen

WILLY WAS STANDING by the window waiting to hear the sound of the carriage on the drive, just as he had every single day since Ned had begun the search for Josefina. Before setting off early that morning, Ned had informed them that he was going to look in Jarrow, for he had already searched Shields and Newcastle, as well as all the surrounding villages.

Tilly always made sure that none of the furniture was ever moved out of place now, for as the sight in Willy's one good eye continued to deteriorate he was prone to bumping into things. He had been standing there for hours as if he had been cast in stone and Tilly could feel his pain, for it was written on his face.

Suddenly turning towards the vague shape of her that was all he could distinguish now, he asked, 'Do you think we shall ever see her again, Mama?'

'I . . . I hope so, Willy, for I feel her loss as much as you do.'

'Oh no, you don't. You couldn't. You see, now that it is too late, I realise that I love her – but not as a brother should love his sister. I love her as a man should love a woman. Are you shocked, Mama?'

'No, Willy, I'm not shocked. I think I realised it even before you did, but then when you fell in love with Noreen I thought . . . Well, I thought that I must have imagined it. On your part at least. Josefina never tried to hide her feelings for you. I just wish . . .'

When her voice trailed away he asked hoarsely, 'What do you wish, Mama?'

'I wish that you had known your true feelings sooner, then she might never have felt the need to run away. Not that I am placing any blame on you, of course, my darling boy. But once she came back from America you seemed so cold towards her. Why, Willy?' It was a question she had been longing to ask.

'Because of the guilt I felt over Noreen's death,' he mumbled. 'I felt somehow that it was wrong to express my feelings for anyone else and so I tried to contain them. You of all people should understand, Mama, for did you not go through the exact same feelings yourself when you promised Matthew on his deathbed that you would never marry again – and now you have agreed to marry Steve?'

His remark hit home, and she told him, 'Yes. Yes, I did, Willy – and still do, from time to time. But life is for the living and we have to go on. Promise me one thing. If Josefina does come home . . . will you tell her how you feel about her?'

Silence weighed heavy for a time until he whispered, 'Yes, I will tell her. I will also ask her to marry me. Will we have your blessing, Mama?'

Tears pricked at the back of her eyes now as she replied, 'Oh yes, Willy. You will have my blessing. But for now let us just pray for her safe return.' And going to the window she took her place at his side as they waited together for Ned's return.

When Ned finally reported to them in the drawing room, his despondent figure told its own story. 'Not a sign of her, Tilly. I've near worn the soles off me boots trailin' the streets, but all fer nothin'.'

'Oh, Ned, you look worn out.' Tilly drew him to a chair before crossing to the bell-pull at the side of the fireplace. 'We do appreciate what you're doing, but you mustn't make yourself ill. I'm going to get you some tea and then I want you to have a day off tomorrow.'

He smiled wearily. 'Yer a good lass, Tilly, but I'll be fine. Every day counts, so when I need a break from the searchin' I'll tell you. Just let me get a good night's kip an' I'll be bright as a button in the mornin' an' rarin' to go again.'

'Oh, Ned, I'm so lucky to have you all,' Tilly told him and the words were spoken from the heart, for she knew without a shadow of a doubt that her staff were also her loyal friends.

As Willy stumbled past them and the door closed behind him, Ned shook his head. 'Master Willy's takin' it bad, ain't he?'

'Yes, he is. We all are, particularly now that Sarah and Lucy have returned to the farm. Anna and John left for Felton Hall yesterday too so the house suddenly feels rather empty.'

'Aye, I know what you mean, lass. But keep yer pecker up. I ain't given up yet and there's still lots o' places left to look.'

Tilly was well aware that what he said was true, but she was also well aware that if Josefina didn't want to be found then he would be on a fruitless quest.

The following morning, they were given a ray of hope. Mother and son were just leaving the dining room following breakfast when they heard a commotion in the hall and looking towards the door, saw Phillipa striding towards them.

She was wearing a dull brown riding-habit and her cheeks were glowing, for she had urged her horse into a gallop for most of the way.

Too excited to bother with the nicety of a greeting, she told Tilly, 'I need to speak to you right away. I have some news that may throw some light on your daughter's whereabouts.'

Tilly felt her hand begin to tremble as she ushered the young woman towards the morning room. Once inside she asked abruptly, 'What is it? What have you learned?'

Phillipa took a deep breath. 'I had occasion to go into Durham yesterday. After I had done what I went to do, I decided to have a stroll as it was such a pleasant day . . .'

When she paused, Tilly told her impatiently, 'Do go on.'

'Well, during my stroll I strayed from the main town and I came upon a pawnbroker's in the back streets. These places have always held a certain appeal for me so I paused to look into the window . . . and that was when I saw it.'

'Saw what?'

'Josefina's butterfly brooch. It is so distinctive that I would have recognised it anywhere. I always used to comment on it whenever she wore it, if you recall? It was on a velvet pad in the front of the window. Anyway, after the initial shock of seeing it there I went into the shop and asked if I might look at it. On close inspection I had no doubt at all that it *was* Josefina's, so I bought it there and then. There was a rather unpleasant man behind the counter and whilst he was wrapping it up I enquired how he had come across it. That's when my suspicions were aroused, for he became . . .' she paused to search for the word she sought '. . . *cautious*,' she said eventually. 'He muttered that he couldn't recall whom he had bought it off, which I found rather strange to say the least, for from what I could see it was the only item of any real worth in the whole of the shop. The rest of the jewellery there amounted to nothing more than a few plain wedding bands, that no doubt some poor unfortunate women had been forced to pawn or sell to feed their family.'

All the while she was talking she was fumbling in the pocket of her jacket, and when she withdrew the item of jewellery and placed it into Tilly's hand she saw the colour drain from her face.

'It *is* Josefina's brooch, isn't it?'

'Oh yes, there's no doubt about it,' Tilly gulped. 'I commissioned a jeweller in Sunderland to make it for her some Christmases ago so I doubt very much if there would be another one like it. I even chose the diamonds that are set into the wings.'

'I *knew* I was right!' Phillipa declared triumphantly. 'I wanted to ride over and give it to you last night, but Lance would not hear of it because it was getting dark by then.'

Taking the brooch from his mother's hands, Willy traced his fingers across it.

'My sister would never have parted with this unless she was in dire straits,' he muttered fearfully. 'It was one of her favourite pieces.'

'I know,' Tilly agreed. 'But what can we do now?'

'We can go into Durham and search every corner of it until we find her. Has Ned left yet?'

'I'm not sure,' Tilly answered. 'Go and ask Biddle if he would go round to the stable-block and see. And if Ned hasn't gone yet, tell him that I need to see him.' Then to Phillipa, she said urgently, 'Can you remember where this pawnbroker's shop was?'

'Oh, yes,' she hastened to assure her. 'I could take you straight to it.'

'Right then, in that case we have not a moment to lose. Would you come into Durham again with me, Phillipa?'

'Of course,' the young woman replied without hesitation. 'I will come with you every day until we find her, if that's what it takes.'

At that moment, Willy tore back into the room, almost overturning an occasional table that was standing to the side of the door in his haste.

'Ned was just leaving,' he told them breathlessly. 'I've told him what's happened and he's bringing the carriage around to the front for us.'

'Good, you go and get in with Phillipa then whilst I have a quick word with Ellen and Fanny. I want to let them know what is going on. We may not be back until late and I need to make sure that a basket of food is sent over to the cottage for Steve this evening. If I don't arrive he will think that something is wrong.'

Phillipa took Willy's arm and led him towards the front door as Tilly set off in the direction of the kitchen. And all the while she was praying, 'Oh, dear God, please let us find her safe and well!'

When Josefina's eyes blinked open she found herself staring up at a sooty skylight set high in the roof. Her mouth was dry and her limbs felt stiff. She lay for a moment trying to remember where she was, and then as the events of the previous evening flooded back, she was engulfed in panic. In her mind's eye she relived the journey to the tall three-storey house with Alfred, and the strange, sweet-smelling tea she had drunk. She could remember vividly being carried up the long flights of stairs and the terror she had experienced as her limbs refused to do as she told them. Gingerly, she flexed her fingers and almost cried with relief when they responded to her command. They still felt as if she had pins and needles in them but at least they were working again.

At that moment a face swam into her vision and she started as she found herself looking up at a dark-haired girl of about sixteen or seventeen. Her hair was greasy and tied back from her face, and a strong smell of body odour was emanating from her, but despite this she had the face of an angel.

'So, 'ow yer feelin' today then?' she asked with concern.

Josefina ran her tongue around her dry lips before trying to answer. 'A little strange, to be honest. But what is happening? Why . . . am I here?'

' 'Cos yer fell fer that sweet-talkin' Alfred's offer o' help, that's why,' the girl told her through gritted teeth. When Josefina made to pull herself up, she placed her arms around her and helped her into a more comfortable position. 'Just lie still fer a bit if you can,' she advised. 'You'll still feel strange fer a time if yer anythin' like I was when they did this to me.'

'But . . . but why are we here?'

The girl's face drew into a frown. 'I asked meself that when I first woke up here,' she admitted. 'But then the other night, that Jake turned up wi' this sea captain who looked me over like I were a slab o' meat. From what I could gather I'm to go aboard his ship at the end o' the month, an' when I get to wherever it is they're takin' me, I'll be sold to the highest bidder. No doubt they've got the same in mind fer you an' all.'

'Oh, no!' A look of terror settled across Josefina's features as the girl squeezed her hand reassuringly.

'Don't worry,' she urged. 'They ain't got us on the ship yet an' now there's two of us there's more chance of us gettin' away.' As she eyed Josefina's pretty dress she suddenly asked, 'What's yer name anyway? I'm Beth, remember?' She was consumed with curiosity, for Josefina was like no one she had ever seen before. Her dark skin gave her the look of a Red Indian squaw, the kind she'd seen in picture books, and yet she was dressed and spoke like the gentry.

'My . . . my name is Josefina. Josefina Sopwith. My mother lives at Highfield Manor, near South Shields.'

'Stone the crows.' Beth was awestruck. 'So if you come from such a posh family, how did you end up 'ere?'

'I've been a fool,' Josefina told her, and looking back now she realised just how true that was, in so many different ways.

When she made no attempt to enlarge on her statement Beth drew in a deep breath and after scuttling away she returned with a piece of bread in her hand. 'Try an' eat this,' she said. 'I saved it fer you when Nell brought it up this morning. It's as dry as a bone but it'll keep yer strength up, an' we're gonna need our strength if we're to get out o' here.'

Josefina took the bread and obediently nibbled on it as Beth sank onto her backside to sit cross-legged at the side of her.

Eventually, Josefina asked, 'How did you come to be here?'

Sadness shone in Beth's eyes now and for a moment Josefina thought that she wasn't going to answer her, but then she said quietly, 'I lived in the back streets wi' me parents. I were the youngest, an' all me brothers an' sisters had left home so I suppose I were spoiled up to a point. Anyway, last year, me ma pegged it. Dicky ticker, yer know? So I stayed on in the house wi' me da. He worked down the pit an' some months ago there was a fall there an' . . . well, me da were dead when they finally dug him out three days later. Him an' half a dozen others, may I add. The house we lived in were tied to the pit, as are many o' the houses hereabouts, an' a few days later, the heavies turned up an' kicked me out onto the street wi' nothin' but the clothes I stood up in an' a few pots an' pans. They're ruthless bastards, I don't mind tellin' yer. Since then I've lived between me brothers' an' sisters' houses, kippin' down wherever I could, which ain't always been easy, fer they've all got more bairns than they know what to do wi'. Still, at least it was better than endin' up in the work-house. An' then I met Alfred an' I thought me luck had changed. He told me he knew where there was work goin' in a respectable house an' that I would get to live in. I jumped at the chance an' came along to meet Nell. The rest you can guess.'

'But won't your brothers and sisters be looking for you?' Josefina asked.

Beth shook her head. 'I doubt it. I'd told 'em all I had the chance of a live-in position so they won't think nowt of it if I don't show up.'

Josefina's teeth nipped down on her lip, and feeling slightly stronger now, she leaned up on her elbow to look about the room. Apart from the lumpy flock mattress that she was sitting on there were two more thrown down on the floor. A bucket stood in the far corner and even from here Josefina could smell it, for this was obviously what they were to use for their water closet. She shuddered. Fortunately, she had not needed to use it yet, but that time would come soon. There was not a single stick of furniture in the room. She thought that things could get no worse until Beth suddenly informed her, 'There's somethin' else you should know, an' all. Jake, the bloke who owns the pawnbroker's an' this place, he . . . well, he might come up an' try to . . . *yer know.'*

When Josefina looked puzzled, the younger girl sighed. 'Blimey, you are green, ain't yer? What I'm tryin' to tell you is he's partial to us young bits. He turned up here late the other night, an' if I hadn't fought like a wild cat he'd have taken me down, so be warned. Not that he's likely to try it now there's the two of us up 'ere. He wouldn't want his missus to find out, would he?'

Josefina screwed her eyes tight shut at the predicament she found herself in. It was made worse for knowing that she had brought it on herself. She had no time to ponder on it, however, for Beth was eyeing her curiously before she said tentatively, 'So, if yer don't mind me askin', how come you're er . . .'

'Black?'

'Well, aye. That is what I were wonderin'. No offence meant, o' course.'

'My mother adopted me during a trip to America when I was still very young.'

'Ah, that explains it then. The way you talk an' whatnot.'

'Yes, I suppose it does. I have been very fortunate.' And what she was thinking was, Oh, why didn't I realise it before?

The journey into Durham was made in almost total silence as each of the people in the swaying carriage watched the countryside flash by the window. Willy looked as if he had just come back to life after a long, long sleep, and Tilly's hands fidgeted nervously in her lap. Phillipa too, was restless and as Tilly looked across at her she realised how much the young woman had come to mean to her. It was odd to think now, how jealous she had been of her before she discovered that she was Steve's daughter and not his mistress as she had at first presumed. Darling Steve. He had been so understanding during the last difficult weeks, and he hadn't once pressed her for a date for the wedding, as if he sensed that she could not go ahead with it, with everything else she had on her plate. But soon, she promised herself as the carriage trundled along.

Sarah's face was healing well, though she would bear the scar of her Christening Day to the grave. All Tilly needed to do now was return Josefina to her rightful place at the Manor and then at last she could retire to the cottage and find the peace she had always craved with Steve. A little voice nagged her, *But you are Tilly Trotter, the witch.* She pushed it from her mind as she prepared herself for the search that lay ahead – and she *would* search for her daughter – until she dropped dead, if need be!

Chapter Fifteen

'I WERE READIN' THAT Mr Disraeli has a programme o' social reforms lined up to improve conditions fer the workin' classes,' Arthur commented as he took a bite of the huge doorstep sandwich that Ellen had just placed in front of him. 'What do you reckon to that?'

'I'm all for it, of course,' Ellen replied, wiping her floury hands down the front of her starched white apron. 'And I know that Tilly is, too.' She was in the process of kneading dough, but had welcomed Arthur's intrusion when he appeared at the kitchen door. He often came into the kitchen during his lunch-break now and she looked forward to their conversations, for as she had soon discovered, Arthur was a very intelligent man, who followed politics and the happenings in the country religiously. *The Times* and any other publications that were sent to the Manor were shared and read by everyone in the house.

'Of course,' she added, 'I do wonder if, at seventy years of age, he will have time to do all he plans to. It seems a shame that he couldn't have taken over as Prime Minister from Gladstone a little sooner.'

'Aye, I know what you mean,' Arthur agreed, 'but I think his idea of cutting down the working man's week from sixty to fifty-six hours will be well met.'

'Yes, and also his instructions to local authorities to rip down the slums and rehouse the workers in better accommodation.' Now that she had covered the dough with a wet cloth, Ellen left it to rest and swell. Picking up the tea caddy, she carefully measured four spoons of tealeaves into the large brown teapot, tipped the boiling water in and left it to mash, covered by a bright knitted cosy.

Aware that Arthur's eyes were following her about, she felt a faint blush of colour stain her cheeks. Arthur always had that effect on her.

'So, how are you enjoying it back in England again then?' he asked when she was just beginning to think that the silence would stretch on forever.

Lifting the lid of the teapot she stirred the tea before answering. 'I'm really enjoying it, although I have to admit to it feeling a little strange after all the years I spent in Africa.'

'Aye, I can well imagine that,' Arthur conceded. She had often spoken to the staff in the kitchen of the adventures she had been on whilst there and Arthur could have listened to her stories forever. Or gazed upon her forever, if it came to that, for as yet he had found no single thing that he disliked about her.

'You must miss your husband?' he said softly, and now her hand became still as she thought on his question.

'Yes, I suppose I do miss him – but not perhaps as you would think. George and I had a rather strange relationship after leaving England. Especially after he became firm friends with David Livingstone. Months at a time could pass without me so much as seeing him when they were off on their expeditions. And of course, he died a long time ago.' She paused reflectively. 'Did I ever tell you that following David's death, the natives cut out his heart and buried it in Africa?

You see, they believed that was where it belonged. They then embalmed his body and carried it overland for nine long months to the shores of the Indian Ocean where he was put on a ship and returned to England for burial in Westminster Abbey. It's quite remarkable when you come to think of it, isn't it?'

'He must have been very well-loved,' Arthur remarked and her head bobbed in agreement.

'Oh, he was. He built a chapel, and set up a printing press for them, as well as running his mission. He also spent a lot of his time preaching and healing. One of his greatest wishes was to abolish slavery. He was a truly remarkable man, considering he came from such humble beginnings.'

'I didn't know that,' Arthur said, his interest aroused.

'Oh yes, he was raised in poverty. The family consisted of nine people and they all lived in a single room in a Lanarkshire cotton-mill tenement, which makes his achievements all the more impressive, don't you think?'

Arthur nodded and would have gone on with the conversation, but at that moment Fanny bustled into the room. Her face was creased with worry and as Ellen and Arthur looked at her their thoughts returned to the person who was uppermost in their minds.

'Do you reckon they'll ever find Miss Josefina?' she asked fretfully.

Ellen placed a comforting arm about Fanny's broad shoulders. 'I'm sure they'll do their very best to. Try not to worry too much, love.'

'I can't help it.' Taking a handkerchief from her apron pocket, Fanny loudly blew her nose on it. 'She's had such a sheltered upbringin', the poor little lamb,' she sniffled. 'She'll wonder what's hit her now she's out in the cruel wide world.'

'Well, worrying isn't going to change anything,' Ellen told

her wisely as she poured her out a cup of tea. 'I'm sure that Tilly and the others will be doing all within their powers to find her. Meanwhile, it's up to us to keep things running as smoothly as we can back here.'

Fanny nodded in agreement before noisily slurping at her tea, while Arthur rose reluctantly and stretched his long arms above his head.

'Right then, all good things must come to an end, so they say. I reckon 'tis time as I was gettin' back to work.' He flashed the women a friendly smile as he left the kitchen, and as Ellen lifted his empty mug and carried it to the sink she found herself thinking, Arthur is a lovely man. Oh yes, as far as she was concerned he was lovely . . . in all ways.

They were all standing in front of the pawnbroker's window and Tilly's nerves were stretched to the limit. 'Do you think I should go in alone?' she asked.

Ned shook his head. 'No, I ain't in favour o' that, Tilly. I reckon it would be better if we all went in together. You know what they say, there's safety in numbers an' this ain't such a good neighbourhood.'

'Very well then,' Tilly agreed. 'But when we get in there, let me do the talking.'

Ned was happy to agree to that at least, and so with Tilly leading the way they stepped into the gloomy interior of the shop. The smell of unwashed clothes met them as the shop bell tinkled above their heads, but Tilly held her chin high as a door behind the cluttered counter opened and a large untidy-looking man appeared.

'Good morning.' Tilly's voice was stiffly polite as she looked him coolly in the eye.

'Morning, ma'am. What can I be doin' fer you?' Jake

Hammond was not used to having this class of people in his shop and felt faintly nervous.

'Actually, it is information I'm after,' Tilly told him imperiously. 'My friend here,' she inclined her head towards Phillipa, who steadily held his gaze, 'bought a brooch from you yesterday afternoon. Five guineas, she paid for it. Do you recall it?'

As if it was an everyday occurrence for him to sell an item of such value he stroked his chin thoughtfully and gazed off into space. 'Mmm, now let me see . . .'

'Come along, sir. Let us not waste each other's time. This is the brooch in question.' Taking it from her bag, Tilly laid it on the counter and had the satisfaction of seeing his colour rise.

'Ah, *that* brooch.' He made to take it up, but now Tilly snatched it back.

'I would like to know who you purchased the brooch from.'

'Well now, to be honest I can't quite rightly remember.'

'Would this help your memory to return?' When Tilly placed a golden sovereign on the counter his eyes glittered greedily and he would have snatched it up, but her hand covered it as she told him, 'Information first, if you please.'

His brows drew into a frown as he sought a way out of the predicament he found himself in. These people were clearly class and it was obvious that the woman who was doing all the talking was not one to dally with. But what could he tell her without digging himself deeper into the mess. *Damn* that idiot Alfred! Hadn't he told him a million times to choose his victims carefully?

'May I ask why you want to know, madam?' he prevaricated.

'I want to know, sir, because my daughter – my adopted

daughter, that is – is missing, and this is her brooch. So I ask again, who sold this to you? Was it a young, dark-skinned woman?'

Tilly's voice was so heavy with contempt that he now visibly blanched.

'Now that I come to think on it, I reckon it were,' he told her cautiously, and Tilly could barely contain herself as she leaned across the counter and asked him, 'When was this?'

He chewed on his lip as he considered what to tell her. Having no idea at all how long the girl had been missing, he realised that he was going to have to be careful.

'If I remember rightly, it were some time earlier in the week.'

This answer must have sat well, for she didn't dispute that it could not have been so.

'And did she give you any idea where she might be staying?'

'No, she didn't,' he replied, beginning to feel more in control of the situation again. It was at that moment that Tilly's eyes strayed behind the counter, and when she saw a smart coat hanging there, the breath caught in her throat and the room began to swim around her. Stabbing a trembling finger towards it she told him, 'That is also my daughter's coat. Did you buy that off her too?'

'Aye, I did, an' I give her a fair price fer it, an' the bonnet an' all. Though who would want somethin' of that quality hereabouts I have no idea. I'm too damn soft fer me own good at times.'

Tilly's heart was heavy. What state must Josefina be in if she had been forced to resort to selling the clothes from her back?

During the whole exchange Willy had remained silent, but now he stepped forward and said, 'When someone pawns their things they usually leave an address in case they are able to redeem them in the future.'

'You're quite right there, sir. They do. But that's only in the case of 'em pawnin' 'em. In this case the young lady in question sold 'em to me outright so I had no cause to ask fer an address.'

Snatching some coins from his pocket, Willy flung them onto the counter and demanded angrily, 'Give me her clothes this minute. I cannot bear to see them in such a place.' When the man handed them over without a word, he thrust them at Phillipa and taking Tilly's arm, he turned her about. As a thought suddenly occurred to him he looked back at the pawnbroker. 'Do you have any more of my sister's things? Anything else at all that she might have sold to you?'

'Not a thing, sir. That was the lot.'

They all began to trail dejectedly from the shop but at the door Willy paused to tell him, in a tone he had never used to anyone in his life before, 'Should I discover that you have been lying to us, I promise you before God, you will live to regret it.'

Once outside on the pavement they stared about them. Durham was a sizeable place and they had no doubt that to find someone who had no wish to be found there would be like looking for a needle in a haystack. Nevertheless, they intended to try, so whilst Willy went one way with Phillipa, Tilly and Ned set off in the opposite direction. They came back together as the light was fading, tired and thoroughly dispirited.

'It's useless,' Tilly muttered. 'We'll never find her at this rate.'

'Oh, yes, we will.' Ned was determined. 'There's no point in lingerin' here any longer, but I'll be back at first light an' I won't give up till she's safe home with us again. Of that you need have no fear.'

'Then I'll come back with you,' Tilly told him.

Ned shook his head. 'I'd rather you didn't, to be honest. There was somethin' about that bloke as didn't sit quite right. I got the impression that he was lyin' through his teeth so I've a mind to come back on me own so I ain't quite so conspicuous, an' follow him when he shuts the shop tomorrow.'

When Tilly looked doubtful, he asked her, 'Have you got a better idea?'

'Well . . . no, I haven't to be honest.'

'Then let's say no more about it. We might be clutchin' at straws but at this stage anythin' is worth a try, from where I'm standin'.'

The despondent group turned as one and made their way back to the carriage.

It so happened that, as they arrived back at the Manor, Fanny was just about to set off for the cottage.

Taking the basket from her hands, Tilly said, 'I'll take it, Fanny. I shall only sit about here worrying if I don't.'

'But ain't you too tired, pet?' Word had quickly spread through the staff about the dramatic developments, and Fanny was hurting for her. 'Wouldn't you rather stay here an' put yer feet up?'

'No, as I said I'd rather keep myself busy. Besides, it's just started to drizzle and I don't want you catching your death.' Taking the basket from Fanny's hand she turned to ask Biddle, 'Would you mind getting Ellen to send something to eat through to Willy? Tell her not to go to too much trouble. I'm sure he will be more than happy with cold meat and pickles.'

'Of course, ma'am.' Biddle immediately turned to do as he was bid as Fanny draped a heavy cape about Tilly's weary shoulders. It was Tilly's favourite, a heavy dark green one with a fur-trimmed hood that she had designed herself, perfect for days such as this.

'Don't get stayin' too long now,' Fanny instructed her as a mother might a child. 'You look all in.'

Tilly flashed her a smile and then, after slipping out of the back way, set off for the cottage. She was soon in the woods, where she paused to inhale the unforgettable scent of bluebells. It was too dark to see them now but even so, when she set off again she was sure-footed, for she knew this route like the back of her hand. Staying well back from the edge of the gorge, where Hal McGrath had once met his end, she eventually came out of the woodland and on to the common land.

Lifting her heavy skirts, she began the climb up the steep bank that would lead her to the coach road and on to the cottage. It was there that she paused to cock her ear. She was familiar with all the normal night sounds, but what she had just heard sounded like someone dogging her footsteps. All was quiet again and she shrugged. It was no doubt some poacher, out for a rabbit to make a pie. At the top of the bank she paused again to strain her eyes into the darkness behind her, but all was silent now so she made for the crossroads and hurried on her way.

As her footsteps receded, Randy Simmons came out from the shelter of the trees to stare after her. So, old Ma McGrath had been right then – the witch was off to visit her latest fancy man, as she did almost every night, apparently. It would be a shame, wouldn't it, if she were to have an accident on her way home one night? 'Tweren't safe in the woods, with all these traps about, were it? You caught all sorts o' things in them there traps. Rabbits, squirrels, witches . . .

A crafty leer on his face, the bent figure turned and made off in the opposite direction.

Chapter Sixteen

'NOW STAND WELL clear of the door, else I'll see that you starve, so I will.'

As Nell's voice echoed in the corridor beyond the door, Josefina and Beth looked at each other. The next minute they heard the key turn in the lock and Nell appeared in the doorway with a tray in her hands. But their plans to rush her and make their escape were foiled when they saw the large frame of Alfred standing close behind her.

As if she could read their minds, their jailer grinned, 'Thought you were going to get past me, did you, young ladies? Well, you can forget it. I'm not so foolish as to come up here on my own. Now eat that, and think yourselves lucky to have it. I'll be back up later to collect the tray.'

As she placed it down onto the bare wooden floorboards, Josefina asked, 'Are you aware who I am?' in the most dignified voice she could muster.

'Yes, I'm aware of it. What of it?'

'My mama is a very wealthy woman and I have no doubt that she would pay very highly to get me back.'

'Perhaps you are right,' Nell replied, her eyes as cold as ever as she stared at Josefina. 'But what use would the money do me if I were locked up, eh? And I obviously would be, if our little racket were to come to light. No, my pretty, it's far too late for that now.' Her snakelike gaze flickered over the younger girl critically. 'Speaking of which, the Captain is coming over to have a look at you tonight so try to make yourselves look respectable. Christ, it stinks in here.'

'And just how are we supposed to keep clean with the facilities that are available to us?' Josefina gestured towards the bucket that was now nearly overflowing with urine, and the small rough towel and pitcher of dirty water that was all they had to wash in. 'Couldn't you at least empty the bucket and give us some fresh water and soap for our ablutions?' she said indignantly. 'Even animals are kept in better conditions than we are.'

Nell hesitated, but then nodding at Alfred, she told him, 'Empty that bucket and bring them up a clean pitcher of water. I dare say it's in my own interests to have them looking as clean as I can for the Captain's visit.'

Alfred stepped past her into the room, and as Josefina caught his eye she glared at him. He quickly averted his gaze and once he had the bucket and pitcher, the big man scuttled from the room without a word.

'Well, that's that then,' Beth sighed as the sound of their footsteps faded away. 'There ain't no way we could ever get past the two of them.'

Josefina began to pace up and down. 'There must be *some* way of getting out of here,' she cried in deep frustration, and then a thought occurred to her. She looked up at the filthy skylight. 'Do you think you might be able to reach that if you were to stand on my shoulders?' she asked suddenly.

'I dare say there's a chance, but what if I could? Do you know how high this house is?' Beth sputtered.

'Well, I think I'd rather chance sliding off the roof and

break my neck on the cobblestones than face the future *she* has in store for us,' Josefina said.

Beth looked upwards and shuddered involuntarily. She'd always had a fear of heights, yet she supposed Josefina was right. But they mustn't attempt it yet, for Alfred could reappear with the empty bucket and the clean water at any minute.

'We'll try later on,' she whispered, and then turned her attention to the food on the small tray that Nell had brought up to them. There was a wedge of dry bread and a small chunk of cheese, which no doubt they were supposed to share. To wash it down were two mugs of unsweetened, lukewarm tea.

Josefina turned her nose up as Beth held the bread out to her. 'It would choke me,' she said, as rage began to rise in her like a tide.

'In that case I'll eat it then. Ain't no point in starvin', is there?'

Sinking down onto the smelly mattress, Josefina buried her face in her hands and, for one of the very few occasions in her life, she sobbed as if her heart would break, as hope slipped away.

As Tilly neared the cottage, she saw to her surprise that it was in darkness. Steve should have been home long since, so where could he be? Stepping over the tools that the work-men had discarded when the fading light had stopped them from working any longer, she pushed the cottage door open and stepped inside. The fire was burning low in the grate, so after placing her basket on the table, she crossed to the hearth and tossed some logs onto it. Within minutes, weak flames began to lick at them. She then filled the kettle at the sink and placed it on top of the logs to boil. Dusting her hands off she lit the lamp and turned her attention to the almost completed room. It was strange to see it now, for this room, that had once been the tutor Mr Burgess's parlour, had now been transformed into a kitchen.

In her mind's eye, Tilly began to plan how she would furnish it. She would do away with the small table and replace it with a huge scrubbed oak one that would seat visitors, should she and Steve ever be lucky enough to have them. Then against that wall there she would have an enormous dresser, filled with her favourite china. At either side of the fireplace would be two wing chairs that she and Steve could sit in when he returned home from work each night. She could picture them telling each other of the sort of day they'd had, and it made a warm glow spring to life in the pit of her stomach. In front of the hearth would be a deep pile rug that they could lose their toes in, and she would hang brasses here and there on the beams, that would glow in the light from the fire.

Lifting the lamp, she then opened the door in what had formerly been the outside wall, but which now led into the new parlour. The workmen had just finished putting in the windows, which were leaded to match the rest in the cottage. 'I'll have red curtains in here,' she said aloud, 'and a sofa to match. Then perhaps on that wall, a nice long sideboard where I can put some silver and knick-knacks. And of course we'll need some small tables and pretty rugs.' Moving on to yet another door she entered what was to be her favourite room, the library. She supposed it might appear a little ostentatious to have a library in a cottage, but at last she would have somewhere to house all of Mr Burgess's beloved books. Steve had already started to carry them down for her from the little room beneath the eaves and they were stacked in neat piles all about the room. One wall would be shelved from floor to ceiling and she saw now that the carpenter had almost finished them. Very soon now she would be able to arrange the books in alphabetical order all across the lengths of them. She decided that she would buy a desk for the centre of the room where she could sit to write her letters and keep her accounts. Nothing too large, like the one at the Manor, but something that would complement the size of the room – and perhaps a leather chair to sit on?

Retracing her steps, she made her way upstairs to the room that would be hers and Steve's once they were married. It was going to be a lovely room, a grand room, in fact. She could see it now although this room was nowhere as near to completion as the ones downstairs. The floor was in and the roof was on, but the window frames were standing propped against the walls as yet. Even so she saw that it would afford space for at least two double wardrobes as well as a big chest of drawers and a good-sized dressing-table. And that was without the bed. She blushed as she thought of them lying there together, their limbs entwined and the rest of the world seemingly a million miles away.

In the far wall of the bedroom was a door leading to the only luxury Steve had insisted upon: a bathroom and a water closet, for as he had pointed out, after being used to the life o' Riley up at the Manor, she certainly wouldn't want to have to get used to using an outside closet again. It was the first time that day that she had been able to think of anything but Josefina, and she welcomed the distraction. So much so that when a voice behind her suddenly said, 'Now *there's* a sight for sore eyes,' she almost jumped out of her skin. She spun around, her skirts swirling, and when she saw Steve standing there she almost cried out with relief. Seeing the amusement on his face she blushed like a schoolgirl who had been caught in the act of doing something that she shouldn't.

'I er . . . I didn't hear you ride up. You startled me. While I was waiting for you I thought I'd have a look around at how everything was coming along. I hope you don't mind?'

'Aw, Tilly, if I wasn't all covered in soot I'd hug you. Why should I mind? This is going to be our home. Come over here, woman, and let me look at you.'

She did as she was told, and once she was standing in front of him he looked deep into her eyes and saw the pain there. Taking her two hands in his he squeezed them gently and asked, 'So how did it go today in Durham? Jimmy rode over to the mine to tell me what had happened.'

Her head wagged from side to side. 'It didn't go well. Phillipa took us to the pawnbroker's where she had bought Josefina's brooch, but the man who owned the shop could tell us nothing. Ned is going to go back into Durham tomorrow on his own, and when the shop shuts he's going to follow the man that we spoke to home. Though I can't for the life of me see what that will achieve.'

'Ned is a canny old fox,' Steve assured her. 'I think 'twould be wise to let him follow his instincts. But enough about that for now. What do you think of the way the house is coming along?'

'I think it's looking beautiful,' she said softly, and she meant it. He led her to the hole in the wall where the main window would be and they stood staring out at the moonlit countryside. The rain had stopped for now and everywhere looked peaceful.

'I think you and I are going to know deep contentment here, Tilly,' he told her, and she hoped he would be proved right.

★

Josefina had washed and tidied herself as best she could, and to her deep embarrassment had been forced to use the bucket in the corner of the room. At least it had been emptied. Beth had tactfully kept her back turned, but Josefina was mortified at being put in such a position all the same.

It was dark now, and the only light in the cold attic room was that of the moon that was shining through the skylight far above them. 'Do you want to see if you can reach it now?' Josefina asked Beth.

'Well, seein' as I'm a lot bigger than you, it might be best if I gave *you* a bunk-up,' Beth suggested. 'There ain't nothin' on you, an' you're that skinny you probably wouldn't be able to lift me.'

'Very well, I suppose we have nothing to lose by trying.'

Beth positioned herself directly below the window and bending low she told Josefina, 'Sit on me shoulders an' see if you can reach it like that.'

With some trepidation, Josefina hoisted her skirts up and sat astride Beth's shoulders, and then with a great deal of cursing and grunting, Beth slowly staggered upright with the other girl clinging to her neck for dear life.

'Right,' Beth gasped. 'Stretch your arms up an' see if you can reach it now. An' fer Christ's sake, get yer hands from around me neck! You're stranglin' the life out o' me.'

After gulping deep in her throat, Josefina released her hold on Beth and then, balancing as best she could, she stretched her arms as far as they would go, groaning with the effort.

'It's no good,' she panted. 'I'm still some long distance away.'

As Beth leaned forward they both overbalanced and toppled in a heap onto one of the mattresses that was lying on the floor. Under other circumstances they might have

Rosie Goodwin

found the exercise amusing, but as it was they knew that this had been possibly their only means of escape.

'Looks like we'll 'ave to come up wi' some other plan of action,' Beth mumbled miserably when she finally got her breath back. The words had scarcely left her lips when footsteps sounded on the landing outside and the girls shivered with fear at their narrow escape. Voices reached them. One of them was Nell's, and they heard her say, 'I believe you'll be well pleased with Alfred's latest offering, Captain. This one is very pretty and I'm sure she will fetch a good price. I think you'll agree she's a cut above the sort we usually find for you. But come and see for yourself.' The next sound they heard was the key turning in the lock and then the door squeaked open and they saw Nell standing in the doorway holding a lamp. As Josefina's eyes settled on the pearls fastened about her neck, rage swept through her, and without stopping to think, she leaped to her feet and shouted, 'How *dare* you wear my necklace! You thief! Give it back at once, I order you!'

'*Ooh.*' Nell's free hand covered her mouth as she stifled a giggle. 'Didn't I tell you she was different, Captain? A right little spitfire and beautiful with it.'

There now stepped past Nell one of the largest men that Josefina had ever seen. He was dressed in naval uniform and his long black hair was tied back into a pony tail. Under other circumstances Josefina might have been afraid of him, but at the moment she was so incensed to see Nell wearing her pearls that everything else paled into insignificance.

The Captain watched with amusement as she strode towards Nell, her eyes flashing fire. 'Get that off *now*, I tell you! Or as sure as God is my judge, you will live to regret it.'

His hand came out and stayed her from passing him but she slapped it away disdainfully. 'Get out of my way,' she hissed. And now he laughed – a loud sound that bounced around the walls and echoed back from the ceiling. Catching her wrist in a vice-like grip, he swung her about and tossed her onto the mattress as if she weighed no more than a feather. When she sprang back up and glared at him indignantly, his laughter increased.

'You will not get away with this!' she told him as she stabbed a trembling finger towards him. 'Has she told you who I am?'

Seeing the bemused look on his face she went on, 'I am Josefina Sopwith and my mother owns Highfield Manor near Jarrow. At this very minute she will be looking for me, and when she learns of the way I have been treated, it will be all the worse for you.'

He looked questioningly back at Nell and Josefina had the satisfaction of seeing the woman quake in her shoes. 'I er . . . I was meaning to talk to you about that, Captain,' she stuttered. 'Alfred didn't know that she was gentry when he brought her here. But you need have no fear. There is nothing to link her to us.'

'There had better not be,' he ground out. And then, turning his attention back to Josefina, he narrowed his eyes. 'Perhaps, given the circumstances, it might be better if I arranged for her to sail earlier in the month on one of my other ships?'

'Yes, yes. That might be a good idea,' Nell simpered as she backed from the room, keeping the lamp held high.

Suddenly unable to bear it any longer, Josefina rushed towards the doorway – and had it not been for the Captain, she might have made her escape. As it was, he simply waited until she was level with him and then caught her around the waist and swung her off her feet. Her hands balled into fists and she pummelled his chest with frustration as her feet kicked out at fresh air. 'LET ME DOWN! DO YOU HEAR ME?'

Once again she was slung onto the mattress and this time he did not look quite so amused. 'Do you know,' he panted, 'I think I might quite like to break this one myself. Have her put into a room on her own for me on Friday. I shall enjoy taming her spirit.'

'Yes, Captain, and now if you'd care to come back downstairs we might perhaps discuss her worth?'

'You bastards!' Josefina sobbed as the door closed on them and once again the girls were plunged into darkness.

'Don't cry.' When Beth's arm snaked around her shoulders, Josefina sobbed all the louder.

'That man will not touch me. Do you hear? I would rather *die* than have his hands on me.'

Beth hung her head, for there was nothing she could say. During the day the heat from the sun had shone through the skylight and turned the attic room into a furnace, but now it was chilly and the two young women clung together for warmth and comfort.

Tilly returned to the Manor that night to find Willy still up and staring down into the empty fireplace in the drawing room.

'Are you all right, pet?' She watched him closely as she slipped her heavy cape from her shoulders.

'I shall never be all right, Mama, until we find Josefina and bring her home safe and well.'

There seemed to be no answer to that, so turning about she left him standing there. Apart from Josefina, she had something else to worry about now, for during her visit, Steve had admitted that there were grave problems at the mine. Number three shaft was still shut, which had meant men had had to be laid off, and now number four was flooding as well. She undressed with a heavy heart, and as the hours of that long night passed, she plunged in and out of nightmares, in which she was trapped in the mine, surrounded by eternal darkness.

Chapter Seventeen

'MA, ARE YOU all right?' Eddie Bentwood's face was a picture of concern as he hurried to Lucy's side. She was leaning heavily on the handle of the butter churn in the dairy and her face was a sickly ash-grey as she clutched at her stomach.

After taking a moment to compose herself she smiled weakly at him. 'Aye, I'm fine, son. Just give me a minute. I came over all funny there, but 'tis passing now.'

It was almost macabre, his mother having a child after his father's death. By, it had taken some getting used to, the notion of a new brother or sister in the house. But no one could ever replace his beloved poor, dead sister, Noreen. Christ, if he could get hold of his father, he would kill Simon Bentwood all over again . . . It was his fault that the girl had run away from home and died in childbirth after months of deprivation.

His eyes came to rest on her swollen stomach. After chewing on his lip for a time he asked tentatively, 'Shouldn't we be starting to get things ready for the baby coming soon, Ma? I mean, it's er . . . more than obvious that it won't be that long now. You should be restin' more, I reckon. Tilly did say that she'd get a girl in from the village to help you if need be.'

'I don't need any help!' Lucy snapped and then, instantly repentant when she saw his face drop, she lifted her workworn hand and tenderly stroked his cheek. 'Sorry, I didn't mean to bite your head off, pet. I'm just a bit tired and out of sorts, that's all.'

He nodded before turning on his heel and striding away, and looking towards the window, Lucy fought back the tears as she asked, 'Oh, Lord, what am I going to do?'

After a time, she crossed the yard and entered the kitchen to check on Sarah. She was still fast asleep in her crib at the side of the fireplace, and as Lucy looked down on her the tears that she had held back spurted from her eyes and ran in rivers down her pallid cheeks. The child was lying snuggled up, with the unscarred side of her face visible, and she looked so beautiful that Lucy had the urge to snatch her into her arms there and then. 'Oh, my poor little bairn,' she whispered. 'What will happen to you when . . .' She stopped her thoughts from running any further ahead, for when the time came she would make provision for the child, just as she would for Eddie. 'But not yet,' she muttered. 'Please God, not yet!'

Ned had spent the whole of the day scouring the streets of Durham without success, but as the light began to fade he made his way back across the cobbled streets to the pawn-broker's. Once in sight of it, he hid in an alley, from which he had a fair view of the shopfront, and there he waited. The streets were full of men making their way home from their shifts at the pit, their heavy boots clashing on the cobbles. Workworn women in crude wooden clogs and thin shawls tied about their shoulders scuttled past with raggedy-arsed children clinging to their skirts. More than one of them entered the pawnbroker's shop and Ned guessed rightly that they would be pawning their weddings rings or anything else they had of worth to put food on the table for their children until pay day.

At one stage, a great ugly-looking man with one eye stitched shut went in too, but though Ned watched the doorway diligently he did not see him come back out. By this time a lamp had been lit in the shop, but as the minutes ticked away there was no sign of the owner closing up. Ned's stomach was rumbling with hunger, and as the sun sank below the rooftops, the damp seemed to set into his bones. He was just thinking of calling it a day and starting the journey home when the shop window was suddenly plunged into darkness.

He shrank further back into the shadows of the alley and was rewarded for his patience when some moments later, the door opened and Jake Hammond appeared, along with the tall man whom Ned had watched enter the shop some time ago.

Luckily, the gas-lamps had not yet been lit so it was easy for him to follow the men as they started through the labyrinth of stinking back streets.

They had not gone far when they entered a public house, and Ned cursed softly. There was nothing he would have liked better than to follow them in and order a jug of ale to quench his thirst, but he was too afraid of Jake Hammond recognising him from his visit to the shop the day before. And so he stood there as the night grew colder by the minute and waited yet again.

At last, Jake Hammond reappeared, alone this time. His steps were slightly unsteady now and slower as Ned once again began to follow him. When they turned into a street of tall, three-storey houses, Ned saw the man start to fumble in his pocket. Shortly afterwards, he stopped in front of one of the houses and after clumsily inserting a key into the lock, disappeared inside it.

Ned stood there staring up at the windows. They were all in darkness, save for the one that overlooked the cobbled street, but nothing could be seen of the room beyond, for the curtains were drawn against the night, with only a slither of light showing through a slight gap.

It was as Ned was standing there, at a bit of a loss now, that he saw the man who had accompanied Jake Hammond into the pub coming up the street towards him. He was walking beside another man who looked out of place in this area, for he was dressed in a fine melton coat and a patterned waistcoat. He was elderly and even in the dim light, Ned could see that his portly face was ruddy and somehow strangely familiar. Thrusting his hands into his coat pockets, Ned strolled on so that it would not appear that he was loitering, and seconds later he peeped over his shoulder just in time to see the two men disappear into the same house that Hammond had entered.

Time passed and eventually Ned turned to leave. There seemed nothing more that he could do tonight and he was so hungry by now that his stomach felt as if his throat had been cut. He had gone no more than a few steps, however, when a piercing scream rent the air and he glanced back. The houses on either side of Jake Hammond's were boarded-up and empty. Could it be that the scream had come from the house he had just been watching? He stood as still as a statue for a while, then shrugging, went on his way.

The staff were all in the kitchen when he returned to Highfield Manor late that night, and Fanny jumped up from her seat and gazed at him expectantly as he entered the room. 'Well, did you see any sign of her?' she demanded.

He shook his head, his weariness evident in his every movement as he flopped down onto a chair at the side of the table. 'Not so much as a sniff, though I did find out where that Jake Hammond lived. Still, there's always tomorrow, isn't there? And who knows what that might bring.'

'I'll get you something to eat,' Fanny offered, her disappointment evident in her voice. 'I've had your dinner keeping warm in the oven, though I'm not sure 'twill be edible by now. It'll probably have turned into a burnt offering.'

'Ah well, a bite o' bread an' cheese will do me if it has,' Jake told her with a tired smile. 'I'm that hungry by now I could eat a scabby horse an' the rider along with it. I'd better pop through an' tell Tilly how I got on first though. No doubt she and Master Willy will be waitin' up fer me.'

'Aye, they are. And so is Ellen. You'll find 'em all in the sittin' room.'

He sighed then slowly trailed towards the door as Fanny lifted a cloth and hurried to the oven. Just as she had said, he found Tilly pacing up and down and Master Willy resembling something like a powder keg that was about to explode. But it was Ellen who asked first, 'Any luck, Ned?'

'I'm afraid not, although I did find out where that pawnbroker lives.'

'I *knew* I should have come with you!' Willy cried with frustration, for the day that had just passed seemed to have been one of the longest of his life, made far worse by the fact that just a few short months earlier, it had been Noreen for whom they had been searching.

'No point in goin' down that road,' Ned said plaintively. 'You know as well as I do that you'd stick out like a sore thumb back there. No, it's best I go on me own, or if need be, take Arthur or Jimmy wi' me. I'll go back first thing tomorrow, an' I'll watch that Hammond like a hawk, never fear.' He said nothing of the scream he had heard.

'Thank you, Ned,' Tilly told him. 'Now go and get your supper. It has been a long day for you too.'

Ned nodded, and after wishing them good night, he plodded wearily back to the kitchen and his 'burnt offering'.

'You – come with me!'

As Beth blinked in the light of the lantern, she saw Nell standing at the door and realised that it was she the woman was addressing.

'What if I ain't a mind to?' she asked, but the cockiness dropped away when Alfred appeared over Nell's shoulder and took a threatening step towards her.

'All right, all right, keep yer hair on,' she muttered, rising stiffly from the mattress. 'Where are you takin' me to? Is Josefina comin' an' all?'

'Just come along and stop asking so many questions,' Nell said irritably.

Feeling that she had very little choice, Beth took a few faltering steps towards the door. She had longed to be out of this room for days, yet now that she was about to leave, something didn't feel quite right.

'Where are you taking her?' Josefina demanded as she sensed Beth's fear.

Nell ignored her as she took Beth's elbow and yanked her out onto the bare landing. Then the door closed and was locked, and Josefina listened to their footsteps fading away as the darkness closed around her yet again.

Beth found herself on the next landing down, where a bright carpet drugget was laid across varnished floorboards. Nell drew her to a halt in front of a door halfway along it and told her. 'You will find a visitor in there. His name is Mr Rosier and I want you to be nice to him.'

'What d'yer mean . . . *nice?*'

'Oh, just get in there, girl, and use your imagination.' Nell opened the door and pushed her forward, and as the door slammed behind her, Beth found herself face to face with an elderly gentleman. He rose from the side of a large brass bed and approached her with a broad smile on his face.

'Hello, my dear. Just as Nell said, you are indeed a pretty little thing, aren't you?' Her eyes dropped to the buttons of the waistcoat that were straining across his bloated stomach, and she shivered with revulsion. After walking around her three or four times he asked, 'How old are you, my dear?'

'What's it got to do wi' you?' she snapped.

As if she hadn't spoken, he went on.

'What are you . . . eighteen, nineteen perhaps?'

When his hand reached out and squeezed her breast she angrily slapped it away and cried, 'Leave off me, you dirty old bastard! I've heard about old blokes like you.'

'Now, now. There is no need to be like that, my dear.' His voice had a wheedling quality to it. 'If you were to be *nice* to me I could be very *nice* to you in return. You would actually be amazed at just how generous I can be.'

'*Piss off.*' The words seemed to have no effect on him, for now to her horror he grabbed her hand and began to rub his stiff member with it, through the material of his trousers. It was then that she screamed, an ear-shattering sound that echoed around the room as she turned and began to pummel on the door with her clenched fists. '*Let me out! Let me out! Do you hear me?*'

On the floor above, Josefina heard her loud and clear, and she began to sob for her friend. How long would it be before there was a visitor for her, she wondered.

It was much, much later when the door opened yet again and Nell thrust Beth back into the stinking attic room without a word. But this Beth was nothing at all like the cheeky girl Nell had dragged from the room earlier, for her spirit seemed to have been broken. As the door slammed shut behind her, Josefina ran towards her and took her trembling frame into her arms. In the dim light she saw that the front of Beth's cheap dress had been torn open, exposing one small breast, which Beth made no effort to cover. One cheek was swelling even as she looked at it and a trickle of blood was running from a split in her lip.

'Oh, my poor dear. Whatever have they done to you?' Josefina was shaking almost as much as Beth was now, and so they stood with their arms wrapped around each other.

The following morning, Ned was up with the lark to find Tilly waiting for him in the kitchen. She was enjoying an early-morning cup of tea with Ellen.

When he raised his eyebrows questioningly at her she blushed before saying, 'Forgive me, Ned, but I have to come with you. Arthur is coming too in case he should be needed. I just have this awful feeling that Josefina is in grave danger and I can't seem to shake it off. Perhaps I am a witch, after all? I've had no more than an hour's sleep all night long, and think I must have worn a hole in the carpet with my pacing up and down.'

The refusal that sprang to his lips died away as he saw her distress, so quietly he told her, 'Very well then. But you must stay out o' sight. We don't want this man to know we're following him.' He too had passed a miserable night as the sound of the scream he had heard in the street where Jake Hammond lived rang in his head again and again.

'I think it might be a good idea if you wore one of my dresses,' Ellen suggested to Tilly. 'They are nowhere near as fashionable or of the quality of yours and you would be more inconspicuous in it.'

Tilly grinned for the first time that morning. 'They will also be about a foot too short for me,' she pointed out, and Ellen laughed.

'Oh dear, you are quite right. I hadn't thought of that. But then you could perhaps borrow my plain cape instead? That would at least cover most of your outfit.'

When Tilly nodded in agreement, Ellen rushed away to fetch it as Arthur appeared looking fresh as a daisy. He had sluiced his face under the pump in the yard, and now his wet hair stuck to his head, the droplets of water on it sparkling like dew in the early morning sun that was filtering in through the window.

When they had breakfasted and were ready to leave, Ellen handed a laden wicker basket to Tilly. 'I've filled it with food,' she told her. 'There's no reason why you should go hungry. And don't worry, if you aren't back in time this evening I shall prepare another one for Steve and get Fanny to take it over to him.'

Tilly impulsively leaned over and kissed Ellen on the cheek. Her life had taken a turn for the better now that Ellen Ross was back in her life. Oh aye, she had no doubt about that at all. At the door she told her, 'You might have a bit of a job on your hands today when Willy finds out that we've gone without him.'

Ellen waved aside her concerns. 'You just go and do what has to be done, and God speed. I can handle Willy, never you fear. I'll read to him and keep his mind occupied somehow.'

By the time the carriage rattled into Durham town the sun was riding high in a cloudless blue sky. After leaving the horses and carriage in the care of a small hump-backed man at the local farrier's, the small group set off in the direction of the pawnbroker's shop.

'Now you two stay 'ere while I have a meander past the window,' Ned instructed Arthur and Tilly, as he ushered them into the alley where he had passed most of the day before.

They obediently did as they were told as Ned thrust his hands in his pockets and strolled across the cobbles. He had been gone no more than a matter of minutes when he shot back to them, his eyes wide with concern.

'What's the matter?' Tilly asked as she saw how ruffled he was.

'I can't be sure, but I could swear there's one o' Miss Josefina's rings in the window,' he told her slightly breathlessly after his sprint across the road.

'But it can't be,' Tilly frowned. 'The owner of the shop assured Willy that he hadn't bought anything else from her.'

'Perhaps she's been back and sold some more of her things?' Arthur suggested.

Ned firmly shook his head. 'There's no way she could have done that yesterday wi'out me seein' her.' He was adamant. 'I stood here in this very alley for that long watchin' that shop doorway that it's a wonder as I didn't take root. I know Miss Josefina an' I'm tellin' you now, as sure as eggs is eggs, that she never came nowhere near.'

When Tilly chewed on her lip he said, 'What I want you to do now, lass, is pull the hood o' your cape over that hair o' yours an' stroll by the window an' see if it *is* Miss Josefina's ring. Do you think you could do that?'

Even as he spoke, Tilly was already pulling the hood over her head, and once she was quite sure that her hair was concealed she strode from the alley, and with her head bent, crossed the cobbled street. As she passed by the window, she glanced in to see Jake Hammond sorting through what appeared to be a pile of rags on the counter. Happy that he was occupied, she slowed her steps and peered into the window. Her eyes found the ring at once and her heart leaped into her throat. Jake had been right. It *was* Josefina's ring – there could be no doubt about it. It stood out amongst all the other tat just as her brooch had; a small emerald with diamonds on either side of it that sparkled in the morning sun. She was about to turn away when her eyes fell on something else – her daughter's gloves. There was no mistaking them, for they were very distinctive: fine kid leather in a soft brown, trimmed with black buttons and black cord.

Retracing her steps to the alley, she told Ned urgently, 'You're right, it *is* Josefina's ring. And her favourite gloves are in the window too. But where could he have gotten them? She would never have parted with that ring for all the money in the world, even if she were starving. I know she wouldn't. You see, Willy bought it for her about two years ago, and she loved it. In fact, it was rarely off her finger. Oh, Ned, something bad has happened to her, I know it has!'

Seeing her deep distress, Ned kept his voice calm, although he too was now afraid for Josefina. 'What we're goin' to do is bide our time,' he told Tilly and Arthur. 'I've got the strangest feelin' that Jake Hammond knows exactly where Josefina is, an' if my hunch is right then it's only a matter o' time till he leads us to her. Can you try an' hold yourself together an' do that, Tilly?'

'I'll try,' she whispered brokenly, but the terrible sense of foreboding she had been feeling for days intensified.

When Nell opened the door, a small, dirty-faced boy, who was clutching a letter in his hand, confronted her. 'Are you Mrs 'Ammond?' he asked, and when she nodded, he thrust the envelope towards her. 'The Cap'n asked me to fetch this to you.'

She nodded and shut the door in his face as he muttered beneath his breath, 'Tight-fisted old cow!'

Ripping the envelope open in the hall, her eyes scanned the page. Its contents brought her thin lips curving upwards in a smile.

'Thank God for that,' she muttered, and then grabbing up her skirts she began to climb the stairs as fast as her legs would take her.

When she unlocked the door to the attic room she wrinkled her nose in distaste as the overpowering smell of stale urine met her. But then she stared down at Josefina and Beth, who were huddled together on the mattress, and told them, 'You will be leaving us tonight. Off on a nice little sea voyage no less, you lucky girls. The nice Captain who came to visit you the other night has managed to get you on an earlier passage.'

Josefina scowled at her. 'I don't think so,' she said haughtily. 'You'll never get me on it.'

'Oh, I think you'll find I will,' Nell told her spitefully. 'You'll be having a nice little drink to calm you both down afore you leave, and before you know it you'll be enjoying a life on the ocean waves.'

'I shan't drink it,' Josefina told her firmly as her chin jutted in defiance.

Nell shrugged and as she backed from the room her parting shot was, 'Well, you have two choices. You either drink it of your own accord else Alfred will hold your nose whilst I tip it down your throat. Think on it, eh?'

Beth's body began to shake with sobs as Nell's footsteps faded, and Josefina hugged her. It was strange now that she came to think of it, for she had never had a friend to call her own until she'd met Beth. But somehow she knew that no matter what happened to them now, she would think of Beth as such from this day on. Equally as strange was the fact that she now realised she had never before hated anyone in her whole life; unless the feelings she had felt towards Noreen could be construed as hate, when Josefina had viewed her as a rival for Willy's affections. That silly jealousy paled into insignificance now, compared to the feelings she had towards Nell Hammond, and she knew without doubt that had she had a knife concealed about her, she would have stabbed the woman through the heart without a pang.

Tenderly now, with no thought for herself, she rocked Beth gently to and fro. 'Don't cry,' she urged her. 'They will never get us aboard that ship, I promise you. My family will be looking for me and they will find us.' And deep down she was praying, 'They have to!'

As darkness cast its shadow across the cobbled streets, a lamp was once again lit in the pawnbroker's shop and shortly afterwards, the hidden trio saw a short, smartly dressed woman slip through its door. Peering across the gloomy street, they watched her waving her arms about and her mouth working as she talked to Jake Hammond, who was standing beside the counter with her. They saw him run his fingers through his hair as if he had heard something that disturbed him, and then he snatched up his coat and in the next instant the shop was plunged into darkness. Seconds later, he and the woman, who was still talking nonstop, emerged onto the pavement, and after hastily locking the shop door they set off together across the slippery cobbles. It had begun to rain and Tilly was glad of the cape that Ellen had insisted she wear.

Keeping a safe distance, the three retraced the journey Ned had made the night before until eventually they saw Jake

Hammond and the woman disappear into the same three-storey house that Ned had told them about. A light appeared in the hallway as the woman lit a lamp and then the large bay window of the room that looked onto the street was illuminated as she carried it into there.

For minutes that seemed like hours they stood well back for fear of being seen, but after a while when no one appeared in the window they crept forward and peered into the room beyond. And it was then that Tilly's hand flew to her mouth and she stifled a cry as she saw a familiar object in pride of place on the windowsill.

'Oh, my God! Ned, Arthur – *look*! It's Josefina's jewellery box!'

As they followed the trembling finger that was pointing to the intricately inlaid box, a sound akin to that of a wounded animal escaped from Arthur's throat. 'Right, that's it! There's somethin' fishy afoot here, an' I think it's about time we found out what it is, even if I have to beat it out o' the devil. Ned, go an' get the police. I'm goin' in there . . . Tilly, you stand well back.'

Before either Tilly or Ned could stop him, Arthur approached the door and started to hammer on it with his fists. Ned turned and scuttled away, intent on doing what Arthur had asked whilst Tilly stood and watched with fear shining from her eyes.

Despite Arthur's prolonged pounding, no one came to answer the door so after a while he muttered, 'Have it your own way. If you won't open up I'll break the bloody thing down.'

Tilly had never seen Arthur in such a towering rage in all the years she had known him, but she made no move to stop him as her eyes once again settled on Josefina's treasured jewellery box. He was right. Something was badly wrong here.

He ran at the door, hitting it with the full force of his shoulder but when it showed no sign of yielding he then lifted his foot and started to kick at the lock. By now, people were appearing on the steps of the houses that were occupied in the street, though no one came forward to make an effort to stop him, and slowly the whole awful predicament Tilly found herself in began to take on an air of unreality.

Suddenly the wood gave way with a resounding crack and the door flew inwards. Arthur hurtled into the hall to find the woman he had followed standing at the top of a flight of stairs looking down at him with a lamp held high in her hand.

'You'll be sorry for this,' she spluttered fearfully. 'Breaking into folks' houses. What is it you're after? Is it money you want?'

'No, I ain't after your money, missus. I want to know how you come across that box in your front window an' what you know o' the lass that owns it.'

'I . . . I don't know anything.' Her voice was laced with fear now as, paralysed, she stared down at him, like a snake faced with a dangerous predator.

It was at that moment that a scream floated down the stairwell, and like a bullet from a gun, Arthur shot up the stairs, shouldering the woman aside.

When yet another scream erupted, Tilly darted into the house and followed him, ignoring the woman he had pushed aside. The screams led Arthur to yet another set of stairs, which he took two at a time. He found himself on a long narrow landing and when, some way along it, he came to a door that was swinging open he rushed into the room, and what he saw brought him to a shuddering halt. Jake Hammond was leaning over a young lass on a bare mattress, forcing some drops from a bottle down her throat, as Miss Josefina pummelled at him with her fists.

For a moment, Arthur was so astounded that he could only stand and stare, but then as the horror of what he was seeing struck home, he sprang forward and yanked Jake to his feet. Then, pulling back his fist he swung it at the man's face and sent him spinning across the room. Jake fell against the bucket that had served as a latrine for the girls, and as it overturned he slid on the foul-smelling mess that spilled out onto the floor and went his length in it.

It was at that moment that Tilly appeared in the doorway, and for as long as he lived, Arthur would never forget the look on her face as her eyes came to rest on Josefina.

'It's all right, hinny,' she said brokenly, opening her arms wide. 'I'm here now. You're safe.'

'Oh, Mama,' Josefina sobbed, and suddenly she was pressed tight in her mother's arms and she never wanted to leave the safety of them again.

A clatter of boots then sounded on the stairs and Ned ran into the room with two police constables, who looked around the room in amazement as they wrinkled their nose at the smell. Ned had told them what he suspected on the way, and now, as Arthur pointed towards Jake Hammond, who was still flailing in the stinking mess on the floor, the larger of the two crossed to him and after dragging him up by the scruff of his neck, he handcuffed him. 'You'd better come with me,' he said grimly. 'An' I promise you, you're going to have to be a very good talker to talk yourself out o' this mess.'

'Th . . . there was a woman too . . .' Tilly told him in a shaking voice.

'Aye, I know there was, missus. Never fear, our colleague copped her rushin' down the street as if her feet were on fire.

She's on the way to the station even as we speak. An' if I'm right in what I think has been goin' on here, I can safely promise you it'll be a long time afore either o' those two walk free again.'

Arthur had now turned his attention to the young girl on the mattress who seemed to be out cold. Gazing over Josefina's head, Tilly asked fearfully, 'Is . . . is she dead, Arthur?'

'No, lass, no. I don't think so.'

'He . . . he drugged her,' Josefina managed to tell them. 'They w . . . were going to put us on a ship tonight and we were g . . . going to be sold abroad.'

'Oh my dear God.' Tilly screwed her eyes up tight at the thought of it. Her legs were as weak as water.

'Do you want me to get a doctor to take a look at the lass?' one of the policemen offered as the other marched Jake Hammond from the room. And it was then that Josefina asked, 'Can Beth come home with us, Mama? Please! Just until she has regained her strength? She . . . she has no one now and . . .'

'Hush, hinny. Of course she can. Ned, would you mind going to fetch the coach?'

'Aye, Tilly, I'll be but a tick.' Ned rushed from the room as Arthur lifted Beth's limp form into his arms. And then one behind the other they made their way down to the hallway.

Whilst they were waiting for Ned to return, the constable asked Josefina some questions, but she was so deep in shock and so weak from her terrible experience that she was unable to answer most of them, although she named and described Alfred, and the way he had tricked her and Beth.

'Never mind, lass. I have your mama's address. All this can be done at a later date,' he told her with compassion. 'You girls just go home now and get your strength back. And think yourself lucky that these brave people found you when they did. Had they not turned up here until tomorrow it would have been a completely different kettle of fish. You girls would never have been seen again.'

Some minutes later, the carriage wheels sounded on the road outside and Arthur carried Beth out, with Tilly following close behind.

'Come along, my bonny lass,' Tilly whispered in Josefina's ear. 'Let's get you home where you belong.'

Chapter Eighteen

THE VILLAGE WAS alive with gossip once more as news spread of the latest goings-on up at the Manor.

'Like mother like daughter,' they said smugly. That there half-caste that the witch had waltzed back from America with, had been on the game in Durham, hadn't she, and word was out that Arthur Drew had been forced to go and drag her back home! Still, it was no more than they could expect from the likes o' them! Livin' like royalty in their fancy house when they were no better than the scum of the earth!

It so happened that Fanny had cause to go down to the village shop, Butterworth's Stores, for half a stone of flour one day and heard a conversation along those lines. Her first reaction was to snap their heads off and tell them that they didn't have a clue what they were talking about, for it was more than obvious that the talk was all for her benefit. But Fanny had lived with Tilly for a long time now, and some of Tilly's common sense had rubbed off on her, for once she had got what she came for, she just put her nose in the air and marched past them as if they were nothing more than a dirty smell under her nose.

Of course, this had the desired effect, for now, Amy Laudimer's wrath turned on her. 'An' them Drews 'ave turned out to be no better than they should be,' she said loudly. 'Take that Arthur fer a start. They reckon as he's a bit too close fer comfort wi' Ellen Ross. It's absolutely disgraceful that she should stoop to his level, when she were married to a man o' the cloth! Plus she's near old enough to be his mam. An' then there's Jimmy. Now *there's* a strange bloke if ever there was one . . . The age he is, an' yet he's never looked the side a lass is on, when it's common knowledge that little Gwen would 'ave him tomorrow. Makes you wonder where his preferences lie, don't it?' This was her parting shot as Fanny walked regally from the shop.

Fanny's chin stayed high all through the village, but once she had turned onto the road leading to the Manor it drooped to her chest and she could barely see where she was going for the tears that were spurting from her eyes. When were they ever going to leave Tilly alone? Or anyone connected with her, for that matter?

By the time she reached the drive she had composed herself. Tilly had enough on her plate at the minute without having to hear idle tittle-tattle, so she would say nowt about it. As far as she was concerned, it was a case of 'least said, soonest mended'.

'So what will happen to Beth now, Mama?'

The doctor had just left after giving Beth a clean bill of health, and now Josefina was concerned for her future. She was in the morning room with Willy and her mother, who was sitting in the sunshine that was flooding through the huge bay window, reading her mail at the bureau.

Tilly's hands became still in her lap as she looked across at her daughter, and now, more than ever, she would always consider Josefina as such, for when she had thought for a time that she had lost her, it had been almost too much to bear.

It was now a week since the dreadful night in Durham when they had rescued her from the evil clutches of Jake Hammond, and thankfully, Josefina was looking a little more like her old self with every day that passed. It had come as somewhat of a surprise to Tilly, and Willy too, if it came to that, to see the girl's deep concern for Beth, for Tilly had never known Josefina to form a friendship before. Not that she looked upon it as a bad thing. She, more than anyone, knew that everyone needed a friend, so what she said now was, 'Well, do you think Beth might consider taking a position over at the farm with Lucy and Sarah? I have an awful feeling that Lucy is struggling. I've already asked her if she would allow me to get someone in from the village to help out, but she wouldn't hear of it. However, if it were Beth that I was asking her to employ, she might look upon it as her doing me a favour, thereby killing two birds with one stone. It would mean that you and Beth could stay in touch too. So what do you think of the idea?'

Josefina was unable to conceal her delight. 'Oh, Mama, I'm sure that Beth would jump at the chance. She has nowhere else to go, and at least if she was there we would know that she is safe. Would you like me to ask her?'

'No, pet. I shall ask her myself. But does she have everything she needs for now?'

'Oh yes, I sorted out some of my clothes that have become a little tight for me and they fit her as if they were made for her. Well, except for being a little too short for her, that is, but Gwen is going to let the hems down on them for her.'

During this conversation, Willy sat with his head cocked to the side listening, a contented smile on his face. Since Josefina's return, the pair had slipped back into the easy relationship that they had shared before her trip to America.

And this time, Willy was determined that nothing would spoil it.

'What if you were to tell Beth that she could come here on her days off to see us?' he suggested now, and as Tilly turned her head thoughtfully towards him, she nodded.

'That's an excellent idea, Willy! I think Beth would like that. She's certainly a pleasant enough girl, and it would be nice if she and Josefina could remain friends. I shall go and put it to her this very minute.'

Once Tilly had left the room, Willy rose from his seat and fumbled his way towards the shape that was Josefina. Even her features were blurred close up now, so he lifted his hand and tenderly stroked her cheek, his face breaking into a smile when her hand came up to cover his. They'd had very little time alone together since she had arrived home, and so now he intended to make the most of every second.

'I don't know how I would have gone on living if you hadn't come back to me,' he told her softly, and now her face creased with pain as she replied, 'You are still grieving for Noreen, and so I didn't think you would even notice that I was gone.'

A mixture of emotions flickered across his face before he finally answered. 'I will always have a place in my heart for Noreen. I would be a liar to tell you otherwise. And I will always feel a measure of responsibility about her death . . . but when you disappeared it made me realise that I . . .'

'Yes?' Her voice was expectant and her face so close to his that he could feel her warm breath on his cheek and smell the clean sweet scent that she always wore.

'I . . . I realised that I love you, Josefina. I think I always have, but it took this to make me understand just how much. I cannot envisage my life without you now, and so . . .' He sank down onto one knee as she held her breath and what he asked her was: 'Josefina, will you do me the very great honour of marrying me? I am aware that with my handicap I am neither use nor ornament, but even so, I love you with all my heart . . . so again I say, will you marry me?'

Time seemed to stretch as he knelt there with his heart wildly pumping, but then she suddenly dropped to her knees too, and her skirts billowed around them like a silken balloon as she laughed and snatched his hands into hers.

'Oh, Willy. If you should live to be a hundred you will never know how much I have longed to hear you say those four little words. So the answer is . . . yes! Yes, I will marry you and I promise you will never regret it.'

He leaned awkwardly forward and his lips came gently down on hers, but then she clasped him to her and the sheer passion of her kiss left him breathless. When they eventually broke apart they were both laughing and crying, all at the same time.

'What do you think Mama will have to say to our news?' he asked, and she smiled through her tears.

'I think it will come as no surprise at all to her. She recognised a long time ago where my heart lay, even before I told her of my feelings towards you. But . . .' Josefina became solemn now. 'I think we should wait until Mama is wed before we make our announcement.'

'Oh.'

Hearing the disappointment in his voice she caught his hands to her breast and then kissed them. 'Think of it, my love,' she urged him. 'It is only a few more months and then we will have the rest of our lives together to look forward to. Let Mama make the plans for her own wedding and get settled into the cottage with a clear mind. And then she can start to worry about *our* wedding, and we both know that she will.'

Willy chuckled now as he saw the sense in what Josefina said. 'As always, you are right. I suppose I am just so happy that I want to tell the world.' But then there was no more time for words, for as his lips again found hers, she gave herself up to the pleasure of knowing that her dream was about to come true.

Tilly tapped softly on the bedroom door next to Fanny's and when a voice answered, 'Come in,' she opened it and entered the room.

Beth was sitting at a small chair in the window looking out at Arthur who was busily trimming the topiary trees. But when she turned her head and saw Tilly standing there she was instantly on her feet and colour flooded into her still-pale cheeks.

'It's all right, pet. You needn't look so worried,' Tilly told her, as she perched on the edge of the bed. 'I've come to talk to you about what you plan to do in the future, now that you are recovered from your ordeal.'

A look of great sadness washed over Beth's face as she shrugged, and Tilly thought how pretty she looked. She was wearing a summer gown in a soft shade of yellow that Josefina had given to her, and now with her long dark hair washed and twisted into a shining coil on the back of her head she could almost have been taken for a lady, until she opened her mouth, that is, for what she said now was, 'I ain't sure where I'm gonna go yet. But if you want me out, then you've only to say the word.'

'Dear Beth, you don't have to go anywhere, for I am deeply indebted to you. Josefina has told me how kind you were to her when she found herself locked up with you. And so for that reason I have a proposition to put to you.'

Beth's eyes were wide with expectancy now as Tilly went

on, 'I was wondering if you would consider going to live at Brook Farm to help out with my baby granddaughter, Sarah. There would, of course, be some light household duties you would be expected to undertake as well. And I haven't cleared it with Lucy, her other grandmother yet, though I'm sure she will raise no objections. So . . . would you like some time to think about it? When you have decided, if the decision is favourable, of course, I shall approach Lucy and see what she thinks of the idea. We can then discuss your wages and days off, et cetera.'

'Oh no, missus! What I mean is, I don't need no time to think about it. Me answer is yes, an' I thanks you kindly fer askin'. I promise I'll do anythin' you ask an' you can depend on me. I won't let you down.'

'Do you know, Beth, I don't think you will,' Tilly told her with a light tone of amusement in her voice. Rising from the bed she now said, 'Give yourself another week to fully recover and then we will get you over there to meet them – if Lucy is in agreement, that is . . .'

'Yes, ma'am.' Beth bobbed her knee, and the smile on her face was brighter than the sunshine that was streaming through the window as Tilly turned and made her way out of the room.

Tilly's happy mood became somewhat subdued that evening when she walked over to the cottage to find Steve standing with a dark frown on his face as he looked down the rise from one of the new windows.

'So what's wrong with your health and temper then?' she asked mildly as she laid the basket containing his supper on the table and slipped her cape off. She was surprised to see that he had not washed as yet, and was still covered in coal dust from head to foot.

217

'Ah, hello, lass. I didn't see you coming.' He walked towards her and would have taken her hands but then suddenly seeing the state he was in, he laughed. 'Just give me a few minutes to get spruced up, eh? An' then we'll talk.'

Crossing to the fire, she pushed the kettle into the flames as Steve moved to the sink and began to sluice his hands and face in the bowl of cold water he had put ready there. By the time he rejoined her some minutes later she had prepared the teapot and the mugs and was looking at him expectantly. '*So*, are you going to tell me what's wrong then?' she asked.

'Well, the truth of it is, I've had to lay some more men off today,' he answered, and just as he had expected she stared back at him in horror. Tilly was well aware that the men who worked down her mine relied on their wages to put food into their children's bellies. If they didn't work, they didn't eat – it was as simple as that.

'But why, Steve? Surely you could have found work for them somewhere else?'

'Don't you think I would have done if it were possible?' he snapped, and then was instantly contrite as he ran his hand distractedly through his damp hair. 'It's like this, pet. As you know, number three an' number four shafts have been prone to flooding for some time, despite the fact that I've kept the pumps going down there round the clock. I shut number three down some weeks ago and moved most of the men from there into numbers one, two and four. Anyway, last week I had no choice but to close number four down as well. It was either that or put lives at risk, an' I knew you wouldn't want that.'

When her head bobbed in agreement he went on, 'You were up to your neck in it all last week tryin' to see to Josefina so I didn't want to worry you by telling you how bad things really were. So I then put the men from number four into one an' two as well. But it's hopeless, Tilly. They were fallin' over each other an' tempers were flarin' so I had no choice today but to lay some of 'em off. I've got men working flat out even as we speak to try to clear the flooded shafts, but until they have I can't risk another accident. That mine has claimed enough lives as it is. You do understand, don't you?'

She nodded sadly. 'Of course I do, and you did quite right. But I worry about how the ones that have been laid off will cope.'

'Aye, well hopefully it won't be for too long, though I have to say it as much as I hate to. The mine has about had its day from where I'm standin', an' I sometimes wonder if we shouldn't have sold it to Rosier when he asked. As I once told you, it's a bloody bad-tempered little mine.'

Tilly told him indignantly, 'I *would* have sold, Steve, had he offered a fair price. But you know what Rosier is like. He always wants something for nothing. Added to that, he barely pays his men enough to keep the wolf from the door. If it were up to him, he would still be sending children down.'

'The thing is, pet, I reckon you should start looking around for another buyer then, for I have a bad feeling about the place now. We both know that should you sell it, we could invest the money in the steelworks with Jim Coleman an' no doubt be better off. Though the choice is yours, of course.'

A silence settled between them for a time as Tilly thought on his words until Steve suddenly told her, 'Happen I've got some other news that might put the smile back on your face.'

Lifting the kettle that was now bubbling on the coals she poured the water into the teapot before looking at him quizzically. 'Oh yes, and what would that be then?'

'Well, I had a visit from Anna and John last night. Just

turned up out of the blue they did – though I was right pleased to see them, of course,' he chuckled. 'But anyway, I'm going off the point. While they were here, Anna made a nice suggestion concerning the wedding.'

Tilly was intrigued now, and laying her hands flat on the smooth wooden table they became still as she looked back at him.

'The thing is, as she quite rightly pointed out, Parson Portman is unlikely to want to marry us in the church in the village after what happened at Sarah's christening, is he? And even if he did, we can hardly expect a very warm reception from the villagers, feeling as they do about us. So, she wondered how you might feel about getting married over her way at Saint Bartholmew's and us having the reception at Felton Hall?'

'Oh!' Tilly was so shocked that she was rendered temporarily speechless. Now that she came to think of it, she had given very little thought as to *where* they would be married. She had simply looked beyond the actual ceremony to the time when they would be together. But now she saw that Anna's kind offer might be for the best all round.

Seeing that she wasn't immediately opposed to the idea, Steve went on, 'She's offered to arrange the church, the wedding breakfast, the flowers and everything. She says that all you'll have to do is choose your outfit and concentrate on looking beautiful, which as I told her is already a foregone conclusion.'

Taking Tilly into his arms he now kissed her tenderly and told her, 'You know, I think I'm a very lucky man. Shall I tell her to go ahead then and arrange everything for September? This place should be all done and dusted by then.'

She hesitated for just a fraction of a second before slowly nodding. 'Very well then. I shall write and tell her I would be most grateful to take up her kind offer, and could she please go ahead with the arrangements.'

'Excellent!' Steve now held her at arm's length and asked, 'How is Josefina, and that youngster Beth?'

'Much better, though I still shudder to think what might have happened if we hadn't arrived at that house when we did.' A shudder passed through her as she recalled that terrible attic room and the way the girls had narrowly missed being sold into the white-slave trade.

'So what will happen to Beth now?' Steve asked, and the smile was back as Tilly told him, 'As it happens, I'm going to see Lucy tomorrow, to see if she will allow Beth to move into the farm to help out with Sarah. Beth seems really taken with the idea and if Lucy will only agree to it I wouldn't worry about her quite so much. She really does look very poorly.'

'Aye, she does,' Steve agreed soberly. 'Poor lass. She's had it hard, that one. An' what of Jake Hammond an' that wife of his? Have you heard what's happening to them?'

'Yes, I have, as a matter of fact. The police paid us another visit to take statements from the girls yesterday and informed us that Jake and his wife are still safely behind bars, along with their procurer and assistant, Alfred Coggins. Personally I wish they would throw the key away, for it seems that they had a right little racket going on. As soon as they locked Jake up he squealed like a pig and gave the officers the name of the sea captain who was involved with shipping the girls abroad. Ugh! I pity the poor souls who he *did* manage to get aboard the ship. He was selling them to the highest bidder, and it seems that most of the poor lambs ended up in brothels in North Africa.'

'Eeh, you mustn't torture yourself with that. At least there will be no more going the same way, thanks to you and yours, and you *did* get to the girls in time, thank God!'

'Not quite. It seems that Josefina came out of it all better than Beth did,' Tilly admitted, and gulping deep in her throat she went on, 'Apparently, the night before we found them, the poor girl was forced to . . . entertain a gentleman! Hence the split lip and the bruises. Still, as you say, they are both safe now and it's best not to dwell on such things.'

'All I want *you* to dwell on now, madam, is getting ready to become Mrs Steve McGrath. Do you think you could do that for me?'

'I might be able to,' Tilly answered with a twinkle in her eye, but she had no chance to say more, for suddenly he had her in a tight embrace again and his lips were locked on hers.

Chapter Nineteen

THEY WERE SEATED around the breakfast-table and the atmosphere was lighter than it had been for some long time. As Tilly wiped her mouth on a snow-white linen napkin, she saw Willy and Josefina exchange a look that set her to thinking, So it's finally come about then?

It was no surprise, for hadn't she sensed their feelings for one another long before they did? Her eyes moved on to Beth and she was pleased to see that the bruises on her face had now faded from being a livid purple and black to dull yellow and lilac. Another week or so and there would be no sign of what the poor girl had been forced to endure – at least, not outwardly.

Addressing her now, she said, 'I was wondering, Beth – if you feel up to it, that is – whether you would like to come with me to Brook Farm this morning? It would be a good opportunity for you to meet Lucy and Sarah, while I put our proposition to Lucy. Oh, and there's Eddie, of course – he is Lucy's son. I normally ride over, but if you'd like to come I'll ask Ned to get the trap ready for us, seeing as it's such a beautiful morning.'

'Oh, I'd love to,' Beth told her, and now Tilly looked

towards Willy and Josefina. 'Would either of you like to come with us?' she asked them.

'Thank you, Mama, but no. I think I'll stay in today,' Willy replied politely.

Josefina too declined the offer. 'I shall stay here with Willy, Mama. I promised to read *Punch* to him.'

'As you wish.' Tilly was just about to rise when she suddenly remembered she had something to tell them, and they were all amused when she muttered, 'I er . . . that is, Steve and I agreed to set the date for the wedding last night. It will be sometime in September and we will be married in the village where Anna and John live before attending a reception at Felton Hall.'

'Why, that's wonderful news, Mama!' She was relieved to see that Willy looked genuinely pleased. 'And what a splendid idea to get married there.'

'Well, I have to admit we have Anna to thank for that. I thought it was really kind of her.'

'Yes, yes it was, though knowing Anna as we do I've no doubt she'll be in her element arranging it all. She loves parties, doesn't she? How many people will be coming?'

'I hadn't really given that side of it much thought yet,' Tilly admitted. 'But I dare say there will be all of us, and the staff here. After all, the Drews have been the closest thing to a family that I've had for many years. Then there will be Phillipa and Lance and the boys, and Sarah, Lucy and Eddie, of course.' Suddenly embarrassed she said, 'That's enough about us for now anyway. We have your twenty-first birthday party to think of first, Willy. Beth, I'll just go and get Ned to prepare the trap for us. Can you be ready to leave in say, fifteen minutes?'

When Beth nodded eagerly, Tilly straightened her skirts and hurried from the room, leaving Willy and Josefina with wide smiles on their faces. It was nice to hear good news for a change after all the dramas of the past months.

Beth was totally enchanted with the countryside all the way to the farm, for after being used to the overcrowded streets of Durham town she felt as if she had died and gone to heaven. Her delight was even more in evidence when Brook Farm came into view with a plume of smoke rising lazily from the chimney into a cloudless blue sky.

'Why, it looks just like a picture on the front of a box o' chocolates me ma had once,' she declared as Tilly brought the trap to a halt in the yard. As she stepped down, some chickens went clucking indignantly out of her way, and it was as she was turning to watch their progress across the yard that she saw a young man striding towards her. He was very handsome, and for no reason that she could explain, she felt the colour rise to her cheeks and she hastily lowered her head. Could she have known it, she was having the exact same effect on Eddie, for as he stared at her he was sure that he had never seen a prettier girl in the whole of his life.

'Hello, Eddie,' Tilly greeted him as she lifted a basket full of treats from the trap. 'How is your mother this morning?'

Glancing towards the open kitchen door to make sure that they were not being overheard, he lowered his voice and told her, 'She's not good, Tilly. Not good at all, to be honest. She was in so much pain last night I was all for fetching the doctor out to her, but she wouldn't hear of it. You know how stubborn she can be!'

'I see.' Tilly took a deep breath and then fixing a smile back onto her face she strode into the kitchen. Sarah, who was almost six months old now, was sitting contentedly on the hearthrug playing with a wooden rattle that Eddie had carved and smoothed for her from a piece of wood. The instant she saw Tilly she raised her arms up to be lifted, and only too happy to oblige, Tilly deposited the basket on the table and hurried across to her. Once the child was comfortably seated on her hip, Tilly then looked towards Lucy, who was now rising from the fireside chair.

'Lucy, my dear, I've brought someone to meet you. This is Beth, the girl who helped Josefina through her ordeal in Durham.'

Lucy smiled at her and Beth liked her instantly. There was a gentleness about her and a kindly light in her soft brown eyes.

'Hello, pet.'

'Hello, Mrs Bentwood.'

'Ah, call me Lucy, everyone else does,' she told her, lifting the kettle to make tea for the visitors.

'Here, let me do that. You can point out to me where everything is,' Beth told her as she took the kettle from her hand. For a moment Tilly thought that Lucy was going to refuse but then she smiled and sank back into the chair as Beth carried the kettle to the sink. In no time at all she had made the tea and now as she placed the knitted tea cosy over the pot she asked Lucy, 'Is there anythin' else that I can do fer you while we're waiting for it to mash?'

'Actually, there is.' Lucy pointed to a basket standing at the side of the door. 'Would you take that out to Eddie in the yard and ask him to go into the henhouse and collect the eggs for me?'

'Of course.' Lifting the basket, Beth almost skipped from the room and as Lucy's eyes followed her she remarked to Tilly, 'What a pleasant girl.'

The words were like music to Tilly's ears, for they paved the way nicely for what she was about to say. 'I'm glad you think that, for I have a favour I'd like to ask of you.'

'Oh yes, and what would that be then?' Lucy asked curiously.

And so Tilly began, 'As you already know, Beth is the girl who was imprisoned with Josefina in Durham. The poor lass is an orphan, and now that her health is improving we find that she has nowhere to go. And so I was wondering . . .'

'You were wondering if I would let her come and work here at the farm?' Lucy finished for her.

Tilly grinned as Lucy smiled wryly back at her. And then Lucy's eyes moved to the open door to follow the girl's progress across the yard. She seemed a nice girl, she had to admit, and the extra help would be very useful. Eventually she said, 'What if I was to take her on a month's trial?'

Tilly beamed. 'I think that would be an excellent idea. Are we agreed then?'

'Yes, we're agreed.' And so it was decided.

Within minutes of Beth returning to the kitchen, with a red-faced Eddie hot on her heels, she had Sarah chuckling as she leaned down to tickle her.

'Oh, Mrs Sopwith. Ain't she just beautiful?' she sighed, and Lucy warmed to her even more. The girl seemed to have looked beyond the ugly scar on the baby's face to her sunny disposition. Perhaps having someone in to help wouldn't be such a bad idea after all, she thought. Ah well, it was agreed now so no doubt time would tell. She had nothing to lose, for if at the end of a month it was not working out for either of them, then the girl would be free to leave.

The conversation moved on to Willy's forthcoming birthday and the wedding, and by the time Tilly and Beth rose to leave they were all easy with each other. Lucy had grown to like Beth more as the morning passed and now she found herself looking forward to the time she would move in.

With Sarah in her arms, her plump legs sitting astride Lucy's swollen stomach, she followed them outside to the trap. Once in the yard she pointed up to two narrow leaded windows beneath the eaves at which hung pretty flowered curtains.

'That will be your room once you move in,' she told Beth. 'I dare say I should have shown it to you. It was our Noreen's room . . .'

Seeing the sadness settle across the woman's face, Beth leaned over the side of the trap to squeeze her hand. 'It's all right,' she told her. 'I didn't need to see it. I'm sure it will be lovely.'

'So, when do you think you'll be coming then?'

It was Tilly who answered for Beth now when she told Lucy, 'I'd suggested giving her another week or so to fully recover at the Manor and then perhaps she could move in?'

But Beth took them both by surprise when she told them, 'I'm fine now. Really I am. So . . . would tomorrow be too soon?'

'Well, no. Not if you're quite sure you feel up to it,' Lucy told her and she could have sworn that she saw a flicker of a smile lift the corners of Eddie's mouth. Ah, she thought, so that's the way the land lies, is it? She had never known Eddie to have his head turned by any girl before, but all the signs were there to show that he was smitten with this one. Well, it might not be such a bad thing. And Beth *did* seem like a lovely lass. The sort she might have chosen for him, in fact. So, all in all it was turning out to be a good day!

Turning about, Lucy hurried back inside. Anna was visiting again in the afternoon, though she had no doubt it was more to see Sarah than herself. She found herself smiling, despite the niggling pain deep down in her stomach that seemed to be constantly eating away at her. Sarah adored her and Anna was so patient with her that it was touching to see them together. What a shame it was, Lucy found herself thinking, that Anna had not as yet produced a child of her own. She would have made a wonderful mother.

Beth was almost bubbling over with excitement on the way back to the Manor and chattered away nonstop.

'I think I'm goin' to like workin' there,' she told Tilly. 'An' I'll give her no cause to regret takin' me on. You just wait and see.'

'I'm sure you won't,' Tilly replied with a trace of amusement in her voice.

However, her mood took on a solemn edge when Beth next asked, 'When is Lucy's baby due? I couldn't help but notice that she's pretty far gone along the way.'

'I'm not sure.' Tilly kept her eyes straight ahead as she steered the pony and trap along the lane. 'Lucy always changes the subject whenever I ask, for some reason. But it can't be due later than August or September as her husband died just before Christmas. I can't help but worry about her though. She really does look dreadful, doesn't she? I think Eddie is concerned about her too. But Lucy can be very stubborn and refuses to see a doctor.'

'Well, happen once I'm there I'll be able to take a bit o' the weight off her shoulders,' Beth said sensibly. 'It can't be an easy time for her, can it? What with all she's been through recently, I mean.'

'I could say the same about you,' Tilly pointed out. 'It hasn't exactly been easy for you either of late. I just hope you aren't starting work too soon. You are more than welcome to spend a little more time at the Manor if you feel that you need it.'

'Aw, that's really kind of you,' Beth said quietly, and

hearing the emotion in her voice, Tilly took her eyes from the lane ahead to glance at her. She really was a very pretty girl, she found herself thinking, and good-natured too from what she had seen of her. She was sure that the arrangement with Lucy would work out well for all of them.

The happy mood was broken the instant she pulled the trap to a halt outside the steps that led up to the front door of the Manor. Jimmy hurried towards them to take the trap to the stable as Peabody opened the door with a look of grave concern on his face.

'Mister Steve had this delivered for you, ma'am,' he told her, handing her an envelope. Beth skipped away to find Josefina and Willy, intent on telling them all about her new post, whilst Tilly slit the envelope and started to read. A frown settled on her face as her eyes scanned the page. There was trouble at the mine and he wanted her to get there as soon as was possible. She knew that it must be something very bad for Steve to send for her, so intent on not wasting a minute she hurried upstairs to get changed.

'Peabody, could you get Jimmy to saddle Lady for me, please?' she called down. 'I have to go out immediately.'

'Yes, ma'am. I'll see to it straight away.'

When Tilly emerged onto the steps some minutes later in her riding breeches, Jimmy was waiting for her with Lady impatiently pawing at the ground.

'Thank you, Jimmy.' She put her foot into his hand and the next second he had hoisted her up and she was sitting astride the horse. Reining her expertly in the direction of the gates she shouted across her shoulder, 'Tell Fanny not to wait dinner for me! I'm not sure how long I shall be.'

'Consider it done,' came the answer and then she was urging Lady into a gallop and they were flying past the rowan trees. By the time she had covered the five miles to the pit, her cheeks were rosy, and strands of snow-white hair that had escaped from her hat were curling damply on her forehead.

A large group of men, whom she instantly recognised as some of her workers, were standing in a straggling line in front of the entrance to the pit, and when they saw her, they began to shake their fists in her direction.

'It's all right fer the likes o' you, livin' like bloody royalty in yer fancy palace,' one of them shouted. 'But what about us as have bairns to feed, eh? What do we tell 'em when their bellies are rumblin' wi' hunger?'

Tilly climbed down from the horse and after tying it to a post outside the office she drew herself up to her full height and turned to face them full on. 'I am aware that this is distressing for you,' she told them calmly. 'But if you will allow me to have a word with my manager then we will see what can be done to resolve the situation.'

As she turned, a voice came clear on the air and she screwed her eyes tight shut though her steps never faltered.

'Huh! Who'd 'ave thought the day would ever dawn when we were all reliant on a witch, eh? P'raps *we* should 'ave made up to the Master an' his son, an' then happen *we'd* be livin' like kings, an' all.'

With her head held high, Tilly strode into the office where Steve was waiting for her, and only then did she allow her shoulders to sag as she asked him, 'What is it, Steve? I knew it must be something bad for you to have sent for me.'

'Aye, it is bad, lass,' he told her as he ran his hand distractedly through his soot-black hair. 'The water has seeped into number one shaft now an' it's risin' by the minute from what I can see of it. I've been down there meself for most of the day and in the end I had no choice but to ask the men to make their way out. But they won't budge, Tilly. They're too afeared of bein' laid off like the rest of them out there.' As he nodded towards the window, his head wagged from side to side in despair. 'I'm telling you, if the water continues to rise as it is for much longer, the whole roof is going to come down on top of them. But what can I do?'

Tilly's mouth set in a straight line as she pensively tapped her riding crop on the edge of the table, and then making a decision she told him, 'I'll go down and speak to them. They'll listen to me.'

'*You will not.* I'm telling you, it isn't safe down there.'

'Then that is all the more reason for us to get them out while we still can,' she told him.

Backing two steps away from him, she kept her eyes tight on his face and then without another word, she slung her riding crop onto the table, turned and stepped out through the door. The air of unrest amongst the assembled men was so tangible that Tilly felt she could have cut it with a knife. They were staring towards her – no, glaring, she thought, might be a more apt description. As she walked towards them, they parted to let her through and a silence descended as she told them, 'Steve tells me that number one is now in danger of flooding, too. I am going to go down to try and persuade the men to come out. If they don't there is a grave danger that the roof will come down on top of them. I'd like you to stay here, for if that should happen they'll be trapped down there. And don't worry. When . . . or if, I come back out, I shall be making provision to ensure that you and your families will not starve while we try to get the mine into operation again.'

A ripple of shamefaced approval passed through the men, and one was heard to say, 'Yer have to admit, the lass has got some guts. There ain't many as would want to venture down there wi' things as they are, is there?'

With Steve at her side now she made towards the incline

that led down into the bowels of the earth and as she went it took every ounce of courage she had, for in her mind's eye she was back down there trapped with Mark Sopwith, in darkness so black that she had convinced herself she had gone blind. She entered what appeared to be a tunnel with two sets of iron rails running down the middle of it, knowing of old that she must keep to the side of the rolley way or risk being ploughed over by one of the horses that would rise from the depths pulling bogies of coal behind it.

As they descended ever deeper, lanterns hung at regular intervals on nails hammered into the thick wooden supporting pillars lit their way. Daylight was far behind them now and Tilly had to resist the urge to reach for Steve's hand. Eventually, the rolley line met up with others coming out of different roads, two of which were closed off, and she and Steve had to press themselves against the dirty wall as another weary horse pulling three full bogies of coal slowly tramped past them. Men in moleskin trousers and bare chests stared dully back at them from black faces as they passed, though not a single comment was made. It might have been an everyday occurrence to see the Lady of the Manor down in the depths.

Now as they moved on into number one shaft the incline became even steeper and they had to bow their heads to stop themselves from banging them on the low pit props. The larger horses were no longer evident here, for in the lower depths small Galloway ponies were used. Tilly averted her eyes from a skinny little man who was labouring towards them. He had a harness made of chain strapped around his waist and attached to it was a shallow skip loaded with coal, but as he passed them he didn't even raise his eyes. And then they came to the widening and found themselves in what appeared to be a large chamber. The noise hit them as they looked about at the figures scurrying here and there, but it wasn't this that caught Tilly's attention. It was the deep water in which the men were working. In some places it reached way above their waists and she could see rats swimming about them as bold as brass.

'My God, Steve.' Her fear was evident in her voice as her eyes slowly took in the scene before her. She stepped forward, feeling the water, which was curiously warm, seep into her boots and above them as she moved on. In no time at all it was up to her knees and then past them, but still she did not hesitate until she came to what appeared to be a huge blank wall with men hacking away at it. Other men were reaching down into the dirty water and feeling about on the floor for lumps of coal, which they then threw into a waiting bogey.

Tilly walked to what she judged was roughly the centre of the chamber and there drew the air, what there was of it, deep into her lungs before shouting, *'Could I have your attention, please?'*

For long seconds it appeared that no one had heard her, or if they had they were choosing to ignore her. But then slowly the sound of banging and hammering and cursing slowly died away and one by one the men looked towards her.

'Thank you.' Tilly was now covered to the waist in the scum that floated on the water, but heedless of the fact she went on, 'You must all be aware that you are putting yourselves in mortal danger by staying down here. The pumps are having little impact on the level of water at the moment and so I must ask you all to make your way to the surface for your own safety.'

'Oh aye, an' then we'll be no better off than them other poor buggers standin' up there wi' no work,' one man shouted.

Tilly looked calmly back at him. 'I will tell you the same as I have told them. If you will all make your way to the surface I will ensure that you and your families are paid a retainer whilst the mine is made safe again.'

'What – yer mean we'll still be paid though we're not workin'?' There was incredulity in his voice as he looked back at her.

'That is *exactly* what I mean,' Tilly said firmly. 'Of course, I can't promise to give you as much as you would normally take home. But I will make sure that you each have enough to put food on the table for your families. You have my word on it.'

Another man now shouted, 'Sounds a bit fishy to me!'

'Very well then. Have it your own way.' She spread her hands across the black water that seemed to be rising by the minute and pointed towards the rotting timbers that were groaning against the weight of it.

'None of you are fools,' she went on. 'You must all be aware that the pit props cannot take the sustained pressure for very much longer. But there, I have made the offer and now it is up to you. Perhaps you would all rather stay down here and leave your families without mothers and fathers?'

Turning to Steve, she nodded in the direction they had come. 'There is no more I can do,' she told him. 'If they choose to stay here and be killed, that is up to them. At least I cannot be accused of having their blood on my hands if they are. Come.'

Without another word, she turned, setting the murky water swirling about her as she headed back towards the incline that would lead them up to daylight and safety.

For some long minutes the men stood with their picks dangling idly in their hands. Then Jack Forest was the first to make a decision, when he said, 'You lot can please yerselves, but my missus is due to drop another bairn any day now an' I'd like to be around to see it.' Hoisting his pick over his shoulder, he began to follow Tilly and Steve, and very soon, the other men did the same.

As Tilly and Steve came out of the gaping hole into daylight, it was all Tilly could do to stop herself from crying with relief. She followed Steve into the hut that served as an office and when the door had closed behind them, she leaned heavily against it.

Eyeing her up and down, he told her admiringly, 'That took some courage, Tilly, considering that you were once trapped down there for three long days.'

His eyes were on the small window that overlooked the entrance to the pit, and when she saw the smile break out on his face, she looked towards it. The men were emerging one by one. Thank God! She looked down at the sorry state of herself. Her long brown leather boots were now a dirty black, and her riding breeches were covered in coal scum and clinging to her legs. Even her jacket as far as the waist up was wringing wet and filthy.

Turning her attention now to the ledger that lay open on Steve's desk she told him, 'I want you to keep as many men back as you need to man the pumps, and then until the mine is fit to work in again I'd like you to give each person a quarter of what they normally earn.'

'What?' Steve was staring at her as if she had taken leave of her senses, but he saw by the jut of her chin that she was not going to be swayed from her decision.

'It's only right that they shouldn't starve for something that is beyond their control,' she said now, and although he secretly thought she was going the right way about breaking herself, still he could not help but admire her.

'Have I told you lately, Tilly Trotter, what a truly remarkable woman you are?' he asked with a twinkle in his eye.

As she looked back at him with all the love she felt for him shining in her eyes she replied, 'Well, not today. But after I have been home and changed and come over to the cottage tonight, you might perhaps remedy that?'

'You're on.' He watched her straight figure walk out into the sunshine, thinking, I am indeed a very lucky man!

As she mounted her horse she looked back to see Steve walking over to the men who were gathered at the entrance to the opening of the mine. After slipping her feet into the stirrups she dug her heels into the horse's sides, and as she grasped the reins and turned Lady in the direction of home, a voice carried to her on the air, and what it said was, 'There must be sommat in what they say about her bein' a witch, yer know. She led them men from that pit like the Pied Piper himself. Who would ever 'ave thought a woman could do that, eh?'

Smiling wryly to herself, Tilly Trotter the witch rode away down the lane without once looking back.

Part Three
A Time to be Born and A Time to Die

Chapter Twenty

'HERE, LET ME help you with that.' Taking the log basket that Beth had just filled, Eddie swung it effortlessly through the kitchen and on to the hearth.

It was a warm July day, and Beth had been living at the farm for over three weeks. In many ways they had been the best three weeks of her life – and for more than one reason. The first reason was that Lucy treated her with great respect and kindness, which Beth had only ever known in short supply. The second was that Beth was now totally enthralled with Sarah, who had her wrapped around her little finger, to the point that Lucy sometimes scolded her, saying, 'You are spoiling her, miss!' The third reason was the fact that Lucy gave her every Sunday afternoon off and she was able to visit Josefina at the Manor. As for the fourth and final reason . . . she blushed prettily as she thought of it now. The fourth reason was Eddie. She glanced at him now as she crossed to the sink to swill her hands. He had bent to chuck Sarah under the chin, and the baby was gurgling up at him.

Eddie was kind. Oh aye, there was no doubt about it, and so was his mother too if it came to that. Sometimes Beth would wake in the little bedroom under the eaves to the sound of birdsong, and as she looked towards the tiny leaded windows and the pretty flowered curtains, she would think that she had perhaps died and gone to heaven. Then she would get up and stare out across the rolling fields and her heart would sing, for after being brought up in cramped conditions in the heart of Durham town, she knew that she would never tire of living in such beautiful surroundings.

Beth sighed with contentment, then her thoughts returned to her favourite subject. Not only was Eddie kind, he was handsome, too – the most handsome man she had ever seen. And yesterday, he had asked her if she would like to go to a barn dance in the next village on Saturday night. For a moment, she had been tongue-tied – unable to utter a word. And when the answer did pour out of her, it came out nothing like she had intended it to.

'I . . . I can't,' she had stuttered, and then felt instantly remorseful as disappointment flashed briefly in his eyes. He had concealed it almost immediately with a shrug until she had cried, 'It ain't 'cos I don't *want* to, Eddie. Never think that. I ain't never been to a dance before an' I'd love to go. But . . . the thing is, I don't get Saturday nights off an' yer ma might not be able to spare me.'

'Oh, I see.' She couldn't be sure but she thought he looked relieved. 'Well, how about I ask her then?' he had asked next, and she had hardly known where to put herself.

'I er . . . I'm still on me month's trial an' I wouldn't want her thinkin' that I were a fly-be-night,' she had muttered.

This had caused Eddie to throw back his head and laugh. 'I doubt she'd think that,' he assured her. 'Why, only yesterday I heard her telling Anna she didn't know how she'd ever managed without you. If anything, you do too much – easily the work of two people at least. So . . . shall I ask her then?'

'All right then. Aye, if yer sure it'll cause no bother.'

And so Eddie had asked, and when Lucy readily agreed to it without so much as a single quibble, Beth was so happy that she hardly knew how to contain her excitement. But first, of course, was Willy's twenty-first birthday party tomorrow up at the Manor and they had all been invited to that too. So there was something else to look forward to. The heat in the kitchen was oppressive, for Lucy had been forced to keep the fire in the range lit to bake the cakes that would be her contribution to the party. Wiping the sweat from her brow, Beth nodded towards the cakes that were now spread out on wire racks to cool on the table.

'Your ma is such a lovely cook,' she smiled, wiping her sweaty palms down the front of her apron. 'This frock Miss Josefina gave me is bulging at the seams an' I've only been here for three weeks. I'll grow to the size of a house at this rate.'

'Well, you'd be the best-looking house I've ever seen,' Eddie told her, smiling widely. 'Truth is, you look better with a bit of flesh on your bones. You were too skinny by half when you first arrived.'

Beth looked away so that he wouldn't see the effect his back-handed compliment had had on her. Gesturing now towards the stairs door, Eddie asked her, 'Ma still having a lie-down, is she?'

'Aye, she is.' Worry was heavy in Beth's voice now as she told him, 'She ain't been so grand today.'

'I had noticed. I'm getting really worried now, but as you've seen she's as stubborn as a mule. She won't let the doctor within a yard of her.'

'Happen once the bairn arrives she'll be all right again,' Beth told him hopefully. 'There's been a big gap between you an' this one, so it's bound to take its toll on her.'

Scooping Sarah onto his broad lap he asked, 'So who is takin' the cakes over to the Manor?'

'I am. But your ma is goin' to ice 'em first. An' . . . well, whilst I'm there, your ma said I'm allowed to try a dress on Josefina has sorted out for me to wear fer the party an' fer the dance on Saturday.'

'Huh! It'll be like gilding a lily,' he teased her. 'You'd look beautiful in a sack.'

'Aw, Eddie. You don't have to say such things. I'm as plain as a pikestaff.'

'*You* . . . plain? Why, whoever told you that must have been blind.' He looked away, and slightly embarrassed now, he told her, 'The truth is, Beth, I've er . . . Well, I've taken to you. I know you might be slightly older than me, but I'm older up here, I promise you.' He tapped at his head as sadness settled across his face and she had to stifle the urge to run to him and comfort him. 'I weren't no more than fourteen when me da's back started to play him up. An' from that day on I had to take over the main work on the farm. There ain't nothin' like that to make you grow up quick. But all that aside, do you think you could ever look kindly on me?'

The girl had the sensation of floating, and for a moment she was speechless. Was Eddie really saying what she thought he was? Could this wonderful, kind, handsome man *really* be interested in her?

She opened her mouth to answer him, but at that moment they heard the sound of Lucy's footsteps on the stairs and the words died on her tongue. All she had time to do was smile at him shyly and then Lucy was entering the room as she knuckled the sleep from her eyes.

'Good Lord,' she gasped as she glanced towards the clock on the mantelpiece. 'I must have gone out like a light. I only intended to have half an hour. Has Sarah been good for you, Beth?'

'Oh, aye, missus,' Beth assured her. 'She's been like a

little angel.' At that moment Sarah smiled up at her and her heart was heavy as she saw the way only one side of the child's face responded to the smile. The side that was scarred seemed to stop the corner of her lip from lifting, giving her a lop-sided appearance. Even so, Beth still considered her to be beautiful.

'I suppose I should set to and get those cakes iced,' Lucy said as she looked towards the cooling racks.

'I could do it for you,' Beth offered, but Lucy flapped her hand at her.

'You'll do no such thing, miss. You've been up since the crack of dawn and you've barely stood still, let alone sat down. I think it's time you had a break now or you'll be calling me a slave-driver.'

'Never! I can't remember a time when I've been so happy.'

As Lucy looked into the girl's radiant face she could well believe it, and she warmed to her yet further. Beth had been there for a relatively short time, but already Lucy could not envisage life at the farm without her. Perhaps it was having another female to talk to again that was the charm, she thought to herself, and her heart twisted in her chest as a picture of her Noreen's face swam before her eyes. Of course, Beth wasn't Noreen, and she could never take her place in Lucy's affections. But it was so nice to have her there . . . and if she wasn't very much mistaken, there was someone else who felt very much the same.

Beth and Eddie had left, and were now crossing the yard together. Beth was carrying a bucketful of pigswill and she was laughing up into Eddie's face with her heart in her eyes. And he . . . well, Lucy couldn't remember seeing him look this happy since he was naught but a bairn.

Her hands came to rest on the swollen mound of her

stomach. It was nice to think that there would be someone there for him, should anything happen to her. Now there was just Sarah left to worry about.

When Beth skipped into the kitchen of the Manor late that afternoon she found it alive with activity. Ellen was just removing some pies from the oven and the room was filled with the aroma of apples and cloves. Fanny was busily decorating a trifle, and even Tilly was there, looking very harassed as she carved a huge leg of pork that would be served cold on the buffet table at tomorrow's party. Willy and Josefina were sitting at the table having fun icing little buns and sipping from glasses of ginger beer, but the minute that Beth appeared, Josefina slid from her seat and hurried to meet her with her hands outstretched.

'Beth! I was beginning to think that you wouldn't make it today,' she said, her eyes expressing her pleasure at the sight of this girl whom she now considered to be her close friend. 'I got Fanny to press and let down the hem of the dress I thought you might like to wear for the party. Do you have time to try it on?'

'Yes, I do,' Beth told her happily. 'The missus told me to take as long as I like, though I wouldn't want to take advantage, o' course.'

'Then let's go to my room right now,' Josefina suggested brightly. 'I have the feeling that this dress is going to be just perfect on you.'

Flashing a smile at Willy, who was looking indulgently on, she then grabbed Beth's hand and hauled her through the green baize door and into the hallway.

'You're certainly lookin' pleased wi' yerself,' Beth remarked.

Glancing back across her shoulder, Josefina whispered, 'I

have something to be happy about. But I'll tell you all about it when we get to my room.'

Beth was intrigued, and the moment they entered Josefina's room and the door closed behind them, she hissed impatiently, 'Well then?'

Josefina walked to the window and stared down into the grounds for a moment before eventually confessing, 'Willy has asked me to marry him . . . Oh, Beth, I can't even begin to tell you how happy I am! I think, looking back, that I have loved him all my life, but I never dared to hope that he would love me. But you mustn't tell anyone just yet. We've decided to wait until Mama has married Steve before making the announcement.'

'Ah lass, that's wonderful,' Beth told her, then giggling behind her hand she blushed before telling her, 'I've got some news fer you an' all.' She could sense Josefina's eyes boring into the top of her bowed head. 'The thing is,' she said shyly, 'Eddie has told me that he has feelin's fer me.'

'And . . . is that a good thing?' Josefina's voice was hesitant but she had her answer when Beth's smile lit up the room.

'Oh, yes! I think I fell fer him the first time Mrs Sopwith took me over there to meet 'em. The only thing is . . .'

When her voice trailed away and her brow creased into a frown, Josefina came to her side and taking her hands in her own now, she looked deep into her eyes before asking, 'The only thing is . . . what?'

Beth seemed to be wrestling with some inner demon before she suddenly blurted it out. 'What if he were to find out what happened to me that night at the house before they found us? The night that that awful man . . .' As the memories rushed back, tears of shame and humiliation spurted from her eyes. 'Eddie might not want me, were he to know what that bastard did to me,' she said bitterly.

'I think you're quite wrong there.' Josefina's voice was soft. 'If Eddie loves you, he will know that what happened was not of your choice. You were forced into it through no fault of your own. You must try to put it behind you now.'

'But I *can't*.' Beth began to pace up and down the room. 'Sometimes when I'm abed of a night I can feel his filthy hands all over me an' I have to get up an' go an' sluice meself down under the tap in the yard. I dare say I'm spoiled goods now, ain't I? What do you think Lucy would have to say if she knew I wasn't goin' to Eddie pure?'

'You *are* pure.' There was an edge of anger in Josefina's voice now. 'And you *must* try to forget what happened now, otherwise it will spoil the rest of your life. Here!' After pressing a handkerchief into Beth's hand she stood aside until the other girl had mopped her face and noisily blown her nose. And then Josefina smiled encouragingly at her. 'That's better. Don't let's spoil such happy news. I think love must be in the air, for there are two others who I think might be coming together soon too.'

When Beth raised her eyebrow, Josefina confided, 'I think Ellen and Arthur are getting close.'

'*Never?*'

'Oh, yes. I've seen the way she looks at him and the way he looks at her, though I don't think they've done anything about it.'

'Well, I'll be blowed.' Beth was smiling broadly again now. 'At this rate there'll be enough weddin's to keep the parson happy fer a year!'

The two girls fell together in a heap on the bed and their laughter joined for a time. But after a while, Josefina rose and, crossing to a dress that was hanging on the wardrobe, she held it up for Beth's inspection. 'This is the gown I had in mind for you,' she told her, and Beth stared at it in awe. It was one of the most beautiful dresses she had ever seen. It was made of a pale-blue linen that was so fine it might have been silk. A tight, embroidered bodice fell into a big crinoline skirt, trimmed with a heavy broderie anglaise in a darker blue.

Beth could only gaze at it in wonder, until Josefina urged, 'Well, come and try it on then. And we shall have to do something with your hair, too. I thought we might pile it on top of your head like this.' Catching the long silken tresses that were spilling free about Beth's slim shoulders, she twisted them up on top of her head, securing the topknot with hairpins before teasing out some loose curls with her fingers, to frame her pretty face. Beth could scarcely believe that it was her own self looking back at her from Josefina's dressing-table mirror.

Gulping deep in her throat she asked falteringly, 'Don't yer think it might be a bit too posh fer the likes o' me?'

'Absolutely not,' Josefina told her firmly. 'Trust me, you're going to be the belle of the ball. Now try the dress on and do as you're told for a change.'

Only too happy to oblige now, Beth slipped out of her cotton work dress and gave herself up for a time to the joy of being pampered and spoiled.

The party was a great success and everyone thoroughly enjoyed themselves. The following day it was the talk of the village, for Randy Simmons had concealed himself in the bushes outside the dining-room window of the Manor and watched the whole proceedings, almost from beginning to end. ' 'Tis naught better than a whorehouse up there,' he told the rapt villagers, and of course the news spread like wildfire and was the main topic of conversation for days.

'They reckon as the women were hoistin' their skirts up an' cavortin' about the room like spring lambs,' Amy

Laudimer was heard to say. 'It don't bear thinkin' about when yer look at us lot down here in the village, havin' to live on next to fresh air while they eat an' drink their fill like pigs at a trough!'

The fact that Tilly was still now paying the men a quarter of their normal wages for doing nothing, whilst those who had volunteered to stay on to rectify the problems at the mine worked round the clock, seemed to go no way at all to curbing Amy's spite, nor the ill-will of those listening to her.

'The one that shocks me the most is that there Ellen Ross,' she grumbled on, well into her stride now, and aware that she had their undivided attention. 'But then I suppose 'twas to be expected. They should have hanged her when they had the chance, 'tis my opinion. They reckon as how Parson Ross died a broken man 'cos of her goin's-on. I dare say she was consortin' with them black savages along of Africa, too. There'd be devil-worship too, I'll be bound.' A gasp went up from the band of listeners as she lowered her voice and said, 'An' now word has it that she's set her cap at Arthur Drew. I tell yer, she's wanton, that Mrs Ross. Huh! I wouldn't spit on her if she were afire.'

Heads bobbed in agreement, but she wasn't finished yet. 'Randy reckons that there wench Tilly Trotter brought back from Durham were makin' eyes at Widow Bentwood's Eddie all night long. They couldn't keep their hands off each other, from what Randy were sayin'.' She paused for effect before going on, 'At some stage durin' the proceedin's, Randy saw Tilly take that bastard son of hers into the library an' hand him an envelope.'

'What were in it?' This from one of her audience, whose eyes were almost starting from her head.

'I can tell you *exactly* what it was,' Amy said importantly, 'for as Randy told me, it was a warm evenin' an' the windows were wide open so he could hear every word that was said as clear as a bell. The boy is now near-blind, as you know, so his ma had to read the documents out to him – an' it were no less than the deeds to the Manor, lock stock an' barrel, along wi' some shares that Mark Sopwith had left to her just afore he died. How's that fer a legacy, eh? She told him she wished him to have his inheritance now rather than after she were gone!'

'*No!*' A sigh of amazement rippled through the crowd as Amy hitched up her ample bosoms and smiled smugly. 'I'm tellin' you it's true as sure as I'm standin' 'ere. *She* ain't no longer the Lady o' the Manor. The blind bastard 'as took over from her.'

'So what will she do now then?' one of the village women asked eventually.

Amy tossed her head scornfully. 'Huh! She won't starve, more's the pity. She still owns the mine *an'* all the surroundin' farms, as well as that cottage that Steve McGrath is turnin' into another mansion in readiness fer Her Ladyship when they're wed. But listen to *this*. I've saved the best bit fer last. You see . . .' She looked round at the sea of faces before playing her trump card, 'Would you believe that, accordin' to Randy, that strange little black bitch *she* brought back from America an' her other bastard were all over each other like a rash. Ugh! It don't even bear thinkin' about, does it? I mean . . . they're brother an' sister, ain't they? An' that to my mind adds up to incest, so what do you think o' *that* then?'

It was not immediately evident what her captive group thought of it, for the silence that settled was so profound you could have heard a pin drop.

Chapter Twenty-One

PHILLIPA AND TILLY were sitting in the drawing room of Phillipa's beautiful home sipping at iced tea as the welcome breeze from the open French windows played over them.

'Oh dear, if it doesn't cool down soon I'm sure I shall melt away,' Phillipa complained as she took up a fan from the table at the side of her chair and began to waft it in front of her face.

Tilly laughed as she looked out at the lawn where Steve was playing croquet with Gerald and Richard. She and Steve had decided to pay the couple an impromptu visit and, as always, had met with a warm welcome. Eventually Phillipa asked her, 'Is the wedding still planned for September?' and instantly she saw a frown cross Tilly's face.

'Well, there may be a delay,' Tilly told her hesitantly.

Phillipa raised an eyebrow. 'Is there a problem then?'

Rising from her chair, Tilly began to pace the room. She stopped before the writing bureau and fiddled with the pots of brown and blue ink. The blotter was covered with faded words that made no sense, written backwards. 'Not a problem exactly,' she said eventually. 'But the thing is, Lucy is still far from well. The baby must be due in August or September at the very latest, according to my calculations, and I do *so* want her and Sarah and the new baby to be present at the wedding. So . . . I thought it might be better to postpone it until some time in October, perhaps. That way, Lucy would have had time to recover from the birth and be back to something like her old self.'

Phillipa chuckled. 'Oh dear, are you quite sure this isn't just a case of cold feet?'

'Oh no, no,' Tilly hastened to assure her. 'I've spoken to Steve about it and he understands, and so does Anna. She's already agreed to speak to the parson at Saint Bartholomew's to try and get us a later date. I'm not saying Steve is happy about putting it off for yet another month, but it would mean so much to me to have Sarah and Lucy there.'

'I can understand that,' Phillipa conceded, but her next words brought Tilly's brows together into a frown.

'I hate to say this to you, Tilly, but at some point you must learn to put yourself first. My father has waited a long time for you, and you owe it to him, not to make him wait too much longer now. Neither you nor he are what could be termed as old, but then you are not in the first flush of youth either. Time is precious, as I am learning. Lance is seventeen years my senior, as you know, and I terrify myself daily with visions of how I would cope, should anything happen to him.'

As Tilly thought on her words, she knew, deep down, that what Phillipa was saying was perfectly true. Walking to the open doors, she followed Steve's progress as he paused to tap a wooden ball through a hoop. His grandsons cheered. And then he turned his head and looked back across his shoulder at her, as if he had sensed her eyes on him, and his face was bright. Steve was such a kind man; a good man in all ways, and Phillipa was right: it was not fair to delay the wedding for a second longer. Come hell or high water, they would be married in October. This was the vow she made to herself as she moved away from the sunlight into the welcome cool of Phillipa's splendid drawing room.

Rising from the floor of the earth closet that stood at one end of the farmyard, Beth swiped her hand across the back of her mouth. She had been sick every single morning this week and her breasts were sore and tender. Added to that was the fact that, this month, she'd had no need of the rags that were folded in the corner of her drawer. Whilst living in Durham she had seen the signs of pregnancy many times, for the women who lived in the warren of back streets tended to breed like rabbits.

Screwing her eyes tight shut, she tried to stop her tears from flowing. Why, oh why did this have to go and happen now, just when everything was going so well? In the few weeks that she had lived at Brook Farm, she had been happier than at any other time of her life. Not only that, she had met a young man with whom she could happily have spent the rest of her life – and now this! He wouldn't want her when he discovered that she was carrying another man's bastard inside her, and she asked herself, could she really blame him? No, the answer came back. Eddie was lovely and could have had the pick of any lass he fancied.

Her sorrowful mind drifted back to the night of her deflowering, and once again she saw the rapist's face in her mind's eye. She would never forget that face for as long as she lived, for it was branded into her brain, as was the feel of his smooth hands on her body. She remembered thinking at the time that she had never before met a man with smooth hands, but then he had been of the gentry so he had probably never had cause to work. No doubt he had others who earned his fortune for him. She remembered his swarthy complexion and his thin hair that was touched here and there with a trace of grey, but most of all she remembered his nose, for it was long and protruding and seemed to be too big for his face; his frame as well if it came to that, for he had not been a tall man.

'Beth!' The sound of Lucy's voice brought her springing from the closet, and when she was outside in the fresh air again she saw Lucy standing at the doorway of the kitchen, looking up and down the yard for a sight of her.

'Ah, there you are, lass. I wondered – could you pop into the village for me? I would get Eddie to take you in the trap but he's working up in the top field. I need some tea and some dry goods.'

'I'll go gladly, missus. But will yer be able to cope wi' Sarah whilst I'm gone?'

'Of course I will, pet. I'm not an invalid, you know.' Lucy looked deep into the girl's eyes. They seemed to have sunk back into their sockets over the last couple of weeks, and Beth looked pale and drawn. Added to that was the fact that she suddenly seemed to be holding Eddie at arm's length, which was strange when Lucy came to think of it, for until recently the pair of them had been getting on like a house on fire. They had twice been to the barn dance in a nearby village and Beth had returned with her cheeks glowing and her eyes as bright as buttons. Yet only last week when Eddie had asked her if she would like to go again she had turned him down flat, saying that she was in need of an early night. This in itself was strange, for as Lucy had discovered, the girl's strength belied her small frame, and had Lucy let her, she would have worked from dawn till dusk.

Dusting her hands down the front of her coarse calico apron, Beth stepped past the missus into the shade of the kitchen, and after picking up the money that was laid ready for her on the table, and a large wicker basket, she then held her hand out for the list of goods Lucy had written down for her. She could read most of the things on the list now, for Eddie had been teaching her the alphabet and her letters each night when the work was done.

'Right, I'll be as quick as I can then, missus,' she told Lucy, and as she made to step past her, Lucy's hand settled on her arm and momentarily stayed her.

'Is everything all right, lass? You don't seem . . . quite yourself these past few days. I'm not overworking you, am I?'

There was a trace of the Beth she had come to know and love, as the girl now told her, 'No, missus. You don't overwork me.'

Lucy made an obeisance with her head and then, as she watched Beth walk away in the direction of the farm gate, a thought suddenly occurred to her. 'Oh dear God, please let me be wrong,' she muttered to herself. But now that the idea had formed it would not leave her. How long was it that Beth had been here now? She began to calculate the weeks in her head and her suspicion became stronger. Hadn't Tilly told her that the girl had been raped shortly before she, Ned and Arthur had rescued her and Josefina from that dreadful house in Durham? Could it be that the rapist had left her with her belly full?

At the sound of Sarah crying plaintively for her breakfast, Lucy turned to make her way back inside to feed her, but the worries that had sprung to life in her head would not be so easily quieted.

As the doorbell heralded Beth's entrance into Butterworth's Stores, a silence settled over the people assembled there. They stepped aside to give her access to the counter and Beth moved between the sacks, boxes and shelves to put her list down on the wooden counter. She found herself stammering as she read off the items she wanted to Molly Butterworth, deeply aware of the fact that all eyes were upon her. And then it started, just as she had known it would.

'Ah, word has it that the witch up at the Manor is plannin' her weddin' to Steve McGrath fer October. Huh! Now there's a farce if ever there was one,' said one voice.

Beth studiously ignored the gibe as she began to load into her basket the tea, bootlaces and blue bag of Demerara sugar that had been slapped down on the counter for her. But the gossips were only just warming up, and now Mrs Fairweather's voice declared, 'You can expect no better from the likes o' *her*, but I were shocked to hear that Lucy Bentwood were thick in wi' her now. I would 'ave expected better o' Lucy, but then she is bringin' up the blind one's bastard, ain't she? You would 'ave thought the witch would see to her own, wouldn't you, given the circumstances – but then Lucy has always drawn the short straw where *she* were concerned.'

Beth's hands had begun to tremble now and she had to grip the packet of candles she was placing in the basket very tight to stop it from showing.

'Funny we never see Lucy down in the village any more an' all, ain't it, when you come to think on it. But then 'appen she's too ashamed to show her face.'

It was no good, the rage that had started deep in the pit of Beth's stomach was now lodged in her throat, and if she didn't give it free rein she knew that she would choke. Raising a big bar of Pears's soap, like a weapon, she turned to face them, her face as dark as a thundercloud.

'Haven't you got anything better to do than stand about in here picking holes in people?' she spat furiously. 'Why . . .

it's no wonder your homes are like hovels. Let me tell you that Lucy Bentwood is one of the kindest ladies I have ever met and another is Tilly up at the Manor. I'll tell you something else an' all fer nowt: fer all that you've pilloried her, there is not *one* of you here who is fit to lick her boots. So now why don't you all just go back to your sties and grovel in the muck where you belong!'

Tossing some coins at Molly, she snatched at the last item, a box of bicarbonate of soda, hefted the basket from the counter and flounced from the shop without even bothering to wait for her change, as open-mouthed they stared after her.

Her rage carried her more than half the way home, but then as it gradually ebbed, her steps slowed and she hung her head. It had been evident from the second she set foot in the shop that they had been trying to goad her and she, fool that she was, had fallen for it hook line and sinker, which would now give them something else to gossip about. Worse than that was the fact that she had stormed out without even waiting for the missus's change! Aw well, she could always tell Lucy to stop it from her wages if the worst came to the worst, she decided.

As she passed the top field, she paused to stare across it, and there was Eddie repairing a break in one of the drystone walls that surrounded it. She could vaguely recall the missus asking him to do it, now that she came to think about it, for the gap had been the cause of them losing two of their sheep over the last weeks. Hidden by a small cluster of gorse-bushes, she watched the way the muscles in his arms rippled as he lifted the heavy rocks and dropped them expertly into place. His broad, bare back was shiny with sweat and deep brown from the long hours spent in the sun. A wave of love washed over her and her sadness increased, for she knew now that if she could not have Eddie, then she would never have anyone.

By the time she turned into the yard, Sarah was enjoying her mid-morning nap, and guessing where the missus would be, Beth directed her steps towards the dairy. Just as she had expected, she found Lucy bending over the churn, sweat dripping down her brow.

'Get yourself away to the kitchen for a cool drink,' the girl urged her. 'I'll take over wi' that now.'

As her eyes fell on the laden basket, Lucy smiled gratefully. 'I reckon I might just do that, hinny. But only if you come over and have one with me first before you start.' Stretching her back, she ran her hand across her face and then side-by-side they turned towards the farmhouse.

Once inside, Lucy hurried away to fetch a jug of sarsaparilla from the thrall in the pantry, and after she had poured them both generous measures she handed one to Beth and asked, 'What's wrong, pet?'

'I er . . . I didn't stop to get yer change in the shop,' Beth mumbled, keeping her eyes fixed on the table. 'But don't worry. You can take it from me wages.'

'Oh, I don't think there will be any need for that,' Lucy said comfortably. 'It would have been hardly worth waiting for anyway. But as a matter of interest, why didn't you wait for it?'

The lie hovered on Beth's lips, but then bracing herself, she admitted, 'The women in there were havin' a poke at Tilly . . . an' at you. An' I sort o' just lost me temper an' gave 'em what-for!'

'*You did what?*'

'I er . . . told 'em to go back to their sties an' grovel in the muck where they belonged!'

For a moment Lucy said not a word, as Beth looked at

her shame-faced, but then her head went back and her chin began to tremble, and unable to hold it in a second longer, she burst into laughter. In fact, so loudly did she laugh that tears rolled down her face.

Beth looked at her employer incredulously. 'Ain't you mad at me then?' she finally dared to ask as Lucy bent across the table, with her hands held tightly into her sides.

'Oh Beth, I bless the day you entered this house, for I swear you do me more good than any tonic ever could,' Lucy managed to say through peals of laughter. 'An' oh, what I wouldn't have given to be a fly on the wall when you were laying into that lot.'

Her laughter was so infectious that slowly Beth's lips tipped into a smile too and soon they were both hanging onto the table as the sound of their joined laughter echoed around the rafters.

The mood was still light when Eddie returned from the fields. Carrying a steaming meat pie and a large pan of potatoes to the table, Lucy wasted no time in telling him of Beth's encounter in the village. He grinned as she loaded his plate high, before winking at Beth, 'Now that's what I like to hear,' he told her. 'Someone who isn't afraid to stand up for those they care about. Now I know you're really one of us.'

Thankfully he did not see the look that flickered in Beth's eyes at his last comment. If what she feared was true, she could never be truly one of them now. In fact, once they found out, she had no doubt that Lucy would send her packing. Her eyes roved around the room she had come to consider as home and her heart was heavy. Inside, she was thinking, Oh, why did this have to go and happen now, when my future looked so very bright? All she had ever wanted was stability and someone to care for, and now that she had found it, it seemed that it was just about to be snatched away from her again.

It was dark by the time Tilly and Steve steered the horse into the drive of the Manor that night. The only light they had to show the way ahead was the light of the moon and the lantern that was swinging on the side of the trap. They were both tired but happy, as with her head resting on his shoulder she asked him, 'Are you quite sure that you don't mind me postponing the wedding till October?'

He looked away from the drive ahead just long enough to tell her, 'Well, I can't pretend to be happy about it, Tilly. But as long as you don't come up with another excuse as October approaches, I dare say I would be classed as mean if I didn't agree.'

'There will be no more excuses,' she promised him softly. 'As Phillipa pointed out, we are neither of us getting any younger and I want to spend what time I have left with you.'

He nodded, but in his mind he was thinking of the long lonely years that they had already wasted.

Chapter Twenty-Two

'ANNA, M . . . MY D . . . DEAR, I have something to t . . .
tell you.'

'Yes what is it?' Anna looked back at John
expectantly. He had been into Newcastle that morning and
had only just returned, looking quite unlike his usual happy
self.

'W . . . well, the thing is, I t . . . took the oppor . . . tunity
of calling in at the or . . . or . . . orphanage while I was there.'

'Oh, John, how *could* you? We agreed—'

'N . . . now just w . . . wait until you've heard wh . . .
what I have t . . . to say, please,' he implored her.

Putting her hand unconsciously up to her birthmark, she
became silent, but with a sulky expression on her face. And
now as he saw that she was at least prepared to listen to him,
he went on, 'I . . . I didn't p . . . plan to go, I swear it. But
when I h . . . happened to glance from the c . . . carriage
window, there it w . . . was, and s . . . so I thought, W . . .
where is the h . . . harm in making enquiries? And Anna, th
. . . the sights I saw were enough to b . . . break your heart.
T . . . tiny b . . . babies, lying in c . . . cribs, who no . . . longer
cry, f . . . for they know that no one w . . . will c . . . come to
them.' His voice became gruff and he wiped away a tear.

Despite the fact that she had rejected his suggestions of adoption before, Anna found that she was curious to hear more. 'How many babies were there?' she asked, trying hard to hide her interest.

He spread his hands wide with a look of great sorrow writ on his face. 'I d . . . didn't stop to cou . . . count them, but the room w . . . was full of c . . . c . . . cots. And then, in an . . . another room, were ch . . . children ranging in size up t . . . to this height.' He lowered his hand to a level that was just above his knee as she shrugged.

'And why would I want to know this?'

'B . . . because I h . . . have seen w . . . with my own eyes how y . . . you are with S . . . Sarah. Could y . . . you tell me truthfully, w . . . with your hand on your he . . . heart, that you would n . . . not take her and love her as your own, if the ch . . . ch . . . chance arose?'

'That is different. Sarah is family!' she snapped uncharacteristically, and then felt instantly contrite when she saw his face fall. 'I'm sorry, darling. I know you mean well . . . But the thing is, I still haven't given up hope of us having a child of our own yet.'

Crossing to him in a rustle of silk lavender skirts, she smiled sadly into his eyes before telling him, 'I sometimes feel selfish, John, wishing for more when I already have so much. We have this beautiful house and grounds, and more money then we could ever spend in a lifetime, not to mention each other, and yet . . .' Tears sparkled on her lashes now as her hand went to her heart. 'I still have this yearning deep in here. This *awful* nagging feeling that something is missing. And yet when I am with Sarah and I hold her in my arms, the hurt goes away.' She tossed her head restlessly, but then after a moment she asked, 'What exactly is involved in adopting a child?'

'It is f . . . far easier than I ant . . . anticipated in actual f . . . fact.' His eyes were animated as he turned her back towards him and looked deep into her eyes. He loved this woman with all his heart and would have moved heaven and earth to please her if need be.

'Th . . . they w . . . would ch . . . check that we are who w . . . we say we are, an . . . and then it is just a m . . . matter of ch . . . choosing a child, and making a donation t . . . to the orphanage. Of c . . . course, nothing c . . . comes free. But I warn you. It w . . . would not b . . . be easy to ch . . . choose. In the short t . . . time I was there, I saw at least half a d . . . dozen ch . . . children that I could happily have br . . . br . . . br . . . brought home.'

Dragging her eyes away from his, she gave a deep sigh and murmured, 'I make you no promises, but I will think about it.'

And so for now at least, the subject was closed.

It was halfway through the following week, when Anna was visiting Tilly, that she raised the subject herself. Beth had brought Sarah over to the Manor for the afternoon to give Lucy a break, and the child was crawling across the grass with Beth chasing after her as Tilly and Anna sat in the shade of an oak tree sipping homemade lemonade.

'Tilly, I was wondering . . . what do you think of adoption?'

Tilly looked at Anna curiously. 'Why, I think it's a wonderful idea. I adopted Josefina, didn't I? And I have to say, despite the controversy it caused when I first arrived back in England, I look upon it as one of the best things I ever did. But why do you ask?'

'Well, last week John called into an orphanage in Newcastle whilst he was there, to make enquiries. He seems very taken with the idea of adoption, but I'm not so sure how

I feel about it. What I mean is, I haven't yet given up hope of having a child or children of my own.'

Tilly laughed softly. 'If you were to adopt, it would in no way affect your chances of having your own children, Anna,' she pointed out. 'And I have to say, living in a house the size of Felton Hall, you have enough empty rooms to accommodate a dozen children.'

'There is that in it,' Anna agreed as she followed Sarah's haphazard progress across the lawn. As her eyes came to rest on Beth, who had now collapsed in an exhausted heap in a bed of buttercups, she said musingly, 'Don't you think that Beth looks rather unwell? She has gained weight, admittedly. But it's her eyes – they look so . . . empty,' she finished lamely.

Tilly nodded in agreement as she too looked towards Beth, who was staring off into space with a blank expression on her face. 'She seems to have lost her sparkle, doesn't she? Although I think she is happily settled at the farm. Lucy is forever singing her praises and between you and me, until recently I truly believed that she and Eddie were becoming more than friends. But according to Lucy, Beth is suddenly holding him at arm's length and it's breaking his heart. Poor boy. I think he's in love with her, and they make *such* a lovely pair.'

'Mmm,' Anna sighed, and then suddenly she asked, 'Why is it that nothing is ever straightforward, Tilly?'

The older woman's laughter rang across the lawns now as she responded with, 'Now you really *have* asked the wrong one that question! I seem to have lurched from one crisis to another throughout my life. But then, seeing as I am supposed to be a witch, it's hardly surprising, is it?'

Seeing the twinkle in Tilly's eye, Anna smiled, and then, her thoughts returning to the orphanage, as they had been prone to do since the night that John had informed her of his visit there, she asked suddenly, 'Do you think I should visit the orphanage?'

'Well, what harm could it do?' Tilly replied simply.

And as hard as she tried, Anna could not think of a single good reason why it should.

'If – and I only say if – I decide to go, would you consider coming with us, Tilly?'

'Whyever would you want me there?'

'I . . . I just think I'd feel more comfortable if you were, somehow,' Anna said quietly.

'Then in that case I'd be delighted to come with you,' Tilly told her as she gently stroked her hand. 'But just remember, Anna. You don't have to do anything that you feel uncomfortable about.'

It was at that moment that they saw Ellen appear at the far end of the lawn. She was carrying a glass in one hand and what looked to be a plate of food in the other, and they saw her approach Arthur, who was weeding a flowerbed full of hollyhocks, which happened to be amongst Tilly's favourite flowers.

As Ellen drew near, he lifted his hand and tenderly touched her cheek as she smiled up at him. Ellen had been to visit her mother the day before, and it was obvious from the way Arthur was looking at her that he had missed her.

'Mm, things might not be going so well for Eddie and Beth, but it certainly looks like there's a hint of romance in that direction,' Anna commented with a wry smile.

And Tilly was thinking, Oh, please let it be so – though she said not so much as a single word. From where she was sitting, Ellen – and Arthur, for that matter – were long overdue a little happiness, and they *did* make a very pleasant-looking couple.

★

Later on that afternoon, when John collected Anna, and Jimmy had set off in the trap to deliver Beth and Sarah back to the farm, Tilly entered the shade of the house and began to walk from room to room. She touched the treasured china and paused in front of the silver cabinets, thinking how well polished Fanny kept everything. Until the night of Willy's twenty-first birthday, the house and everything in it had belonged to her, but now it was Willy's, along with a share of the mine. She had no regrets. She had started her life in a cottage and would soon be returning to one, and to her mind that was as it should be.

As usual, when Sarah was present, Josefina had kept out of the way for most of the day. Soon, she and Willy would be the master and mistress of Highfield Manor and she wished them well, though she felt that she had little need to, for they were so taken up with each other that sometimes Tilly felt as if she had already gone from them.

The smell of the lamb that Ellen was roasting for dinner that night was wafting through the green baize door that led to the kitchen, making Tilly's stomach rumble. Feeling at a loose end, she decided to go in and seek Ellen out for a chat.

She found her shelling peas into a colander. The doors and windows were thrown wide open, yet her face was pink with the heat. She smiled when Tilly entered the room and teased her, 'Much more of this weather and you'll be making do with salad and cold cuts. Speaking of which, Arthur is in the vegetable garden now and he says we have so much come on with the warm weather that we'll never eat it all. Do you want to take some over to the cottage with you this evening? I've already sent a basketful back with Beth for Lucy.'

'Yes, that would be lovely,' Tilly said and then added coyly, 'I couldn't help but notice that you and Arthur seem to be getting on rather well.'

Ellen did not come back at her with denials as Tilly had expected. Instead, she nodded rather bashfully. 'We are getting on well, Tilly. In fact, I've – that is, Arthur and I – have been meaning to have a word with you. You see, the thing is, he has asked me to marry him and I've said yes. I do hope you feel all right about it, Tilly?'

'*All right?* Why, I think it's wonderful, and I hope you'll be very happy together, though I can't pretend that your announcement is completely unexpected. I would have had to be blind not to see the way you two feel about each other. When is the great event to be?'

'We thought around Christmas-time.' Ellen's eyes were shining like a young girl's, and Tilly's heart swelled with happiness for her. Although Arthur Drew was as different from Parson Ross as a body could imagine, being an out-doors man, and lacking the Oxford degree that had made the parson a well-read man, he nevertheless had a strong, sensible mind, and a generous, kindly disposition that no university degree could ever bestow. To Tilly's sage mind, both Ellen and Arthur had done very well for themselves. This was the second bit of good news she had heard today – the first being Anna's possible change of heart towards adoption.

'Right,' she announced. 'I have a proposition to put to you now, so leave what you're doing and come and hear me out.' Once Ellen was seated in front of her she went on, 'If you and Arthur are to be wed you'll need a home of your own to live in, and I have just the place in mind for you. Do you recall me telling you some while ago of the little cottage in the bluebell wood beyond the vegetable garden?'

When Ellen nodded, intrigued, Tilly went on, 'Well, it needs more than a little work doing to it, because it has stood empty for some years. But then Arthur is very handy at repairs and so on, and I've no doubt if he worked on it of an evening and at weekends he could have it habitable for when you're wed. Would you like to go and see it?'

'Oh, yes, please!'

'Very well. It won't take long and there's no time like the present, so let's go and look at it now,' Tilly suggested.

Ellen needed very little persuading. After basting the lamb, she followed Tilly. They skirted the Manor and headed towards the vegetable garden, where Arthur was busily at work.

'Arthur,' Tilly said briskly, 'put that hoe down and come with us,' and he immediately dropped the tool, snatched up his coarse cotton workshirt and followed her as meekly as a lamb.

When they came to a small copse, Tilly led them into the heart of it, confiding, 'This is my favourite part of the grounds. I love this little wood, especially in the spring when the bluebells are all in bloom. It's like walking on a blue carpet in here then, and the scent of them is enough to knock you out.'

It was cooler here and they slowed their steps as they moved yet further into the woods. Squirrels hopped effortlessly from branch to branch above them, and little rabbits with snow-white bobtails scampered out of their way. And then, just up ahead of them, they spotted a little clearing and there was the cottage. The picket fence that surrounded it was broken down in places, and the garden was an overgrown tangle of weeds, but even so Ellen gasped with delight when she saw it, and running forward she stood staring up at the thatched roof in awe.

'Why, Tilly, it's absolutely beautiful,' she breathed. Turning to Arthur, she grabbed his hands in her excitement as she told him, 'I've just explained to Tilly about you and me getting married, and she suggested that if you were prepared to work on this cottage we could live here and have our very own place.'

'Aw, Tilly, lass. That's right kind of you,' he muttered, but brushing his thanks aside she ushered him now towards the door. 'Don't thank me till we've seen how much needs doing to the place,' she said wisely, then pushing open the door they all trooped inside to what appeared to be a comfortable-sized kitchen-cum-living room. There was still furniture scattered about but it was thick with layers of dust, and the windows were festooned with cobwebs, though seemingly in good order with no broken panes.

Crossing to the large pine table that stood in the centre of the room, Ellen declared, 'Why, this will be just beautiful when it's scrubbed, and the chairs are sturdy too. I shall only have to recover the seats and they'll be as good as new. I could perhaps get matching material to make curtains for the window . . . oh, and look, Arthur, there's a cooking range here, too! A bit of blacklead on that and it will shine enough to see your face in it.' Skipping through a door that was set into the far wall she then found herself in a small but pretty parlour. Two fireside chairs still stood at the side of a tiled hearth with a moth-eaten hearthrug between them. 'Well, perhaps the rug is beyond saving,' she giggled, 'but we can soon buy a new one.'

Without even waiting for the others, Ellen trotted back into the kitchen and across the stone-flagged floor, to disappear up a wooden staircase that led directly from the rear. At the top of the stairs she looked around a large room with two windows on either side of it. The ceiling followed the shape of the roof outside, and against one wall was a large brass bed. The bedding that was slung across it was as moth-eaten as the rug in the parlour had been, but on close inspection, the bed was seen to be in very good condition, as were the oak wardrobe and chest of drawers that stood against the end wall. Most importantly, the room was dry. No damp had entered over the years to stain and destroy. Lowering her head, Ellen crossed to another door that led into a smaller bedroom, which she declared would be just perfect for storage. And so the inspection went on until they all ended up back downstairs in the kitchen again.

Tilly was almost as pleased as Ellen was. 'All in all, there doesn't seem to be *too* much that needs doing,' she declared. 'The chimney will need sweeping, of course, and everywhere will need a thorough scrub, but there doesn't seem to be any damp in here, or none that a few good fires won't dry out, at least. It looks as if most of the work is on the outside. The fence will need replacing and the garden is thoroughly overgrown, which is to be expected, I suppose, when you think of how long it has stood empty. But at least it would be a place to come back to at the end of the day where you would have your own privacy. So . . . do you think you're up to tackling it, Arthur?'

His arm settled around Ellen's slim shoulders. 'After bein' used to keepin' the grounds o' the Manor spick an' span, this will be a piece o' cake,' he teased her. 'An' thanks, Tilly. It will be nice to have somewhere as we can feel is our own.'

'You won't have to *feel* it's your own,' she told them solemnly. 'It *will* be your own. Willy and I have decided that we shall be giving the deeds to the cottage to you as a wedding present.'

'But . . . but we can't take this,' he stammered. 'It . . . it's too much!'

She brushed his comment aside. 'Don't talk so daft. Ellen was my first real friend, and you and your family have been that to me over many years. In fact, to tell you the truth, I don't know what I would have done without you all at times,

and you are just like my own family. This is mine and Willy's
way of saying thank you, so take it in the spirit it is given and
may you both know nothing but contentment from the day
you move in.'

'Aw, Tilly, lass.' When his head bowed, Tilly saw that he
was deeply moved as Ellen turned to comfort him. Suddenly
feeling somewhat of an intruder, she called out a goodbye,
and quietly slipped out of the cottage and back to the Manor,
where she made some gravy and finished shelling the peas!

A week passed, and then another, and there was still no sign
of the weather breaking. The lawns surrounding the estate
were becoming yellow in the heat and everyone was feeling
it.

'Phew.' Fanny, who was sitting at the kitchen table,
mopped her brow and looking towards the open kitchen
door, complained, 'I can't remember when we last had such a
scorcher. I reckon if it don't cool down soon I shall melt
away. You'll come in one day to find me nowt more than a
great lump o' lard on the flagstones.'

Ellen, who was in the process of kneading dough,
answered, 'I know how you feel. It would be lovely to stand
out in the rain and get soaked through. But then, we're never
happy, are we? When it's raining we want the sun and when
it's too hot we want the rain.'

The green baize door at the end of the kitchen opened
and Tilly joined them, looking very fresh and pretty in a
white blouse decorated with a row of tiny pearl buttons all
down its front, and a full dark-grey skirt trimmed with black
binding.

'Ellen, I'm going into Newcastle with John and Anna
tomorrow, and wondered if you would like to come too, as it
would be a chance to look at some material for the cottage.'

'Ooh, yes, Tilly, that would be lovely. I know what I want. I thought perhaps some pretty flowered cotton? Gwen has offered to make the curtains and seatcovers up for me, which I have to say was a great relief, as I've never been that good at sewing.'

'Tell you what: why don't I go over there now and do some measuring up?' Tilly offered, adding, 'I can't say I'm altogether looking forward to visiting the orphanage. John has booked their appointment but Anna still seems in two minds about the whole thing.'

'Well, happen she'll know if it's right or not for her when she gets there,' Fanny said sensibly, rinsing some rhubarb. 'An' even if it's not, at least it will put that option to rest. It's a shame though, 'cos from where I'm standin' Mister John an' Miss Anna would make wonderful parents. Just look how she is wi' little Sarah. Why, the lass adores her. It's a cryin' shame that they ain't been blessed wi' what they want most of all, when there's young girls havin' babbies out there that they don't want. Still, not all things are fair in this life, are they? Take me fer instance.' There was a twinkle in her eye now as she looked towards Tilly. 'Here's me been pantin' after Stevie McGrath fer the whole o' me life, an' then you goes an' snatches him away from right under me nose! Now I ask you, where's the justice in that, eh?'

Tilly playfully swiped at her plump arm with a stick of wet rhubarb as Fanny bellowed with laughter. 'Right, I'll go and measure up for these curtains then,' she told them. 'And then Josefina and I are going to go into Shields this afternoon to see if there is anything we fancy for the wedding outfits.'

'Have you thought what you might like?' Ellen asked her as Tilly paused in the doorway.

'Nothing fancy,' Tilly told her, 'so get that out of your mind right away. I'm hardly a blushing bride, am I? So I shall be choosing something plain but elegant that I can wear again.'

'Spoilsport!' Ellen and Fanny chorused in unison, and laughing, Tilly tripped away to find the tape-measure.

Once she reached the canopy of trees leading to the cottage, the heat was not so intense and Tilly sighed with relief. The prolonged hot spell had become oppressive now, to the point that everyone was feeling lethargic and having to force themselves to perform their chores. She was strolling along, enjoying the sound of the birdsong, and the cottage had just come into view, when she suddenly narrowed her eyes. Someone was outside, peering through the window, and whoever it was had two dead rabbits dangling from their hand. For a moment, she paused, wondering if she should run back to the Manor to get help. But then as indignation got the better of her, she stormed forward and shouted imperiously, 'Hey, you! Just what do you think you're doing? Are you aware that you are on private land?'

The man almost jumped out of his skin before turning startled eyes towards her, and it would have been difficult to say who was the most shocked of the two as they recognised each other.

'Randy Simmons. What are you doing here?' Tilly's voice covered the distance as he stared back at her open-mouthed.

Eventually his face hardened as he answered her. 'I were out fer a stroll an' noticed there were work bein' done on the cottage, an' I were just bein' curious, see? There ain't no law agin that, is there?' he spat.

'Perhaps not. But there is certainly a law about you poaching on private land!'

As she spoke she stabbed her finger towards the two dead rabbits, and for a time it appeared he had been struck dumb. But then he composed himself yet again and retorted, 'What's a couple o' dead rabbits to the likes o' you? Rather see folks starve, would yer?'

'I was informed that you had been employed at Mr Rosier's pit,' she told him coolly, 'so if you are in employ, why would you starve?'

'Ah, well, the thing is, me an' Rosier didn't see eye to eye so he give me me marchin' orders.'

Tilly was not surprised when she thought back to the comments Simon Bentwood had frequently made about how work-shy the cowman had been whilst employed on the farm. 'I am sorry to hear that,' she told him now, 'but that is still no excuse for you to trespass on this property. If you leave now I will say no more about it – but I warn you, should I find you poaching on my land again I shall have no choice but to inform the authorities.'

His lips curled back. 'Yer think yer so high an' mighty, don't yer, Tilly Trotter?' he sneered, 'but it won't be long now afore yer toppled from yer throne, an' as far as I'm concerned it can't come a day too soon.'

'And just what is *that* supposed to mean?' Although Tilly's heart was thumping painfully, her head was high as she stared back at him.

He made no reply, but merely turned on his heel and strode away.

Tilly watched until he had disappeared into the thicket of trees, then on legs that had suddenly turned to jelly she crept into the cottage, closing the door and locking it behind her. Crossing to the nearest chair, she sank down onto it and took a deep breath. What had Randy meant? Was he making a veiled threat? As she sat there drumming her fingertips nervously on the tabletop, she gazed around the room and was amazed at the transformation in it.

The windows had been washed and now sparkled in the

sunshine that filtered through the trees, and the grate had been blackleaded until it looked like new: she could almost see her face in it. What furniture Ellen and Arthur had decided to keep was now dragged into the middle of the room, and the flagstoned floor had been scrubbed clean. Rising to peep from the window, Tilly saw that Arthur had made a start on the garden too. Most of the fence had now been repaired, and he had cut the weeds down, revealing the little twisting path that led to the door.

Tilly pictured her two friends there on dark winter nights, with the fire blazing cheerfully in the grate and the curtains drawn tight across the window. The thought brought her mind back to the reason for her being there, and so taking a small tape-measure from her pocket, she began to measure the windows and chairs, jotting the figures down in a little notebook. She then hurried back outside again. There was no sign of Randy Simmons but his threats still rang in her ears, and the birdsong no longer sounded so sweet, nor the shade seem so inviting.

Shrugging, Tilly tried to push the unpleasant encounter from her mind as she made her way back to the house, the bright day tarnished.

Chapter Twenty-Three

'OH, MAMA, *PLEASE* try it on,' Josefina implored, as the sales assistant held out a flowing dress in a soft shade of cream. 'It's such a beautiful dress, and perfect for a mature bride.'

'But I told you I only wanted something simple,' Tilly objected as the assistant looked patiently on. They were in a large emporium in Shields and Tilly felt as if she had looked at half of the shop's contents already. Josefina had turned her nose up at every single one until the assistant had carried in this particular dress for them to see. It had been ordered up, she told them reverently, from the Liberty's store in London's Regent Street.

Yes, it was a beautiful dress, Tilly was forced to admit, but she pointed out, 'I am getting married in October, you know, and whilst this dress would be lovely for this hot weather, I envisage it would be rather cold to wear then.'

'Oh, that needn't be a problem, madam,' the stout assistant hurriedly assured her. 'We also supply a wide variety of accessories, and I know of a short fox-fur stole with a matching muff that would be perfect for this dress and an autumn wedding.'

Seeing the excited sparkle in Josefina's eyes, Tilly knew that she would have no peace unless she at least tried it on, so turning towards the fitting room yet again, she sighed, 'Very well, you may help me to try it on. But if I don't feel comfortable in it, we shall have to continue looking.'

When she re-emerged in the dress some minutes later, Josefina's eyes filled with tears. 'Oh, Mama, you look like one of the princesses out of the storybooks you used to read to me when I was a little girl. It's absolutely perfect on you.'

Tilly looked into the pier-glass and had to admit that the dress was indeed very fine. Made of a very heavy silk, it rustled invitingly as she walked. The bodice was fitted tight into her waist, and the low-cut neckline was trimmed with thick lace. The skirt was the very latest fashion, with a full bustle – a far cry from the half-crinolines that Tilly was used to wearing.

The sales assistant promised to fetch the fur stole now, calling over her shoulder, 'Stay right there, madam. I shall be back directly.'

Some minutes later, she panted back into the room holding a beautiful short fur cape in one hand and a matching muff in the other.

'Try these on with it, madam,' she pleaded, and as she set the cape about Tilly's slim shoulders and slipped her hands into the pretty matching muff the outfit was complete. The furs were in a glorious shade of russet-brown that made a perfect contrast to the cream of the dress and the snow-white mass of Tilly's hair.

'Well . . . I must admit it *is* rather beautiful,' Tilly said dubiously, and then as she thought of Steve she suddenly smiled. 'Oh, very well then. I'll take them.'

When she was once again dressed in her own clothes she told Josefina, 'Now we have to find you an outfit.'

Josefina shook her head. 'Yes, we do, Mama. But not

today. It's so hot. We'll leave my outfit for another time, shall we?'

'Very well then.'

The dress and furs were packed carefully into two enormous boxes and carried by two shop boys to where Ned was waiting with the carriage a short distance away.

Tilly smiled from ear to ear. Not only had she chosen her bridal gown, it wasn't often that she was able to prise Josefina from Willy's side, and so she was enjoying having her daughter all to herself for a change.

As the carriage bowled towards home, Tilly was feeling quite light-hearted. Tomorrow she would be visiting the orphanage with Anna and John. Ellen and Arthur were obviously more than happy, and it seemed that Willy and Josefina were, too. Steve had informed her only last night that they were finally managing to get the water levels down in the mine, so all in all things were going well for a change. She put the memory of her encounter with Randy Simmons into a box in her mind, and then locked it.

When the carriage set off for Newcastle the next day, Anna was so nervous that she could barely sit still. 'I'm still not sure that we're right in even going there,' she fretted. Never having been blessed with children herself, the parson's wife recognised some of her turmoil.

'I . . . it will b . . . be fine,' John assured her as he caught her hand in his. Tilly and Ellen smiled at her reassuringly and then a silence settled as they rattled on their way.

Having deposited Ellen in the centre of town, where she was to choose her curtain material, the carriage moved on, and finally drew to a halt in front of a dark, forbidding-looking building with bars across its windows. Anna shuddered as John helped her down.

'It looks more like a prison than an orphanage,' she commented, and although Tilly said nothing she silently agreed with her.

They climbed the dirty grey steps and rang a bell that jangled inside, and seconds later the door was opened by a mousey-haired girl in a dress that was at least two sizes too small for her.

'Mr and Mrs Sopwith, is it?' she enquired, goggling with envy at the fine clothes they were wearing.

'Y . . . yes, it is. We h . . . have an appointment with M . . . Miss Hale, the Superinten . . . dent of the home,' John told her solemnly.

'Please come in, sir.' The girl held the door wide and when they stepped past her, they found themselves in a gloomy corridor with doors all painted in a dull brown colour leading off it.

'This way, if you please.' With a last longing glance at the dresses that Tilly and Anna were wearing, the girl led them along, until she paused at a door and tapped on it softly.

'Come in,' a voice boomed, and after pushing it open, the girl bobbed her knee as they all filed past her.

'Ah, Mr Sopwith.' A woman who was so large that she seemed to be bursting out of her clothes rose from a desk to greet them. Her thinning grey hair was pulled into a tight bun on the back of her head, and though she smiled, her eyes remained calculating.

Wasting not a minute, the woman went on: 'What age of child are you looking for?'

Anna became flustered and so Tilly answered for her. 'I don't believe Mr and Mrs Sopwith have a specific age in mind, Miss Hale. Perhaps they could meet some of the children and then we could go from there?'

Miss Hale ruled the orphanage with a rod of iron and was

known to be a very strong-minded woman. Normally the prospective adopters who came to see her were shivering in their shoes, but in Tilly she sensed a will as strong as her own. 'Very well then. We shall start with the nursery. I shall get Miss Thomas to show you around and, should you find a child that might be suitable, you can come back to me and I shall tell you what I know of their history.'

'Thank you, that is most kind of you,' Tilly responded.

Miss Hale rose from her seat, setting her huge breasts rippling across her waist, and after pulling on a rope that dangled at the side of the door she joined her hands across her enormous stomach and they all waited. Seconds later, there was a tap at the door and a young fair-haired woman entered the room. As Anna looked at her, she found herself thinking how attractive she might have been. As it was, the drab grey dress she wore and the tight bun that her hair was tied back into made her appear much older than her years.

'Ah, Miss Thomas,' Miss Hale greeted her. 'These dear people are thinking of taking one of our little treasures off our hands. Will you kindly escort them to meet the children? Those that are not working, that is. Start with the nursery.'

Miss Thomas bobbed her knee. 'Certainly, ma'am,' she said, and then turning to Tilly, Anna and John, she asked, 'Would you like to follow me?'

After inclining their heads in Miss Hale's direction, they all filed out into the corridor again. Once out of earshot, Anna instantly asked, 'What did she mean, those that are not working?'

Miss Thomas, who seemed a pleasant sort, sighed. 'The older girls and boys are sent out to work, apart from some of them that work here, that is. The boys tend the vegetable gardens at the back and the girls work in the laundry to pay for their keep.'

'I see,' Anna replied, hating the place more by the minute. When they came to a large room that was laid out with long tables on which were rows of tin bowls with spoons laid at the side of them, they rightly guessed that this must be the dining room. At the head of the room was another table, which was where the staff must sit. Tilly averted her eyes from the split cane that lay across it before Miss Thomas led them straight through it into yet another corridor, and then they were climbing a bare wooden staircase that seemed to go on forever. 'The nursery is along here,' Miss Thomas told them, and soon she came to a door, which she then threw open. The visitors found themselves in a long narrow room with only one window, set high in the wall and which let in very little light. Rows of wooden cots were placed the length of the two long walls, and as Anna peeped into the first one she thought that her heart would break. A tiny baby stared up at her, but even when she reached into the cot to stroke its hand the expression on its pale little face didn't change.

'They become used to having very little human contact,' Miss Thomas explained to them sadly. 'Apart from when they are fed or changed, they never come out of their cots.' Hearing the trace of weariness in the girl's voice, Anna's heart warmed to her.

'Have you worked here for long?' she asked softly.

Miss Thomas laughed, a low bitter laugh that made Anna's flesh grow cold. 'I started up in here,' she told her. 'I was left on the orphanage steps when I was just a baby – but I was one of the unlucky ones. No one ever adopted me so I've been here ever since. When I reached fifteen I was given a choice. I could stay on here as one of the staff or I could go to live in the workhouse. So, I chose to stay.'

'Oh, I'm so sorry,' Anna said, embarrassed, and now the girl's shoulders moved into a slight shrug.

'I dare say it's been better than having to live on the streets and beg for a living or worse, as some children are forced to do. But anyway, that's enough about me. Have a look around and if there's any particular child that catches your eye, let me know.'

John, Anna and Tilly walked slowly along the rows of cots and by the time they rejoined Miss Thomas at the door, Anna's eyes were bright with unshed tears and John's face was solemn.

'I would like to take them all home,' Anna told her truthfully.

'Aye, the nursery usually has that effect on folks,' Miss Thomas agreed. 'But come and meet the little ones now. They are back downstairs.'

On the landing they passed doors that led into dormitories with rows of beds that were all neatly made, and Anna was saddened to see that there was not so much as a single toy or teddy bear to distinguish one child's bed from another.

Once they had retraced their steps back along the gloomy hallway they entered a large room where children ranging from toddlers to five year olds were sitting cross-legged on bare wooden floorboards. Anna and Tilly were appalled to see that they had nothing whatsoever to entertain them, for there was not a picture book or toy in sight. A woman sitting at a large desk with what appeared to be a ledger open in front of her looked briefly up at them, but then almost instantly she returned her attention to what she was doing, and the visitors had the impression that they might have been invisible.

Slowly the little ones began to inch across the floor towards them and soon they were staring up at the visitors hopefully as they touched the women's smooth skirts and smiled tremulously.

Tilly felt as if she would choke on the lump that had formed in her throat, and when she glanced towards John and Anna she saw that they too were deeply upset. John began to fumble in his pocket, and when he produced a small paper cone full of pear drops, the children's eyes lit up with excitement. After glancing at Miss Thomas for her permission, he then began to distribute them into eager little hands, and once he had done so, the children all then returned to their original seats on the floor with a look of wonder in their eyes as they sucked on their sweets.

It was Anna who first noticed a little boy sitting alone in a far corner. He had not come forward for his treat as the other children had, and as she then looked towards Miss Thomas with a frown on her face, the young woman explained, 'That's Joseph – or Little Joe, as we call him. I'm afraid Little Joe is a cripple and so he doesn't like to come forward for fear of being made fun of.'

'What is wrong with him?' Anna asked, and Miss Thomas told her, 'He has one leg shorter than the other, which tends to throw him to the side when he walks. Poor little chap.'

Anna now took another sweet from John and crossing to the child she bent to his level and pressed it into his hand. He looked to be about two years old and for a moment he simply stared at the sweet before looking back up at her from huge dark eyes. His hair was also dark with a tendency to curl, and she had to resist the urge to swipe a stray lock from his forehead. And then suddenly his face broke into a smile and it was totally transformed as he held his hand out towards her. She hesitated for just a fraction of a second before taking it and now the tears were falling again and she wanted to snatch him into her arms.

'Well, I'll be . . .' Miss Thomas muttered as she crossed the room to join them. 'I could count on one hand the number of times I've seen that little boy smile. He must like you. It's such a shame he has a handicap. I'm sure that someone would have adopted him by now, had he not been a cripple.'

Suddenly, it was more than Anna could bear, and she had the urge to pick up her skirts and flee. 'John, I'd like to go now,' she said in a panic.

'But you haven't seen the rest of the children yet,' Miss Thomas objected in dismay.

'I know, and I'm so sorry, but I . . . I can't bear it!'

Anna was stumbling blindly towards the door now, and Tilly and John hastily followed her. They didn't manage to catch up with her until they were at the main entrance and there they found her sobbing bitterly, tears raining from her eyes.

Hearing the commotion, Miss Hale's door flew open and she wobbled towards them like a battleship in full sail.

'Have you seen a child that you like?' she asked hopefully and Tilly had to answer, for Anna was too upset to speak.

'I'm sure that Mrs Sopwith has seen any number that she would like,' she replied as calmly as she could. 'But I'm afraid it has all been a little too much for her. However, I have no doubt that you will be seeing us again, so thank you for allowing us to meet some of the children here. And now on behalf of us all, I will wish you good day.'

As the same shabby girl held the door wide, Anna escaped out into the warm sunshine with a sigh of relief. She gulped deeply at the fresh air and then, without even waiting for John, she bunched her dress into one hand and lifting it high, clambered back into the carriage and sank in a tearstained huddle against the seat.

Once Tilly and John had joined her, and were on their way to meet Ellen for lunch, John comforted his wife as best he could. He was feeling so very guilty, and not a little tearful himself.

'Oh, m . . . my poor d . . . dear!' he exclaimed. 'I had no idea that the vi . . . visit would upset you so, or I w . . . would never have su . . . suggested it. I am s . . . so sorry.'

Anna stared blankly from the window as images of the children's poor little faces swam round and round in her head. Eventually she broke the silence that had settled over them when she said, 'How can children ever be expected to survive in such places, Tilly? I had always thought I was hard done by, having to contend with this.' Her hand moved upwards to stroke the purple birthmark that stained her neck. 'But now I realise what a privileged life I have had, and I feel so ashamed.'

'You shouldn't, pet.' Tilly's voice was gentle as she felt Anna's pain. 'And nor should you feel obliged to take a child if there were none there with whom you felt you could bond. You must try to put the visit from your mind and forget about it now.' But even as the words were uttered Tilly knew that Anna would never forget the things they had seen that day, and neither would she.

It was a sombre party that arrived back at Felton Hall, and as soon as they had got inside, Anna pleaded a headache and escaped upstairs. John, Tilly and Ellen sat and took tea in the drawing room.

John looked as if his world had ended as he told Tilly brokenly, 'I would n . . . never have up . . . upset her like this f . . . for the world.'

'Hush, pet.' Tilly placed her arm around his shoulders. 'If my premonition is right, the way Anna is feeling right now is more to do with a certain child we met there.'

As John raised an inquisitive eyebrow, she went on,

'Didn't you see the way she reacted to the child they called Little Joe?'

When he nodded slowly, Tilly said, 'I think there was something about that little boy that touched a chord deep inside her, and right now she doesn't quite know how to deal with her feelings. But bide your time, pet, and it'll all come out in the wash, you just mark my words.'

'I h . . . hope you're right, Tilly. H . . . he was a grand l . . . little chap, wasn't he?'

'Oh, he was that all right,' Tilly agreed. 'A right bonny little fellow, if ever I saw one.'

At that moment, Anna was not in her room but on the top floor of Felton Hall, which she had always planned to turn into nursery quarters. There were four rooms in all, the first being a water closet. The second was a large airy room with a huge window that overlooked the lake. It opened onto a slightly smaller room that would be perfect for a nursemaid to sleep in. The fourth was an ideal size for a schoolroom when the children grew older. Anna had lost count of the times she had been up here, and each time she did, she had pictured a cot with a contented baby lying in it. But now as she stood there, she was seeing instead a little bed, in which lay a small boy with large soulful eyes and a mop of dark curly hair. A small boy whom nobody would ever want because of his crippled leg.

She could see herself reading him a story and tucking him into bed as he smiled up at her. She could see them both playing on the rolling lawns that stretched down to the lake and hear them laughing together. But what sense was there in dreaming? She knew that John had taken her to the orphanage in the hope that she would choose a baby, not a little boy who looked to be already about two years old.

Rosie Goodwin

But oh, he was such a *bonny* child. Perhaps it would be worth putting the idea to John, after all? At the end of the day, the worst he could say was no, wasn't it? She decided to wait for the right moment, for she knew now without a shadow of a doubt that she could love Little Joe as if he was her own flesh and blood.

It so happened that the right moment presented itself far sooner than she had anticipated, for she and John were lying side-by-side in their old four-poster bed in their room that night, when he tentatively broached the subject they had both studiously avoided all evening.

'I . . . I'm so sorry about the v . . . visit t . . . to the orphanage,' he stammered as he stroked her smooth cheek. 'I thought y . . . you would like t . . . to see the babies.'

'Oh, I *did* like seeing the babies, John,' she assured him, and then, taking a deep breath, she blurted out, 'But it wasn't one of the babies that I felt drawn to. It was Little Joe. Do you remember him – the boy who sat in the corner?'

She looked so beautiful, lying there with her dark hair fanned out across the pillow that John felt as if his heart would burst with love for her.

'Wh . . . what are you trying t . . . to tell me?' he asked.

'I'm telling you that I would like to bring him home and adopt him,' she said boldly. 'Do you think you could ever come to love a child his age? I mean, I know you had your heart set on a baby that we could bring up as our own from an early age, and I know that he has a crippled leg, but—'

'Sshh.' His eyes were smiling now as he told her, 'I too f . . . fell in love w . . . with the li . . . little chap, but I d . . . didn't dare to say.'

'Oh, John!' She bounced from the bed now and began to pace the room in her excitement as her fine lawn nightdress billowed around her legs in the soft breeze from the wide-open window. 'Do you think they would let us adopt him?' Her voice was anxious now.

John chuckled as he leaned on his elbow to watch her; he would never tire of watching her, he knew. 'I sh . . . should think th . . . they would let us ad . . . opt the whole lot of them if we g . . . gave a large enough do . . . donation to the ben . . . benefactor of the orphanage. But th . . . there's only one way t . . . to find out. We sh . . . shall pay another visit.'

'When?' she asked, as she tried to curb her impatience.

'Well, th . . . they say th . . . there's no time like the p . . . present, so we shall g . . . go back first thing in the m . . . morning. Will that b . . . be soon en . . . enough for you?'

'Oh, John!' she cried as she flung herself into his arms. 'Just think, very soon we could have our very own little boy. "Joseph Sopwith" has a nice ring to it, don't you think?'

He nodded fondly, but then all thoughts fled as she placed her sweet lips on his.

Chapter Twenty-Four

BETH WAS JUST leaving the milking shed when she almost collided with Eddie. Had he not reached out his arm to steady her, the jug of milk would have spilled all over the yard.

'Whoa! Slow down there,' he told her, but his eyes were smiling.

'Sorry,' she muttered. 'I didn't have my mind on what I was doing.'

His face became solemn now as he said, 'You don't seem to have had your mind on things for some time, lass. And I've had the distinct feeling that you've been avoiding me. Have I done something to offend you?'

'Oh, no, Eddie, *never*!' When the words came out in a rush, the colour flooded into her cheeks and she lowered her head, tightly gripping the jug of warm milk.

Eddie scowled, then after glancing towards the open kitchen door he took her elbow and drew her back into the milking shed. His voice had a stern edge to it now as he said, 'Right then, Beth. This has gone on for long enough. I know something is wrong, so why don't you just tell me what it is?'

Her head wagged from side to side. 'I . . . I can't tell you,

Eddie. I mean . . . 'tis nothing, really. Happen it's just the heat getting me down,' she gabbled.

His eyes narrowed into slits as he watched her hovering like a bird that was about to take flight. Then his hand dropped from her arm and dangled at his side as he stared at her helplessly. And then, deciding to take the bull by the horns, he cleared his throat before declaring, 'I love you, Beth. I think I have since the very first moment I set eyes on you. I know this isn't the most romantic of places to make a proposal, but the thing is . . . Well, I want to marry you.'

'You . . . you mustn't say that, Eddie.' Her eyes were wide with fear now as she backed away from him.

'Mustn't say what? That I love you or that I want to marry you?'

'Either – you mustn't say either. You see, I couldn't marry you even if I had a mind to. I . . . I can't marry anyone, so get it into your head and don't let us have this conversation again.'

Heedless of the milk that was slopping over the lip of the jug, she elbowed past him, and as he watched her almost running across the yard, his heart was crying. Until recently he would have sworn that his feelings were returned, so what had happened to make her change in such a short time? Sinking down onto a bale of hay, Eddie buried his face in his hands and did something he had not done since the death of his sister. He wept.

As Beth came back into the kitchen, where Lucy was resting on the long wooden settle, the older woman could tell that something was wrong. The girl looked on the verge of tears. She watched as Beth carried the milk into the deep pantry on the north wall and placed it on the thrall, and her eyes stayed on her when she walked back out and began to tie a large coarse apron across her work dress.

'Right, missus. I'm off to the washhouse to make a start on the laundry,' Beth told her, and then she was gone without another word, leaving Lucy to stare after her in bewilderment.

Once she was in the washhouse, Beth crossed to the boiler to check that the water was hot enough to start the sheets. Eddie had lit a fire under it earlier in the morning, and now the small lean-to structure resembled something close to a furnace. Grabbing a white cotton sheet, the girl rammed it viciously into the water with the poss-stick as the injustice of what was happening to her made her want to cry out in despair. She had hoped to stay here for a longer period of time – at least until the bairn was showing – but she knew that this would be impossible now, following Eddie's declaration. Oh, *why* had he to go and ask her to marry him like that? It would have been so very easy to say, 'Yes, yes, I will marry you,' and, 'Yes, I love you too,' for she did love him with all of her heart. But that was the problem. She loved him too much to saddle him with another man's bairn, even if it *had* been conceived against her wishes.

Crossing to the mound of washing that she had flung onto the hard-packed mud floor, she began to sort it into piles. The sheets and the towelling squares that served as Sarah's nappies, along with the white cotton underwear, would be boiled until they were spotless in the copper. The rest she would wash in the poss tub on the washboard. Lifting some of Sarah's tiny clothes, she now dunked them under the water and rhythmically began to push them up and down the wooden washboard in the hot soapy water, then when they were clean she threw them into a large tin bucket full of clean water that she had placed ready at the side of the poss tub and rinsed them before carrying them outside and feeding them through the mangle.

It was as she was pegging them onto a long washline that stretched from the side of the barn to the corner of the washhouse that her hands became still as an anxious fluttering feeling sprang to life in her stomach. She needed no one to tell her that this was the baby. Now she looked sorrowfully across the yard. She would have to leave very soon now, but where would she go? The only place she could think of was the workhouse in Shields and she shuddered at the thought of it. She had heard tales of the conditions that the people there were forced to endure, and had caught glimpses of the women, some in their late twenties and early thirties, who looked at least sixty, old before their time and riddled with disease. But then she supposed it would be better than winding up on the streets with nowhere to lay her head, and it would ensure that the bairn had a home of sorts when it put in an appearance.

Her eyes swept past the barn to the wide-open spaces, and she wondered how she would ever again adjust to living in cramped, confined, conditions? Every day she had spent here had been like a holiday, and the people – Lucy and Sarah, not to mention Eddie – had become like her family, and she knew that she would never get over the loss of them. Turning back to the copper she wearily hoisted a steaming sheet from its depths with the large wooden tongs, then after plunging another in, she immersed the first one in cold water before carrying it out to the mangle. Before she left she would make sure that everything was on top with the work; she owed Lucy that much at least.

As Miss Hale eyed the banker's draft, placed on the desk in front of her, her eyes sparkled with greed as she secretly calculated the gratuity she would receive as her share. 'I can see no reason at all why you cannot take Joseph away with you right now,' she simpered. 'If only all our orphans could be so fortunate as to go to such loving homes. And such a generous donation, Mr Sopwith! Our benefactor will be most grateful.' She heaved herself from the chair now before telling them, 'If you would just be so kind as to wait there, I will go and get Miss Thomas. She is helping with a school class today. You can spend a little time with Joseph whilst she packs his things.'

'Thank you.' Anna inclined her head politely as Miss Hale wobbled from the room, but the second she had gone she turned to John, scarcely able to contain her excitement. 'Do you think that Joe will be happy when he knows that he is coming home with us?' she asked him.

'I sh . . . should think s . . . so. After all,' John spread his hands to encompass the bleak surroundings, 'any . . . w . . . where is preferable t . . . to living h . . . ere.'

The smile slipped from her face as her eyes followed his around the drab room.

Seconds later, they heard footsteps in the corridor outside and Miss Hale reappeared with Miss Thomas close behind her.

'Miss Thomas will take you to the day room now,' the older woman wheezed. 'When you are ready to leave, perhaps you would be so kind as to come back here and sign some forms that I shall have ready for you?'

'Of course.' Anna and John rose from their seats and followed Miss Thomas through the winding corridors until they were back in the bleak little room that housed the younger children during the daytime. The woman in charge took the opportunity to leave the room at that moment.

Although the children recognised John as the kindly man who had given them a pear drop the day before, none of them made a sound. But he hadn't forgotten them; a peppermint lozenge and a liquorice dragee were put into each small land.

Joe was sitting in the same corner, almost as if he had never moved from the spot since the last time they had visited, and Anna's heart went out to him. He looked so little and vulnerable – and so very unhappy.

She and John stood back whilst Miss Thomas crossed to him and knelt down to his level. Then, taking his hand in hers, she gently told him, 'You are going to live with these nice people, Little Joe. Won't that be lovely? I'm sure you'll get to have a bedroom all to yourself and . . .' Her voice suddenly trailed away and Anna was distressed to see that the young woman's shoulders were heaving. Hurrying across to her, Anna now also sank to her knees, and draping one arm around Little Joe and the other around the girl's shoulders, she hugged them both and asked, 'What is it, my dear?'

Deeply embarrassed, Miss Thomas swiped the tears from her cheeks as she tried to compose herself. 'I'm so sorry,' she apologised. 'It's just that I get so attached to the children who live here. I . . . I am the one who has looked out for Little Joe since he arrived and I'm . . . I'm going to miss him so much.'

'Oh.' Anna was now almost as distressed as Miss Thomas. She looked helplessly across her shoulder at John, who was wringing his hands in the doorway. And through it all, Little Joe had not shown so much as a sign of understanding what was going on, but simply continued to stare at Miss Thomas from dull eyes.

The young woman suddenly pulled herself together and rose, straightening down her drab grey skirt as she did so.

'Please excuse me,' she gulped. 'It won't take me long to pack Joe's possessions, and then I shall be straight back. I'm so glad that you are offering him a home. I feared that no one would ever want him, with his leg as it is, but I'm sure you won't regret it. Once he has settled with you, I have no doubt he will bring you great joy.'

She quietly left the room now, and it was then that an idea occurred to Anna and the corners of her mouth suddenly rose in a smile again. 'Whyever didn't I think of it before!' she exclaimed quietly. 'We are going to need a nurserymaid for Joe. Who better than Miss Thomas, with whom he is already acquainted?'

John immediately saw the sense of this but even so he pointed out, 'I c . . . can't see th . . . that Miss Hale will be too h . . . happy to lose Miss Thomas.'

'Neither can I,' Anna admitted, but there was a determined jut to her chin. 'All the same, what can she do to stop her leaving if the girl has a position to go to? Think of it – it would be a chance for her to get away from this place too, and I'm sure that she could be happy living with us, and Little Joe. Oh, won't you *please* let me put it to her, darling? If she is unhappy with the proposition, I swear I'll never mention it again.'

At that moment, the woman who had been in charge of the children swept back into the room and took a seat at the desk, so lowering his voice now, John whispered, 'Very well. But as I said, d . . . don't ex . . . pect M . . . Miss Hale to be p . . . pleased about this.'

Squeezing his hand, Anna turned her attention back to Joe, who she now saw on closer inspection, was painfully thin. 'We'll soon have you with some roses in your cheeks,' she told him, smiling at him kindly. 'And we'll have to sort out a little pony for you for when you're a bit older. Would you like that, Joe?' She kept up her reassuring chatter, with the other youngsters listening in, until Miss Thomas joined them some minutes later with a small carpetbag in her hand and a face as long as a fiddle.

'Ah, Miss Thomas. I wonder – might I have a quick word with you in private?'

Miss Thomas looked deeply uncomfortable as the older woman behind the desk glared at her, but she allowed Anna to lead her back out into the corridor, where the latter asked her without preamble, 'Miss Thomas, would you consider coming to live with us, to be a nurserymaid to Little Joe? I know my suggestion will have taken you completely by surprise, but as I just pointed out to my husband, we will need to employ someone to help, and who better than yourself? I shall quite understand if you need a little time to think about it, but I *do* so hope you will agree.'

Miss Thomas's eyes were almost popping out of her head, but finally she managed to mutter, 'You are asking me to come and live with you . . . at Felton Hall?'

'Yes, I am,' Anna told her gaily with a trace of laughter in her voice. 'I can't think of a better nurserymaid for Joseph, can you? You would be doing us a tremendous favour, I assure you. John and I have never had children, so having someone on hand who knows how to care for our son would be a tremendous help. And I promise you, we would treat you fairly. You would have a room of your own next to Joseph's, we would supply you with some nice new clothes, and of course, we would pay you a fair wage and you would have a certain amount of time to yourself.'

Miss Thomas had long since resigned herself to the fact that she would grow old and die within the confines of these dark walls. But now suddenly a whole new life was being offered to her on a plate and she hardly dared to believe it.

'I . . . I don't need time to think about it,' she finally managed to say. 'I would love nothing more in this world than to accept your generous offer, but the thing is . . .'

'Yes?' Anna was watching her face closely, and now Miss

Thomas whispered, 'I don't think Miss Hale would agree to it. As you've probably already realised, she rules this place and the people in it with a rod of iron. If I were to leave, she would have to find someone to replace me, and on the wages she pays, that could prove to be difficult.'

John's face hardened and he said, 'Y . . . you just le . . . leave her to *me.*'

'But she—' Miss Thomas opened her mouth to warn him, but he was already striding away down the corridor with his back as stiff as a broom-handle.

Anna watched him go with pride, loving him even more in that moment than she ever had before. Then, unable to contain her excitement a second longer, she turned back to Miss Thomas. 'Go and pack your things as quickly as you can,' she urged her. 'Then hurry back here to us. We shall be waiting for you. The sooner we are all away from this god-forsaken place the better, as far as I'm concerned.'

Still hardly able to believe her luck, the young woman ran off down the corridor in a most unladylike manner, thinking, I'm going! I'm really going at last.

In less than ten minutes she was back in the corridor clutching a small valise. Just as she had promised, Anna was waiting for her with John gripping Joseph tightly in his arms. Joseph was looking slightly bewildered. However, the same could not be said for Miss Hale, who was also waiting with them, her face as black as a lump of coal.

'Are you quite sure that this is what you want, Miss Thomas?' she enquired coldly, and when the younger woman's head wagged in answer, she drew herself up to her considerable height and width, and shrugged. 'Very well then. I just hope that you will not live to regret your somewhat hasty decision. You are leaving me in the lurch and I find your ingratitude quite incomprehensible.

However, Mr Sopwith has now signed all the necessary forms so I will wish you all goodbye.' With that she turned and waddled away as John ushered the two women in front of him towards the door.

Miss Thomas felt as if she was dreaming as John helped her into the carriage before handing Joseph up to her, then once he and Anna had joined her on the opposite seat, the carriage began to pull away and Miss Thomas gazed wonderingly from the window onto the bleak façade of the orphanage. Would this really be the last time she would ever have to look on it, she wondered, and however had Mr Sopwith managed to persuade Miss Hale to let her go? Eventually her curiosity got the better of her and she dared to ask, 'How did you manage it, sir? I would have staked my life that she would put her foot down and refuse to let me leave.'

John's eyes twinkled as he looked across the now swaying carriage at her. 'There's an old s . . . saying – money t . . . talks – and it certainly d . . . did the trick wi . . . with that one back th . . . there.'

Anna now fell against his shoulder as their laughter joined and Miss Thomas found herself smiling, really smiling, as she never had before. Oh, these were nice folks, she would have staked her life on it, and somehow she knew that she was going to be happy with them.

When, some time later, the carriage rattled through the gates of Felton Hall, the whole day began to take on a fairytale quality for Miss Thomas, for never in her life had she dreamed that places such as this existed. And *she* was going to be living here!

'What do you think of the Hall?' Anna asked her as she saw the girl's astounded expression.

'Oh, it's lovely, ma'am,' she gasped.

'Do you mind me asking what your first name is?' Anna enquired, and the girl smiled tentatively.

'It's Meg, ma'am, though I can't remember the last time anyone addressed me as such.'

'Well, I shall call you Meg – with your permission, of course,' Anna told her. 'It's so much more informal than Miss Thomas, isn't it? If that's all right with you, that is?'

'Oh yes, ma'am. I'd like that,' the girl agreed, and from then on Meg it was.

John was already jumping down from the carriage and as he helped first Meg and then Anna down, then lifted the child from his seat, where he had been asleep, his face broke into a smile. 'Look over there, J . . . Joseph,' he said to the little boy, pointing in the direction of a large pool surrounded by weeping willows. 'Th . . . there are some f . . . fish in there that are almost as b . . . b . . . big as you are. When you're a little older, I shall t . . . teach you to fish, my lad.' Strange how his stutter had weakened as he tried to reassure the little chap, who was looking ready to burst into tears.

'Only if you promise not to let him get too near the edge,' Anna told him, and John's heart warmed as he saw the protective look on her face as she picked the small boy up and cradled him against her slim shoulder.

In that moment, John Sopwith knew that their son Joseph had come home.

That evening, long after Meg and Little Joe had been fed and watered, bathed and bedded down, Anna and John went up to their room, feeling tired but overwhelmingly happy.

'What do you think Tilly will say when she discovers what we've done?' Anna asked as she sat down at her dressing-table to brush out her long dark hair.

John, who was watching her adoringly from the bed,

chuckled. 'I d . . . don't think she'll be in the least surprised,' he told her confidently. 'I th . . . think she knew even before y . . . you did that you'd l . . . lost your heart to that little chap up there.' It had happened again, he noticed; the words were coming more easily.

'Oh, but he is such a bonny little boy, isn't he?' Anna sighed with a faraway look in her eyes as she thought of the child she had earlier tucked into a nice clean bed, with her old teddy bear to cuddle. She'd fed the sleepy little boy spoonfuls of bread and milk, and read him a story. Meg, worn out with the excitement of the day, had been only too happy to let her employer take over.

John nodded in agreement. 'Y . . . yes, he is, but there's n . . . nothing to say we sh . . . shouldn't still go on trying to m . . . make a little brother or sister for him, so c . . . come here, woman.'

Anna giggled, then tossing her hairbrush onto the dressing-table she ran across the room to join him.

'Pardon me, ma'am. I have a note here that has been sent by carriage from Miss Anna. Shall I ask them to wait in case you wish to send a reply?'

'Oh, yes please, Peabody.' Tilly glanced at Steve, who was sitting in the bay window of the smoking room enjoying a cigar, before taking the envelope from the silver tray that Peabody was holding out to her. She withdrew a single sheet of paper as Steve watched curiously. 'It's an invitation from Anna and John, asking if we will join them for tea on Sunday,' she told him when she had read to the bottom of the page.

'Does it say why?' Steve asked.

Tilly shook her head. 'No, it doesn't, but I have a curious feeling I might know the reason.' Then, turning to Peabody, she instructed him, 'Please inform them that we would be delighted to join them, and look forward to seeing them then.'

'Certainly, ma'am.' Tilly hugged herself as a little feeling of excitement settled around her like a mist.

Chapter Twenty-Five

TUCKED UP IN her bed beneath the eaves, Beth stared towards the two slits of windows, through which the moon was shining. It was a wonderful evening, and the sky was bright with stars. Added to that, a breeze had blown up, and after the intense heat of the day it was more than welcome. Her cheeks were wet with tears, for tonight when the house was asleep she planned to leave forever. Far better to do that than risk seeing the disgust that would surely cross Eddie's face when he discovered that she was carrying a bairn. Before coming to bed she had hugged Sarah close to her for the very last time and she had pecked the missus awkwardly on the cheek, which had led to Lucy asking in happy surprise, 'And what did I do to deserve that then?'

'Aw.' Deeply embarrassed, Beth had flapped her hands as she walked towards the stairs. 'I just felt like it, that's all.'

'Then I can only live in hope that you feel like it a little more often,' Lucy had teased, and as she watched the girl climb the stairs she had thought, as she often had, It was a good day when Beth came to this house. Oh aye, a very good day indeed. But then the pains that had growled deep down in Lucy's abdomen all day long had brought her doubling over, and springing from his seat, Eddie had rushed from the settle and led her to a chair. 'What can I get you to ease it, Ma?' There had been a trace of fear in his voice as he looked on her chalk-white face, but she had rustled up a weak smile for him, whispering, 'It's nothing, my love. You just get yourself off to bed now, eh? You've had a long day and I'll be fine when I've had a good night's sleep. I expect I've just overdone it a bit, that's all.'

Eddie hovered at her side as he chewed distractedly on his lip and then he asked fearfully, 'Are you quite sure it isn't the babby coming, Mother? I could always saddle the horse and get down into the village for the doctor.'

'No, no – I told you, I'm all right. Now stop fretting and get yourself away to bed and do as you're told for once, will you?'

His eyes settled on her stomach. It was so swollen now that it looked in danger of bursting out of the smocked nightdress that was strained across it. Shaking his head, and turning about, he slowly and anxiously climbed the stairs to lie in the room next to Beth's.

Alone once more, Lucy looked towards Sarah, who was fast asleep in a cot next to the large dresser that displayed Lucy's treasured china. The baby had outgrown the rocking crib that both Noreen and Eddie had once slept in, and Eddie had fetched the cot in from the barn, where it had been stored for many a long year, and then stood back and watched as Beth scrubbed every inch of it.

Leaning forward, Lucy buried her face in her hands. What would become of the little mite, when her time came? What would become of all of them, if it came to that? She had no time to ponder on it, however, for just then a pain the like of which she had never known before seemed to lift her from the chair and brought her lips stretching wide in a rictus of agony. She felt as if she had a knife twisting inside her, and trying to be as quiet as she could, she staggered towards the door that led into the farmyard. Maybe if she could just make it to the tap she could sluice herself with cold water and that might help a little. But she was only halfway across the room when the next pain struck, and this time no matter how she tried she couldn't stop herself from crying out. She stopped and screwed her eyes up tight at the sharpness of it, and then vomit was rising in her throat and blackness was rushing towards her as she fell heavily onto the floor in a dead faint.

Both Beth and Eddie heard the commotion, and after jumping from their beds, they almost collided in the narrow space that separated the two small attic rooms.

'Did you hear that?' Eddie was bare-chested and his trousers, which he was hastily pulling on, made Beth avert her eyes as warm colour crept into her cheeks.

'Aye, I did,' she nodded. 'It sounded like someone in pain.'

Shoulder to shoulder, they spilled down the staircase, but the sight they saw when they reached the bottom brought them both skidding to a temporary halt. Then Eddie was springing towards his mother, who was stretched out on the cold flagstone floor.

'Ma! Ma – what is it?' His cheeks were wet as he picked up her hand and started to rub some warmth into it. Beth, meantime, sprinted to the sink and taking up a small tin bowl that they used for washing Sarah in, she quickly poured some cold water into it and snatched up a clean rag. Dropping to Lucy's side, she dipped the rag into the bowl and proceeded to wipe it around the woman's waxen face as she told Eddie, 'Saddle the horse an' get down to the village fer Doctor Murray, would you? Tell him we need him straight away.'

Hearing the urgency in her voice, Eddie jumped to his

feet, his face now nearly as white as his mother's. 'Can you cope till I get back?'

'Yes, yes. Now just *go*, will you?'

He turned on his heel without another word, throwing a shirt over his head on the way out.

'Willy, I was wondering if you and Josefina would care to join Steve and me when we go to Felton Hall for tea on Sunday?' Tilly asked as she lightly buttered a slice of toast.

Willy and Josefina exchanged a secret glance. 'As it happens, Mother,' Willy replied, 'Josefina and I were thinking of taking a little trip. We thought we might take a train to the Lake District for a few days – if you have no objection, of course? There are plenty of good hotels there.'

If Tilly was surprised by this she managed to contain it well, for her voice was light as she replied, 'I think that would do you both a power of good. I believe the Lake District is supposed to be quite beautiful at this time of year. But it's a rather sudden decision, isn't it?'

Josefina had the grace to look embarrassed as she turned her attention to her breakfast and said, 'We only thought of it yesterday. It seems sensible to take advantage of the fine weather. It can't last for much longer, can it? Besides, I would rather be away while the case comes to court about the brothel. I've given the police so many statements now that I just want an end to the whole thing. By the time we get back, it should all be over. Can you understand, Mama? I know it's rather unorthodox for us to just go off unchaperoned like this, but—'

'It's all right,' Tilly cut in tenderly. 'You don't have to explain. I can quite understand how you must feel – and don't worry about what people will say. As for the weather, let's hope the hot spell doesn't last for too much longer. The wells are running dry and everything in the garden is dying from lack of water. I never thought I would say it, but I think we would all benefit from a little rain . . . When exactly were you thinking of going?'

'Well, you know the old saying, Mama – there's no time like the present, so we thought we would leave today,' Willy told her.

Tilly was dumbfounded, but the conversation was stopped from going any further when Fanny burst into the room. 'You'd better come quick, Tilly,' she told her breathlessly. 'Young Eddie from Brook Farm is in the kitchen an' it seems that Miss Lucy has been took bad.'

Dropping her toast onto her plate, Tilly pushed her chair away and hurried towards the door. Once there she turned to look back at Willy and Josefina, and what she said now was, 'I think your idea of a break is an excellent one. Don't let this stop you going. There are more than enough of us here to look after Lucy if the baby is coming. I shall be going over to the farm now and am not sure how long I shall be gone. But if you should leave before I return, have a wonderful time and I shall look forward to seeing you when you get back. How long do you plan to be away?'

'Oh, not more than a couple of weeks or so,' Willy told her, and she wondered if she had imagined the trace of something akin to guilt in her son's tone. 'Do give Lucy our best wishes won't you, Mama?'

'Of course, pet,' Tilly promised him, then with a last fond smile at both her children she followed Fanny down the hallway to the kitchen door.

Eddie was leaning heavily on the kitchen table with his head bent low when she entered, and when he looked up at her she saw the fear in his eyes. 'It's Mother, Tilly,' he told her quietly. 'She was taken bad last night so I rode into the village to get the doctor out to her. There's something badly amiss 'cos he's sent for a specialist from Shields to come and see her later this afternoon.'

'I see.' Tilly chewed thoughtfully on her lip before suddenly turning about and announcing, 'Wait there for me, Eddie. I'm going to get changed and then I'll ride back to the farm with you. And Eddie . . .' she paused. 'Try not to worry too much. Your mother isn't a young woman any more, which is probably what has made this pregnancy so difficult for her, but she'll come through it just fine, you wait and see.'

He nodded politely, but as a picture of his mother's pain-wracked face swam before his eyes he wasn't so sure that Tilly was right.

When some time later, they reined their horses to a halt in the yard of Brook Farm, they saw that the specialist the doctor had sent for must already be there, for a fine trap drawn by a tall white horse that was pawing impatiently at the ground, was tethered there alongside the doctor's horse.

Tilly climbed expertly down from the saddle and passed the reins to Eddie, who then led the horses to the water trough before tying them to a post and following her into the kitchen.

Beth was sitting at the table with Sarah on her lap and she nodded solemnly up towards Lucy's bedroom. 'The doctors are in wi' her now. Oh, Tilly, I'm so scared. The poor missus looks like death warmed up.'

Tilly could find no response so instead she gripped Beth's shoulder and planted a hasty kiss on Sarah's springy curls before beginning to pace up and down the room as she waited for the doctors to finish their examination. Eddie, meantime, sank down into the chair next to Beth and allowed his hands to dangle slackly between his knees.

It was some time later when the village doctor appeared,

and said gravely, 'Tilly, Lucy would like you to join us, please.'

Hiding her surprise, Tilly followed him upstairs, to where Lucy was propped up on feather pillows in a large brass bed.

The specialist was packing his instruments away into a large black bag and his eyebrows rose into his hairline as he saw Tilly standing there in riding breeches. However, he made no comment other than to say, 'I have told my colleague what I fear is the problem, Mrs Sopwith. And Mrs Bentwood wishes you to be present whilst the doctor tells you of my findings. So now I will wish you all good day, and should I be able to be of any further assistance to you, please do not hesitate to call me.'

'Thank you.' Tilly inclined her head towards him as he made for the door, adding, 'If you would be so kind as to send your bill to Highfield Manor, I shall see that you are paid immediately, sir.'

Grim-faced, he nodded and then the door was closing behind him and Tilly was approaching the bed where she took Lucy's hot hand in her own.

'Well?' Her words were addressed to Dr Murray now. 'What is wrong with Lucy? Is it the baby?'

Before the man could reply, Lucy surprised them both by saying, 'Doctor, would you mind very much if I told Tilly myself?'

'Of course not, dear lady,' he assured her, getting up ready to leave. 'The pill you have taken should give you a good night's rest. Please ask your son to call if you should need me.' And then he too was gone, leaving the two women to stare at each other.

The silence seemed to stretch between them for a time until Lucy finally told her, 'Tilly, I think what I have to tell you may come as something of a shock. You see . . . I am not pregnant and I have always known this.'

Rosie Goodwin

'*What?* But . . .?' As Tilly's eyes settled on the mound beneath the blankets, Lucy squeezed her hand, and the irony of the situation was not lost on her, for here she was now, in her darkest hour, confiding in the woman who had always stood between herself and her husband as surely as if she had resided with them. But then, as she had always known, Tilly could not be blamed for that. It was Simon who had never been able to get over his obsession with her, and for that reason, no other woman, including herself, had ever been able to hold a torch to Tilly in his eyes.

Speaking slowly, for the drug was beginning to work, she explained: 'Simon and I had not lain together since long before Noreen left home, and so I knew that I couldn't be expecting a child. At one time I would have laid down my life for him, even though I knew that I would always play second fiddle to you in his eyes. But then, when Noreen fell in love with Willy, his obsession seemed to switch from you to her, and he made all our lives unbearable. He could not endure the thought of seeing Noreen happy with the son of the woman whom he had never been able to claim as his own.'

When Tilly's head wagged from side to side in silent denial, Lucy whispered, 'Don't upset yourself, hinny. The blame did not lie with you but with Simon. Strangely enough, I knew the first time I ever met you that day in the marketplace with Simon, that under other circumstances you and I were destined to be friends. And that has been proven a thousand times over since Simon and Noreen died, for you have been better to me than my own family – apart from my Eddie, of course. That is why I need to talk to you now. You see,' she paused and gulped deep in her throat before going on, 'this thing growing inside me,' her finger stabbed at her stomach, 'is not a baby as everyone presumed, but a growth.'

'Oh, no! No!' Tilly's deep distress was evident, but Lucy knew that she must finish what she had started to tell her. 'My time is short now, Tilly. But please do not distress yourself. Death will be a welcome release from the pain I have been forced to endure over the last months. But first I must make sure that those I leave behind will be provided for. I have hopes that Eddie and Beth will wed, for from the day that girl breezed into this house she has been like a breath of fresh air and I've come to look upon her as my own. It is Sarah who I am worried about, for as much as Beth and Eddie both love her, it would be unfair of me to ask them to take her on. So I ask you, Tilly: will you promise me that when I go she will be well-provided and cared-for?'

'Oh, my dear.' Tilly could not go on for a time as tears ran unchecked down her cheeks. But then, when she had managed to compose herself, she vowed, 'She will never want for anything. This is my solemn promise to you.' And this death-bed promise was one she would have no difficulty in keeping.

'Thank you.' Lucy sank back against the pillows as Tilly asked, 'Why did you never tell me about this before?'

'What good could it have done?' the sick woman asked. 'I sensed that there was nothing that could be done, no curing this, so I suppose I closed my eyes to it, hoping that it would go away. I would like to rest now', she murmured. 'Would you excuse me?'

Tilly gently laid her hand down on the coverlet and then tiptoed from the room.

When she entered the kitchen, she found Beth crying into her apron and Eddie looking almost as pale as his mother, and she knew that the doctor had told them of Lucy's condition. 'Would you like me to take your mother back to the Manor with me?' she asked the young man. 'I promise that she would be well cared for.'

His chin firm, he shook his head proudly. 'No. Thanks for the offer, Tilly, but I think my mother would wish to spend her remaining time here in her own home.'

'In that case, I shall ensure that you have all the help you need,' she told him.

Again he shook his head. 'We can manage between us, can't we, Beth?'

The girl nodded without hesitation. There was no way that she could leave him now, or Lucy for that matter, despite the plans she had made. 'Of course we can,' she said stoutly.

'Then would it help if I took Sarah?'

Eddie shook his head for a third time. 'She's the bright spot in my mother's life,' he said quietly. 'But rest assured, if we find her too much to cope with, we will tell you.'

'Very well.' Tilly made her way towards the door on legs that felt as heavy as lead. Of a sudden, she recalled a verse from *Antony and Cleopatra*, the Shakespeare tragedy that she had studied with Mr Burgess. The words were so heartbreakingly beautiful that she had never forgotten them, and somehow, they seemed so very appropriate now.

Raising her face to the sun, she whispered:

> *'Finish, good lady; the bright day is done,*
> *And we are for the dark.'*

Chapter Twenty-Six

NED WAS WAITING for Tilly when she reined the horse to a halt outside the stable-block.

'How is she, lass?' he asked.

Climbing nimbly down, Tilly said, 'Not good, Ned. I fear that her days are numbered now.'

Her old friend let out a great sigh. 'You'd think the poor lass had suffered enough, wouldn't you? An' now for this to go an' happen. Is there a problem wi' the bairn she's carryin'?'

Tilly wondered what she should tell him, but then guessing that he would find out sooner or later anyway, she decided to be truthful.

'Lucy isn't having a bairn, Ned. The thing that is growing inside her is a tumour and it has gone too far now for anything to be done.'

'I see.' His kind eyes grew sad as he thought on what she had confided to him. 'Then we can only pray that her end will be quick an' merciful,' he said. 'She ain't the first I've heard of to suffer wi' sommat like this, an' the other poor devils I know of ended their lives writhing in agony praying fer death to take 'em.' When he saw tears start to her eyes he instantly wished he could take back what he had just told her, and now he tried to soften it by saying hurriedly, 'O' course, there's no sayin' it will take Lucy that way. Pay no heed to me, lass. You should know by now that me tongue has a habit o' runnin' away wi' me.'

'It's all right, Ned. I know you meant no harm,' Tilly told him, and he hung his head in shame as he watched her walk towards the back of the house and the kitchen entrance.

Ellen and Fanny were waiting for her, and when she repeated what she had just told Ned, they too became upset.

'What will it mean for little Sarah?' Fanny asked eventually, and now Tilly shrugged as she joined them at the huge scrubbed oak table.

'That is something I shall have to discuss with Willy,' she told them solemnly. 'She is his daughter, after all. Have Willy and Josefina left, by the way?'

'Aye, lass, they've gone. You've just missed them. They were both in fine high spirits. Now come on, get this sweet tea down you. You look as if you're in need of it, an' sugar is good for shock. I bet you ain't had a bite past your lips since you left here neither, have you?' As Fanny spoke she was cutting a shive of bread from the fresh baked loaf on the table. Cutting a good wedge of cheese, she placed it on the plate with the bread and then pushed it towards Tilly with the butter dish and a jar of homemade pickle. 'Now come on,' she ordered as a mother might to a child. 'Get that down you else I'll not let you leave the table.' In the meantime, Ellen had filled the big old black kettle, and had put it on the hob to boil.

Tilly managed to force the food down, although it tasted like sawdust and kept threatening to lodge in her throat. Lucy's news had affected her deeply. That and the vow she had made about her little granddaughter. What would happen to her if Willy was not willing to take her? she found herself thinking, and then she instantly felt guilty. Poor Lucy was not even dead yet – nor, God willing, would she be for some long time to come.

'If there's just you for dinner tonight, what would you like me to cook for you?' Ellen asked. 'I can make you up a special recipe from here.' She tapped her copy of Mrs Beeton's *Book of Household Management*.

'Oh, it isn't worth cooking just for me,' Tilly said tiredly. 'I'll tell you what, why don't you put a little extra into Steve's basket and I'll have supper with him over at the cottage tonight?'

'Of course,' Ellen agreed and then hesitantly she reminded her, 'We were supposed to be meeting the men who are working on the schoolhouse down in the village this afternoon. Would you like me to go alone?'

'Oh no, no. I'm interested in seeing how it's coming along,' Tilly assured her. 'I'll just finish this tea and then I'll go and get changed and then we can be off. There's no point in sitting about moping, is there? All we can do is go on as normally as we can.'

Ellen looked on this woman whom she had known since she was a parson's wife and Tilly was just a girl, and her admiration for her grew even more. Tilly Trotter could take whatever life chose to throw at her with dignity and grace. And once again, the older woman found herself thinking, as she had done so many times before, Our Tilly is more of a natural-bred lady than many of the gentry who are born with silver spoons in their mouths!

It was late afternoon by the time Tilly and Ellen rode into the village. The heat of the day had passed its peak, yet still it was stifling with no breath of wind to cool them even as they bowled along in the trap. When they came to the cottage that was being converted into a small schoolhouse, they found the men Steve had instructed to do the job still busily working there. The sound of banging and hammering ceased as Tilly drew the horse to a halt, and a tall black-haired man wiped the sweat from his brow as he stepped from the open door and hurried forward to meet them.

'Afternoon, ladies,' he greeted them politely.

Tilly inclined her head as she and Ellen followed him back into the shade of the cottage. Once inside, it was all Ellen could do to contain her excitement, for what had formerly been the kitchen-cum-parlour was now transformed into a tidy room with a number of tiny tables and chairs laid out in neat rows. The sink was still in the corner, where the children could wash their hands, and the fireplace was still intact, with its chimney all freshly swept in readiness for the winter. The walls had had two new coats of distemper and looked clean and bright, and flagstones had been laid on what had formerly been a mud-packed floor. A carpenter was just completing a large store-cupboard that would house the books and pencils that Tilly and Ellen would supply, and now as they looked around in awe, Ellen clapped her hands together with delight. 'Why, Mr Cartwright, it looks wonderful! You have surpassed all my greatest expectations.'

The dark-haired man's chest swelled with pleasure at the praise. 'Why, it's nice of you to say so, ma'am. We do pride usselves on doin' a good job, even when it's a rushed 'un, as this was. I thought over there . . .' he pointed next to the cupboard, 'I might get Bob to build you a good stout bookcase, an' o' course we've also cleaned up the outside water closet, should any o' the little 'uns get took short durin' lessons. If you don't mind me sayin', I think it's a grand thing you two ladies are plannin' to do. I'm all fer learnin' meself an' I don't mind tellin' yer, if I lived closer I'd be askin' you to take my brood on.'

'Why, thank you, Mr Cartwright.' Ellen was positively beaming. 'It's so good to hear that people are finally showing an interest in learning. I believe even the pit-owners are no longer frowning on people who can sign their name, which is most encouraging.'

'Well, we can't be expected to live in the Dark Ages forever, can we?' he replied.

'Quite!' Ellen now looked at Tilly with a happy smile on her face. 'Steve is to be congratulated too, for employing such conscientious workers.'

'I had no doubt that they would do a good job after the work I have seen them do on the cottage,' Tilly told her truthfully. As she looked towards the window, her heart sank, for a small figure in a dirty shawl was standing in the road outside. It was Mrs McGrath, there could be no mistaking her. No doubt this meant she had yet more abuse ready to hurl at her. As Ellen followed her friend's gaze, she too recognised the woman who had scarred Sarah for life on her Christening Day.

'Would you like me to go out and ask her to move on?' she suggested in a hushed voice.

Tilly shook her head resolutely. 'It would do no good if you did,' she replied. 'I know Mrs McGrath of old. In fact, looking back, I think she has always been a thorn in my side. The longer I leave her to simmer out there, the worse the abuse will be, so I may as well go out there now and get it over and done with.'

'Not on your own, you won't!' Ellen declared, as a vision of Sarah's face flashed before her eyes. 'That woman should be locked up. She must be insane to harbour a grudge against you as she has all these years. No, Tilly, you stay here. *I* shall go out and see what she wants, and don't argue, for I insist.'

So saying, she swept up her skirts and sailed from the

cottage. Once she was standing opposite Mrs McGrath, Tilly heard her ask, 'May I help you with anything?'

The old woman glared past her before saying, 'An' just what could the likes o' *you* 'elp me wi'? Why, yer no better than that whore in there who's bewitched me son. Had it not bin fer *you*, your poor 'usband wouldn't have had to leave the village in disgrace. But then, Parson 'ad no choice, did he? Not wi' you standin' trial, you hussy, wi' blood on yer hands. Yer almost as near to a witch as that one in there, but then they say that witches have covens. Come back from your godless goin's-on in Africa, have you, to join hers, is that it?'

'Why!' Ellen spluttered indignantly, and her voice was rising to match her temper now as she wagged a finger in Mrs McGrath's face. 'You *silly* old woman, you. Why can't you let the past be the past? Do you take pleasure from inflicting misery on people?'

'Only one person in particular,' the woman smirked. 'But takin' it a step further, just who do you think is goin' to trust their bairns to the care o' two murderers? You've wasted yer time an' money doin' that there cottage up, fer there'll only be the pair of you in it.'

'That remains to be seen, doesn't it?' Ellen's eyes were now like chips of ice, and seeing that her friend's temper was about to get the better of her, Tilly hurried out to join her.

A small huddle of people were beginning to gather, and ignoring the old woman as if she wasn't there, Tilly now lifted her chin and addressed them. 'Within the next few weeks, Mrs Ross and I will be opening a small school here.' She pointed back towards the cottage. 'If any amongst you wish your children to make the best of themselves, then they will be very welcome to send them to us. If, on the other hand, you wish them to remain in ignorance, then do as Mrs McGrath here says and keep them away. Once the school is open, it will be entirely up to you.' With this said, she took Ellen's elbow and led her towards the pony and trap as the villagers watched her open-mouthed. Mrs McGrath, meanwhile, snorted and stamped away up the road to her own cottage without so much as another word.

As the trap pulled away, Lily Lawrence was heard to say, 'Well, you have to hand it to her – the witch has got some guts, if nowt else!' A ripple of agreement moved through the crowd as they slowly dispersed.

The two women had gone some way beyond the village before Ellen could trust herself to speak again. 'I don't know why you have stayed around here, Tilly, knowing that the villagers feel about you as they do!' she said passionately.

Tilly grinned ruefully. 'Circumstances, lass. We don't always have a choice in these matters. I have come to accept that they will always look upon me as something of an oddity.'

Ellen crossed her arms across her small chest and frowned, and the rest of the journey home was made in thoughtful silence.

The sun was riding high in a sky full of powder-puff clouds when Tilly and Steve arrived at Felton Hall on the following Sunday afternoon. Ned helped Tilly down from the carriage before taking it round to the stable-block as Tilly and Steve mounted the impressive curved stone steps that led to an enormous oak door, and rang the bell. The sound of banging and hammering came to them from above even before the door was opened, and Steve raised a questioning eyebrow at Tilly. Within seconds the butler opened the door, telling them pleasantly, 'The master and mistress are expecting you. They instructed me to show you to the day room, madam.'

'Thank you, Bright.' Tilly handed him her bonnet and

then she and Steve followed him along the carpeted hallway. A young maid scurried past them, a smile on her face. In fact, the whole atmosphere of the place seemed to be lighter somehow, despite the din that was floating down the wide staircase. When the butler carefully opened the door of the day room, Tilly and Steve stopped dead in their tracks at the sight that met their eyes.

John was down on his hands and knees with a little dark-haired boy sitting astride his back, giggling uncontrollably. Anna was leaning forward from the edge of the chaise longue and she too was laughing. When she looked up and saw Tilly and Steve, she instantly rose to greet them with her arms outstretched.

'You're never going to believe what we've done,' she told them gaily.

'Oh, I think we will,' Tilly replied as she recognised the little fellow from the orphanage. Oh, it did her heart good to see them all so happy!

'We have decided to adopt Joseph,' Anna said proudly as she watched the antics of her husband and the child gambolling like spring lambs around the floor.

'It's wonderful news,' Steve said sincerely. 'He really is a beautiful child, Anna. He could be your own, with that shock of dark hair.'

'He *is* my own,' Anna retorted as colour flooded into her cheeks, then she laughed self-consciously again. 'Oh, you'll have to forgive me. The whole house seems to have been turned upside down in the last few days. We have men working on the nursery floor, as you no doubt heard when you came in, and Joseph already has the whole of the staff eating out of his hand, not to mention his new daddy.'

'I can see that,' Tilly beamed as Steve approached the new father and child for an introduction.

John lifted the boy onto his lap as Steve sat down at the side of them.

Although Tilly had instantly recognised Little Joe, he was so changed in the few days he had spent with Anna and John that she could scarcely believe it. Gone was the tiny dull-eyed boy they had found cowering in the corner, and in his place was a little chap whose eyes were alight with mischief. His hair had been washed and now sprang about his head in a halo of curls, and the clothes he was wearing would not have looked out of place on a little prince.

'Oh Anna, he really is so beautiful. I'm sure he's going to bring you both so much happiness,' Tilly told her sincerely.

'You don't look too surprised to see him here,' Anna remarked, and now Tilly chuckled as she told her, 'I would have been most surprised to arrive and *not* find him here. It was obvious from the moment that you set eyes on him in that dreadful place, that it was a case of love at first sight.'

'Then you must have seen it before I did, for it wasn't until we got home that I found I couldn't put him from my mind,' Anna admitted. Then her eyes twinkled as she went on, 'But Joseph wasn't the only one we brought home from the orphanage!'

Now at last she had the satisfaction of seeing Tilly's mouth gape in surprise. 'What? You mean you brought more than one child home with you?' she asked.

'Not a child exactly,' Anna giggled. 'Do you remember Miss Thomas – the young woman who showed us around the orphanage?'

'Yes. Yes, I do.'

'Well, it was whilst we were collecting Joseph that John and I got to thinking. We would need a nurserymaid, and who better than someone who Joseph already knew and trusted?'

'You mean you . . .'

'Yes, we brought Miss Thomas home with us too, though we call her Meg now. You'll meet her over tea before she takes Joseph for his bath. Oh Tilly, I can't even *begin* to tell you how happy we are. If only I had listened to you before, when you suggested we might adopt a child.'

'Better late than never,' Tilly smiled, and then forgetting all about Anna for now she hurried across to introduce herself to her new nephew.

That night as the carriage carried them homewards, she leaned her head contentedly against Steve's shoulder.

'Didn't I always tell you that Anna and John would make wonderful parents?' she sighed happily.

'Aye, you did, lass,' Steve chuckled. 'But I hope that Little Joe isn't going to make you go all broody?'

She punched him playfully in the arm. 'Give over with you. My days of bearing bairns are long past.' But then as her thoughts shifted to Sarah her mood became sombre. It might just be that she would have no choice but to raise yet another child as things stood at the minute.

Beth leaned Lucy forward and slipped a clean nightdress over her head, keeping her eyes averted from the missus's swollen stomach. She seemed to be weakening by the day, yet still she made no complaint, even when Beth was forced to administer the laudanum that the doctor had supplied for when the pain became too much to bear.

Settling her back against the pillows, Beth lifted the bowl and towel that she had just used for washing Lucy and turned to leave, when the sick woman asked feebly, 'Are you coping, hinny?'

'Oh aye, missus. Everythin' is ship-shape an' Bristol fashion!'

Lucy's eyes grew tender as she gazed on the girl who looked so ill herself. 'If it should get too much for you, Tilly has offered to send Gwen over to help you with the chores,' she told her.

'Aye, well, I'll bear it in mind, but fer now I'm managin' fine. I just wish . . .' As Beth's voice trailed away, Lucy looked at her inquisitively.

'You just wish what?'

'I just wish as there were more I could do fer you to ease your pain,' Beth told her in a trembling voice.

Lucy held out her hand and when Beth placed the tin bowl and coarse towel on a small table and crossed back to her, Lucy now took hers and squeezed it gently.

'My dear, I feel I have to say something to you and I hope that you won't take offence. You see, the thing is, Eddie loves you and until recently I had thought that you returned his feelings. Would I be right in thinking that?'

Beth's chin dropped to her chest as she nodded slowly.

'Then why is it that you suddenly seem to be holding him at arm's length?' Lucy asked urgently. 'Nothing would please me more than to see you two come together before—'

'That can never happen, missus,' Beth told her more sharply than she had intended as she snatched her hand away.

'But why? You have just admitted to me that you love him, so again I ask . . . *why* can't you come together?'

Resisting the urge to run from the room, Beth looked down on the face of this woman she had come to love as a mother. For a moment, she wrestled with her conscience. Then her shoulders suddenly sagged. 'I can't marry Eddie,' she told her in a low voice. 'Nor anyone else, for that matter . . . Ever.' Sinking onto the edge of the bed, she felt Lucy's hand settle gently on her arm and slowly she told her,

'I'm goin' to have a bairn.'

She waited for Lucy to storm at her but when she remained silent she dared to peep at her from the corner of her eye.

'I thought as much,' Lucy told her regretfully. 'I'm so sorry, pet. Now, I know you are a good girl, so I assume this is to do with the kidnapping you endured.'

Miserably, Beth nodded. There seemed no point in trying to hide it, nor yet deny it any longer. 'Aye,' she whispered, as tears started to flow. 'It happened when me an' Josefina were locked away in Jake Hammond's house. The night before Tilly an' Arthur came an' got us out, Nell – that's Jake's missus – came an' put me in another room . . . an' then . . . this man came an' . . . he forced me to . . .' She could go on no longer.

Lucy dragged herself up in the bed and took Beth in her arms, rocking the weeping girl to and fro as she felt her humiliation and pain. 'Why didn't you tell me before?' she asked tenderly.

Beth swiped a dewdrop from the end of her nose. 'I were too ashamed,' she snivelled.

'But why should *you* be ashamed? It is not as if you had gone willingly to this . . . this man. Though it is an insult to other men to class this rapist amongst them. I don't suppose he told you his name, did he?'

'No, he didn't. But I know what it was 'cos I heard Nell call him by it.' She cast her mind back to that terrible night. 'He were gentry,' she sighed. 'An' Nell called him Mr Rosier.'

Shock registered on Lucy's face. 'Are you quite sure of that, Beth?' she asked.

'Oh aye, I ain't likely to forget, am I? Not when he's left me wi' me belly full.'

'No, of course you're not,' Lucy soothed her, but her mind was working overtime. So, George Daniel Rosier had finally tired of his greedy, social-climbing wife, had he? No doubt Tilly would be interested to know of this latest development. But first she must help Beth, so what she said was, 'You need to talk to Eddie about the predicament you find yourself in, Beth. I'm sure he would understand.'

Beth now shot from the bed like a bullet from a gun, and hands on hips she told her, 'No! I don't want Eddie ever to find out. I couldn't bear it. He'd only take me then 'cos he felt sorry fer me. I was all fer runnin' away to the workhouse but then you took bad an' . . . I couldn't bring meself to leave you. But I will go if yer tell Eddie. Promise me that you won't!'

'But hinny, it can only be a matter of time before he notices,' Lucy pointed out. 'You can't hide something like this forever.'

Seeing the sense in what Lucy said, Beth nodded. 'I know that, missus. But just for now . . . can we go on as we are? We'll have to cross the next bridge when we come to it.'

Somewhat reluctantly, Lucy agreed. 'Very well then. But you *must* slow down. It's not good for someone in your condition to work as hard as you do.'

'Huh! Every night afore I go to sleep I pray that I'll lose this.' The girl stabbed a finger towards her belly and her voice was full of venom now as she said, 'If work could make me shift it then I'd gladly work till I dropped. An' every single night I promise meself I'll have me revenge on the bugger that give it to me. An' I will an' all, you just wait an' see! I know that Jake Hammond an' his missus will get their comeuppance next week when the case comes to court. But Rosier! Well, one way or another I'll bring him down 'cos he's ruined me life. When I met your Eddie I knew straight off that he were the one fer me, but that will never be now. An' if I can't have Eddie then I'll have no one.'

Lucy closed her eyes as she heard the hurt in the girl's voice, and she who had never been known to curse, found herself thinking, Life can be a cruel bugger at times. Oh aye, there is no doubt about it!

Chapter Twenty-Seven

I T WAS THE second week in August when the weather finally broke and the heavens seemed to open. The ground was so parched that for a time the rain lay in great pools on the lawns before it slowly began to soak in. There was still no sign of Josefina or Willy returning, although they had sent postcards to say that they were well and enjoying themselves. The week before, the newspapers had been full of the trial of Nell and Jake Hammond, who had been sentenced to ten years' hard labour each for their part in transporting young girls abroad to be sold into prostitution. Tilly could muster no pity for them, for every time she thought of how dangerously close Josefina and Beth had come to suffering that fate, she had the urge to be sick. Of course, the village had been agog with the news, but that was no more than she had expected so it did not really trouble her. Now her thoughts were on other matters, for today was the day when she and Ellen planned to open the doors of the village school for the very first time.

Taking a last glance in the long cheval mirror in her bedroom she nodded with satisfaction. Her snow-white hair was coiled neatly on the top of her head and she had chosen to wear a plain bombazine dress that she felt was fitting for the day ahead. Making her way down to the dining room, she found Ellen waiting for her, her eyes alight with excitement.

'Oh, Tilly, it's quite exciting, isn't it?' she gushed.

'Don't speak too soon. We don't know if anyone is going to turn up yet,' Tilly said.

'Oh, of course they will,' Ellen said confidently. 'Even the villagers wouldn't be fool enough to make their children miss out on free education.'

'Well, we'll soon find out, won't we?' Lifting a pile of books that Mr Burgess had once used to teach Matthew, Luke, John and Jessie Anne, in the nursery above them, Tilly now strode into the hall. 'Come along then,' she grinned. 'We may as well go and get the first day over with.'

'Ned has pulled the carriage round to the door for you, madam,' Peabody informed her as he slipped a long cape over each woman's shoulders. 'It is unfortunate that the weather should have chosen today to break when you both have to make the journey into the village.'

'I've been out in far worse, Peabody, but thank you for your concern.' The words had barely left her lips when Fanny appeared from the kitchen door with a broad smile on her face. 'Eeh, Tilly, you look every inch the schoolmarm,' she declared, highly amused.

Sheltering the precious books beneath her cape, Tilly ran lightly down the steps with Ellen close on her heels. Once they were in the carriage and Ned had slammed the door they both shook off the hoods of their capes and grinned at each other.

'Perhaps the weather will work to our advantage?' Tilly said.

'What do you mean?'

'Ask yourself. If you were stuck in a poky cottage with a herd of children under your feet, would you not be glad to get them out of the way for a time?'

As they gazed out at the drenched landscape, the two women made the rest of the journey in silence, concentrating on keeping on their seats as the carriage slithered along the muddy road.

The sight that met them when they pulled up outside the schoolhouse wiped the smiles from their faces immediately, for the doors were wide open to the weather and the small leaded windows were hanging off their hinges.

Tilly almost spilled out of the carriage as she ran the short distance to the room that they had spent the whole of the day before preparing. The small tables and chairs were overturned, some of them smashed to smithereens, and the chalks and the pencils that they had lovingly laid out were snapped in two and scattered across the waterlogged floor. Even the bookcase had been ripped from the wall and the books that it had contained now floated on the muddy water that was seeping into the room by the minute. Ellen had picked a bunch of dog daisies and cowslips the morning before and stood them in a jar on the windowsill, and as she saw them now floating amongst the debris on the schoolroom floor she clapped her hand across her mouth. Tears sprang to her eyes, whilst Tilly could only stand and stare at the devastation before her. And then she muttered two words and the way she said them struck terror into Ellen's heart.

'*Mrs McGrath!*'

'Oh no! No, surely even *she* would not be so cruel as to do such a thing.'

'I assure you, Ellen, if she thought it would hurt me, she would,' Tilly told her, grim-faced.

Ned had come to join them and he scratched his head in bewilderment at the scene of destruction. His voice heavy with distress, he said, 'Come on, ladies. Let me get you home.

I don't know why you even bother to try and help this lot down here.'

But Tilly tossed her head, fumbled with the clasp of her cape and once she had managed to undo it she then hung it on the row of little coat-hooks that the carpenter had fashioned and rolled her sleeves up with an air of determination. Ellen and Ned looked on open-mouthed.

'Wh . . . what are you doin'?' Ned stuttered.

'I'm doing what needs to be done, of course. I came here to open a village school and that's exactly what I shall do. You don't think I'm going to let that wicked old woman beat me, do you?' As she spoke, Tilly was righting one of the overturned chairs and then with a tone of authority in her voice, she said, 'Ned, would you mind collecting the books together? Lay them on the floor of the coach as carefully as you can and when I get home I'll see what may be salvageable. Fanny might be able to dry out those that are still intact in the kitchen for me.'

There was a light of admiration in his eyes now as he bent to do as she asked, and now Tilly addressed Ellen. 'Go back with Ned,' she instructed her. 'And perhaps you could call in at the mine? Steve will be there and I'd like you to ask him if he would send the men back down here to do the repairs to the furniture and the windows.'

'I'll do no such thing,' Ellen snapped indignantly and now she too was removing her cape. 'We started this together and we'll put it to rights together!'

Two hours later, the schoolroom was once again tidy. They had managed to fix the bookshelves back to the wall and righted the furniture, removing the broken items. They had then mopped the floor, and now the workmen had arrived and were busily repairing the windows and any furniture that had been damaged but was still usable. And still the rain was coming down with no sign of ceasing, to run in muddy torrents along the hard-packed earth lane outside the door.

'There y'are then, missus,' a tall lanky workman called Ted Baker informed her. 'That's yer windows all fixed up good as new.' He pulled one closed as he spoke and wiped the rain from his face.

Tilly flashed him a grateful smile. 'Thank you. I do appreciate you coming so promptly. I dare say you'll be going back to work on the cottage now, won't you?'

'Aye, we will,' he nodded. 'Though it's all but done now. Sayin' that, every time we get to this stage, that man o' yourn comes up wi' sommat else as he wants doin'. I were only sayin' to the lads the other day, if the place grows much bigger it'll be a match fer the Manor.'

He chuckled as Tilly smiled at him before asking, 'I dare say you wouldn't say no to a nice cup of tea before you go, would you?'

'Eeh, you're not wrong there, missus,' he agreed eagerly.

Crossing to the little stove in the corner, Tilly struck a match and lit the gas and then after placing the kettle on it she looked around with satisfaction.

The workman's face was solemn now as he twisted his cap before suggesting, 'It might not be a bad idea to let me fit a nice stout padlock on the door fer you, missus. At least it would deter whoever did this from doin' the same again.'

'I think that's an excellent idea,' Ellen agreed as she placed some fresh flowers back on the windowsill.

Tilly had no time to answer, for just then a dark shadow blocked out the light from the open doorway and they glanced up to see a bent figure with a sack across its head and shoulders to keep out the rain.

'So, the openin' o' yer school got delayed then, did it?' Mrs McGrath chortled with glee.

'Only temporarily,' Tilly informed her calmly. 'That is, unless you intend to burn it down next as you did my grandparents' cottage?'

Mrs McGrath glowered at her before suddenly turning about and splashing away through the deep puddles back the way she had come.

Tilly was standing with her hands tightly entwined at her waist, but then as Mrs McGrath disappeared into the driving rain, she turned and began to prepare the tea without so much as another word. And as the workmen and Ellen looked towards her they found themselves admiring her courage and dignity all the more. Many women might have flown at the old crone for what she had done, and they could have been excused for it; yet Tilly had somehow managed to belittle the ancient harridan with a mouthful of words.

As Ted Baker was to tell the men in the Royal Arms later that night when he was sitting with a well-earned tankard of ale in his hand, 'She is certainly some lady!' and no one argued with him.

That evening, as Tilly and Steve were placing yet more of Mr Burgess's books onto the bookshelves in the now completed library at the cottage, Tilly could not fail to notice that Steve was unnaturally quiet, so after a time she asked him, 'Is something troubling you, pet?'

'Aye it is, lass.' He ran his hand through his hair in the manner she had come to love as she looked into his troubled eyes. 'It's me ma. I can't believe what lengths she'll stoop to, to hurt yer, Tilly. It . . . it's frightenin'. I thought once our Hal were gone she'd let bygones be bygones, but it looks like I were wrong.'

'I can cope with your mother,' Tilly told him confidently as she took his hands in hers and gently entwined her fingers with his, but his face remained solemn. There was a bad feeling on him that he couldn't seem to shake, and the nearer it got to their wedding, the worse it became.

'Look, this is only a suggestion, but why don't yer let Ellen run the schoolhouse on her own fer a while?' he said tentatively. 'I know this is somethin' you wanted to do together, but the thing is . . . Well, there's more chance o' the village folk lettin' their bairns go along if Ellen is there on her own, ain't there? Just fer a time at least. Will you think on what I've said?'

'Yes, yes I will, Steve,' she told him sorrowfully. She had so looked forward to this venture, but after today she was forced to admit that if she were present in the schoolroom, just as Steve had said, the villagers might never let their children attend, and then all that work would have been for nothing.

There was a teasing note in his voice now when he told her, 'You'll have to busy yourself up here instead. The new furniture we ordered from Newcastle is arrivin' tomorrow, an' no doubt you'll want to be here when it arrives so as you can tell the men where you want it puttin', lass.'

Her face was lighter now as she nodded in agreement. 'Yes, you're right. I can hardly leave it up to you, can I? Or I just might find the bed in the parlour.'

He had his arms tight about her as they walked back into the kitchen where the kettle was singing on the hob, and as she hurried to make his tea she asked him, 'So, how are things going at the mine?'

'Not too bad. At least, I've managed to get all the shafts reopened and the men back to work . . . but you know, Tilly, I wonder how long we can keep it going now. Some o' the seams are dryin' up, an' should we have another flood, well . . . I don't need to tell you this weather doesn't help.' He looked at the rain lashing against the windows. The recent dry spell had gone a long way to enabling the men to pump the water from the flooded shafts, but if this rain kept up, the river would rise again and they could end up back at square one. 'Why don't you and Willy consider Rosier's offer?' he said gently. 'I know you've no time fer the man an' nor have I, fer that matter, but he seems keen to acquire it, and as I've told you before, I could put the money into Jim Coleman's steelworks an' probably double it in no time for you both.'

'I do realise that, Steve, but I have no need to tell you how badly Rosier treats his workers. Added to that, he would probably only offer Willy and me a fraction of what the mine is worth, if I know him – particularly now he is aware of the problems we have had there recently.' She was carefully measuring two spoonsful of tea into a brown earthenware teapot as she spoke. Once she had mashed it, she then began to unpack the basket that Fanny had prepared for them, and Steve rubbed his stomach as he gazed down on the feast. There was a large, fresh-baked rabbit pie, which just happened to be one of his favourites, and griddle-cakes that he would smother in butter fresh from the dairy.

'Ellen make this, did she?' he asked as he helped himself to a large slice of pie.

'Yes, she did, though Fanny still does the main part of the kitchen work. I really don't know what I'd do without her.' Tilly was now pouring milk into two mugs but her hand suddenly became still and her eyes twinkled as she told him on a happier note, 'Anna and John spent the afternoon at Brook Farm yesterday. Oh, you should have seen Joseph and Sarah together. They get into all sorts of mischief and absolutely adore each other. Anna and John have taken Joseph to a doctor in Durham who is going to have a special built-up boot made that will bring his crippled leg on a level with the other. It will be wonderful for him to walk without that lopsided gait, won't it?'

'Aye it will, but how is Lucy?' he now asked.

Tilly shrugged. 'Holding her own, though she rarely gets out of bed any more. I don't know what she would do without Beth. She's been an absolute treasure.'

'And are things back to normal with Beth and Eddie?'

'It didn't appear so, not while I was there at least. I feel like banging their heads together because it's obvious that they love each other.'

He chuckled. 'Well, you know what they say, the course of true love never runs smooth – and it was certainly the case with us, wasn't it?'

'Yes, it was,' she told him regretfully. 'But we'll be remedying that in just a few short weeks, won't we?'

An involuntary shudder ran up Steve's spine as a picture of his mother's malicious face flashed in front of his eyes, and he found himself thinking, Oh, please, dear God, let it be so this time! For he knew in his heart that if anything should happen to keep them apart yet again, it would be the death of him.

It had now been raining for a solid week, with no let-up, and whereas through the dry spell the rivers and the wells had shown signs of drying up, they were now full to overflowing.

Ellen was down in the village in the schoolhouse, for Tilly had thought on Steve's wise words and decided to keep away for a time. Even so, as yet only one child had turned up. Tilly found it very disappointing, but Ellen remained optimistic. 'Where there is one, others will follow,' she had declared confidently, and so Tilly left her to it. She herself was spending a lot of time up at the cottage, and with every day that passed it was beginning to look more and more like home. Only yesterday she had hung red velvet drapes at the windows in the parlour, and they had instantly given the room a cosy feel. The library was all but finished and set out just as she wanted it to be, and she was really looking forward to the time when she and Steve would be living there.

She was working on the accounts in the library at the Manor when a commotion in the hallway outside caught her attention. Laying down her pen on the large mahogany desk, she hurried from the room and was thrilled to see Peabody taking Willy's and Josefina's coats from them. Completely forgetting herself, she ran down the hallway and then they were all laughing at once as they clung together in a warm embrace.

'Oh, I've missed you both so much. You look so well – have you had a wonderful time?' she cried as she held her children close. She really had no need to ask, for they were both positively glowing, especially Josefina. Tilly thought her daughter had never looked more beautiful.

'Oh, we had a *marvellous* time,' Willy assured her. 'But come into the morning room, Mama, and we'll tell you all about it. And Biddle, I could kill for one of your lovely cups of tea.'

'Straight away, sir,' Biddle told him, hurrying away with a happy gleam in his eye. It seemed that everyone was smiling, and as Tilly walked between her two children into the day room, she could hardly take her eyes off them.

There was a roaring fire in the grate to combat the cold, damp weather, and lifting the poker she stabbed at the coals before telling them across her shoulder, 'I was surprised when I received your last postcard informing me that you were in Scotland! I thought you were going to the Lake District?'

'Oh, we did, Mama,' Willy assured her. 'But then we decided to move further north.'

'Well, the holiday has obviously done you both a power of good,' Tilly smiled. 'I can't remember ever seeing you both look so very well.'

They were sitting side-by-side on the settee and Tilly was happy to see that they were once more totally at ease with each other.

When Biddle trundled a laden tea-trolley into the room a few minutes later, Tilly began pouring the tea out, all the while aware of them exchanging loving glances.

'So,' she asked innocently, 'did anything exciting happen whilst you were away?' As she turned to press a china cup and saucer into Willy's outstretched hand she was surprised to see a deep blush spread across his cheeks.

'Yes, Mama. As a matter of fact, it did.' He seemed slightly ill at ease now and Tilly noticed that Josefina had hung her head.

'Then come along and tell me all about it,' she encouraged as she now passed a cup to Josefina. However, what Willy said next caused her own tea to slop over the side of her cup and into her saucer as he blurted out, 'Look, Mama, whilst we were away, Josefina and I . . . Well, we were married. At Gretna Green.'

Her mouth gaped. She must have been hearing things! But no, as her eyes fell on the third finger of Josefina's left hand, she saw a plain gold wedding band nestling there, and knew that what her son had told her was true.

The silence seemed to stretch between them as Willy and Josefina both held their breath, wondering what her reaction would be. And then Tilly clumsily slid the cup and saucer back onto the trolley and fumbled in her sleeve for her handkerchief.

'Oh, Mama, *please* don't be upset!' Willy exclaimed as he leaped from his seat and placed his arm around her waist.

'I . . . I'm not upset. J . . . just surprised,' Tilly stuttered, noisily blowing her nose.

'I assure you, we had no intentions of doing this when we set off,' Willy said hastily. 'But then when we thought about it, this seemed to be the easiest way. In fact, the only way. We three know, Mama, that Josefina and I are brother and sister on paper only. But an English church would never have let us take our vows.'

'That's true,' Tilly tearfully admitted. 'The whole place will be a hotbed of gossip as it is when the news gets out. But what I have to say is, I am pleased for you, for I realised long ago that you were made for each other. I . . . I wish you well and you have my blessing. Now come here, the pair of you, and let me give you both a hug.'

And so Mr and Mrs Sopwith did just that!

Chapter Twenty-Eight

URING THE AFTERNOON that followed, Tilly came to realise just how deeply Willy and Josefina cared for each other, for they could barely take their eyes off one another and their hands were constantly joined, just as newlyweds should be. Only once did the smile slip from Josefina's face, and that was when Tilly told her of Lucy's illness.

'So what will happen to Sarah when Lucy is gone?' she had asked coldly, and a bad feeling settled in the pit of Tilly's stomach.

'I . . . I had rather thought that seeing as Willy is her father, that he would take charge of her here.' It was something that had to be said. Josefina had looked away through the window, to the rain that was pouring down outside, and her face had set into a mask.

Not wishing to spoil their homecoming, Tilly had quickly changed the subject. She knew that for Josefina, any issue involving the Bentwood family and Willy's relationship with Noreen would always make her prickly. A kindly girl at heart, her passionate jealousy always got the better of her where Willy was concerned. But there would be time to discuss this on another day.

'I think you two should move into the master bedroom,' Tilly decided. 'I shall go and ask Fanny to prepare it and light a fire for you in there straight away.'

And now she was standing in the doorway of that very room and her heart was sad as she pictured Mark Sopwith, her first lover and the father of Willy, lying there in the great four-poster bed so many years ago, enduring the life of an invalid after the mine disaster in which he and Tilly were trapped underground in rising water for three long days. The room had never been slept in since the day he died, but tonight, Willy, who had been conceived in love in that very bed, would lie in his late father's place. It felt strangely fitting, somehow.

The rest of the day was spent in transferring Willy's and Josefina's clothes to their new room and so it was that as the evening darkened, Tilly made her way to the kitchen. Fanny was sitting at the table chatting with Ellen.

'So how's the honeymooners then?' Fanny asked with a cheeky grin.

'Do you know, Fanny, that's just what I've come to see you about,' Tilly replied. 'I was wondering, would you mind taking Steve's basket over to the cottage while I carry on helping them to get settled into their new room? I'm sure Steve won't mind if you explain to him what's happened. I'll get Ned to take you in the carriage, seeing as it's such a filthy night.'

Fanny smiled good-naturedly. 'I don't mind doin' that at all, but you can forget about the carriage. A drop o' rain never hurt anybody. But if you've no objection, Tilly, I'll borrow that nice thick cape o' yours. It'll be warmer than mine an' there's a hood on it.'

'Of course you can. And thanks.' Without quite knowing

why, Tilly suddenly bent to plant a kiss on the other woman's plump cheek.

'Whatever were that for?' Fanny laughed as she glowed with pleasure.

'I'm not sure – probably because I'm feeling happy and I know how lucky I am to have you. But promise me you'll mind how you go. It's like a quagmire once you get beyond the copse.'

'Oh, get off wi' you. I've walked through worse than this,' Fanny said, and so Tilly flashed her a final smile and hurried back upstairs to help with the move. And as she went, she was thinking, Oh, it's been a grand day! The people beyond these walls might have no time for her, but here she was surrounded with love and kindness, there was no doubt about it!

As well as the driving rain, the wind had now also risen, and it was all Fanny could do to stay upright as she concentrated on putting one foot in front of another. She was clutching the basket to her with one hand, and trying to keep the hood of Tilly's cape from blowing off her head with the other as she struggled along the sodden lawns in the direction of the copse. At least in there the trees would provide her with some shelter from the rain, she thought. She was proved to be right, for once she was beneath the overhanging branches, the rain at least was no longer lashing into her face, though the wind was whistling through the trees making a sound like a banshee. Added to this it was very dark, for the rain had obscured the moon.

Normally, Fanny would have made this trip with her eyes shut, but tonight for some reason she found herself glancing nervously into the blackness that had settled around her more surely than the cape she was wearing. She moved on, her eyes going constantly from left to right until at last she saw a break in the darkness up ahead, which told her that she was almost at the edge of the gorge. If she took the path that ran along the top of it she would be up on the coach road and at Steve's cottage in no time, then she could hurry back to her own warm kitchen with a clear conscience. A fox suddenly shot out in front of her and startled her so much that she almost dropped the basket containing Steve's evening meal. Me boyo wouldn't have liked that, she thought to herself with a grin, as she paused to allow her heart to settle back into a steadier rhythm.

She had almost reached the break in the trees when she thought she heard something behind her. Stopping again, she peered back over her shoulder from under the hood of the cloak, which was pulled down over her face as far as it would go. There was nothing, and thinking that it must have been just another night animal on the prowl for its supper, she shrugged and lifted her foot to go on again. It was then that an arm suddenly caught her around the throat and lifted her bodily from the ground. The basket went flying, scattering Steve's supper into the muddy puddles that had soaked into the bottom of her dress. She opened her mouth to scream, but the arm that had tight hold of her was constricting the air and she had the sensation of suffocating. Anger took over from her fright and she began to lash out blindly with her arms and legs. And it was then that she felt herself falling to the ground with her attacker on top of her. The fall momentarily winded her, but then as the hold on her throat loosened she opened her mouth to scream and this time it echoed around the surrounding countryside.

'What the 'ell do you think you're pl—'

The words stopped abruptly as she felt something cold

suddenly plunge into her chest, chasing the air from her lungs. She was so shocked that for a moment she could do nothing. Then as her fingers found their way beneath the cloak, they closed around the handle of what appeared to be a knife and she realised that she had been stabbed. With a superhuman strength, she rose to her feet, and with the hood fallen away, she faced her attacker. The eyes of murderer and victim met in a stare of mutual horror, and then, as the cold rain fell on her face, a strange sort of warmth stole over her and she felt her eyelids, and her knees, begin to droop. And then she knew no more.

It was now gone ten o'clock. The newlyweds had retired some time ago, but Tilly could not rest until Fanny was safely home. She looked at the clock on the mantelshelf and there was this strange feeling on her again that usually warned her when something was wrong. Fanny should have been home hours ago, even allowing time for her to stay for a chat with Steve. Tilly stamped along the hallway to the kitchen and when she walked in, Peabody, who was enjoying a pipe at the side of the fire, made to rise.

'It's all right, you needn't get up,' Tilly assured him, and then, 'Is Fanny still not back?'

Gwen was sitting darning by the light of the lamp at the table and it was she who answered. 'No, she ain't, ma'am.'

Ellen had long since gone to bed with a headache, but Arthur and Jimmy were in the middle of a game of cards on the other side of the table, and with a trace of concern in his voice, Arthur asked, 'What time did she leave, Gwen?'

'Ooh, now let me see . . . 'twould have been about sixish.'

'*Sixish?* She could have been there and back half a dozen times by now!' Rising from the table, Arthur started to shrug his muscular arms into the sleeves of his work coat. 'I'll just go an' have a scout round an' see if there's a sign of her,' he told Tilly. 'The ground is that slippy underfoot she could have fallen an' twisted her ankle or sommat, an' not been able to get home.'

'I'll come wi' you, man,' Jimmy volunteered, and the two brothers made their way to the door together as Gwen pressed a lantern into Arthur's hand.

'I'll come with you too,' Tilly told them, feeling worried and guilty, but they both rounded on her.

'You'll do no such thing,' Arthur said. 'It's hardly fit weather for a dog to be out in this! I've no doubt we'll find her up at the cottage wi' Steve. You know what a chatterbox our Fanny can be. She's probably got talkin' an' just lost track o' time.'

Once the two men had disappeared into the black night, Gwen pushed the kettle into the heart of the fire. 'We'll have us a nice cup o' tea while we wait for 'em to get back, eh?' she suggested kindly.

'What? Oh . . . yes, that would be very nice. Thank you, Gwen.' Tilly wished with all her heart that she'd insisted on Ned taking Fanny there and back.

The minutes ticked away until suddenly, some time later, the kitchen door flew open, sending the flames on the fire leaping up the chimney. Jimmy staggered into the room, his sodden coat leaving puddles on the floor. His hair was plastered to his head and his boots were caked with mud, but it was his eyes that struck terror into Tilly's heart, for they were wide and full of panic.

'Peabody, Biddle – I need you to come with me,' he said gruffly. 'We've to get an old door from the stable an' take it back to Arthur. We . . . we've found Fanny!'

'Is she all right?' Tilly's voice was shaking, but Jimmy didn't stop to answer her, for he was already heading back out into the pelting rain. Peabody and Biddle grabbed their coats and pulled their boots on before rushing off to join him, leaving Tilly and Gwen to stare after them with fear on their faces.

It was then that Tilly's head bounced on her shoulders and she declared, 'It's no good, I can't just stand about here doing nothing. I'm going with them!'

'But, ma'am, you can't go out in this,' Gwen objected, but her words fell on deaf ears. Tilly was already snatching up a cape.

'Get some water on and plenty of it,' she flung across her shoulder. 'If she's had an accident, she'll be cold when we get her back and we'll need to warm her up.' Gwen chewed on her lip and wrung her hands as she watched her mistress disappear into the black night.

It was almost an hour later when Gwen heard the weary procession making their way back across the yard. Hoisting a lamp high, she went outside to see the men at each corner of a door, on which lay Fanny's still figure. Tilly was walking at the side of them holding tight to Fanny's hand, but something about the sight made a shiver run up Gwen's spine.

It took the men some time to manoeuvre the door into the room but at last they managed it and laid it across the table, which Gwen had cleared in readiness for their return.

Lifting the bowl of hot water she had ready, in preparation for stripping and washing her friend, she asked tremulously, 'Why ain't Fanny movin'?'

Tilly said not a word as she gently undid the cloak beneath Fanny's chin and then as it fell open, Gwen gasped with dismay as she saw the knife that was protruding from her chest.

'She's gone,' Tilly muttered dully.

'Bu . . . but who would do this?' Gwen was crying now as she looked down on the still face of the plump and pretty woman who had shown her nothing but kindness since the day she had stepped into the house.

'I don't know, but I have a pretty good idea.' Tilly grasped the knife-handle, and with a quick twist she jerked it from Fanny's chest as her life's blood flowed across her fingers. Then turning to the men, who were all openly crying, she told them, 'When dawn breaks, you'll have to ride into Jarrow and fetch the Constable. In the meantime, you'd better go and get changed into some dry clothes. There'll be no sleep for any of us tonight. Now please leave us. Gwen and I are going to lay Fanny out.' There was a catch in her voice as one by one they all bowed their heads and trooped in file from the room.

Turning back to Fanny, Tilly then steeled herself to do the last kindness she would ever perform for this dear woman who she had for many long years looked upon as a sister. Gwen helped her to cut free the clothes, then together they washed every inch of her body from top to bottom, placing a pad over the ugly wound. Once she was clean, Tilly and Gwen slipped one of Tilly's own fine lawn nightdresses across her head and settled it around her. Then Tilly released Fanny's long greying hair from its clips and brushed it till it shone, before twisting it into two long plaits. She placed pennies on the closed eyes and finally she crossed Fanny's arms across her still chest. And in that moment she knew without a doubt that the knife that had killed her much-loved friend had really been intended for herself.

'You daft bugger you! It were supposed to be the witch yer were out for, not the Drew woman!' Mrs McGrath's voice grated on the nerves of the man who was cowering at the side of the fire.

'I thought she were the witch!' he cried, with a trace of panic in his voice. 'She had Trotter's cape on, so how were I supposed to know as it weren't her, the silly bitch?'

Mrs McGrath hobbled to the window and looked up and down the village street as she had a hundred times already that morning. Dawn was breaking and all was deserted. 'You'll have to get yerself away,' she told him. 'It'll be only a matter o' time afore the pollis come here, knowin' how I feel about that 'un up there. If they do come an' catch you here then yer'll be fer the noose as sure as eggs is eggs.'

Randy Simmons began to tremble. 'But where will I go?'

She tossed her head, keen now to get him out of her cottage. ''Ow should I know? Why don't you get yerself aboard a ship? You might be a bit long in the tooth but they're always glad o' men to work down in the engine room stokin' the boilers.'

It sounded like hard work and Randy shuddered at the thought of it. He was afeared of the sea – allus had been. But then what other option was open to him now? As old Mother McGrath had said, if he stayed here, he would end up dangling from a rope on the gallows.

Lifting his meagre bundle from the table, he crept towards the door. 'Is it all clear?'

Again her eyes travelled up and down the road before she nodded. 'Aye, it is. Now get yerself away – an' if you have any sense you'll not show yer face round here again.'

He slipped from the room without a word, and once she had watched him scurry away, Mrs McGrath then returned mumbling and grumbling to her fireside, where she cursed the day the idiot had been born. How could he have got it so wrong? Not that the loss of a Drew counted. Hand in glove with the witch, they'd been, for many a long year, and they deserved everything they got. Still, the fact that he had murdered the wrong woman meant that the witch was still walking. But she would have her day with that one! Oh, aye, if it were the last thing she ever did, Bella McGrath would make sure that Tilly Trotter got her comeuppance.

Once again the village was up in arms. Fanny Drew had been stabbed to death, but worse than that, rumour had it that Tilly Trotter's bastards had gone off on holiday together and had come home as man and wife! It made any decent person sick to even think of it – and how could it be allowed, they asked. Surely it was incest for a half-brother and sister to wed? But then, it was no more than they could have expected from the likes of them up at the Manor. It was a den of vice and it seemed that the witch made her own rules up as she went along. After all, hadn't she borne the bastard to the master up at the Manor after acting as his wife for years? And then when he had died, what had she done? She had only run off and married Matthew, the master's son, with the latter barely cold in his grave, too. Ugh, it hardly bore thinking about, and now her children were dabbling in debauchery too!

Someone had heard that the parson was conducting the burial service for Fanny Drew. Now *there* would be a farce if ever there was one, they muttered. But of course, they still had every intention of being there. It was common knowledge that the police had paid a visit to old Mrs McGrath, but seeing as she was still in her cottage as far as they knew, it couldn't have been her that had done it, could it? That only left Randy Simmons, and as he seemed to have suddenly vanished off the face of the earth, yes, he must have been the murderer, and if so, good luck to him, they said. It was just a crying shame that it hadn't been the witch he had stabbed, for if ever there was a bad 'un that roamed the earth, 'twas she!

Anna and John broke the news of Fanny's death, and of Willy and Josefina's marriage to Lucy, on their next visit to Brook Farm, and the sick woman was so stunned that for a time she was speechless.

'How is she taking it?' she eventually asked when she'd had time to digest their news.

'Badly,' Anna told her. 'I think Tilly looked upon Fanny as a sister and she is struggling to come to terms with her death.'

'Aye, I can believe that,' Lucy said faintly. 'And fancy Willy and Josefina getting wed. Life is a funny thing at times, isn't it? Not so long ago, he and our Noreen had eyes only for each other, and now here we are, with Noreen dead and buried and Willy married to the lass who has been brought up as his sister.'

Anna bowed her head, as grief washed over her. It couldn't be easy for Lucy. The black mood was broken just then when Joseph came tottering into the room with Sarah crawling in hot pursuit after him.

'Mama, Mama,' he cried, and laughing, Anna swung him up into her arms as Sarah squatted at her feet. She now bent to lift Sarah too and with one on each arm she told them fondly, 'Oh, you two! There's no stopping you when you get together, is there?'

'How is Joseph settling with you?' Lucy now asked.

'Oh, I can't remember what it was like without him now.' Anna placed both children back on the floor and laughed when they immediately began to chase each other again. Then turning back to Lucy she asked, 'And how are you feeling?'

'Oh, I can't complain,' Lucy told her, although Anna was very aware that she had just cause to.

'I just worry about what will happen to Sarah when I . . .' Her voice trailed away as a look of deep sadness settled across her features.

Drawing Lucy's thin hands into her strong, warm ones, Anna now told her, 'You musn't worry about her. There are more than enough people who love her to ensure that she will be well taken care of.'

'Yes, yes, I know, and Tilly has promised to take care of all that, but still . . .' The conversation was abruptly halted when Beth entered the room carrying a tray, on which were two mugs and a plateful of fresh-baked lardy cakes.

'Come on, missus.' Her words were brisk yet said with a wealth of affection. 'You know what the doctor ordered. A little an' often, so let's see you get at least one o' these down you, please!'

'Yes, Miss Bossy Boots.' Lucy heaved herself up onto her pillows, then addressing Anna, she asked, 'Do you hear how she speaks to me?'

'I hear,' Anna laughed as the girl turned to leave the room with a cheeky smile on her face, taking the little ones with her to give them a cup of milk and a homemade ginger biscuit.

They drank their tea in silence for a while until Lucy then asked, 'So how are things going up at the mine now? When I spoke to Tilly a few days ago she was telling me that Steve was concerned about the possibility of it flooding again.'

'That's true, unfortunately,' Anna said, solemn once more. 'Between you and me, I think Steve has had enough of it now. He must feel as if he's fighting a losing battle. In fact, I believe he's trying to get Tilly to sell it to Mr Rosier.'

The mention of the man's name brought colour creeping into Lucy's cheeks as she thought back to what Beth had told her. Perhaps it was time to have a word with Tilly? As she sipped at her tea she decided that was exactly what she would do, and at the earliest opportunity.

Chapter Twenty-Nine

F ANNY DREW WAS laid to rest in the village churchyard in the first week in September. The rain was coming down in sheets, and the needle-sharp drops mingled with the tears on the cheeks of the mourners. At one point, one of the villagers was heard to say that it was a wonder as Tilly hadn't slid into the grave with her, for the ground was so muddy that the mourners could barely stand.

In the days leading up to the burial, Fanny had laid in the drawing room in a fine oak coffin. It was the best that money could buy, it was rumoured, for Tilly would settle for nothing less. Four matching black horses with enormous black feather plumes on their proud heads had drawn the glass hearse containing Fanny's body on her final journey to the church, and the villagers had remarked that they had seen nothing like it since the death of the master up at the Manor.

Once again, Tilly had gone against tradition when she insisted on attending the funeral to say her goodbyes. And so it was that she now stood shoulder to shoulder with Arthur and Jimmy at the side of the grave, the only woman present. Peabody, Biddle, Willy, Ned, Eddie and Steve were also there, and they stood with their heads respectfully bowed as the parson intoned the solemn words of the funeral service.

The villagers meanwhile stood in a saturated little huddle at the lych-gate, longing to be back in the warmth of their cottages, yet afraid that they might miss something.

And then at last it was done and the mourners were walking towards them. The villagers parted to let them pass, and for some long time afterwards, the expression on Tilly's face would be talked about, for her eyes when she looked upon them were brimming with raw hatred. The only consolation she had was the fact that Fanny had been laid to rest in consecrated ground, just as she deserved to be.

'So, what do you think of it now?' Ellen turned to look at Arthur who was stacking the soaked logs he had just chopped into a neat pile on the side of the hearth.

As his eyes followed hers to the pretty flowered curtains she had just hung at the cottage windows his face broke into a smile. 'I think they look lovely,' he told her as he crossed to take her into his arms. 'Gwen made a grand job of making them up. We're just about all done now, ain't we?'

She nodded as her eyes played about the cosy little room. The furniture was set out and the colourful peg rugs she had made lent warmth to the stoneflagged floor. The dresser that stood against one wall was stacked with china that Tilly had insisted she should take from the Manor, and the chairs at the side of the roaring fire were now newly padded and covered with the same material as the curtains.

'Right then, so when are you goin' to make an honest man o' me then?' he now asked teasingly.

'I thought we'd agreed to wait until after Tilly and Steve were married next month?'

'Aye, I believe we did. But ask yerself, does it make any sense? I just happened to pass through Allendale the other day when I picked that lass up that Tilly has set on in the kitchen, an' I happened to notice they have a lovely little church there. It got me to thinkin', why don't we just sneak away an' get wed quietly, as Willy an' Josefina did? 'Twould feel more respectful-like to our Fanny, too.' Arthur was still broken-hearted by the loss of his much-loved sister.

Taken by surprise, Ellen chewed on her lip. What Arthur was suggesting actually made a lot of sense, for as he had quite rightly pointed out, the cottage was ready and waiting for them now. And the church in Allendale *did* sound appealing, for there was no way that she would want to get married in their own village church.

'If I agreed to it, and I say *if* . . . would you have any objection to Tilly and Steve coming along to the service to act as witnesses?' she enquired.

'None at all.' He grinned as he saw her softening to the idea, then he went on persuasively, 'Just think of it – I could ride over there tomorrow, get the parson to read the banns out, an' we could be livin' here in less than a month. Husband and wife.'

As she stared up at him she thought what a lucky woman she was, and said, 'Very well then. Let me have a word with Tilly tonight, and if she has no objections it shall be as you say.' There was no time for further discussion, for his lips then came softly down on hers and she gave herself up for a time to the sheer pleasure of his nearness.

'Why, I think it's a wonderful idea!' Tilly told her later that evening when Ellen put the suggestion to her as they sat together in the drawing room. 'It will put a little brightness back into our lives – give us all something to look forward to. Goodness knows, this place has seen enough sadness to last it a lifetime, and between you and me, Ellen, I too long to be gone from it now.'

Ellen lifted her cup and after drinking from it, she asked, 'Is it tomorrow that Mr Rosier is coming to see you and Willy?'

'Yes, it is. He's coming early in the morning as I'm going over to Brook Farm in the afternoon. But I'm not expecting a happy conclusion to the meeting. Mr Rosier has been after the mine for as long as I can remember, but now that it's prone to flooding again he will have the whip hand, and Willy and I have a feeling that this will be reflected in his offer.'

'Mm.' Ellen lifted a book from the small table standing between them and lightening the mood again she said, 'By the way, Tilly, take a look at this. Little Ben Morris actually managed to write his name today. I've got five pupils turning up regularly now, so things are finally looking up.'

Tilly was delighted. 'You said it would happen if we gave it enough time. Well done, Ellen!'

'The credit must go mainly to you. After all, you are the one who set up the facilities and supplied all the books and things,' Ellen said fairly, but then as her thoughts returned to Arthur, she asked, 'Are you really quite sure that you don't mind Arthur and me getting married before you?'

'Of course I don't.' Tilly waved aside her concerns. 'I think things are going to work out really well for all of us. Willy and Josefina will be here, you and Arthur will be in your cottage, and Steve and I will be in ours, and all within a stone's throw of each other.'

The two friends smiled at each other and a companionable silence settled between them as they sat in the glow from the fire, each contemplating their future.

'Good morning, Tilly, and how are you today?' Daniel Rosier asked as Peabody showed him into the library where Tilly and her son were waiting for him.

Drawing herself up to her full height, Tilly told him coldly, 'It is Mrs Sopwith, if you don't mind, Mr Rosier.'

He inclined his head at Willy, who was standing behind his mother, before looking back at her with a touch of amusement playing about his lips. 'Oh come now, Tilly. You and I have known each other long enough to do away with the formalities, don't you think?'

Ignoring his comment, she kept the desk between them as she beckoned him to a chair, and once he was seated she said, 'Well, Mr Rosier, I think we are all fully aware of the reason for this meeting, so shall we get down to business?'

'Of course.' Flicking an imaginary speck of dust from the trousers of his expensive tweed suit, he now steepled his fingers and looking across them at her, he said, 'I'm pleased that you are finally prepared to see sense, Tilly. Word has it that you have already passed the mine and the Manor over to your son Willy here, which is just as well. I mean – whoever heard of a woman being able to run a mine properly?'

When she bristled with indignation, he grinned. 'Now, now, don't go getting on your high horse with me. It is commonly known that the mine hasn't been doing too well lately, and were it to flood yet again it would scarcely be worth the price of the land it takes up. So, bearing that in mind, this is what I am prepared to pay you for it, and you should think yourself lucky I am being as generous as that.' He now withdrew a folded sheet of paper from the inner pocket of his jacket and after making a great show of straightening it out, he laid it in front of mother and son, and sat back in his chair to await their reaction to his offer.

He didn't have to wait for long, for Tilly's eyes almost started from her head and her hand flew to her throat as she stared at him in disbelief. 'Why, this is nothing short of an

361

insult!' she spluttered. 'It is worth at least *four* times that amount, even if it is prone to flooding!'

'Be that as it may, I don't see anyone else queuing up to buy it, do you? But now, I shall leave you both to think on it. Should you see the sense of my offer, my solicitor assures me that the transaction could go through within a matter of days.' He was standing again now and she was glowering at him across the desk, which only served to heighten his amusement.

'The thing you need to learn, Tilly, if you are ever to be a good businesswoman,' he said, lowering his voice confidingly, 'is that you should seize an opportunity when it is offered. Only a matter of months ago I made you an offer that was treble the amount I am prepared to pay now, and you turned me down flat. I hope your son will forgive you for that mistake. Do you understand what I am saying?'

Her hand was visibly shaking now as she seized the bell-rope and stabbed a finger towards the door. 'Kindly leave! You insult me, sir!' Willy was already at her side, peering at the mine-owner's blurred face and longing to plant his fist in it.

He chuckled as he rose and ambled slowly towards the door, but once there he paused to look back at her. 'I think you will both be ready to talk again when you have seen sense, Tilly Trotter, Master Sopwith. Until then, I wish you both a very good day.'

The second the door had closed behind him, Tilly lifted the sheet of paper and crumpled it into a ball before flinging it as far across the room as she could. Her hands then clenched into fists as she muttered, 'You will buy the mine for that measly amount over my dead body, Daniel Rosier!'

Her temper had subsided somewhat by the time she reached the farm that afternoon. Thankfully, the rain had stopped and the ground was slightly firmer, although the sky overhead was leaden and overcast. Beth was crossing the yard with a bucket of pigswill in her hand when Tilly rode into the yard, and the girl waved and shouted over to her, 'I'll be back in a minute. Push the kettle onto the fire, would you?'

Tilly nodded and then after dismounting and tying the horse to a post she went into the kitchen. Sarah was playing on the hearthrug with some wooden bricks that Eddie had carved and painted for her, and her eyes lit up at the sight of her grandmother, who she had now come to realise never came to visit without a twist of barley sugar in her pocket for her.

After depositing the treat into the child's hand and kissing her dark curls, Tilly filled the kettle at the sink and as she was doing so, Lucy's voice wafted from the next room, 'Is that you, Tilly?' A week or so ago, Eddie had moved her bed downstairs so she could be nearer to the family and the heart of her home.

'Yes! Just give me a moment to put the kettle on and I'll be through.'

Once the kettle was bedded on the fire and the fireguard was safely back around it, Tilly picked up Sarah and moved into Lucy's room. She saw at a glance that Lucy was highly agitated.

'What is it?' she asked immediately.

'Are we on our own, lass?'

'Yes, we are, apart from this one here.' She hugged the child, who was sucking on her sweet. 'I think Beth was off to feed the pigs when I arrived.'

'Good, then pull the chair up to the bed. I have something I need to tell you,' Lucy urged her. Her next words had Tilly in a state of shock, for what she said was, 'Beth is pregnant. It happened when the poor girl was raped at that whorehouse she and Josefina were locked up in, in Durham.'

'Oh no!'

Tilly's hand had flown to her throat but Lucy was not finished yet. She went on, 'Seems that's been the problem between her and Eddie. The girl says she doesn't want to saddle him with another man's bairn, so she's giving him a wide berth. But that isn't the worst of it. You see, Tilly, the man that raped her was Daniel Rosier, and from what Beth could make out he was a regular visitor there – so what do you make of that then, eh?'

Tilly was in a turmoil. And to think that only that very morning, the man had had the audacity to look down on her as if she were some idiot that didn't warrant his time! But he wasn't her first concern at the moment and so, leaning towards Lucy, she asked, 'Does Eddie know that she's carrying a bairn?'

'No, she made me promise not to tell him. But it's breaking my heart, Tilly. I know he would still take her, despite the circumstances. She won't be able to hide it for much longer anyway – and then what's going to happen?'

Tilly pondered for a while and then, squeezing Lucy's hand, she said, 'Would you like me to have a word with her?'

Lucy panicked. 'If you did that, she would know I had broken my promise to her. I've only done so because she won't be able to go on with the workload here for much longer, and then what will we do?'

'Well, if Eddie is able to keep up the outdoor work here, you, Sarah and Beth will have to come to the Manor to stay with us. And don't say no! Ask yourself, what other option is there? If Beth is unable to care for you, who will? Eddie will have his hands full, seeing to the animals and such.'

It was at that moment that they heard the kitchen door open and within seconds Beth appeared in the bedroom doorway, looking pale and tired.

'Ooh, 'tis enough to cut you in two out there,' she declared. 'Never mind, I'll make us all a nice brew an' that will warm us up, won't it?'

As she wearily turned away, Tilly and Lucy exchanged a worried glance but for the next half an hour they had no further chance to discuss the situation, for Beth was busy in the kitchen and they were worried that she would overhear them. It wasn't until she had gone back out into the yard to collect the eggs from the chicken house that the subject was raised again. And then, in a hushed voice, Tilly quickly told Lucy of Daniel Rosier's visit to her that morning.

'The cheeky devil!' Lucy exclaimed indignantly. 'And to think that all the time he's been playing the high and mighty he's been visiting houses of ill-repute. I just wonder what his wife would think, were she to find out.'

Tilly nodded in agreement, then a thought occurred to her. 'You know, Lucy, I might just be able to use this information to my advantage. For myself, I want nothing more than a fair price for the mine. What is more important is ensuring that the employees are treated well, for it's common knowledge that Rosier abuses his workforce. However, if he were to think that news of his escapades were to become common knowledge, he might be a little more agreeable about signing a legal contract as to what he would pay them and what their work hours would be, and so on, don't you think?'

Seeing the wicked gleam in Tilly's eyes, Lucy's face broke into a smile, which stretched yet further when Tilly went on, 'Furthermore, it wouldn't hurt him to settle a sum of money on Beth to ensure that she and the bairn, when it comes, are well provided for, would it?'

'No, it wouldn't, and as you say, it would help Beth. But can you really see him agreeing to it?'

'After I've finished with the lecherous old devil he'll be

glad to agree to anything!' The firm jut of Tilly's chin told Lucy that she meant every word she said, and now she was laughing again, with relief and gratitude.

'Oh Tilly, I'd give anything to be there when you put these things to him,' Lucy told her.

'Yes. The sad thing is, of course, that none of this will change the position Beth finds herself in. But if we can at least ensure that she won't have to struggle, that's something gained, isn't it?'

'Aye, it is,' Lucy readily agreed, and then their conversation moved on to other things as they heard Beth re-enter the kitchen.

Tilly relayed the conversation she'd had with Lucy later that night when she was sitting in the cottage with Steve in front of a roaring fire.

'By, who would have thought the self-righteous Daniel Rosier would sink so low, eh?' he muttered in amazement as he stared into the flames.

Tilly nodded in agreement before telling him, 'I might just be able to use this to our advantage now, as well as Beth's.'

'Aye, you might.' He nodded vigorously. 'The poor girl. Imagine how she must be feeling. Why, I've half a mind to go and lay the dirty old devil flat out.'

'And what good would that do?' Tilly asked him. 'No, Steve, I think you're going to have to leave this one to me. Don't you worry. By the time I've finished with him he'll not be so keen to take advantage of young girls again!'

'But what will happen to Sarah then, if Beth is having a bairn too?' he asked, and now Tilly looked anxious.

'I was going to talk to you about that,' she said hesitantly. 'You see – the thing is, Lucy is fading fast now and as you say, if Beth is going to have her own bairn to care for, there is no way that she could cope with Sarah as well. Very soon now, I think I shall have to move Sarah up to the Manor and then we'll have to see how it goes with Willy and Josefina.'

'Huh!' Steve snorted. 'I wouldn't count on those two giving her a home. They're too taken up with each other. Not that that's a bad thing, of course. I just can't see Josefina wanting her around, for the bairn is a constant reminder that Willy loved someone other than her, and you of all people should know that it would be too hard for her, and not at all the right atmosphere for a child.'

Seeing the distress on Tilly's face, he placed his arm around her and said comfortingly, 'Don't look so worried, lass. If the worst came to the worst she would have to come here and live with us. I would never see her out – you should know that. She is your flesh and blood, after all. Now, I'm not sayin' I *want* that to happen. I'd be a liar to say otherwise, for I've waited all me life for you, Tilly, an' I had hopes that we would spend whatever time we have left together here on us own. But as we both discovered long ago, Him up there sometimes has other plans lined up for us.'

As he cocked his head towards the ceiling, a wave of sadness washed over her. Steve was a good man. Oh aye, there was no doubt that he was a lovely man. Just lately, she had found herself longing for the time when it could be just the two of them locked away together in this little cottage he had turned into a home. She had hoped that she had seen to the needs of all those who were dear to her. She had bequeathed Willy's legacy on him on his twenty-first birthday. She had settled Beth in at the farm, and for a time it had looked as if everything would work out there. Ellen and Arthur had their little cottage and each other. And Fanny . . . well, her beloved Fanny was beyond helping now and she still felt her loss every single minute of every single day. Anna and John now had Little Joe to brighten their lives and fulfil the longing they had always had for a child of their own. And now for this to happen, and with the wedding only weeks away!

Still, she asked herself, when did my life ever run smoothly? Looking back, it felt as though she had simply lurched from one crisis to another. Caring for her grandchild would be yet another. It wasn't that she didn't love her, of course, for as Steve had pointed out, Sarah was her own flesh and blood. It was just that, deep down, she had longed for a time when her responsibilities would be lifted. Ah well, the way she saw it, she would be best to take a day at a time, for who knew what the future had in store?

Chapter Thirty

THE WOMEN IN the village shop were once more doing what they loved best, which was gossip, and today their subject was Randy Simmons.

'I'm tellin' you it's right,' Ada Flavell told her rapt audience, including Molly Butterworth, who was leaning on the counter listening to every word. 'My chap were on the docks in Shields lookin' fer work when they pinned up the names o' those lost on board the *Mermaid*, an' Randy Simmons's name were amongst 'em. They reckon the fever swept through the crew like wildfire, wiped half of 'em out within days, accordin' to the word goin' round. Poor buggers all got buried at sea apparently. Well, think about it – if it were sommat contagious they could hardly have brought the bodies ashore for burial, could they? So, the long an' the short of it is, old Randy ended up as fishbait. Perhaps it were preferable to havin' his neck stretched though, eh?' She gave a cackle. 'I mean, that's what would have happened, had he stayed around here, ain't it? Everybody knew it were him as done fer Fanny Drew, an' we all have a good idea who put him up to it an' all, don't we?'

A ripple of agreement passed through the women and when it began to wane, Ada ploughed on, 'Lucy Bentwood is about on her last legs. So who will take charge o' the bastard's brat then, eh? Can't see him or his sister-wife wantin' it, can you? No doubt 'twill be shipped off to an orphanage somewhere, an' if it is, happen it'll have to stay there, 'cos no one's goin' to want a child wi' a scar all down one side of its face, are they? You can bet the witch won't take to it wi' her weddin' to Steve McGrath only a few weeks away, whether it's her grandchild or not!'

'Aye, well, the weddin' ain't happened yet,' one of the other women now piped up. 'An' knowin' how old Mother McGrath is simmerin', there's no sayin' it ever will!'

Again the women's heads bobbed in agreement. Would the wedding ever take place, or would old Mrs McGrath finally have her revenge?

To say that the expression on Daniel Rosier's face was smug as Peabody showed him into the library would have been putting it mildly, for he almost swaggered into the room.

'Ah, good day, Tilly, my dear. I wondered how long it would be before you and your son saw sense and sent for me,' he smirked, as uninvited he sank into the chair opposite the desk. He noted that the blind son was nowhere to be seen. Probably canoodling with his sister. Pshaw! the older man thought contemptuously.

Once the man was seated, Tilly said graciously, 'Good day, Mr Rosier.'

Leaning forward, he drummed the fingers of one hand on the edge of the desk as he said, 'So . . . are you and your son ready to be sensible and consider my offer?'

'Yes, Mr Rosier, I rather think we are. Or what I should say is, we have already considered it.'

'Ah, good, good. In that case I shall instruct my solicitor to start work on the legal documents right away.'

It was Tilly's turn to smile now as she inclined her head towards him. 'That would be most acceptable, sir,' she said smoothly. 'Perhaps you could inform him that this is the price you will be paying us. And I assure you, it is a very fair price.' As she spoke, she slid a sheet of paper across the desk towards him and after looking at it, his eyes widened as he snapped, 'Is this some sort of a joke?'

'Oh, no, Mr Rosier. I can assure you it is no joke. That is the price you will pay for the mine.'

He was red in the face now as he jerked himself to his feet. 'You must be mad, Trotter, if you think I would pay that sum for your godforsaken dump!'

'SIT DOWN!'

Rosier was so shocked as Tilly rose up from her chair and barked at him, that he did as he was told. She glared at him across the desk. Her knuckles were white, so heavily was she leaning on the smooth mahogany surface as she now reared towards him, and he was temporarily rendered speechless, for this was no lady looking across at him now, but a banshee, full of fury.

'You will not only pay the price we are asking for the mine,' she hissed, 'but you will also sign an agreement my solicitor is drawing up, stating what working conditions and wages our employees can expect from you when you take over the mine.'

'Have you taken *complete* leave of your senses, Trotter?' he snarled, as her eyes flashed fire at him. 'Why, I would have to be completely *mad* to agree to this!'

'Yes, as you say, you would have to be mad . . . or perhaps just a man with something to hide?' Her voice was low again, and somehow this was more disquieting than before.

'And just what is that supposed to mean?'

Tilly straightened, never taking her eyes from him. Had

she imagined the flicker of fear she thought she had seen flit across his face?

'A certain piece of information has come to my ears that could have dire consequences for you, should it become public knowledge,' she said. She waited for him to erupt but when he remained quiet she went on, 'No doubt you are aware that some time ago my daughter, Josefina, fell into the hands of an unscrupulous pawnbroker in Durham, by the name of Jake Hammond. The papers were full of it at the time. Anyway, Mr Hammond had another, rather profitable little business going on at the same time, *didn't he*, Mr Rosier? A brothel with under age prostitutes – innocent girls abducted from the streets, drugged and imprisoned!' Her voice was rising again now, as she thought of her beloved daughter possibly being deflowered by this . . . creature! Beth's troubled face came to mind as she thundered, 'You visited this brothel regularly, did you not?'

'How dare you suggest such a thing?' Rosier choked, but one look from her silenced him as she went on, 'It just so happens that on the night I fetched Josefina from that den of vice I also brought home with me another young woman who had been violated only the night before by a "gentleman" by the name of *Daniel Rosier*. And that very same young woman is now unfortunate enough to be carrying his bairn.'

'It's a lie, a downright lie!' he blustered. 'Why, it's her word against mine. I'll—'

'Deny it? Is that what you were about to say? Then so be it, Mr Rosier. You may be aware that Jake Hammond and his wife are now serving ten years' hard labour. I have no doubt whatsoever that they would be more than happy to disclose the names of some of their regular clients to get their sentences reduced. Of course, I could always approach the police and ask—'

'*No!* Dear God! There will be no need for that.' Daniel Rosier rose from his chair and began to pace up and down the room like a caged animal.

It was then that Tilly delivered her parting shot. 'And I wonder what your wife would think of all this, should it appear in the newspapers? Goodness me, it hardly bears thinking about, does it? Why, the shame of it! You would have to move far away at the very least, or be charged with some criminal prosecution.'

Daniel Rosier's shoulders sagged and he sank heavily back into the chair as he realised that she had him over a barrel. His head was pounding; there was a pain in his chest.

But even then Tilly had not quite punished him enough. 'Of course,' she said musingly, 'we have not yet discussed what you are going to do for Beth. After all, it is your bairn she is carrying, and neither she nor the child will be able to live on fresh air, will they? I thought perhaps we might negotiate a single payment that will ensure that they might live free of financial worries.'

'How much?' he asked dully, and Tilly once more scribbled a sum on a scrap of paper before pushing it across the desk to him.

'Five hundred pounds?' he muttered disbelievingly.

'Yes – or perhaps you think that is not quite enough?'

Rising from his seat again, he now moved towards the door slowly, holding one hand against his heart. Once there, he paused to look back at the witch. 'You will be hearing from my solicitor within the week,' he told her, all bravado gone.

'Good, good, let's hope I do. Otherwise . . .'

Rosier's nostrils flared as he barged out of the room, slamming the door resoundingly behind him. Only then did Tilly slump into her chair and, burying her face in her hands, she sobbed until she had no tears left.

★

The day dawned bright and clear, though there was a cold breeze as they all clambered into the carriage for their trip to Allendale. It was Ellen and Arthur's wedding day and Tilly was unsure whether the roses in Ellen's cheeks were due to the cold air or the fact that she was marrying the man she loved. Whatever the reason, she was positively glowing and the atmosphere was light. Only the week before, Tilly had taken her into Durham and treated her to the outfit she was now wearing, which might have been made for her. It was a dark blue skirt and jacket trimmed with cream ribbon that matched the ribbons on her bonnet, and it set off her still-dark hair and smooth skin to perfection, as did the bouquet of cream roses that Tilly had ordered especially for her from a flower shop in Shields. Because they were out of season the flowers had cost almost as much as her outfit, but Tilly considered them worth every penny, for Ellen had squealed with delight when they had been delivered earlier that morning.

'You two next,' Ellen smiled as the carriage bowled along and Tilly peeped at Steve shyly from the corner of her eye. As Ellen had said, it was only three weeks to her own wedding now, but it had been many years since Tilly had lain with a man, and she was looking forward to the loving with a feeling of excitement mingled with apprehension.

Back at the Manor was a buzz of activity, for Tilly had insisted that they should hold a small reception there following the service in the church. Once more, the table had been placed against the wall in the dining room, and the staff had been busily piling it with food in readiness for the guests who would be arriving throughout the day. Phillipa, Lance and the boys would be coming, and Anna, John and Little

Joseph. Eddie and Beth had promised to come too, for an hour, bringing Sarah, though sadly, Lucy was not well enough to make even so short a journey. A buffet meal had been agreed upon, so that the rest of the staff could join in the celebrations, and it looked set to be a happy occasion.

Steve was in fine high spirits, and this showed now as he leaned towards Tilly and said, 'Just think, this time next week I shall be a man of leisure and Daniel Rosier will be taking over the mine. I can still hardly believe you got him to agree to your terms, my dear.'

Tilly grinned. 'It wasn't nearly as hard as you think. And the good thing is, I won't have to worry that he will work the men into the ground when he is in charge. They have all been issued with their terms of employment and know exactly where they stand.'

'Huh! Not that they will thank you for it,' Ellen mumbled.

'It doesn't matter. At least I shall be able to sleep easy knowing that I haven't sold them into slavery. And the way Daniel Rosier is known to work *his* men is nothing short of slavery,' Tilly replied.

'So will you be retiring altogether now, Steve?' Arthur asked.

Steve grinned widely. 'As it goes, I've plans to buy into the steelworks with Jim Coleman, but I thought perhaps I'd wait until the New Year and spend a bit o' time wi' me new wife first.'

Tilly blushed becomingly as the little feelings of excitement wormed their way around her stomach again. 'New wife' – it had a nice ring to it, a safe ring, for surely in the cottage with Steve she would find the peace she had always craved?

★

The party was in full swing and the wine was flowing like water. The only dark spot on the day had been the fact that Eddie and Beth had failed to put in an appearance. The service in the little church in Allendale had gone without a hitch and had been so touchingly simple that Tilly had a lump in her throat as she listened to Ellen and Arthur take their vows. They could still barely take their eyes from one another, and Tilly sensed that they were longing for the moment when they could take their leave and retire to their little cottage in the woods.

Peabody had just swept past with Gwen in his arms, dancing to a waltz played on the piano by Ellen, when the dining-room door opened a crack, and Tilly saw Eddie urgently beckoning to her. Slipping unobtrusively from her seat, she hurried across and followed him out into the corridor.

'What is it, Eddie?' she asked. 'We were worried when you didn't show up.'

'It's Beth,' he told her and she could hear the concern in his voice. 'There's something wrong with her, Tilly. She's been doubled over in pain all day long but she won't let me fetch the doctor to her, so Mother told me to ride over and ask for your advice. I know it's their wedding in there, and I'm sorry to barge in on the party, but I'm at my wits' end. Dear God! She looks as if she's dying.'

Tilly chewed on her lip for a moment. 'Let me just have a quick word with Steve and I'll come back with you in the trap. Wait there, would you?'

'Aye, Tilly, I will – and thanks.' The young man was almost out of his mind with the worry of it all.

Minutes later, he was helping her up into the trap and they were rattling along the drive towards Brook Farm. Eddie seemed nervous and on edge, and Tilly could sense his fear.

Once they had pulled into the farmyard she asked him, 'Where is she?'

'She's upstairs in her room, but she won't let me go into her. I can hear her groaning, Tilly! Oh dear, Sarah has just woken up. I'll take care of her and Mother, Tilly, if you can see to Beth.' The baby was screaming now, and Lucy was calling for her son.

Bunching her skirts into one hand, Tilly hurried through the cottage and climbed the stairs to Beth's little room, entering without knocking. Lowering her head to avoid the sloping roof, she approached the bed where Beth was lying with a face that was whiter than the sheet that was laid across her. It was the sheet that Tilly's eyes were focused on, for even in the dim light she could see that it was heavily bloodstained.

'Beth, can you hear me?' She leaned over the girl who appeared to be only semi-conscious, and was relieved when Beth turned pain-filled eyes towards her and whispered, 'I'm losin' the bairn, Tilly.'

'Yes, yes, lass. It looks likely.' Tilly stroked her damp hand as she looked around the small room. Beth was going to need help, and there were not the facilities here to provide it. Making a hasty decision, she told her, 'Try to stay calm, hinny. I'll not be more than a minute.' Once more she lifted her skirts and clattered back down the stairs to where Eddie was pacing up and down the length of the kitchen, holding a distraught baby. Sarah's cheeks were red with teething.

'What is it that's wrong with her, Tilly?' he asked wretchedly, and she found herself in yet another dilemma. Eddie had no idea as yet that Beth was carrying a child. Should she tell him?

Lucy's voice came weakly to them from her open bedroom door. 'Tilly, is that you?'

'Yes, it's me.' Tilly glanced across at Eddie apologetically before hurrying into the bedroom and to Lucy's side. 'She's losing the bairn,' she whispered, and Lucy's hand flew to her mouth.

'I feared as much,' she muttered. 'What can we do for her?'

'I think it might be best if Eddie lets me take her back to the Manor in the trap. She's having a bad time of it and needs a doctor. As soon as we arrive there, I'll get Ned to ride into the village to fetch Doctor Murray, and then on the way back he can collect you and Sarah.'

'Aw, Tilly. Couldn't we all stay here, lass?' the tired voice asked.

'Aye, you could,' Tilly admitted, 'but I don't have to tell you that there's more space up at the Manor. There's barely room to swing a cat around up there,' she thumbed towards the ceiling. 'And tell me, if Beth is laid up, who is going to see to you and Sarah?'

'Very well then,' Lucy sighed, 'but will you manage to get her back safely on your own?'

'Yes. I can get Eddie to lay her in the space at the back of the seat, and once we've gone he can prepare anything that you and Sarah will need to bring with you in readiness for when Ned comes back with the carriage. Now I have to go. She's in a bad way, Lucy.'

'All right then, lass, it shall be as you say. You just see to Beth.'

Tilly had turned to leave but she suddenly turned back and what she said now brought tears stinging to Lucy's eyes.

'I think you should speak to Eddie,' she said on a whisper. 'He has no idea what's going on and is sick with worry. We'll not be able to hide it from him any longer, and it's better that he should hear it from you . . . Do you think you could do that?'

'Aye, I'll do it,' Lucy said softly. 'As you say, the time for hiding it is past. Now you go and do whatever has to be done for Beth.'

Tilly nodded and hurried away, and minutes later Eddie, who had put the crying baby in the bed with his mother, was tucking Beth into the makeshift bed they had prepared for her on the trap. He was almost as white as Beth as he stared at the bloodstained sheet Tilly had wrapped her in, and even more terrified to see that Beth was almost delirious with pain.

'She's dying, isn't she?' he choked as he wiped the sweat from her brow.

'Not if I can help it.' Tilly took up the reins. 'Now go back into your mother, Eddie. She will explain everything and I just hope that you will understand, because if Beth pulls through this, she's going to need all the support she can get.'

Eddie frowned as he watched Tilly whip the horse into a trot, and then as the trap disappeared round the corner, he slowly turned and made his way back into the farmhouse to hear what his mother had to tell him.

Chapter Thirty-One

BETH LAY AT death's door for two whole days and nights as the doctor battled to stem the blood that was flowing from her as if from a tap, but then on the third morning, she suddenly let out a piercing scream as a pain lifted her from the bed and the dead child slithered out of her, along with the small afterbirth.

'That's it, the worst is over now,' Tilly soothed her as she wiped the sweat from the girl's brow with a cold flannel.

'I . . . I'm glad I lost it,' Beth muttered through the tears that were flowing down her cheeks.

'Ssh, you just lie back and rest. Concentrate on getting better.'

Beth suddenly grasped Tilly's warm hand in her icy one and asked, 'D . . . does Eddie know what is happenin'?'

'Yes, hinny, he does. His mother had no choice but to tell him. The poor lad was going out of his mind with worry.'

'That's it then. I hope I die too, for he'll never look at me again, now. 'Twould be better if I went too.' She turned her face to the wall.

'Don't you *dare* let me hear you say that again,' Tilly scolded her harshly. 'None of the blame for what has happened can be laid at your door, and Eddie will understand that!'

'No, no he won't,' Beth sobbed fretfully, and then suddenly grasping Tilly's hand again, she asked frantically, 'You won't let him in here, will you? I couldn't face him. Promise me you won't!'

'All right, all right, calm down now. I shall go and fetch us all a strong cup of tea.' Tilly raised her eyes to those of the doctor, who was still trying desperately to stem the bleeding, which wasn't quite as fierce now. When he acknowledged her look with a reassuring nod, she rose and slowly made her way from the room to tell everyone the good news, if a miscarriage could be classed as that. At least it meant that Beth now had a chance of a life again.

Lucy was the first one she made for, as Josefina took her place at Beth's side. And the sight of Josefina raised yet another concern, for while she was happy to pander to Beth, she had made it more than obvious that Sarah was not welcome in the house, to the point that the poor child had been banished to the kitchen and the care of the staff there for most of her stay up to now. Deciding that she must have a word with Willy about it at some stage, Tilly tapped on Lucy's bedroom door and walked wearily inside.

'Aw, lass, you look all in.' Lucy's face creased with concern, noting the shadows under Tilly's eyes and the crumpled dress. 'How is Beth?'

'I think the worst is over, God willing.' Tilly sank onto a chair at the side of the bed and ran a hand across her aching brow. 'The poor girl has had a terrible time of it. The bairn wasn't even formed enough to fight its way out of her. She lost it a short while ago.'

Lucy made the sign of the cross on her chest before saying, ''Tis just as well.'

'Did you tell Eddie about her predicament?' Tilly now asked.

'Aye, I did. But it's hard to say how he took it. He just went sort of quiet, like. But then it no doubt came as a shock to the lad. He had put Beth on a pedestal and thought she was pure.'

'And she would have been, had it not been for Daniel Rosier forcing himself on her!' Tilly snapped, then softening she said, 'I'm sorry, Lucy. I think I must be more tired than I thought.'

'Of course you are, lass. No, *I'm* sorry – I let my mouth run away with me. You go now and get some rest. God knows you've earned it.'

As weariness washed over Tilly in a wave she nodded. 'Do you know, Lucy – I think I might just do that,' she said quietly, and without another word she walked from the room.

It was later that evening that Eddie arrived in his Sunday best to see his mother. Tilly was still resting, so Gwen showed him up to Lucy's room then hurried away with a promise that she would be back in no time with some tea. Eddie stood by the door for a time, twisting his cap in his hands and looking utterly lost until Lucy patted the side of the bed and said, 'Come on, lad. Come and sit down and take the weight off your feet. You look fit to drop.'

Eddie did as he was told and for a time he studiously avoided mentioning Beth, but then he could not keep up the pretence of not caring any longer and he suddenly blurted out, 'Is she going to be all right? Beth, I mean?'

'Aye lad, we reckon so. She lost the bairn earlier today and had a terrible time of it, but the worst is past now and once she's recovered she can get on with her life. The thing you have to ponder on now is, will that life include you? Or are you going to let something wonderful – for what was between you two *was* wonderful – are you going to let it slip through your fingers?'

Eddie looked towards the window and his eyes were full of unshed tears as he asked his mother, 'What if Beth still doesn't want me?'

'You daft ha'porth,' Lucy scolded him. 'She never *didn't* want you! Can't you see, the poor girl thought you would despise her because of what had happened to her! Go to her now and tell her how you feel about her, lad. If not for yourself, do it for me, for I know I'm not long for this world now and my dearest wish is to see you settled afore I go.'

'Don't talk like that, Ma. You have years in front of you yet!'

'No, lad. Believe me, I know what I'm talking about, but don't be upset, for I'm not afraid. In fact, if I can only see you happily set up I shall welcome death, for this pain is getting unbearable now. So, Eddie, I ask again: will you go and see Beth . . . for me?'

'All right, Ma.'

With a weak smile on her face now, Lucy lifted the bell on her bedside table and shook it. When Gwen appeared seconds later, Lucy asked her, 'Would you take Eddie along to see Beth please, Gwen?'

'Of course, ma'am.' Gwen bobbed her knee and then scuttled away along the landing with Eddie in hot pursuit. Eventually she stopped outside a door and told him, 'Beth is in there. Just give me a call when you need me to show you down, sir.'

'Thank you. Yes, I will.' He waited until she had walked away, then plucking up every ounce of courage he had, he rapped at the door and, without waiting for a reply, strode in.

★

It was some while later, when Tilly entered Lucy's room to check that she had all she needed for the night. The sick woman was quick to note that she had a smile on her face.

'So what's tickling you then?' Lucy asked curiously.

'Well, if I were to tell you that I just popped in to see how Beth was, only to find your Eddie sitting on the side of her bed, and them both staring into each other's eyes like a pair of lovesick cows, would you think that was enough to make me smile?'

'Oh yes, yes I would.' Lucy's pain-ravaged face lit up for the briefest of seconds, and in that time, Tilly caught a sight of the Lucy she had known before this terrible disease had claimed her. And then the dying woman said something that Tilly was to think of long after Lucy was gone. Leaning forward, she muttered, 'You know, Tilly, I sometimes think that you *are* a witch, for whilst sorrow seems to be your constant companion, you can yet make everything seem right. And I want you to know, that despite all that has happened, my life has been enriched for having known you.'

'Aw, hush now.' Tilly's chin trembled as she forced back the tears, but then after a while she rose, and tucking the counterpane more closely around Lucy's poor swollen abdomen she bent to kiss her on the cheek, whispering, 'And you, Lucy Bentwood, are a most remarkable woman. Good night, my dear.'

At the door, she turned to look back at Lucy one last time, and it was as well that she did, for the next morning when she carried in her morning tea, she discovered that Lucy had slipped away from them peacefully during the night.

It was decided that Beth should stay with Tilly at the Manor until after she and Eddie were wed, which Tilly was delighted to hear would be as soon as they could arrange it. At first, Beth had been troubled at marrying so soon after Lucy's death, and thought it might be looked upon as being disrespectful, but as Eddie had pointed out, it had been his mother's dying wish that they should come together, and so she had agreed to it.

It so happened that on the day following Lucy's funeral, Tilly and her son were asked to call in at the family solicitor's in Newcastle to finalise the sale of the mine. Daniel Rosier was present and signed his papers with a bad will, which troubled Tilly not a bit, and some time later she sailed from the offices of Beddows & Nash with a smile on her face, and her arm tucked into Willy's, having just instructed her solicitor to deposit the cheque into her son's account. She had also been handed an envelope containing five hundred pounds in cash, that she had tucked deep in her bag for Beth. The way Tilly saw it, even though Beth was no longer carrying his child, the girl deserved this start in life for all that Rosier had put her through.

Arriving back at the Manor in high good humour, a half-hour later she heard all hell breaking loose as Josefina stood hands on hips in the hallway screaming like a banshee at Willy. 'We will *not* be keeping the child! Do you hear me?' Swinging about in a billow of blue silk skirts she saw Tilly looking at her, and breaking into a sob, she rushed away into the shelter of the day room.

'Whatever is going on here?' Tilly asked irritably.

Willy shuffled towards her, his hand feeling blindly in front of him, and taking his elbow she steered her son towards the day room. Josefina was sobbing uncontrollably in the depths of an armchair, and instantly Tilly's anger melted as she saw how distressed she was.

'Whatever is the matter?' she asked, kneeling beside her.

'I . . . I can't bear it, having the child here all the time,' Josefina told her in a strangled voice. 'I know that I am selfish, Mama, but I cannot help it.'

'Well, I'm sure we could have discussed it privately, without you behaving like a fishwife in front of the staff,' Tilly told her firmly. 'Now come along. Sarah is just a baby, and a lovely little girl at that. Tell me what it is that upsets you so about her.'

'You *know* full well what it is!' Josefina spat as Willy looked helplessly on. 'Every time I look at her I see my husband with Noreen Bentwood, and it is like a knife in my heart. Oh, Mama, when will Beth be taking her back to the farm?'

'Sarah will *not* be going back to the farm.' Tilly's voice was ice-cold now. 'As well as being Willy's daughter, Sarah is also *my* granddaughter, and if he is not going to take responsibility for her, then I feel that I must!'

Willy's head was wagging from side to side in the familiar gesture that told Tilly of his deep distress, and it was he who next spoke when he said, 'It might be for the best if you were to do that, Mama, for as you can see, Josefina will never take to her.'

Turning on her heel, Tilly made for the door. 'It shall be so then, but I'm afraid you will have to endure her presence for a little longer, until after Steve and I are wed.' So saying she bounced from the room, leaving Willy and Josefina to stare after her, shamefaced.

It was the day before the wedding, and Anna and John's butler was seeing that Tilly's luggage was taken up to her room. Tilly meanwhile had been ushered into the day room where Anna and Meg Thomas were doing a jigsaw with Little Joe on the table.

Anna leaped up and hurried to meet Tilly the second she set foot in the room, and her face was alight with excitement as she took Sarah from Tilly's arms.

'Hello, pet,' she said fondly as the little girl's pudgy arms encircled her neck. 'Come over here and play with Joseph and Meg whilst Grandmama and I have a cup of tea, eh?' She deposited the smiling child onto Meg's lap as Tilly looked at her apologetically.

'I'm so sorry I had to bring her with me,' she told her in a low voice, 'but as things are back at the Manor, I could hardly leave her there. Josefina seems to go for Willy's throat every time she so much as sets eyes on her.'

'Oh, you never have to apologise for bringing her to see me,' Anna assured her happily. 'She can go up to the nursery with Joseph, and Meg will look after her whilst we get you in the mood for your wedding. You won't mind, will you, Meg?'

'Oh no, ma'am,' Meg assured her with a smile. 'I think she's a little angel and she and Joseph get on like a house on fire. You just leave her with me and concentrate on enjoying yourselves.' So saying, she lifted Sarah onto her hip and took Joseph's hand, and then the merry little trio left the room, and Tilly and Anna were alone.

'So, how are the nerves holding up then?' Anna teased as she rang the bell for some refreshments.

'I haven't had too much time to think about it, to be truthful,' Tilly replied, and there was a trace of sadness in her voice now as she admitted, 'I was in two minds whether to put it off again, but I didn't have the heart to disappoint Steve. It doesn't feel quite right though. I mean, going ahead with it so soon after Lucy . . .'

'You mustn't think like that,' Anna gently chided her. 'You better than anyone should know that it was what Lucy would have wanted. And besides, have you and Steve not waited long enough? I think you're overdue a little happiness, Tilly.'

Tilly now rubbed her hand down the length of her full skirt as she confided, 'The strangest thing, when I left the Manor today, was to know that I have now spent my last night there. It well and truly belongs to Willy and Josefina now, and she will be the mistress there from now on.'

'And what is going to happen to Sarah?'

Tilly's shoulders sagged. 'I dare say she will come to live with Steve and me.'

'And how do you both feel about that?'

'To be honest, we have little choice. Not that we don't want her, you understand? It's just that we had envisaged living whatever of our lives we have left in peace and tranquillity, for let's be honest, we are both a little long in the tooth to be starting all over again with a baby, aren't we?'

Anna chuckled now as she said, 'You will *never* be old, Tilly, although I admit I know what you mean. Still, with your permission, John and I have decided that Sarah will stay here with us for the next couple of weeks so that you and Steve can at least have some special time together.'

'Oh, my dear Anna. I couldn't expect you to do that—'

Anna waved aside her objections as the maid wheeled the tea-trolley into the room. 'I don't want to hear another word about it,' she told her firmly, and then to the maid, 'Have the caterers arrived yet?'

'Yes, ma'am.' The little maid bobbed her knee, hardly able to keep the excitement from her voice. 'They're setting the tables up in the dining room in readiness for tomorrow right now. An' Cook says to tell you that we have laid a table in the drawing room just for you and your guests for tonight.'

'Very good, Nancy. Tell Cook that will do us just fine, thank you.'

As Tilly looked beyond her into the spacious hallway, she was just in time to see florists arriving with enormous flower arrangements that they were setting down along the length of the hall.

'Oh Anna, I thought I told you I didn't want too much fuss,' she scolded. 'The flowers alone must have cost a positive fortune, let alone the outside caterers that you've brought in.'

'Now, now, Tilly, don't go spoiling it for me,' Anna reproached her. 'I really can't remember when I last enjoyed myself as much as I have while I've been organising this wedding. Though I can't say the same for Cook. She's very disgruntled that she's having to share her kitchen with another cook for a time.'

Tilly sighed and settled back in her seat without further argument, knowing that her objections would fall on deaf ears. And all the while as she sipped at her tea in the elegant day room at Felton Hall, she was thinking, This time tomorrow, I shall be Mrs Steve McGrath!

Part Four
Full Circle

Chapter Thirty-Two

IT WAS DONE, and now as Tilly stood at Steve's side in John and Anna's house, the day began to take on an air of unreality. The wedding service in the little church of St Bartholomew's had gone without a hitch, right from the moment she had stepped from the carriage to float up the twisting path on a carpet of russet and gold leaves on Willy's arm. In her mind's eye, she could still see the look on Steve's face as he had turned to watch her walking down the aisle towards him, and she knew that for as long as she lived, she would never forget it, for suddenly all the pieces of her life had seemed to be falling into place, and she had somehow known that this was how it had been meant to be. She looked at her handsome husband now, as he smiled at her across the top of the three-tier wedding cake, and thought that in his elegant top hat and tails, he could have been taken for the gentry.

Everyone that she cared about was there, smiling back at them, and just for an instant she felt the loss of those absent friends whom she would never forget. But she would not think of sad things today. This was a day for being happy. The first day of the rest of her life with the man she loved – and she *did* love him. Oh aye, she thought, so much so that she felt her heart might burst.

He steadied her hand as he helped her to slice into the bottom tier of the rich fruit cake, and then everyone was raising a toast to them and he was laughing into her eyes. Felton Hall boasted a ballroom, and as an added surprise Anna had booked a quartet to play for them. Soon couples were gliding across the highly polished floor as maids in starched white pinafores and mop caps passed amongst the guests with trays full of champagne and fine wines.

'Well, I think I can rightly say I'll not forget this day in a hurry,' Steve told her as he placed a possessive arm about Tilly's slim waist. Then he added softly, 'Have I told you today how beautiful you look, Mrs McGrath?'

Tilly blushed becomingly. 'I think you might have two or three times, but I'll not be averse to hearing you say it again.'

They were standing on the edge of the dance floor, and at that moment Willy and Josefina twirled past them. 'They certainly seem happier tonight than they have done for a while,' Steve remarked.

Tilly nodded in agreement, 'Aye, they do – probably because Anna has offered to keep Sarah here for a couple of weeks so that we can have some time alone in the cottage.' She still felt uncomfortable about the fact that Sarah would be living with them, though Steve had never so much as flinched when she had told him that Josefina had flatly refused to keep her at the Manor. But then, as she had long since discovered, that was Steve; unselfish to a fault, which only made her love him all the more.

The night wore on and slowly the guests began to drift away until the moment could be postponed no longer, for Steve was turning to her and offering his arm, as he murmured, 'It's high time you and I were away to our bed, woman.'

Tilly felt herself blush like a young girl. It had been such a long time since she had lain with a man, but she was Steve's wife now. The plain gold band on her wedding finger and the vows they had taken had made her so.

Anna was coming towards them and now she beckoned to the butler and told him, 'Would you show Mr and Mrs McGrath to the west wing please, Bright.'

'Certainly, ma'am.' He bowed stiffly before standing aside to wait for them as Anna fondly wrapped her arms around the two of them.

'I don't know how we will ever be able to thank you for all this,' Tilly told her with a break in her voice.

Anna waved aside her thanks. 'Oh, I've enjoyed every minute of it,' she beamed. 'In fact, it will be quite an anti-climax when it's all over. It's kept me busy for weeks. But anyway, you don't want to be standing here talking to me. It's been a long day for all of us. Get yourselves off to bed and I'll see you both at breakfast in the morning. God bless!'

They were following Bright through the guests who had not yet left, and everyone was wishing them well, but inside Tilly was beginning to panic. What was she doing? She had promised Matthew on his deathbed that she would never marry again – and here she was, about to climb the stairs with a new husband. The higher they climbed the quieter it became until there was only the sound of their footsteps to be heard as they followed Bright along a corridor that seemed to go on forever.

'This is your room,' he informed them with a smile as he stopped outside a door. 'Should there be anything else that sir or madam requires, please don't hesitate to pull the bell-rope.'

'Thank you, Bright.' Steve inclined his head and with a last stiff little bow, Bright hurried away with a naughty smile playing about his lips as Steve led Tilly into their room.

A bright fire was roaring up the chimney and the heavy

velvet drapes had been drawn to keep out the chill of the frosty October night. The blankets had been turned back on the bed, and on a small table to the side of the fire was a bottle of chilled champagne in a silver bucket, next to which was laid out a light supper and two cut-glass goblets.

'It seems that Anna has thought of everything, doesn't it?' Steve said quietly.

Tilly nodded. 'I'll er . . . I'll just pop behind the screen and get changed, shall I?'

'Aye, o' course, lass. I'll pour us out a glass of champagne while you're gone, eh?'

Tilly snatched up the nightdress that had been laid out for her across the foot of the bed and shot behind the screen on legs that suddenly seemed to have developed a mind of their own. She slithered out of the beautiful cream dress and her undergarments, and laid them neatly across a chair that had been placed ready; she then pulled her nightdress over her head, and with trembling fingers released her hair from its pins, allowing it to spill down her back. And then slowly she emerged from the screen, and the sight that met her eyes made her nervousness disappear and brought her springing forward with a look of deep distress on her face.

'Steve, whatever is it, hinny?' He was sitting with his face in his hands and his shoulders were heaving with the fierceness of the silent sobs that were shaking his frame.

Sinking to her knees beside him she drew his hands from his face as he told her, 'Forgive me, I . . . I just can't believe that we are really man and wife at last, Tilly. I think I have loved you since the very first minute I set eyes on you, and yet . . . something always happened to keep us apart, until I began to believe—'

'Ssh.' Her voice was soothing as she now took him in her arms and held him tight to her breast. And then after a time it was she who gently pulled him to his feet and led him to the bed. It was she who tenderly helped him to undress before slipping her own nightdress off to stand naked before him. Her nerves had fled to be replaced by a strange sort of calm, for now she knew without a shadow of a doubt that this had been meant to be, since the second they had both drawn breath.

'Now are you quite sure that you have everything you need for Sarah?'

Anna flapped her hand at Tilly as she clutched Sarah tightly to her with the other, 'Will you two just *please* get away to your cottage and stop worrying?' she smiled. Sarah was trying to reach down to tug Joseph's dark curls and didn't seem in the least bit worried by the fact that Tilly was about to leave without her.

'She will be absolutely fine,' Anna insisted as she ushered the newlyweds to the waiting carriage. 'Now be off with you and I don't want to so much as set eyes on either of you for at least two weeks.'

'I'll se . . . second that,' John grinned from his place at his wife's side.

And then Steve was helping Tilly into the coach and they were hanging out of the window waving for all they were worth as it rattled away down the drive. When she at last dropped breathlessly back against the seat, Steve tenderly took her hand in his, and with a twinkle in his eye, he asked, 'Are you happy, Mrs McGrath?'

'Oh aye, Mr McGrath. I have never been more so.' The words were said with such a wealth of truth ringing in them that Steve knew in that moment that he had everything in the world he had ever wanted and more.

★

They had been living in the cottage for over a week now and Tilly was positively blooming. Apart from Willy and Josefina, who had paid them a very brief visit the day before, they had seen no one, and had they been asked, they would both truthfully have said that they wished it could go on like this forever. And so it was a matter of concern when early in the afternoon a carriage pulled up outside and they saw Anna and John alight.

'Something must have happened to Sarah.' Tilly was on her feet, peering at them through the small leaded window as Steve hurried away to open the door.

Anna instantly calmed her fears as she breezed into the room saying, 'Don't panic, Tilly. Everything is just fine.'

Tilly let her breath out as the colour stole back into her cheeks. 'Oh, thank goodness for that. When I saw you, my first thought was that something was wrong with Sarah.'

'Not at all, she's positively blossoming, though I don't mind telling you, she and Little Joe are tyrants when they get together. They are ruling the house and have the whole of the staff wrapped around their little fingers. I had to tell Cook off this morning for feeding them up so. They'll both be the size of houses, the way she spoils them.'

Steve laughed as he imagined it. 'I doubt there'll be much chance of fattening those two up, the way they rampage about. They burn up too much energy for it to have time to go to fat.'

'You're not wrong there,' John laughed. 'But come on, Steve. You and I will g . . . go and put the kettle on, eh? Anna has a pr . . . proposition she wishes to p . . . put to Tilly.'

The two men left the room as Anna sank onto the sofa, smoothing her skirts around her.

'The thing is, Tilly,' she said without preamble, 'Phillipa and Lance came over to Felton Hall with the boys last weekend for a visit. While she was there, Phillipa happened to say that they are off to their house in the South of France next week, where they will stay for the winter. And can you blame them? It's enough to cut you in two here, isn't it?' When Tilly nodded in agreement she went on, 'Phillipa asked if John and I would like to join them with the children, and so if you were willing, we thought we could perhaps take Sarah with us? It would give you and Steve a little more time to get settled in here, and I'm sure the children would enjoy a holiday.'

'Oh!' The offer had taken Tilly completely by surprise and for a moment she was robbed of speech, but then eventually she asked, 'Won't it be rather hard work for you . . . taking *two* children, I mean?'

'Hardly,' Anna laughed as she took off her gloves. 'Meg would be coming with us too, and she's absolutely marvellous with them.'

'I see.' Tilly thought it over before responding, 'Well, as you say, it would be nice for the children to have a holiday – if you're quite sure?'

'Oh, I'm sure all right. I would have been so disappointed if you hadn't agreed to it, and I think Phillipa would have been, too. You know what she's like with the children. I think the biggest worry we'll have is trying to get them back off her when it's time to come home.'

'Very well, then,' Tilly said quietly, and so it was agreed.

Anna, John and their little party left for France the following week, and now that the honeymoon was over, Tilly and Steve's life began to form a routine. He would spend several days a week with Jim Coleman, Phillipa's father, at his steelworks, where he and Tilly had invested their share of the money from the mine that Willy had insisted they should keep, whilst Tilly began to venture into the village again where she helped Ellen out at the school. There were now eight children regularly attending the classes, some from as far away as Allendale, as word of it spread. Ellen seemed to be as happy as a lark, as did Willy and Josefina now that they were finally alone together again. A new cook had been taken on at the Manor to free Ellen to spend more time at the school. She was a pleasant, motherly widow called Clara, from a neighbouring village, and the rest of the staff had taken her to their hearts. Beth and Eddie, who had been married quietly in the village church some weeks before, were also as happy as larks, and so all in all, Tilly was daring to hope that the newfound peace she was finally enjoying in her life might last.

It did just that until almost four weeks after the wedding. It was now well into November, and as Ellen followed Tilly from the little schoolroom to the waiting carriage at the end of a busy day, she shuddered.

'Oh, just look at that sky. It looks full of snow, doesn't it? Arthur has been expecting it for days now.'

Tilly glanced up at the eerie grey blankness above. 'I think he might be right,' she agreed as she crossed to her horse, which was tethered to the fence.

Ellen was following the progress of two of her pupils, who were scampering along the lane. 'Lily Page is doing really well now, isn't she?' she said fondly. Then, without waiting for an answer, she went on, 'She can write half of the alphabet now and read the letters back to me.'

As Tilly placed her foot in the stirrup, Ellen dropped a light kiss on her cheek before turning away. 'I'd best be off then. At least I shall be going home in style today. Arthur wouldn't hear of me walking it because of the weather, though I have to say I've been out in far worse.' She had barely made it to the carriage door, where Ned was patiently waiting for her, when the first flakes of snow began to fall and she chuckled. 'There you are – Arthur was right after all, wasn't he? Will you be safe riding home on your own, Tilly?'

'Of course I will. I know my way hereabouts like the back of my hand. Even if I didn't, Lady does. She's like a homing pigeon when it comes to finding her way back to her warm stable.'

At that moment, a familiar figure came lumbering towards them, and the smiles were instantly wiped off their faces.

'So, that lad o' mine lets you out of his sight occasionally then, does he?' Mrs McGrath was now abreast of them and her face was twisted with malice. 'I'd have thought you'd have invited your new ma-in-law for tea afore now,' she scoffed. 'Or does our Steve reckon as how he's too good for the likes of his own flesh an' blood now?'

Tilly opened her mouth to reply but then promptly clamped it shut again as she turned Lady in the direction of home. She had learned long ago that anything she said to this woman was wasted breath, and so she decided to remain silent.

Raising her hand in farewell to Ellen and Ned, who were watching the proceedings with concern, she dug her heels into Lady's flanks and began to urge her forward. It was then that Mrs McGrath suddenly lunged towards her and swung her wicker basket with all her might at Lady's rump. The startled horse reared, and had Tilly not been such an accomplished horsewoman, there was no doubt at all that she would have been thrown from the saddle. As it was, she had her under control within seconds and now, as she leaned to stroke her side and whisper soothing words into the terrified animal's ear, she glared at Mrs McGrath and said, 'When will you ever let me live in peace? What have I ever done to you?'

The old woman's lip trembled and Tilly's heart grew cold as she ground out, 'You have the brass face to sit there an' ask me that? Why, you've ripped my family apart an' been the cause o' one of my lads going to an early grave. So in answer to your question, I will *never* let you know peace till I see you under the earth. An' never doubt it – I will!'

Tilly galloped away, and it was not until the horse had reached the coach road, which was now covered in a fine coating of snow, that the tears began to rain down her face. These last few precious weeks with Steve had been amongst the happiest of her life, but now she knew without a shadow of a doubt that if old Mrs McGrath could do anything to change it, then she would.

Chapter Thirty-Three

B Y THE MIDDLE of December there was still no sign of the snow ceasing, and Steve was spending most of his days outside keeping the drifts away from the doors and windows. The week before, he had managed to get into the village where he had collected their post, which had contained a letter from Anna telling Tilly that she and John would be returning to Felton Hall with the children in time for Christmas, and asking Tilly and Steve if they would join them.

Tilly had done no more teaching in the village school since her encounter with Mrs McGrath. Instead she had spent the last weeks Christmas shopping in Shields. By now, she was longing to see Sarah again. She had missed her far more than she had imagined she would and had prepared the smallest bedroom in readiness for bringing the child home. Josefina had informed Tilly on her last visit to the Manor that she and Willy had also received an invitation from Anna but they had declined, as they wished to spend their first Christmas as man and wife on their own.

Tilly thought of them now; they were so wrapped up in each other and so very much in love that whenever she visited them she always came away with a smile on her face.

She was smiling now as Steve came into the room on a blast of icy air. Cocking an eyebrow, he asked, 'And what's put that bonny smile on your face then?'

Bending across the table, she laid the knives and forks beside their plates and her voice was light when she answered, 'Oh, I was just thinking about my visit to Willy and Josefina yesterday. You really will have to come with me the next time I go. You will hardly recognise the place. She's had almost all of the downstairs rooms redecorated and had new drapes hung everywhere. Not only that, she's even replaced some of the furniture, though I have to say it all looks most tasteful.'

'Does it bother you, Tilly?' he asked. 'Seeing it all changed, I mean?'

'Not at all. She's just putting her own stamp on the place, I suppose. It's funny, now I come to think about it. I can't recall ever altering a single thing in the whole of the time I lived there.'

'And why was that then?'

'Probably because I never really felt that it was mine,' she decided. 'Oh, I know it was, on paper, but it never felt . . . right somehow. That's why I was happy to sign the whole lot over to Willy when he reached his twenty-first birthday.'

'Well, I only hope he realises how lucky he is,' Steve told her. 'After all, there are not many that get their legacy whilst their parent is still alive.' Suddenly changing the subject he sniffed at the air appreciatively. 'Is that roast pork I can smell cooking?'

Her smile was wide now as she nodded. 'Yes, it is. Are you hungry?'

'Now that's a daft question.' His arms slid around her as he kissed her neck affectionately. She melted back against him before he suddenly pushed her away and told her, 'Go and get me dinner on the table, woman, afore I get an appetite in another direction!'

Warm colour flooded her cheeks as, giggling, she hurried away to do as she was bid, thinking secretly to herself, Eeh, I'm a lucky woman indeed!

It was the afternoon of Boxing Day and Anna and Tilly were sitting in the drawing room of Felton Hall after having eaten a most delicious dinner. The men had retired to the smoking room to enjoy a cigar and the children were playing with some of their new toys on the Oriental silk rug in front of the fire. Little Joe had a pair of built-up shoes for outside, and a special pair of slippers for inside that helped him to walk correctly. A merry little soul, he never stopped chattering and everyone loved him.

'I still can't believe how much Sarah has grown,' Tilly confided as she watched her granddaughter totter unsteadily towards Joseph, whom she barely let out of her sight. 'And to see her walking . . . well, it hardly seems five minutes since she was born! And here she is a year old already.'

'I know exactly what you mean.' Anna looked proudly at the little ones. 'Phillipa and I were enjoying our afternoon tea one day on the lawns of their château when Sarah suddenly just stood up and went haring after Joseph.' She laughed as she recalled it. 'I'm telling you, I don't know who was the most amazed. Phillipa almost dropped her cup in her excitement.'

At that moment, Sarah changed direction and tottered towards them. Tilly eagerly held her arms out, but Sarah went straight past her to deposit a little wooden brick onto Anna's lap before smiling up at her. Tilly felt a pang of jealousy, for were she to admit it, since she had arrived at the Hall, Sarah seemed to be closer to Anna than her. Of course, she was delighted to see the child so happy, and yet deep down she could not rid herself of the feeling that she had lost something precious.

Crossing to the window, she gazed out at the snowy landscape, saying, 'I reckon we ought to think of getting back tomorrow. Otherwise, the way this lot is coming down we might get snowed in here.' As she glanced at Anna, she thought she detected a slight droop to her lips at her words, but then she thought she must have imagined it, for Anna seemed cheery enough as, lifting Sarah and taking Joe's hand, she told Tilly, 'You must do what you feel is right, Tilly, though of course we would love it if you chose to stay for a little longer.'

'Under any other circumstances I would have,' Tilly assured her, 'but look at it! It's beginning to drift now and I'm worried that the roads will become blocked.'

'Well, have a think about it. Meanwhile, I'd better get these two up to the nursery to Meg for their afternoon nap, otherwise they'll be grumpy at dinner tonight.' So saying, she swept the children from the room as Tilly's eyes followed her.

Later that evening they were all once again laughing at the children's antics in the sumptuous dining room. It was a general rule that the children of the gentry ate their meals in the nursery with their nurserymaid, but Anna and John had always enjoyed having Little Joe and Sarah dine with them, even if it did sometimes turn into quite a messy occasion. Tonight looked set to be no different, for despite all Anna's attempts to get the soup into Sarah's mouth, most of it seemed to be going down the front of the large white napkin she had tucked beneath her chin. At one stage Tilly had offered to feed her, but Sarah had clung to Anna's skirts and refused to take a bite of anything until Anna offered it to her.

Sensing Tilly's distress, Steve tried to lighten the mood when he said, 'It's funny how little ones get accustomed to one person, isn't it? No doubt she won't let me near her either, once we have her home and she's gotten used to Tilly again.'

Anna and John exchanged a glance but not a word was spoken until John suddenly asked, 'It will no doubt b . . . be strange for you both, having the responsibility of a child when you are just ge . . . getting used to each other's company?'

'Aw, we'll soon adapt – and no doubt the lass will an' all,' Steve replied good-naturedly. 'I've always thought it was amazing how resilient children can be. Take Little Joe here as an example. Already he's so much a part of your family that it's almost as if he's always been here.'

For no reason that Tilly could explain, the atmosphere for the rest of the meal was strained and she was almost relieved when Meg knocked on the door. 'Are the children ready to come for their baths yet, ma'am?' she asked brightly.

Anna nodded. 'Oh yes, they are, Meg. Thank you.' She bent to kiss the children as they obediently pottered away with Meg, telling her, 'As soon as we have had our coffee I'll be up to read them their bedtime story.'

'Yes, ma'am.' And then the door closed on them and the strange silence was back again as Tilly looked from Anna to John, deeply perplexed.

The silence lasted all through coffee until Anna eventually placed her cup and saucer back on the table and said to Tilly, 'I'm just going up to say good night to the children. And then perhaps John and I could have a word with you both?'

'Of course you can – that goes without saying. But would

you mind if I came up to the nursery with you?'

Anna gulped deep in her throat and glanced at John again, before telling Tilly, 'Not at all.'

The two women rose and made their way to the nursery floor where they found the children sitting at a little table with Meg, who was giving them each a drink of warm milk before bedtime. They were both in their nightclothes, and with their hair brushed and their faces shining after their bath they looked absolutely adorable. The children's faces lit up as the two women entered the room, and before Meg could stop them they had both tumbled off their little chairs in their haste and were speeding towards them. But it was not to Tilly that they ran, but to Anna – and once again her heart sank as she heard them both cry, 'Mama!'

Mama. Sarah had called Anna Mama! It was like a stab in the heart and yet she asked herself, had she not seen this happening since the moment she arrived? She sat down unsteadily and watched Anna take the children to their little cot beds and tuck them in. She listened to her tell them a Grimm's fairy story, which had their eyes popping until their lashes finally began to flutter shut. Only then did Anna close the book, and after tucking the bedclothes up under their chins she kissed them both soundly and beckoned to Tilly to follow her from the room.

Once out on the landing with the door firmly closed between them she grinned as she told Tilly, 'Phew, peace at last, eh?' yet her words were said with such tenderness that Tilly was left in no doubt at all that she adored both of the children as if they were her own.

They found the men in the smoking room and joined them for a glass of port. Steve and Tilly looked at each other, wondering what it was that Anna and John wished to talk to them about. They didn't have to wait long, for Anna soon said, 'Tilly, I know what I have to say may come as a shock to you, but the thing is . . .' She gulped and wiped the spittle from her lips before going on, 'John and I were wondering if you might consider letting us adopt Sarah? Please, before you say no, just think of it . . . she adores Little Joe and he in turn adores her. It goes without saying, I hope, how John and I feel about her. We love her, don't we, John?'

'Oh, yes, we do,' he agreed emphatically. 'And I per . . . promise you she would be well cared for, Tilly. And you . . . you could see her as often as you wished.'

When Tilly's hand settled across her mouth, they could all see that she was deeply distressed.

'I know that you love her too,' Anna said gently, 'but think of the upheavals the poor child has already had to suffer in her short life. And now she is settled here, and John and I are of an age that we can make sure she has everything she needs. I'm not implying that you or Steve are old, of course,' she hastened to add, but now Tilly held her hand up and spoke.

'I know exactly what you are saying, Anna, and have no fear – I am aware that you are saying it with only the best of intentions. If truth be told, until recently I had no desire to take on the care of another child at my age. It's just that . . . well, she is my granddaughter after all, and as Willy and Josefina clearly have no intention of taking responsibility for her, I suppose I had schooled myself to cope. But adoption? You must understand that I will need time to think on what you've proposed.'

'Oh yes, yes of course, we understand you will need to think of it,' Anna gabbled as Tilly slowly rose from the chair.

'Then in that case, I hope you won't mind if we retire? There is a lot to think of now and I'm rather tired.'

'Of course. Take as long as you need to think on our

suggestion. And please, don't let this put a barrier between us, Tilly.'

Tilly's face softened now as she kissed Anna's cheek. 'That could never happen, hinny,' she told her, and then she made her way from the room with a heavy tread.

She slept badly that night, tossing and turning at Steve's side long after his gentle snores were echoing around the room. At one stage she crept from the bed and crossed to the window to stare out into the snowy night. What should she do? Part of her, the selfish side, cried, 'But she is *my* granddaughter!' The other rational side knew that Sarah would be better off with Anna and John, for it was clear that they loved her and she in turn clearly loved them.

By morning there were dark circles under her eyes and she was no closer to reaching a decision. 'What do you think I should do?' she asked Steve as they prepared to go down to breakfast, and he took her in his arms and looked deep into her eyes.

'This is something I can't help you with, lass. It's a decision that only you can make. What I will say is this though: whatever you decide to do I'll be right behind you.'

Anna was pacing up and down the dining room when Tilly appeared, and one glance at her told Tilly that she had not slept either. Not wishing to keep the young woman in suspense, Tilly immediately told her, 'I haven't managed to reach a decision as yet, Anna. You will have to forgive me. I intend to take Sarah home as planned for now and then I shall inform you of what I intend to do as soon as I have decided.'

'Very well.' Although Anna smiled, she could not hide her deep disappointment, and suddenly Tilly longed to be back in the tranquillity of her little cottage. At least there she would be able to think straight again.

As soon as breakfast was over, Tilly asked the maid to pack their things whilst Meg sadly set about preparing Sarah for her journey. Little Joe sensed the tension in the air, and by the time they had all assembled in the hall to say their goodbyes he was fretful and clingy.

Sarah was wearing a little coat and matching poke bonnet that Anna had bought her in France and looked totally enchanting, but she too was fretful as Anna passed her over to Tilly.

'Mama!' The word tore at Tilly's heart as the child leaned towards Anna, holding her chubby little arms out beseechingly.

'I will come to see you very soon, pet,' Anna told her as she forced back the tears that were threatening. Joe was crying too now as he limped along at Tilly's side towards the door. And then they were going down the steps through the ever-deepening snow and Sarah's whimpers had turned to sobs as she struggled in Tilly's arms to get back to Anna. She screamed when Steve held her whilst Tilly climbed into the coach, and she was still screaming as the driver set the horses into a trot and pulled away from the Hall. By the time they were less than halfway home the child had worked herself into a frenzy despite all of Tilly and Steve's attempts to calm her, and it was then that Tilly made her decision. 'Would you ask the driver to turn the coach around, Steve.' A slight tremble of the lip was the only sign that betrayed the deep heartache she was feeling as she added, 'I am going to take Sarah back to where she belongs.'

'Aw, lass. Are you quite sure about this?' he asked.

'Yes, Steve, I am. It's not as if I shall be losing her altogether, is it? I shall be able to see her whenever I wish, and I know she will be well loved and cared for.'

'Aye, there is that in it,' he answered, but deep inside he

was thinking, She will also be yet another loss for you to add to your list. His poor darling. And then lowering the window, he shouted out to the driver, 'Could you take us back to Felton Hall, please? There's been a change of plan.'

Chapter Thirty-Four

I T WAS SIX months later, in the middle of June, and the sun was riding high in a cloudless blue sky as Tilly climbed the steps to the Manor. Her life had fallen into a pattern, and all in all she was content. Earlier in the day, she had driven into Shields to pick up Charles Kingsley's book, *The Water Babies*, which she had ordered as a birthday present for Joseph, whom she would be seeing the next day. But for now, the rest of the day was hers to do as she pleased with, as Steve was visiting Jim Coleman at his steelworks.

Peabody hurried to meet her with a cheerful smile on his face as she entered and told her, 'The master and mistress are in the day room, ma'am, and if you don't mind me saying, you are just in time for morning coffee.'

'Oh, excellent, Peabody, that would be lovely.' She returned his smile, and as she entered the day room, she found Josefina leaning across the tea-trolley.

'Ah, Mama – what good timing. I'll ring and ask Biddle to bring another cup in.'

'It's all right, pet. Peabody is already organising it.' Tilly sank down in the seat next to Willy. He instantly reached out to squeeze her hand and her heart lifted to see him looking so well. He had gained a little weight and it suited him, and Josefina looked radiantly happy.

'No Steve today?' he asked, and Tilly shook her head. 'No, he's in a meeting with Jim and won't be back until later this afternoon.'

'Did you hear about the problems Rosier is having with the pits?' Willy went on. 'Seems the miners' strike in Wales is reaching down here now; word has it that there's a lot of unrest amongst the workers. Personally, I wouldn't be surprised to see his men striking afore long.'

Tilly nodded in agreement. 'Whilst I have every sympathy with the men I can also say I am thankful to be well out of it. Our shares in the steelworks are doing very nicely, and we are more than comfortable on the profits. Also, I'm glad that Steve no longer has to go down the mine. I have seen too many men die of the lung disease over the years.'

Despite the solemnity of the conversation, Tilly sensed that neither Willy nor Josefina were giving her their full attention, so once Biddle had brought another cup and saucer and left the room, she looked from one to the other with an expression of curiosity on her face.

'So, what's happened here then?' she demanded. 'You two can hardly stop smiling.'

The two young people exchanged a loving glance, and after pouring out a cup of coffee for Tilly, Josefina then crossed to Willy's side and took his hand as she told her, 'You must be more astute than we thought, Mama, for yes, as you quite rightly say, something *has* happened; something quite wonderful. You see, the thing is . . . Willy and I have just discovered that we are to become parents.'

Tilly's cup wobbled dangerously in its saucer as her mouth fell into a gape, but then placing it on a small table she covered the short distance between them and snatched them into her arms with a beaming smile on her face. 'Oh, my dears, this is indeed marvellous news! I'm so thrilled for you both. When is the happy event to be?'

'According to the doctor, around the end of December or the beginning of January,' Josefina told her as she blushed becomingly.

'I've told her she's got to slow down a bit now on the redecorating,' Willy said, and this brought forth a sound of glee from Josefina.

'Oh, Mama, will you *please* explain to him that I am not ill, merely carrying a child,' she laughed. 'I'm sure he would put me to bed until after the birth if he could. I feel as fit as a fiddle. In fact, I've never felt better in my life, but still he fusses over me like a mother hen.'

'I think you should forgive him for that.' Tilly's voice was thick with emotion. So, they were going to be blessed with a child. It would be loved and adored, she had no doubt, just as Sarah was by Anna and John. She could hardly wait to tell Steve the good news.

Just as she had imagined, when she did tell him later that evening over dinner, he was as thrilled as she was.

'It feels as if everything is finally falling into place, doesn't it?' he said contentedly.

Tilly nodded, but deep down she knew that her peace could never be complete whilst Mrs McGrath was alive, and she could only imagine what stories would sweep around the village when news of Josefina's condition got out. Once again, she would find herself the target of their gossip, for what would they make of what they termed as 'her bastards' having a child together?

As if he could read her thoughts, Steve said reassuringly, 'Don't worry about what people will say, Tilly.' But her smile was gone now as she admitted, 'I dread to think what your mother will make of this.'

His eyes narrowed into slits and he laid his knife and fork down as he stared towards the ceiling for a while before replying, 'We learned long since that my mother is a bitter, vicious woman. There is nothing we can do about it, but just remember, she is old now, Tilly. And she cannot go on forever.'

She could have answered, 'Yes, yes you are right,' but the words stayed trapped inside her and what she thought was, Yes, she is old, but she will never be happy until she sees me dead. And with the thought, the feeling of foreboding she had come to know so well wrapped itself around her like a shroud.

The children were in fine high spirits when Tilly and Steve visited Felton Hall the next day. Joseph cried with delight at the sight of the book Tilly had bought for him, and Sarah, who was constantly at his side, looked at him adoringly. It was then that Tilly had a premonition, for the look Sarah saved for him alone was the look that Josefina had always saved for Willy. Could it be that history was about to repeat itself in these two innocent children? Joseph was now a fine-looking little boy. The built-up shoes that Anna and John had had made for him ensured that his limp was no longer evident when he walked. As for Sarah, had it not been for the fine white scar that ran down the length of one side of her face, she might have been termed beautiful. Tilly pushed the thoughts away. This was a day for happiness, not for worrying about what the future had in store for her.

'Josefina asked me to share her good news with you,' Tilly told Anna now as Meg led the children out onto the emerald-green lawns for their daily exercise.

'Oh yes, and what's that then?' Anna asked as, taking her

arm, she strolled back towards the drawing room with Tilly, the men following close behind them.

'Well, as it happens they have just discovered that Josefina is going to have a bairn.' Tilly held her breath as she waited for Anna's reaction, but she needn't have worried for Anna smiled from ear to ear, and yet more surprisingly, she blushed.

'I can only say that I am delighted for them. As it is, I have a little news of my own to tell you.' She glanced across her shoulder at her husband before saying, 'John and I have just discovered that we too are about to have a child!'

Tilly stopped so abruptly that Steve almost walked into the back of her. 'You're *what*?' she gasped.

'I know you must be surprised.' Anna's laugh had a tinkling sound to it. 'And I have to admit we were, too. I had been gaining weight, but put that down to the fact that I am now so contented. But I haven't been feeling quite right for some weeks, and so yesterday John insisted that I should see a doctor – and of course when he examined me and told me the reason for my tiredness and so on, I was so shocked that all I could do was stare back at him open-mouthed.'

'Oh, Anna . . . John.' Tilly could think of nothing she could say that would convey how delighted she was for them.

They had now entered the drawing room and as John placed his arm around Anna's shoulders, she explained, 'The doctor told me that this is not as uncommon as you might think. Now that we have Sarah and Joseph, John and I had stopped worrying about the fact that I hadn't conceived, and so because I wasn't always thinking about it, nature obviously took its course.'

Tilly asked for the second time in two days, 'And when is *your* happy event due to take place?'

'Oh, the doctor seemed to think around the middle of October.'

'Then congratulations to you both. It must be something in the air,' Steve declared as he pumped John's hand up and down.

The rest of the day passed happily, especially when Joseph blew out the three candles on his birthday cake, and Tilly was feeling at peace as she and Steve rattled along the coach road in the carriage that night.

'I don't know, hearing about all these new babies that are about to put in an appearance makes you feel a bit broody, doesn't it, Mrs McGrath?' he joked.

Tilly swiped playfully at his arm. 'No, it does *not*, Mr McGrath,' she said. 'As I've told you before, my childbearing days are long past, so you can put that idea from your mind!'

He became serious now as he raised her chin and looked deep into her eyes. 'Actually, Mrs McGrath, I am quite happy with things just as they are. I waited a long time for you and now that I have you I have no wish to share you with anyone.'

'You will never have to,' she told him softly, and then their lips joined in a deep and loving kiss. The horse's hooves and the creaking of the harness were the only sounds in the sweet summer night, and Tilly was happier than she had been for many a long year.

On 18 October 1876, after a trouble-free pregnancy, Anna gave birth to twins, two healthy little girls who were so alike that Tilly could scarcely tell them apart. Anna and John named them Elizabeth Louise, and Emily Eugenie, though they were soon affectionately known as Lizzie and Emmy.

At the time of their birth, the country was in the grip of the worst floods that it had seen for eighty years, and so the babies were almost a month old before Tilly and Steve got to see them on their Christening Day, when they proudly took their place at the font in St Bartholomew's Church and became their godparents. The girls were beautiful, contented babies, and much adored by their older brother and sister. And so now Tilly waited with anticipation for the birth of Josefina and Willy's baby.

The floods subsided, to be replaced with snow in early December, and so Tilly took to walking the distance from the cottage to the Manor each night on foot to check on Josefina.

This Christmas, Tilly and Steve chose to spend quietly at the cottage, for the roads were blocked in many places and the coach road to Felton Hall was impassable. Tilly also declined Willy and Josefina's offer of spending Christmas at the Hall, for Josefina was due to give birth any day now and Tilly could see that she needed her rest.

Steve offered to take Tilly to London for the New Year to stay at a hotel and see a show, but she would not hear of it. 'What if Josefina should go into labour and I'm not here?' she told him aghast, and he laughed at her outraged face.

'Very well then, we'll postpone our trip until the bairn has put in an appearance,' he agreed. 'Though I don't see what you can do even if you are here.'

'I'll just feel better knowing that I am close by,' Tilly told him, and Steve was happy to go along with her wishes, for there was nothing in the world that he would not have done for her.

It happened that in the week between Christmas and the New Year, Tilly had cause to go into the village, where her precious, newfound peace was shattered. Ellen had come down with a bad cold that had Arthur insisting she did not leave the cottage. It was following a visit to Willy and Josefina that Tilly bumped into him in the stableyard as she was about to make the journey back to the cottage through the woods.

'Ah, Tilly,' he hailed her and she stepped into the shelter of the stables out of the snow to have a word with him.

'How is Ellen?' she asked, and he shrugged.

'Still hacking like an old hag,' he told her in his usual forthright manner. ''Twasn't that I needed to talk to you about though, Tilly. She's asking for some books she needs from the schoolhouse, and 'twould be no use me going to fetch them for her. I've no idea what she wants. If I was to take you down there in the carriage, might you sort them out for her? I know it's a lot to ask in this weather, but you know what she's like. She'll only fret till she has what she needs.'

'Oh Arthur, of course I will,' Tilly assured him. 'How about first thing tomorrow morning?'

'Aw thanks, Tilly.' His face broke into a grateful smile. 'Shall I pick you up at the cottage?'

'Oh, no – the top road is impassable,' she warned him. 'I'll meet you here in the stables. Steve says the road to the village is still clear, so it shouldn't take us long.'

'Right you are, Tilly. An' thanks, lass – that'll put the smile back on her face.'

Tilly raised her hand in a final salute and then slipped back out into the snow that was falling so thickly she could scarcely see her hand in front of her.

Steve was waiting anxiously by the window for her when she arrived at the cottage and he came out to meet her. Once inside, he slipped her cape from her shoulders, and led her straight to the fire. 'I'm really not so keen about you walking over to the Manor in this weather,' he told her with a worried frown on his face.

She held her cold hands out to the welcoming blaze. 'Oh, stop worritin',' she said fondly. 'I could do that walk blindfold now, I've done it that many times.' Then, as she remembered her chat to Arthur, she told him, 'I've promised Arthur I'll pop down into the village with him tomorrow morning. There are some books that Ellen needs from the schoolroom, but don't worry – I'll be meeting him at the Manor and he's going to take me in the carriage.'

Steve was staring out from the back window down over the rise. 'He will if he's still able to get the coach through,' he told her. 'The way this lot is coming down, the road into the village could well be blocked an' all by morning.'

Seeing the anxiety on his face she asked, 'Is there anything troubling you, pet?'

He sighed deeply before answering, and then: 'Well, to tell the truth, while you were away over at the Manor . . . I had a visitor.'

'Oh, and who was that in this weather then?'

He hesitated, then said in a low voice, 'It was Fred Laudimer's young lad with a message. Apparently, me ma is at death's door an' she's asking fer me.'

'Oh!' As Tilly's hand settled across her mouth she was unable to hide her distress. 'Then you must go to her, Steve,' she said. 'No matter what has gone before, she is still your mother.'

'Aye, I don't need reminding of that fact, lass,' he told her and his voice was so low that she had to strain to hear it. 'I'll admit that at first I was tempted to take the path you suggest and go to her. But the thing is, Tilly . . . I can't bring meself to do it.' He spread his hands and implored her, 'Think of it – all the misery she has heaped on you and yours, down over the years. Even now she would strike you dead if it were in her power, so bearing that in mind, I've decided that I'll not be going.' He combed his fingers through his hair as Tilly hurried to his side and placed her arms around him.

'Don't do it for me, Steve,' she said softly. 'I could never live with myself if I thought that I had been the cause of you keeping away from your mother in her hour of need.'

'I appreciate that, lass. But my mind is made up. It's best this way, but thanks for your understanding.'

As Tilly laid her head against his broad chest, the words came unbidden to her mind: *If she should die, I would be free of her curse at last!*

Chapter Thirty-Five

'BY, TILLY, IT'S enough to cut you in two, ain't it?' Arthur was waiting for her in the stables when she arrived at the Manor early the next morning, and shaking the snow from the hood of her coat she nodded. 'It is as you say, Arthur. Now let's be on our way, eh? The sooner we go, the sooner we shall be back.'

Within no time at all the horses were picking their way cautiously through the thick snow that lay on the drive, and then the carriage was swerving from one side of the road to the other to avoid the hard-packed snow. It took them twice the normal length of time to reach the village, but at last Arthur drew the horses to a halt outside the schoolhouse. The horses whinnied and tossed their heads, their breath flying in front of them like long lace flumes on the bitter cold air as Tilly clambered down from the carriage. The deep snow immediately found its way across the top of her boots and she shuddered, telling Arthur, 'I'll not be more than a few minutes.'

'Aye, take your time, lass.' He had climbed down from the driver's seat and was now gently talking to the horses, who were nervously trying to lift their hooves from the cold drifts they were standing in.

After hastily lighting the lamp in the schoolroom, Tilly was searching for the books that Ellen had requested. She found them in no time at all and had just extinguished the lamp when there was the sound of a commotion outside. Stepping through the door with the books under her arm, she saw Arthur standing menacingly over the figure of an old woman who was leaning heavily on the picket fence as her gnarled hand held her shawl tightly about her. Tilly's heart sank into her boots. It was old Mrs McGrath. She would have recognised her anywhere, even with her shawl pulled tight across her face.

'I'm tellin' you, just clear off and leave us alone!' she heard Arthur say. Drawing herself up to her full height, Tilly locked the door carefully behind her then trod her way through the snow to the carriage, looking to neither left nor right as she went. But Mrs McGrath was not going to be denied her say.

Seeing Tilly, she croaked out, 'So, you would even deny a mother the privilege of seeing her son when she is on her deathbed, would you?'

Pausing with her hand on the handle of the carriage door, Tilly informed her coldly, 'I deny Steve nothing, Mrs McGrath. If he has not been to see you, then it is purely because he chooses not to. Though I have to say, you do not look to be on your deathbed from where I am standing.'

The woman opened her mouth to spit back a reply, but just then a spasm of coughing shook her frail frame. When she had herself under control once again, she peered at Tilly from beneath her shawl, and what she said next struck terror into the younger woman's heart.

'I might be not long fer this world, witch. But know that you are not either – fer as God is my witness I'll see you go afore I do. Amen.' With that she turned and staggered away, leaving Tilly and Arthur to stare after her with a look of horror painted on their faces.

'Ignore her, lass, she's just letting off steam,' Arthur said, after he was over the first shock. 'Ask yourself, what can she do to you? It's taking her all her time to put one foot in front of the other.'

Tilly allowed him to help her into the coach, but once he was back in the driver's seat, taking up the reins, hot tears came, for what she had seen in the ailing old woman's eyes left her in no doubt at all that her evil mother-in-law meant every word she had uttered.

It was the morning of New Year's Eve and Steve and Tilly were at breakfast when there came a banging on the door.

'Who would that be at this time of the morning?' Steve questioned as he hurried towards it.

They soon found out, for Biddle almost fell into the room when the door was opened. 'Why, man. Get yourself over here by the fire,' Steve urged as he slammed the door on the weather. Then to Tilly: 'Pour him out a nice strong cup o' tea, lass. He looks like he could do with one.'

'Yes, yes,' she said, trying hard to stem the panic that was rising in her like a tide. Fetching a clean cup, Tilly poured the tea with shaking fingers, then carrying it across to Biddle, who gulped at it gratefully, she asked him, 'What is it, Biddle? Is something wrong with the mistress?'

'N . . . not wrong exactly, ma'am,' he gasped, 'but the child has started. Arthur is riding into the village now to fetch the doctor and Master Willy asked me if I would call on you to come too.'

'Oh, I see.' A mixture of excitement and fear took hold of Tilly as she turned to fetch her cape.

'I'll come with you an' all,' Steve offered, and soon they

were all wrapped up against the weather and ready to brave the elements. Steve hastily banked the fire up before placing the guard around it, then turning to Tilly he told her with a note of jocularity in his voice, 'Come on then, woman. Let's go an' wait for this new grandchild that's about to come into the world.'

They walked in single file until they reached the bank that led from the road down to the copse, where they all ended up slithering on their backsides. They then entered the partial shelter of the trees, keeping well away from the edge of the gorge, until they emerged on the other side of the copse and the Manor came into sight. There was no sign as yet of the doctor's carriage, but Tilly rightly guessed that it might take him some time to get through, for the drifts were rising by the hour.

When they almost fell into the kitchen through the back entrance, Tilly told Gwen, 'Get Biddle a hot drink, would you? And then see to a tray for us. Is Master Willy in the drawing room?'

'No, ma'am, he's upstairs with the mistress in their bedroom waiting for the doctor.'

Tilly and Steve entered the hallway, where they then parted – he to the warmth of the fire in the drawing room and a glass of sherry, and she to Willy and Josefina's room.

She found Willy looking even paler than Josefina, if that was possible, as his wife clung to his hand. As Tilly entered the room, her son's head turned at the familiar tread, and she heard the relief in his voice when he cried, 'Oh, Mama! I don't think I have *ever* been so pleased to see you!'

Hurrying across to him she planted a kiss on his cheek before bending to the slight figure on the bed and asking, 'How are you feeling, hinny?'

'Oh, not too bad at all.' Josefina's eyes were feverishly

bright, but Tilly saw that she was calm, which she took as a good sign.

'It's Willy who is the problem,' Josefina joked. 'He keeps flying into a panic every time I have a pain.'

'Have either of you thought to time how far apart they are?' Tilly now asked, and it was Willy who told her, 'Yes, about every ten minutes or so.'

'Good, that means we still have a way to go yet,' Tilly told him. 'That will give the doctor plenty of time to get here. But don't expect it to be over in an hour, Willy. First babies are notorious about taking their time in coming. Why don't you go down to the drawing room and keep Steve company now that I am here? I promise to call you at the first sign of anything happening.'

When Willy looked somewhat reluctant, Josefina flapped her hand at him. 'Go on,' she urged, as she felt another contraction building. 'Get yourself away and do as Mama says. This is women's work.'

He bent to kiss her brow and then slowly left the room, and so began one of the longest days that Tilly had ever had to endure. It took the doctor another two hours to arrive, as he had been busy with a case of pneumonia and one broken arm down in the village.

It was approaching tea-time when Tilly went down to the dining room for a drink and a quick bite to eat. Steve and Willy were waiting for her, and the second she entered the room, Willy almost jumped from his seat to ask, 'How is she? Will it be much longer?'

Tilly pressed him back onto his chair as she told him, 'In answer to your first question, everything is going very well. The second I cannot answer, for babies have a habit of not putting in an appearance until they are good and ready. The doctor is satisfied that all is going as it should, so just try to be patient.' She then turned her attention to Steve and told him, 'It might be as well if you made your way home. I could be here all night, it's getting dark, and we don't want the fire to go out, do we? Lady will need seeing to as well.'

'Aye, you have a point there, lass,' Steve told her, and then with a wealth of affection in his voice he asked, 'And how are you bearing up?'

'Oh, I can't pretend that it's pleasant to see someone you love in pain,' she admitted, 'but it will all be worth it in the end, won't it? Now you take yourself off home and get my bed warm for me, because believe me, I am hoping to be home in time to see the New Year in with you.'

Rising, he planted a tender kiss on her lips before nodding towards Willy and saying jocularly, 'Let's hope tomorrow I shall be back to wet the baby's head with you, eh?'

'Oh yes, let us hope so,' Willy replied, and then Steve went from the room to collect his cape, and Tilly returned to Josefina, leaving Willy to resume his pacing.

At ten minutes to ten that night, Josefina's baby was born, yelling lustily. Tilly peeped over the doctor's shoulder to stare down at the olive-skinned little body and her heart flooded with love.

'It's a little girl!' the tired doctor told them as he cut the cord, and then he wiped the little body and wrapped her in a square of soft clean flannelette and passed her into Tilly's waiting arms. The child had a shock of hair that was as black as a raven's wing, and yet her eyes when she stared up at her grandmother were a striking shade of blue – just like her father's. Tilly was sure that she had never seen so beautiful a child in the whole of her life, and as she gently laid her on Josefina's breast she murmured, 'You have been truly blessed, hinny.'

Josefina made no reply, for she was too busy drinking in the sight of this wondrous creation that she and Willy had made. When the after-birth had been delivered, and the new mother made clean and comfortable in a pretty nightgown, a banging came on the door and Tilly grinned. 'We don't need two guesses to know who *that* is, do we?'

Hurrying across to the door she was confronted by Willy, who was wringing his hands and now looked by far worse than Josefina did. Taking her son's hand in hers, she drew him into the room and whispered, 'Go and meet your daughter, Willy.'

After crossing to the bed, he peered down, and as the shape of his wife and daughter came into his limited vision, he wept with joy as he bent to enfold them in his arms.

'Come on, Doctor, let's go and have a cup of tea and leave them in peace for a few minutes, shall we?' Tilly suggested.

The man wiped a weary hand across his brow, and they crept from the room, for they had no wish to impose themselves on the little family for a moment longer than they needed to.

The next time Tilly entered the room, Josefina was propped against her pillows with her baby lying contentedly in her arms. Willy was sitting at the side of them with a look of pure wonder on his face, and Tilly locked the sight away in her memory.

'So, what are you going to call her then?' she asked, and Willy's answer brought a lump to her throat.

'We are going to call her Matilda Trotter-Sopwith, Mama. And pray that she grows up to be as fine a lady as her grandmama.'

'Oh, my dears.' Tilly bowed her head and now the tears came. Hot, healing tears that momentarily blinded her as Willy and Josefina wrapped their arms about her.

'I am truly honoured.' Eventually she managed to pull herself together and told them, 'Well, I think it's time I should be making my way home. Steve will be beginning to worry. But I shall be back tomorrow. Oh, what a wonderful start to the New Year this has been!'

'Yes, it has,' Willy beamed. 'Happy New Year, Mama.'

'And to all of you too, especially to little Matilda. Now I really must go and leave you all to get acquainted. Good night, my dears.'

She glanced back at the door, but Willy had already returned his attention to his wife and daughter, which was just as Tilly felt it should be.

As she made her way down the stairs, the whole of the staff were waiting to greet her with relieved smiles on their faces, 'Congratulations on your new granddaughter, ma'am,' they chorused and Tilly smiled back at them.

'Thank you. Now, Peabody, go down to the cellar and bring up half a dozen bottles of the best wine, would you? And then I want you all to raise a toast to the newest addition to the Sopwith family, and enjoy yourselves.'

'But won't you be joining us, ma'am?' This was from Gwen.

'No. Thank you for the offer, but it's been rather a long day, and if I hurry I can just make it back to the cottage in time to see the New Year in with my husband.'

'But Tilly, it's freezing out there,' Arthur objected, jerking his finger towards the door. 'Perhaps I ought to walk you back?'

'You will do no such thing,' Tilly told him firmly. 'In the time it will take you to get wrapped up I can be halfway there, and anyway, you should see the New Year in with Ellen.'

'Well, if you're quite sure . . .?'

'I *am*,' she declared. 'Now, good night everyone, and a very Happy New Year to you all.'

She let herself out into the cold night air and for a time breathed deeply. The snow had stopped falling for now and overhead, the sky was full of stars. A full moon was riding high and this, added to the glare of the deep snow, helped her to see her way. In no time at all she was entering the copse, eager to get home and to tell Steve all about the new addition to the family. It was harder to see here, for the trees overhead were blocking out the light. Still she began humming softly as she picked her way through. Eeh, it had surely been a grand day!

She was still in this happy frame of mind when she came to the path that led along the top of the sharp incline. Nearly home now. And it was then that a dark shape suddenly staggered from the trees like an apparition. Tilly's hand flew to her chest as she tried to still the wild beating of her heart, and at that moment the moon sailed from behind a cloud and she found herself staring into the haggard face of Mrs McGrath.

'So,' the old woman's voice sliced through the silence. 'Your bitch has given birth to yet another bastard to carry on the family name, has she?'

'How . . . how did you—'

'How did I know, were you about to ask? Huh! It didn't take too much addin' together when Arthur came haring down into the village fer the doctor, did it? Not knowing that that one up there was due to drop her whelp any day.' The woman's voice was loaded with pure venom.

'Look, why don't you just go home?' Tilly shivered, her mood of exhilaration gone completely. 'You're not well, and being out in this—'

'I'll be going nowhere till I've done what I should have

done a long time ago.' The old woman advanced menacingly, and in the light of the moon, Tilly saw a knife-blade glisten. She began to panic. The woman was stark staring mad – she must be, to behave in this way. And then suddenly the old woman lunged at her and Tilly jumped aside, only to find herself tottering on the edge of the steep incline. She suddenly realised that she was fighting for her life.

'Mrs McGrath, *please* . . .' Her words fell on deaf ears as the old woman lunged at her again, and now Tilly was holding tight to the sinewy arm as her assailant struggled to thrust the knife into her, her deep hatred of Tilly Trotter lending her strength. And then everything seemed to happen at once, for Tilly felt her feet slipping in the snow, and then they were both hovering on the edge of the incline as she desperately tried to gain a foothold. The knife suddenly slashed downwards, and Tilly felt the cold steel slice into her arm, yet strangely she felt no pain, only a curious warmth as the blood began to seep from the wound onto her cold skin. She then had the sensation of flying as they both went over the edge and she was falling . . . but then the air was knocked from her lungs when her fall was broken by an overhanging bush.

As she tried to catch her breath, a bloodcurdling scream echoed in the deep gorge and made the hairs on the back of her neck stand to attention. The scream stopped abruptly, and clinging onto the thorny branches of the bush, Tilly looked below, and there she saw the old woman, lying on a bed of pure white snow at the bottom of the gorge, staring sightlessly up at her. In that moment she knew that it was over. Mrs McGrath was dead.

Sucking the air back into her lungs, Tilly began to sink her hands into the snow and to haul herself back up the steep bank, leaving a thin trail of blood behind her. She had almost reached the top when a lantern appeared above her and a strong voice called, *'Tilly, where are you?'*

Sobbing with relief, she cried, *'I'm here, Steve!'* And then his face was floating towards her as he dropped the lantern into the snow and slithered down to her. In no time at all he had his arm around her and was dragging her back up towards the path. Once there, they both collapsed as they tried to catch their breath, and it was then that the air around them exploded into life as ships' hooters, church bells and pit sirens began to welcome in the New Year.

'Steve . . . your mother . . . I think she's . . .'

'Ssh, hinny. I know. She's dead – and all I can say is, it's not afore time. She died as she lived, a bitter vindictive woman, and I can only thank God that she didn't take you with her.' He wrapped his muffler in a sling for his wife's wounded arm and hugged her tenderly. 'It's over, Tilly. We'll be free to live the rest of our lives in peace now. There'll be no more looking over your shoulder, my darling.'

His arms were tight about her and she was crying as she tried to take in what he had said. *She was free!* Really free at last of the woman who had hounded her and her family for most of her life. And Steve was looking down at her with so much love in his eyes that it shone brighter than the snow, moon and stars combined.

And in that moment, despite the shock, and the cold, and the pain in her arm, Tilly Trotter felt like the luckiest woman in the world.

Just
for You

Rosie Goodwin

Inspiration:
Taking on Tilly

When my editor, Flora Rees, first approached me and asked me if I would like to write a sequel to Catherine Cookson's *Tilly Trotter* trilogy, I was ecstatic! Having always been a huge Cookson fan, and as a relatively new author I could hardly believe my luck.

The phone call was followed by a visit with Flora to meet Sonia Land of the Sheil Land Agency, who was Catherine's agent. I admit I was totally enthralled to hear Sonia speaking of Catherine and it was a very emotional time, especially when, after a lot of discussion on what we wanted the sequel to be, she finally gave me her blessing and sent me on my way to write the book.

I was so excited when we left Sonia's office that I can hardly remember the train ride home from London. I then reread the whole trilogy from cover to cover and it was almost time to start as I was working to a very tight deadline.

It was then that the elation wore off and panic set in. After all, how does *anyone* follow Catherine Cookson? She was the Queen of Sagas and I knew I was up against a huge challenge.

There were so many things I hadn't initially thought of. For example, I would be writing in a different area about characters that had already been created and to do the trilogy justice I would have to stay true to them. With a different location as a setting it would also mean that I would have to use an unfamiliar dialect and terms of endearment.

I realised immediately that to do this I would need to keep the flavour of Catherine's writing without trying to copy her. I read everything I could get my hands on about her and was fortunate at the time to have just finished reading Piers Dudgeon's *The Girl From Leam Lane*, which gave me a wonderful insight into her life. It also brought home to me just how much of Catherine's own life was reflected in her books. For instance, in her *Hamilton* trilogy the main character, Maisie, suffered a number of miscarriages, just as Catherine herself did. Also, many of her characters were what Catherine would term as 'bastards' in her books, and they struggled with adversity to make something of their lives just as she herself and Tilly Trotter did. Much like Catherine, Tilly could be a feisty character and was determined to better herself.

Throughout all this research my admiration for this most remarkable lady grew and I knew that I must do her justice. This book would be my way of paying homage to one of the best storytellers the world has ever known.

I put her photograph above my computer and from that moment on my fears disappeared. Sometimes it was as if the great lady herself was there with me urging me on and giving me her blessing, and so *Tilly Trotter's Legacy* was born.

I think one of Catherine's main talents was that she could bring the characters in her novels to glorious life and now suddenly they were my characters too. I laughed with them and cried with them, just as I'm sure Catherine would have

438

done when she breathed life into them. I would find myself in the early hours of the morning suddenly going into a sub-plot that I had not planned and I would glance up at her picture and smile at her. I felt that she was guiding me and the feeling gave me the confidence to go on. I discovered very early on that this was *my* book. There was no way I was trying to copy Catherine. That would not have worked; there could only ever be one Catherine Cookson. Instead, this was my way of paying tribute to her. Having read almost every book she had ever written I hoped deep down that this might be a way of getting Catherine's fans, along with new readers, to rediscover her wonderful works.

And so, four weeks later, the first draft was finished. I had worked on it every second I could spare and was sad to have to say goodbye to the characters I had written about, just as Catherine must have been after she had finished the trilogy. It was then time to bite my nails when I submitted it to my editor and agent as I waited for their reaction to it.

Thankfully, they loved it and it was a red letter day for me when I first saw the wonderful cover with my name and Catherine Cookson's on the same jacket.

Shortly after the hardback was released I was invited to Newcastle and South Shields, where I visited the museum that houses Catherine's desk, Dictaphone and many more of her personal possessions. I was moved to tears and again regretted the fact that I had never had the chance to meet the great lady herself whilst she was alive.

During my visit I waited for darkness to fall and walked to the River Tyne, which was mentioned in many of her books. There I floated some flowers for her and thanked her for all the pleasure she had given to me and countless readers across the world. It was a very moving time.

If *Tilly Trotter's Legacy* gives pleasure to Catherine's

readers, then I will feel that I have done the job I set out to do. Her novels are timeless classics that can be read again and again and still enjoyed.

I am now delighted to say that I have also completed a sequel to Catherine's *Mallen* trilogy, called *The Mallen Secret*, which will be released in August. I hope all my readers will enjoy reading them as much as I have enjoyed writing them. It was a great honour to follow the Queen of Sagas and wherever she is I hope Catherine will approve. Somehow I feel that she does . . .

Rosie Goodwin xx

Have you read all the novels in the *Tilly Trotter* trilogy?

Tilly Trotter

Tilly Trotter isn't like the other girls in the villages of County Durham. Tall and coltish, but with an unusual beauty, she's not afraid of taking on 'man's work'.

But Tilly only loves one man, farmer Simon Bentwood, and she's heartbroken to discover that he's betrothed to another. Harder times are ahead when a spurned suitor takes a terrible revenge, idle gossip brands her a witch and a betrayal puts her life in danger . . .

Tilly Trotter Wed

Tilly is left pregnant and alone when Mark Sopwith, whom she has devotedly served for twelve years at Highfield Manor, dies.

Tilly is forced to face the prejudices of the local village, and when a vicious attack leaves her baby son, Willy, half blind she follows her heart to America, sure that this will be the beginning of a better life. But new perils await Tilly across the ocean . . .

Tilly Trotter Widowed

Tilly returns from America to the County Durham village where she grew up.

Despite her new status as Lady of Highfield Manor, the locals brand Tilly a witch, and hostility towards her and her children is rife. But Tilly, courageous as ever, is determined, no matter what, that she and her children will find happiness . . .